SPIKE: 35 KILLS AND SMILING

SPIKE
BOOK 1

MIKE SLAVIN

GOLDEN MEAN PRESS

Copyright © 2023 by Mike Slavin

All rights reserved.

No part of this book may be reproduced in any form or by any electronic or mechanical means, including information storage and retrieval systems, without written permission from the author, except for the use of brief quotations in a book review.

❦ Created with Vellum

1

FREE AT LAST
AUGUST

Mexico to New Mexico
Few Miles West of Columbus, NM
Thursday Evening

THE BULLET WHIZZED by his ear. Spike reflexively ducked, felt his ear, and looked at his hand. No blood.

Harry "Spike" Hunter pulled his Glock 40 away from its current position—pressed into Rosa's forehead. With a sprained ankle, she would have to sit and await her fate. He took off running, stumbling down the narrow tracks of the drug cartel's underground tunnel. His world moved in slow motion, and he fully expected to be shot in the back because he had no cover, nowhere to duck and catch his breath. It was a straight shot down the tunnel. But, no matter what, he wouldn't drop the gym bag. That was his start-over kit.

He reached the ladder at the shallow end. Still wired with panic, Spike glanced back down the tunnel. *Rico!* The number-two man in Zorro's cartel stood over Rosa, who was Zorro's wife and partner. She sat on the tracks at Rico's feet.

Spike wasn't sorry that he had to leave her. She was a snake in the grass, guaranteed to turn on him the second he turned his back. Arguably, she was more dangerous than her husband had ever been. Still, leaving her to Rico seemed risky in the long run.

They were talking, paying no attention to Spike. *I wonder who will kill who.* He was too far away from them to hear what they were saying. Spike relaxed for a second as curiosity got the best of him.

Then Rico raised his head. His eyes caught Spike's and bored into them. *Shit. Don't shoot. Don't shoot.* Spike panicked. He shoved his gun into the gym bag and went up the ladder. His forehead slammed on a rung as he missed the first step. *Shit!* Climbing the ladder and escaping the line of fire was his only focus. Fifteen or so rungs and he'd crawl out the open hatch. As he scrambled to pull free, Spike buzzed with haste and worry. Lead could tear through his flesh at any moment. Above him and through the hatch was New Mexico. *So close.*

The twelve-inch cut along his left forearm seared with pain when he used that limb to support his weight. The bag made the climb awkward. Spike clutched it tightly while gripping each rung.

He poked his head through the hatch, pulled his body through, and scooted away from the raised eighteen-inch concrete floor lifted by hydraulics on each corner. It smelled like a warehouse, full of staleness and oil, yet it was sweet US air. The hydraulic top descended slowly and blended into the floor, camouflaged by the junk covering its top. Just as he thought about how odd it was that he hadn't heard a weapon firing since running from Rosa, a gunshot echoed in the tunnel.

Had to be Rosa. Spike shook his head. *Change of management, I guess.*

It seemed Rico and Rosa weren't coming after him. After catching his breath and letting the adrenaline settle, he sighed with a wide smile, picked up his bag, and walked to the door, toward his new life. His arm hurt like a son of a bitch, but he'd get it fixed. *Ahh, back in the US of A. Thank God.*

He paused, got down on one knee, bowed his head, and closed his eyes.

Thank you, God. I know who I am, but I can serve you. Give me the strength. I promise to never kill an innocent again.

Spike stepped outside. To his left, the descending sun hung low against a reddening backdrop. He walked toward a highway he spotted among the flat desert scrub, a double-lane concrete slab cutting a swath through a piece of the Chihuahua Desert and paralleling the US-Mexico border a few miles in. Along the south side of the highway, a dirt road stretched beyond his sight.

He took a deep breath, let the moment fill him, and smiled like a kid, eager to start anew. Spike didn't see any cars. Still, he had to be careful. He knew the border patrol could appear from any direction at any time, and being stopped by them would end badly for someone. The gym bag on his shoulder would cause problems, even if he wasn't a wanted man.

He patted the bag. *Lots of cash, a Glock, no ID, no phone, and a switchblade named "Rosa" with my blood on it. What a day.* The gash Rosa had delivered ached but knowing that her fate was worse ... well, he'd let that balance out.

A sign ahead said, "State Road 9," while another indicated three miles to Columbus, New Mexico. Spike walked toward Columbus on the dirt road beside the highway to the east. With nightfall imminent, he'd have plenty of time to get low and hide if headlights beamed in the distance. But where would he hide in a desert?

His arm throbbed. Otherwise, he felt great. He stopped and stretched, took a breath, and faced south. He yelled, "Thank you, Rosa, for getting my ass out of Mexico!"

Then he turned to the north, adjusted his position eastward, and faced Texas. He yelled, "Thank you, Case, for opening my eyes! I was living too small. You taught me so much." He gave a salute to no one. "Until we meet again."

He kicked up dust on his way to Columbus.

Maybe I'll be there in an hour. Damn! Gotta get this arm fixed. He hissed out a curse as he gingerly eyed the offending wound. *Yup, gotta prioritize me for sure.*

∽

SPIKE WAS IN GREAT SHAPE. During his confinement, he exercised daily and read several books. He even wrote a novel about a serial killer—*Write what you know*—though he never finished it. When the cartel released him, Spike forgot to grab his laptop and lost his work. He planned to eventually recreate what he'd written and finish the novel.

Despite his good health, the day had been exhausting, and it wasn't over yet. He walked under a star-filled sky and closely watched the passing headlights, praying it wasn't the border patrol.

Nearing the town, Spike saw a petite church, decrepit and dressed in what looked like discolored and chipped white stucco, just off the road's edge. His path would take him within a few yards of the church's front door.

God put this church in my path.

The light above the front door shone like a beacon,

glowing eerily yet heavenly. His heartbeat quickened and his breaths shortened.

Spike went to the door and opened it a crack. Conditioned cool air sliced through and gave him pause. He basked briefly in the refreshing breeze, then pushed the door fully open. The smells of paint and fresh wood dominated the room. Canvas cloths covered furniture and pews. Sawdust speckled the floor here and there. At the far end, in a room no bigger than a two-car garage, a man painted a wall, unaware of Spike's presence. Just the two of them alone. Spike quietly walked toward the man.

2

GOTTA KILL SOMEONE

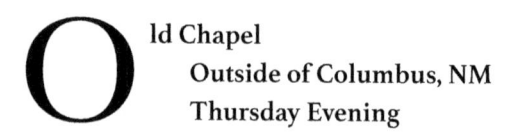

Old Chapel
Outside of Columbus, NM
Thursday Evening

SPIKE STOPPED a few feet from the man.

"Looks like you're working hard. Overtime?"

The man startled and jumped but did not turn. Instead, he laughed. He spoke with an accent. "You surprised me but no. No overtime, just a labor of love."

"Sorry, I move quietly."

The painter—an old Hispanic man wearing paint-splattered overalls—put down his brush and turned to face Spike. The man's weather-beaten face had seen much sun, and his warm and inviting smile drew Spike's attention. *This man knows no strangers.* His white hair and bushy mustache reminded Spike of an older Pancho Villa.

He approached the man, smiled, and extended his hand. "I'm Spike."

The man wiped a calloused palm on a pant leg, then shook Spike's hand. "Miguel."

Spike looked around like a country boy in a city. "I love this place. This is hard work, and you, sir, *are* a better man than me."

"This chapel has a lot of history. It's done a lot of God's work. And it deserves to be made beautiful again and be filled with God's children."

"Oh, sorry, you're a priest, right?"

"Yes, I'm Father Miguel, and I've served the Lord as a priest for forty-nine years now."

Spike pulled up a friendly smile. "Wow. Congratulations, Father. That's impressive."

"You look hot." Father Miguel handed a bottle of water to Spike. "Please, drink."

"Bless you, Father." He opened the bottle and, in one long pull, gulped it down. "That may be the best drink of water I've had—*ever*. Thank you."

The priest removed a canvas cloth from a pew. "Have a seat." He sat and faced Spike. "You look like you have something important on your mind, son. Please, sit. Tell me how I can help you."

Spike smiled, looking down at the priest. *God works in mysterious ways.* "Very perceptive, Father. There has been a big change in my life, and it's all thanks to God. It's like a switch flipped. My life has begun a new phase. It feels good. No, it feels *great*. And believe it or not, you're the first person I've met who I can talk to about this. But I've done some serious sinning."

"We have all sinned and fallen short of the glory of God. Please, tell me about it. You can tell me anything. God is very understanding and forgives those who truly repent."

"Before we get going, as a priest, you can't tell anyone what I say, right?"

"That's correct. Whatever you confess to me stays between us and God. In the Catholic Church, the Seal of Confession is the absolute duty of all priests who hear a confession not to disclose anything."

"I'm not Catholic."

"My son," the priest said, "I would never turn away a person of any faith who wanted to confess. The only thing I *cannot* do, because you are not Catholic, is give you absolution for any sins confessed. But you may ask God in your prayers."

"Good. No absolution is needed here. My deal is directly with God anyway."

The priest gave Spike a half smile and nodded.

Spike paused, lifted his brows, and returned the smile. "I like you, Padre. So, how do we get started? Do we need to get into a confessional box or anything like that?"

"We can, if it makes you more comfortable, but it's under a tarp and needs painting." The priest waved at the pew he sat on. "It's just you and me in this little old church. But—no pressure. Whether you confess is entirely up to you. However, you must have come here for a reason. Whatever it is, just know that God would like to unburden your soul."

Spike sat facing the priest. He slipped the blue bag off his shoulder and placed it on the floor. However, the bag's strap stayed clenched in his right hand. "Okay, Padre. May I call you Padre?"

"Of course, if you like."

"Again, I'm not looking for absolution, or maybe I am. I've had nobody to discuss this with, and you seem to be the perfect person."

"Is there something you would like to confess?"

A hammer the priest had left on the bench rested between them. Spike picked it up and fiddled with it.

"Hypothetically, Padre, what if someone killed a few innocent people, then changed his MO to killing only bad people? Do you think that would please God?" Spike studied the elder before him. He watched the priest's face closely, hoping to intercept micro expressions that gave away his true feelings, but there were none. The priest looked calm, but a gulp and heavier breathing revealed his fear.

The priest glanced at the door, obviously shaken. "I don't understand," he said, gathering his composure. "Are you a soldier?"

"Nope. Not a soldier, just a psychopath, and I get these cravings. The only way to satisfy them is to kill someone. It's my nature."

The priest's eyes went right to the hammer in Spike's hand. "You should never kill anyone, my son. Why did you kill these people?"

"It's hard to explain, Padre. God created me and gave me a need to kill. And God makes no mistakes, right?"

The old man's eyes showed fear and shock. His body tightened and the smile vanished. He straightened and slid back a few inches. Then he shut his eyes, took a deep breath, and paused.

Spike waited. He figured the padre was praying. He wanted to see his brown eyes. Would the eyes hold fear or calm resignation, thinking he would die? *I wonder if he's waiting for the hammer to smash his skull and wondering if he'll meet God.* Spike was very curious to see the priest's eyes again.

The priest spoke with his eyes shut. "Are you going to kill me?"

3

THE PRIEST SINNED

Old Chapel
Outside of Columbus, NM
Thursday Evening

SPIKE LAUGHED SO HARD, he coughed and tears came to his eyes.

The priest's eyes popped open as he stood and stepped backward, away from Spike. The brown eyes screamed fear. Then calm crept over his face, and a smile ... a sad smile ... a resigned smile. "I will pray for your soul, my son." The priest got down on two knees, interlocked his fingers, bowed his head, showing a small bald spot, and started praying out loud. "Our Father, who art in heaven, hallowed be thy—"

Spike stood up with the hammer in his hand. He saw the priest tense up, as he must have heard Spike's movement. None of his kills had ever offered themselves. *So very strange —like a sacrificial lamb.* It would be so easy. Spike walked closer to the priest and used the hammer to tap the priest gently on the shoulder.

The priest jerked from the touch, like a surprised cat leaping across the room. He fell backward. "Please, don't kill me." Then he kept saying a prayer, over and over, too fast for Spike to understand.

"Padre, I told you I only wanted to talk." Spike set the hammer on the floor and kicked it away. He wasn't planning on threatening the padre. "Let me help you up." He held out his hand to the priest. Spike saw the priest trying to compose himself and could see his skepticism. "I promise you ... Father Miguel. I *won't* hurt you."

The priest took a deep breath. "I'm so embarrassed." He brushed himself off with his hand and sat down.

"I'm sorry. Really. Are you hurt, Padre?"

"No, I'm fine. I'm so embarrassed." He wasn't smiling. "So, you were just joking about killing a lot of people."

Spike pursed his lips. Slowly, he shook his head. "No, I'm afraid that wasn't a joke."

"*Really.*" The priest had lost his composure, but Spike could tell he was trying to hold it together. "Please, my son, you should not kill people."

"You know, Padre, we all have things we try to do better. Lose weight, exercise more, gamble less, drink less, and so on. God has created me in a way that gives me the urge to kill now and then. I must. I have no choice. How am I different from everyone else in the world?"

"You kill people!"

"Yeah, but my point is, God made me this way. I want to be good. But it's very difficult. And I didn't know how before, but now I know."

"Did you want to confess? I'm ready to hear your confession. It may help."

"Well, I think I did the confession part, as I said I've killed a few people—well—a lot of people. And let me remind you, in case you forgot, I'm a psychopath and have a need to kill. It's not a choice. But I won't hurt *you*. So, you can relax."

"I'm human," the priest said. "So, I *do* feel fear. It's *hard* to relax now. But I trust in God. I'm a servant of God and feel that you have been put in my path for a reason. So, please, go on."

"Sorry I scared you." Spike curled his lips and shrugged. "But I have a few questions."

"What questions do you have?"

"In the Old Testament killing was acceptable. If we admit that I must kill, then if I kill only bad people, this should please God and give me a place in Heaven or whatever Heaven is, if there is one. How do you feel about that?"

"I'm just a vessel for the Lord's Word," the priest said. "And I cannot judge or give grace, but in Genesis, chapter 19, God sent deadly angels to Sodom and rained fire and sulfur on all its people. God spared none and killed all the heathens in that city because of their blatant disregard for His laws and commandments. It would seem to me that you feel you are doing God's work."

"Am I?"

The priest's response was emotionless. "That is not for me to judge. But that is the Old Testament. The New Testament teaches forgiveness."

"C'mon, Padre, society doesn't even do that. We lock up bad people forever or execute them. I'm just more efficient —we skip the courts. And Christianity is only one version of God. There are many others. There is just no way God could be unhappy about removing evil men and women from the world."

"The things you say. There are no simple answers—"

Spike interrupted the priest. "There are simple answers. My only real question is,

how bad is bad enough to kill someone? You said you've sinned before, Padre. Was it bad enough that you should die?"

4

BAD ENOUGH TO KILL

Old Chapel
Outside of Columbus, NM
Thursday Evening

THE PRIEST TIGHTENED AGAIN. "My son, you make me very uncomfortable when you say things like that. But my sins are not important. God will forgive any sin if sincerely repented."

"Maybe, but I think there's a line where God would look the other way. Maybe *rejoice*.

Like murderers who kill people and keep killing? Drug dealers who sell drugs that kill or destroy people's lives? How about tyrants, bad politicians, and leaders of countries responsible for killing hundreds, thousands, and millions?"

"My son, have you talked to God? You'd be surprised at the insight He'll give you. All you have to do is ask."

"I talk to God all the time." Spike felt confident the priest would have an answer for any question he asked, and most of them would likely be a quote or a request to ask God. Of course.

The padre shifted slightly, then looked up. "My son, I'd be remiss if I didn't share what the New Testament says about revenge. Romans, chapter 12, verse 19, reserves vengeance for God. 'Vengeance is mine. I will repay, says the Lord.'"

Spike peered to his right as if dismissing the padre's last statement. He responded in frustration. "Unless God's way of vengeance is to use me as the means! Maybe God is using me as a tool to exact His revenge."

"This is very unusual. May I ask you a question?"

"Sure," Spike answered with enthusiasm. "Go for it. I like this. It shows you're really interested. Ask away, Padre."

"Do you feel regret or remorse for those you have killed?'

"Tough question." Spike scratched his chin. "To be honest, I'm disappointed I killed innocents. I don't know whether that's regret. Had I thought of it earlier, I would have sought only bad people to kill to quench my thirst. But there's no way I could've known. Plus, I was led down this path, and my teacher killed only innocents."

"Your teacher?" The priest's eyes widened.

Spike nodded and sighed. "Yup, good old Daddy was a psychopath too. He loved to kill and forced me to participate. I often wonder if I'd have this need to kill if it wasn't for him." Spike looked off into the distance for a moment. His mind went to his father, whom he hated.

"I'm so sorry. Is he still in your life?"

"Don't want to talk about that but back to your question about regret and remorse. I have no regret for killing the murderous cartel members who would've gladly killed me. About remorse, if that means a deep and painful feeling of guilt for wrongdoing for anyone I've killed, then, nope. I'm just not wired to feel that way. But since I've found I can kill bad people and quench my unstoppable desire to kill ... I do feel better. I feel good. I feel I can fit into society. At least in my own way."

"But you're killing people, my son." The priest was animated now, moving his hands and showing disbelief on his face. "It's wrong, immoral, and illegal. How do you feel you fit into society?"

"Because I'm doing God's work," Spike said. "I'll no longer kill innocent people. That means I'm saving innocent people—by killing *bad* people. When I walk out of this church, I'll be aware of this choice for the first time. And I have to make it. I have to discipline myself to kill only bad people and never again kill an innocent.

"If we were talking about food, I must eat. Before now, I could eat anything. No control required. But now, no doughnuts, no cookies, no ice cream—you get the idea? I can eat *only* healthy food. Kind of funny if you think about it. The healthy food in this analogy is bad people. I've never been tested. But I want to be good. I really want to be good."

Spike stood and slung the blue bag strap over his left shoulder. "Padre, it's been fun, but it's time to go."

"Did you find what you were looking for?" the priest asked as he walked Spike to the
door.

"I don't know, Padre. You tried, but I think I'm alone in this, just me and God. No middlemen. No offense, Padre."

Spike stood in the open doorway, looking out. He felt the heat coming in from the New Mexico night.

Behind Spike, the priest said calmly, "You must stop killing people. It cannot please God. If you ask God, He will give you the strength you need. I promise."

"Sorry, Padre, you did your best. Don't feel bad, but I have no choice," Spike said over his shoulder. "God and I have chosen the next best thing." He turned slightly to face the priest. "One more thing, Padre."

The priest jolted a tick. His eyes got big, showing a lot of white, and he stepped backward. He swallowed hard and his voice cracked. "Yes, my son."

Spike unzipped the bag on his shoulder and reached into it. With his hand in the bag, he felt the Glock, and then his fingers glided over the switchblade named Rosa. He gripped it tight and looked at the priest. "You won't tell anyone about our discussion. Right?"

The priest's eyes, filled with fear again, were fixed on the bag. "No, never. I'm not allowed to by God."

"Good enough for me." Spike pulled out a bound stack of hundred-dollar bills and handed it to the priest. "Ten thousand dollars for you to do God's work with."

The priest couldn't hide his surprise. He relaxed, got giddy. The smile returned. "*This,* I never expected. *Bless you.*"

"Spend it wisely, Padre." Spike turned to walk away.

"Wait," the priest said. He turned and wrote something on a piece of paper and then handed it to Spike. "If you ever need someone to talk to, please call me. It's my cell number."

"Don't wait up for a call, Padre, but never say never." Spike shook the priest's hand and stared into his eyes. "You're a good man, Padre." Spike turned and walked toward Columbus. His journey was his new freedom and was just beginning.

Lord,

Give me the strength to not kill an innocent, and the will to protect the weak.

And the skill, strength, and cunning to kill all the evildoers I can.

Amen.

He heard the priest shut and lock the door.

Spike looked over his shoulder.

Locked doors don't protect the innocent, but I will.

5

BUCK AND BARBIE

Columbus, NM
Thursday Evening

"Get off me, bitch!" Buck's knees almost buckled when his girlfriend's loser mom, Mary, jumped on his back. The stench of alcohol was strong. One of her fingernails knifed his left ear. With the other hand, she grabbed a fistful of his slicked-back black hair. However, Buck was in his late thirties and tough.

"Get out of here! Barbie's not going with you!" Mary yelled, slurring, riding Buck like a wild horse and screaming between shouts. She was rail-thin but strong. Her knees wrapped around him, squeezing. "Leave my baby alone!"

"Stop! Let go! That hurts! Let go, you crazy bitch!" Buck shouted. He circled wildly, dipping his shoulder, trying to throw her off. There wasn't much room in the old trailer.

"Don't! Mom, let him go!" Barbie yelled.

Buck watched Barbie back into a corner and slide down to a crouch. He knew Barbie had learned to stay back from wild struggles. She was used to violence. Mary's habit of picking the wrong men, combined with the copious drugs and alcohol she typically consumed, created volatile situations. She seemed to believe she would stop, yet never could.

With one hand, Buck tried to pull Mary's fingernail off his ear, while with the other, he grabbed Mary's hand, which was wrapped in and pulling his hair. To lessen the pain, he tightly held her hand against his skull. Then he stopped spinning, threw himself backward, and slammed her against the wall.

The trailer shuddered. Mary wheezed, went limp, and released her hold, then slid down the wall and off Buck's back.

Buck turned, took a few backward steps, and yelled down at her, "Jesus, you're fucking crazy!" He stuck out his bloody hand, clenched her hair, yanked her head back, and banged it against the wall, forcing her to look at him. She didn't struggle. "You fucking cut my ear! I should kill you! Just overdose your ass. Who'd care?"

"Stop it! Stop it!" Barbie yelled, rushing up to Buck.

Without letting go of Mary, Buck swung out his right arm and backhanded Barbie. She fell to the floor and held her cheek. He glared at her. "You want to get out of this shithole, right?"

She nodded.

"Then get your shit and go wait in the truck."

Barbie picked up a small, beat-up suitcase and walked to the door, staying out of Buck's range. "Sorry, Mom, I can't stay here anymore. But don't worry, Buck treats me nice."

Mary didn't answer. She shook her head, then started to cry. She was defeated. Without looking up, she said, "Who's going to take care of me?"

∼

BARBIE PEEKED at Buck as he jumped in and slammed the door of the old truck. He looked furious. Too scared to speak, she avoided eye contact. Barbie had left with Buck for one reason—to start over. She felt horrible about leaving her mom, but she had tried so many times to live a better life.

Buck had an offer from a friend to work construction in Louisiana. He'd told Barbie he would help her get a good job and go back to school if she went with him. Buck was good-looking and mostly treated her well, except when he went nuts from drinking and jealousy. Still, she didn't love him. He was a means to an end. She knew Mr. Right was out there somewhere, but for damn sure he wasn't in Columbus.

She sighed, maybe too loud. "You think my mom'll be alright by herself?"

"Who gives a shit? I oughta buy her a case of whiskey and let her kill herself. She's a fucking wreck!"

"I'm just worried about her."

He hit the brakes. "You wanna stay? Get your ass out, now! I don't need you whining all the way to Louisiana." He reached across and flung open her door.

She hated how Buck treated her sometimes, but he did love her. She was sure of it. Barbie was careful not to roll her eyes.

He pulled the door shut. "I didn't think so." Then he continued, "We'll stay at the La Rosa Hotel tonight and head to Louisiana tomorrow after a good breakfast. I'm tired and horny."

She didn't answer.

"Hey! You hear me?"

She flinched. "Sure, honey, that sounds great."

6
THE NEW BOSS

Chihuahua, Mexico
Thursday Evening

IT HAD TAKEN some outside help, and several deaths, including Zorro's and Rosa's, but Rico was now the *capo*: the head of the Zorro cartel. He didn't regret pulling the trigger on Rosa in the tunnel after Zorro had been killed earlier in the day. She had always treated Rico like shit. Nobody had witnessed Rico killing Rosa, so he told everyone Spike had done it. Regardless of who killed whom, it was a dangerous time for the new boss.

Rico rested for a moment in what, just that morning, had been Zorro's study. One of Rico's first calls was to Zorro's *abogado*. Because the attorney didn't want to lose the cartel's business or his life, Rico knew he'd be eager to help. Rico advised him to make a small revision to the will. The will had never been publicly filed because Zorro had wanted to keep everything private. A brief paragraph stated that if all three died, everything went to charity. After cutting, pasting, and a trip to the copy machine, that charity became Rico.

Once the attorney hung up, Rico called in Toro and Mateo, both of whom were waiting outside the study's closed door. Rico had wanted no witnesses to the will changing.

Toro and Mateo had been regional bosses for Zorro. As the former number two, Rico knew them both well. He had immediately called them, as well as others in the organization, to his new *hacienda*. Most waited outside.

He knew these men must have been nervous earlier, as some changes were harsh when a new *capo* took over, but they seemed more relaxed now. He'd already spoken to Toro and Mateo individually, explaining that he needed trustworthy men beside him. They both knew they were on the inside now.

"Toro, Mateo—has it been done?" Rico asked.

"*Sí, Capo*," Toro and Mateo answered. They dipped their heads almost in unison.

"They're downstairs in the courtyard, all ready for you, boss," Toro said.

Rico hadn't told either man that they were the number two. He had done this on purpose, to see how they would act. *Who will suck up? Who will take charge but not undermine my authority?* He noticed Mateo had frowned at Toro for adding more explanation to their joint answer. Maybe Mateo thought it made Toro look weaker.

Toro was a big man, but that wasn't how he'd gotten his nickname. Instead, he'd earned it after playing "matador" when he was young, and the bull's horns had cut the left side of his face, from his chin to the outside of his eyebrow. Toro proudly wore the scar and didn't explain its origin to many people. He preferred them to see it as a sign of his ferociousness.

Mateo was an average-sized man with scary eyes. He was known for being sly and cunning, but he had no nickname. His name meant "gift of God," and he let everyone know it. Rumor was that when killing someone, he would say, "This is a gift from God," right before pulling the trigger.

"Let's get this over with," Rico said.

He descended the stairs from the balcony of his new study overlooking the ranch. Toro and Mateo followed. Outside, six men were lined up, zip-tied and on their knees. Two cried, one begged, and three were stoic. Their zip-ties were further secured to a stake in the ground. They could only squirm hopelessly. They couldn't escape.

Rico stopped beside the men, with Toro and Mateo behind him to his left and right. Nobody spoke—most notably Rico—for a minute or more. He wanted to raise the tension. Then he issued a loud command to his new lieutenants and whoever was on hand to watch. He knew the word would pass quickly to anyone not there. "These men have been shown to be untrustworthy. No one else will be harmed. This is a one-time cleansing. As long as you are loyal, we will all prosper together. I have big plans for growth. Stay loyal and get rich. Therefore, the men you see before you must die."

Rico gripped a 1911 Colt 45, the weapon perfect for his message. He held the gun about a foot from the back of the first man's head, then pulled the trigger. There was a small kick as the shot rang out. The shell ejected, and the slide set the next round. The man jerked forward and lay in a heap, blood pouring onto the ground from what was left of the front of his head. Rico took his time between men, letting the horror and fear travel deep into all the observers. As he went down the row, each man got a single bullet.

An eerie quiet descended. Only the birds and Rico's steps back to his initial position filled the thick air. Now he was where he'd started, facing Toro and Mateo.

In a fluid motion, he lifted the pistol to Mateo's forehead. Rico pulled the trigger as he said, "This is a gift from God."

Rico knew this was unexpected. *I am the fucking boss.* He held his arm extended for a few seconds longer than needed. Then he slowly lowered the gun and turned to his men.

"That was the last purge!" Rico yelled. "Toro is the number two! Let us all swear to never kill our own again!"

Rico walked around and fixed eyes for a moment with every man, shaking each one's hand.

Once finished, he strode back toward the enormous ranch house. Rico spoke softly to Toro. "You're my man. We live or die together." He knew he had to give trust to someone, and Toro had it, at least as much as possible. Still, Rico knew everyone was susceptible to corruption.

"Until the end," Toro said.

Rico and Toro watched men put the bodies in the truck's bed. Then they walked back to Rico's study and shut the door.

"You heard of the deal going down in Houston yet?" Rico asked.

"Not yet, but Pedro said it's still on, and the sellers knew Zorro was out. They said they didn't care as long as they got the weapons."

"I should be there, but there's no way I can get there before it happens," Rico said. "Way too many moving parts today." He poured two drinks and handed one to Toro. "Here's to our success."

"*Salud!*" Toro downed the drink.

"Have a seat." Rico sat behind the desk. "Toro, have we heard anything about the other cartels trying to make a move on us?"

"Not yet, but we must be ready for it."

"Keep checking with our spies. Also, are you sure Spike has the bitcoin wallet?"

"He has to have it," Toro said. "It was supposed to be picked up from the bank in Chihuahua and brought to us immediately, but the men went to the safe house first. As you know, Spike killed them all. We searched the house everywhere. About three hundred and fifty thousand dollars in cash and the thumb drive are gone."

"I'm willing to write the cash off, but there was about sixteen million dollars on that thumb drive. That's too much to forget," Rico said. "Let's start with El Paso." He called Dante.

∼

EL PASO, TX

Thursday Evening

Dante felt uneasy, waiting for a bullet.

Scared to death, or maybe scared of death. Either way, his stomach upset him. Whenever a cartel changed leadership, it was an extremely dangerous time. About thirty minutes ago, he'd gotten a warning call from a friend in Mexico. "There may be some executions." Often, leadership changes rolled downhill. It was natural that Rico would take over the operation. Dante had no issues with the new boss, and anybody who might've had a problem with the new *capo* was dead.

However, Dante oversaw the El Paso area and was at a

loss for what to do. He'd always hit his numbers, except once, but he'd made up for it in cash.

He debated calling Rico and pledging his loyalty. Finally, he decided he should. He was holding his phone, looking at it, when it rang.

"Dante, this is Rico."

"Yes, *Jefe*," Dante said. He hoped that calling him *Jefe* would express where he stood.

"So, you know?" Rico asked.

"*Sí.*"

"Any issues?"

"No issues. You're the boss. I'm loyal to you."

"Good. Let's move on. With all the confusion today, something has been stolen from us. A gringo came through the Palomas tunnel, maybe an hour or two ago. He was on foot. There's a good chance he's in or around Columbus. He may have a very valuable thumb drive. It's a bitcoin wallet. The gringo goes by Spike, but I don't know if that's his real name."

"What does he look like?"

"He's about forty, average height, seemed to be in good shape, dark hair, and he had a blue gym bag. I need that thumb drive, and him, in case he's already downloaded what's on it. Don't kill him. And be careful. He's probably armed."

"I got it, boss." He almost said congratulations, but it was better to say nothing and just show his loyalty.

Dante left immediately. Now that he'd had time to think, he felt better about his position with the new management. But still, he worried.

7

ALWAYS BE SMILING

Columbus, NM
Thursday Evening

ONE HOUR after he'd left the church, Spike reached the edge of Columbus. The only light he saw came from the trailers spread everywhere. Many had yard lights on poles, illuminating sandy yards scattered with junk. Ahead, he saw an intersection with small businesses on at least one corner. *Gas station? Maybe some snacks and a long-sleeved windbreaker to cover my bloody arm ...or at least something to drink.* Struggling to gather moisture in his mouth to swallow, he realized how thirsty he was.

He glanced at his watch. *Eight o'clock.*

On his approach, he saw there was only one business on the corner, a quaint restaurant called The Borderland Café. *Cute.* The sign on the door said it closed at seven, but people were inside, so he went in.

"Hi, hun," an older skinny waitress said. "You're lucky.

We're usually closed, but we're having a party and decided to leave the doors open." She waved her hand toward a table.

Spike smiled and read her name tag. "Thank you so much, Lilly. You're such a kind person." He hated her strong, spicy perfume. It burned his nose. "I love that perfume. Spice?"

"Why, yes, thanks. Most people don't notice. You know, I think it's time to close it up. The kitchen told me to lock the door twenty minutes ago to keep people from wandering in. You just made it. They'll kill me if I don't lock it."

Spike turned a little and smiled. "You gotta be careful. You never know who wants to do you in, do you?"

"You're right about that." She laughed with Spike for a second, then rushed off to take care of the other tables.

From his booth, Spike took in the small, brightly colored restaurant. *Freedom!* The first thing he'd done was go to the restroom and wash up as best he could with paper towels. It felt so good, but the mirror didn't lie. He still looked rough, though at least now he was clean.

Returning to his table, he found iced tea. Spike took a long sip of the sweet cold liquid through a straw. *My God!* He shut his eyes and held a mouthful for a few seconds before swallowing. He'd been so thirsty that hot piss would have tasted great, which only made the tea better. His mind drifted back to his childhood kitchen, iced tea in the summer and coffee in the winter, and the first time his mother had given him the advice that he would live by.

Always smile. Always be nice to people. Then you will always get what you want. Spike replayed the words in his head. *You can think whatever you want anytime. You can do whatever you want in private. But always be polite and smile.*

He took a breath and let it out slowly, then looked over

his shoulder at a young woman, probably part of the party, who'd caught his eye when he'd walked to his table. *Eighteen, maybe, Hispanic, small breasts, big brown eyes, long jet-black hair, and a delicate throat.* His heart sped up. His breath became shallow. *Too innocent ... I need a rubber band.*

Spike looked away from the young woman and called to the old waitress. "Ma'am," he said, holding up his empty glass a little.

When Lilly looked his way, he smiled and winked. She gave him a vigorous thumbs-up and disappeared.

He tried to forget the young woman. Spotting a red rubber band on the cashier's counter, he walked over and picked it up, then slipped it on his right wrist and pulled it up as far as possible. *Snap!* It stung badly. He moved back to his table, using self-imposed blinders secured by sheer will to not look at her. *Snap!*

He hoped he didn't smell after twenty-four hours of sweat, exertion, travel, desert, guns, killing, surviving, and a tunnel.

"Here ya go, darling, fresh cold tea for my favorite customer."

"Thank you, Lilly. You're as nice as you are pretty."

"You must need glasses. I look horrible." She straightened herself up, brushed her clothes, and ran her hand through her grey hair. Lilly's wrinkled, leathery skin screamed that she'd spent too much time in the sun. She'd seemed overly pleasant before, but now she was falling all over herself. She'd trust him. She smiled with stained teeth.

Never wrong, I can read 'em. "I need something to eat too."

"The menu is kind of limited, but the burger and fries are pretty good."

"That would be great," Spike said with a warm smile. He

touched her hand and let it linger for a second when she took the menu. *I think she blushed.*

"Sure thing, darling," the waitress said. "Anything for a good-looking hunk of a man like you."

Spike glanced at her finger—no ring. *Bingo! Could be a fallback place to flop tonight and a possible ride.* "Thank you, Lilly. You really are a head turner too, you know." Spike winked. He was aware of his good looks, charm, and shape —and he used them. *People like me.*

Lilly giggled like a little girl, lingered slightly too long, and took off for the kitchen. Then she stopped abruptly, turned, and leaned into Spike. "Can I ask why you snap your wrist with that rubber band?"

"You can ask me anything, Lilly. But to answer your question, it's a technique to help people break a bad habit."

"You have a bad habit?"

"Just a nervous habit of tapping my foot." She'd probably prefer that answer to the real one—to control his desire to kill the innocent. He had no issues with using bad people to feed his habit, but he wasn't sure it would work. Without a real test yet, he was quite curious.

He still felt like shit. The last twenty-four hours had started when he'd been freed from his prison, designed by Jeff Case—a pretty damn efficient vigilante. Spike had spent several months in the underground cell in Houston. Then Spike had taken a jet to Chihuahua, Mexico. Later, he'd spent half a day in the desert, running from the cartel. This had been followed by gunfights, a serious cut on his arm, and, finally, an escape to the States through a cartel tunnel while being shot at.

Spike kept the blue gym bag beside him. The bag touched his hip and leg, creating a sensory reminder that almost burned him.

The foot-long cut on his left forearm throbbed with pain. Dried blood crusted at the edges of the duct tape where it had oozed out. Spike had hidden the wound with a windbreaker he'd bought as soon as he'd walked into the diner. He'd seen the sign outside for Poncho Villa State Park, which was likely why his new jacket had the Poncho Villa logo. He'd also gotten a hat with the same logo, which he could wear pulled down over his eyes.

I need to have that arm looked at. Soon! Maybe a vet?

He took a sip of tea. *A lot of people died today. Three were mine.*

His whole body ached.

"Johnny. You okay?" said a female in the background. Then she screamed, "Johnny! Johnny!"

Spike didn't want to look or act interested. Because he wasn't.

"Help! Help! Please! My husband! He's choking!" an old woman yelled.

Spike sighed, then slowly raised his eyes and saw a short woman, about fifty, standing and flailing.

"Help him! I don't know what to do!"

The man at the table with her held both hands to his throat. He looked terrified as he tried to stand.

Funny, the guy's face is turning as red as the tablecloth. Spike smiled, then tried to look concerned in case someone was watching him. He wanted to stare at the man as he fought to live. He'd never seen someone die by choking on food.

The old man bolted to full standing but quickly dropped to one knee. Lilly ran over and slapped him on the back.

Slapping on the back. Jesus ... really! Everyone knows that only makes it worse.

Always be nice. His mother's voice was constantly in his

head. *Shit!* The loving command repeated itself, getting louder. *Always be nice. Always be nice. Always be nice.* He tried to give Lilly an encouraging nod.

No one except the old skinny waitress made a move toward the man in the white shorts and orange polo. Spike didn't feel indifferent, as he wanted to watch the guy die. *Just curious.*

But he kept hearing his mother. *Always be nice. Always be nice.*

Sighing and remembering his promise to God from when he'd crawled out of the tunnel, Spike sprinted over and crouched between Lilly and Johnny. Lilly scampered out of the way, probably relieved to have someone take over. Spike jerked Johnny to a standing position—the man had stopped choking and was now limp—and started the Heimlich maneuver. Nothing happened. The man was now a rag doll, but Spike kept jerking up with his arms around the man and his hands in a fist centered under the ribs. Three times he yanked the rag doll up, popping pressure into the man with his fists together.

Decision time! Ease up a little and let him die or ... fuck it! Though his arm screamed in pain and he was certain he was bleeding all over himself and Johnny, Spike kicked it up a notch, performing the Heimlich vigorously as the limp body flopped around.

The wife started crying loudly. "Oh, my God! He's dead!" The crying quickly turned into a messy, uncontrolled blubbering.

It took three more pumps before Johnny spat out a piece of meat and took a big gasp of air. As Johnny appeared to get his wits back, Spike eased him onto the floor. The wife was all over Johnny with hugs and kisses. Then she stood and hugged Spike, kissing his cheek over and over. "My God.

Thank you so much. I can never thank you enough. You are such a good man. I couldn't live without my husband." She wept uncontrollably again, then put her head on Spike's shoulder and squeezed him. It didn't take long before she regained her composure. Wiping away her tears, the old woman stared into Spike's eyes, piercing his soul. In a calm voice, she said, "God sent you as an angel among us."

Everyone in the restaurant clapped and cheered. This felt extremely odd to Spike. He was still reeling from how the woman had touched him.

She thinks I'm an angel.

With his head down, he gave a casual wave to the applause, then returned to his booth. *Thank God my bag is still here. Wow, all the thanks felt so ... good. They think I'm a hero. Did God just talk to me? Mom was right. I should always be nice. But Dad!*

Before leaving the restaurant, every patron stopped by Spike's table to shake his hand. Johnny and his wife stopped by too, and the tears started again.

"Lilly, sweetheart, is there a hotel in town?" Spike asked.

She leaned down and pushed the bill toward him until her hand touched his. Almost in a whisper, she said, "You know, I got a couch and get off in about thirty minutes." Then she straightened up and said in a normal voice, "Sure but just one hotel. As soon as you go out the door, look to your right. You can see it. Bright yellow and pink, all lit up."

"Thank you, Lilly."

"Oh, the owner said no charge for the meal."

"Thanks again. Tell him for me."

She didn't leave. He turned the bill over. It said, "No charge," and had her phone number.

"I'm awful tired tonight. Is the invitation open for tomorrow?"

"Yes, anytime ... and I mean anytime." She gave him an exaggerated wink that felt like it came out of a sitcom.

Spike squeezed her hand. "You are really terrific. I'm glad I met you, and I'll plan to see you again real soon." He picked up his blue bag, pulled the cap over his eyes, and left.

8

THE GUNN

Houston, TX
Thursday Evening

The Observer

AVA GUNN'S air conditioner had stopped blowing cold air into her car about thirty minutes ago, but she couldn't pull over or try to get it fixed.

August in Houston. It's damn hot.

Ava plucked her wet blouse off her skin to let some air blow in. She couldn't stop driving. *No choice.* She just had to suffer. She had the address of some warehouse and a time, and she was supposed to be there to take pictures. It felt a little strange, but doing surveillance could be weird sometimes. And it was getting dark.

She put her windows down in the Houston heat. *My hair's going to look horrible too.* It was like an oven with the windows up, but even with them down, she still felt miserable.

"Hey, Siri, what's the temperature?"

"It's about ninety-two degrees outside. Hot!"

"No shit! Hey, Siri, call Stanley Lawyer."

The call went through.

"Any problems?" Stan said.

"Since you asked, my A/C's out. It's hot, and I'm sweating like a pig. Can I catch these guys later?"

"That sucks for you, but I really don't care."

"Relax, damn."

"Sorry, but this is a rare chance. A one-time meeting for me to ID a few guys for a case, and I need some pictures. That's all you need to know. And don't forget: Try to get license plates and faces if you can. If it doesn't happen on time, then wait. Got it?"

"I got it, but there might be no water left in my body in a couple of hours."

"Quit bitching. You're getting paid, you know."

"Yes, sir!" she said as he hung up. *Stanley Lawyer, my ass.* Ava had previously looked up the man and found no one named "Stanley Lawyer" anywhere. And she was sure he was using a burner phone.

Soon, she pulled into an industrial park and drove by the address. She didn't see anything or anyone around the warehouse. It was in a line with a bunch of other buildings and didn't look special. The park wasn't an easy place to hide, but she found a spot where she could see the front and not be too conspicuous. The night lights were coming on, which made it easier to see and created shadows. The shadows would help conceal her.

Before long, a van pulled up, and a few guys got out. Even wearing jeans and Dockers with polo shirts, they looked rough. The driver slammed his door shut and walked into one of the buildings.

Ava had parked behind a van that was a block away, but she could still see the entrance. She settled down and waited for him to come back out, getting the address off her cell phone in the meantime. A drop of sweat fell off her nose and onto her phone. She was hot, irritable, and sticky. Only half her bottle of water remained, and she knew it would soon be gone.

She turned off the car. With no A/C, the engine generated extra heat. Ava sat with her head slightly out the window and spread her arms and legs to try to stay cool. *This sucks.* She kept glancing at the rearview and side mirrors.

Then the door to the warehouse ascended. Ava grabbed her camera with the long-range telephoto lens. Just as the door got high enough to clear the vehicles, a semi-truck with a Cadillac Escalade in front rounded the corner. Ava started clicking.

She glanced in the mirror at the smaller bald man with a beard, wearing blue jeans and a blue polo shirt, walking up the sidewalk behind her. He was talking on a cell phone and not looking in her direction. Back to taking pictures. Although not her assignment, she planned on walking up to the building to see if she could get some photos of what was going on inside.

She relaxed as the bald man walked past the passenger side.

Before she had time to turn her eyes back to check the mirrors, something was jerked over her head from behind. *A bag!* She dropped her camera and reached to pull the bag off her head, but a drawstring was already tightening around her neck.

The hands and strength felt like a man's. Big hands quickly grabbed her left armpit and right shoulder, trying to jerk her petite body through the window. In the bag, the world was pitch black, but she grabbed the steering wheel with both hands and spread her legs to prevent her extraction from the car. The man kept yanking her body. Ava's left knee struggled to stay under the steering wheel while her right foot was wedged under the dash. She tried punching the man with one hand, but she always lost ground and ended up regripping the wheel.

He's strong, and God, the gagging BO penetrates even the bag.

She wanted to go for the gun in her shoulder holster, but she was afraid she'd get ripped out of the car and lose it.

"Stop fighting, bitch!" the man said in a loud, deep voice.

Ava could hear it muffled through the bag. *Hispanic accent?* He leaned into the car to get a better grip, then moved his right hand so it no longer pulled on her shoulder but instead reached under her arm. He grabbed her harder and got a handful of her right breast.

"Ouch! You asshole! Let go of me!"

As she struggled, the bag twisted and choked her. Somehow, an odd thought raced through her mind. *Why did I have the window down? Oh, yeah, it was hot!* She had her knee under the steering wheel, trying to keep herself in the car, but it was slipping.

Ava took one hand off the wheel and moved her hand inside the cord around her neck to prevent herself from being choked unconscious.

"Help me, you idiot!" the accented BO man yelled.

Another set of hands—smaller but still strong—grasped her body. She released her second hand from the steering wheel and went for her gun. Just as she pulled the weapon from her shoulder holster, the two men jerked her again, hard. Her hand hit the steering wheel, and she dropped the gun. With her head and shoulders out the window, one hand came off her. Then something hit her face.

Because her head was in a bag and she was wiggling, the blow hit her forehead. It surprised her but didn't do much damage. She tried to reach her ankle holster, but her toe hold was about all she had left as her foot slipped down the dash. She couldn't reach the holster, and she couldn't pull up her leg without releasing her toehold.

The second blow hit her square in the face with a sledgehammer force. Wooziness overtook her. The punch had made her muscles relax enough that, in one swift motion, the men were able to yank her out of the car. Ava was dazed and weightless until her body slammed onto the pavement. She was at their mercy. She could see nothing and lay still on the warm, hard surface. She smelled the asphalt first, then the sweat and BO of the man who had pulled her out of the car.

"Let's take her to Pedro," the other man said.

Same accent. Gotta be the little bald guy.

"Shut up!" BO man said.

Someone slapped her bagged head.

The BO man asked her, "Who are you, lady?"

"Your worst fucking nightmare," Ava said.

"Yeah, right. Who hired you?"

"Santa Claus."

"Now that's funny," BO man said.

Both men laughed.

Ava was regaining her senses. From her ankle holster, she grabbed her pistol: a six-round 9 mm Glock 43. Then she moved the pistol in the direction of the voice of the man holding the bag on her head. When she pushed it into the flesh of a body, probably a stomach, she pulled the trigger.

"Jesus, she shot me!" yelled BO man.

The grip on the bag was gone. Ava scrambled on her ass, then her knees, and then onto her feet, pointing the gun in the direction of the other voice. He said nothing now.

"Shit! Get her, you idiot! Watch the gun!" yelled BO man.

Ava couldn't get the bag off with one hand. She was completely disoriented. *Which way do I run?* She reached up with her gun hand so now both hands worked on the tie string. It loosened.

"Fuck, I'm hurt bad!" BO man yelled.

She started pulling off the bag.

"Too late," a deep voice said.

Those were the last words Ava Gunn heard before something hard hit her in the head. Everything went black.

9

THE BIG DEAL

Warehouse:Houston Industrial Area
Thursday Evening

The Buyer

PEDRO HERNANDEZ CHECKED HIS WATCH. *Soon!* He had overseen the Houston area of the Zorro cartel for three years now. Though Pedro had a new boss, the deal couldn't be called off. Drugs and human trafficking had been their focus, and this evening was their first large arms deal. They would take the delivery today and resell it to a militia group tomorrow. They'd make a huge profit for less than a day's work, moving a semi-truck full of arms.

Pedro's eyes kept darting around at his men. His stomach churned, and he was sure they saw how unsettled he was. He shifted from one foot to the other, then halted, realizing he was too obvious with his unease. But he knew it was too late to do anything other than move forward.

The warehouse was no longer used. They'd rented it for a month, just for this deal. Near the hydraulically controlled industrial-sized door, one of his men yelled and waved.

Pedro gave the man a thumbs-up, then hit "send" on his phone, with Rico's number ready.

The motors kicked in, and the door slowly slid open. It was enormous, reminding Pedro of an aircraft hangar door. When it had opened wide enough, an Escalade entered with windows so dark it was impossible to see the occupants. A semi-truck followed.

Pedro held the phone to his ear. "Rico—I'm sorry—I mean boss." He paused. His gut fluttered, and his heart pounded. A new boss and a big deal—so many things could go wrong. "It's time ... they're here."

Three men stood behind Pedro, all armed: two to drive the truck away and his driver.

Pedro glanced toward a sniper perched high in the warehouse to his right. He couldn't even see him. Pedro smiled. *That's some comfort, knowing he has our back.*

A man opened the door. That made five guys.

Should have brought more.

Once the semi pulled into the warehouse, they'd examine the goods and call Rico. He'd transfer the rest of the money. The buyer would confirm, and everyone would leave.

The truck stopped, and men piled out of it and the Escalade.

The Seller

"Boss, we're here," the man in the Escalade said into his phone. He had an M4 on his lap and a Glock on his hip.

"Good," Gecko responded.

He was an anonymous man. Few knew his real name, but he had a solid reputation as an arms dealer. He always delivered and was notorious for hunting down, at all costs, anyone who screwed him. No one would ever cross him if they had half a brain and an ounce of common sense. The deal had been arranged anonymously, and the fee was to be paid half up front and half upon delivery. Gecko would not be with the truck or the Escalade. Once the merchandise was examined and the funds transferred, his men would leave the truck with the goods in it and depart.

"We're inside. They're standing there. Looks okay. I'm getting out now. I'll call you as soon as they're ready to transfer the rest of the money," the man said.

"Good. Take no chances and be careful. Shoot first if you have to."

"Got it."

Black Ops Team

A SMARTLY LED and well-trained black ops team was tasked with retrieving weapons for the US government. Two weeks before the sale of stolen Switchback drones took place, they had found out which warehouse would be used. Those weeks had given them time to do a thorough recon, which included disabling all the cameras that might get a glimpse of them during preparation or on the way out. No one would leave alive except them. They were off the books and not authorized to operate on US soil, but getting the FBI or ATF involved would lead to a leak that would be extremely embarrassing to the US. The seven-man team, which included four snipers, would get this done and disappear. Ghosts.

The team had taken up position thirty-six hours earlier. The snipers found their shooting positions high in the warehouse, then retreated to hide and see if any of the other parties sent people early to cover the operation. The operatives on the floor also found where they would initiate the attack from their hiding places in the warehouse.

The Cop

JUST A REGULAR DAY for Officer Rodgers, HPD, until he rounded the corner and saw two guys jerk a woman with a black bag over her head from a car window. Rodgers didn't hit the siren but quickly called it in. He wanted to drive up to them, so he'd have a chance to surprise them. He touched his sidearm, a Smith & Wesson 40 caliber, then put his hand on the wheel. *Close enough to hold them, but if they run, I won't shoot ... I'll have to let them go.*

Two shots rang out, and the bigger guy released the woman. The man stumbled backward, holding his midsection as he fell in the center of the street. Rodgers noticed the surprise on the man's face. The woman, still with the bag on her head, had shot him. She started blindly scooching on her ass to get away, holding her pistol and swinging her head to the side. She was looking for the second man, who stepped up and decked her hard in the head with his gun. She fell limp on the street beside her car. The man turned and saw the cop hit the brakes. With his weapon drawn, the cop jumped from his patrol car.

"Drop the gun!" Rodgers yelled. He stood in a shooting stance, aiming his pistol.

Then all hell broke loose. It sounded as if a firefight in a war zone had erupted from a warehouse a block away. Rodgers turned his head and heard a gunshot nearby. Then his shoulder erupted in excruciating pain as he took the baseball-bat-like hit. He stumbled backward, dropped his gun, and collapsed to the pavement.

Officer Rodgers crawled a few feet and picked up his weapon. From his position on his back, still on the ground, he lifted his weapon with great effort and pointed it at the injured man, who was standing over the woman who'd just shot him. Rodgers knew he was going to pass out. Despite his fuzzy vision, he tried to aim, then squeezed the trigger. He heard a shot but felt nothing. It looked like the man was lunging, staggering toward him. Rodgers thought he pulled the trigger, but he passed out before he could confirm a hit.

Black Ops Team

FLUFF LAY PERFECTLY STILL, with controlled breathing. *Not my first rodeo.* He went onto the comms. "This is six. You all know what to do. Take 'em down fast. Wait for my command."

This has to go down fast, or we're all screwed.

Along with his other preparations, a few cameras gave him a feed. He and his men on the floor were hiding in empty wooden crates on all sides of the warehouse, by the walls, behind where the action would take place. These positions would keep them from being spotted by either party during a sweep. They'd find nobody. Fluff's men on the floor would clean up what the snipers missed.

The snipers were also hiding. If either party brought an overwatch, Fluff's men would take them out with knives before they even got set. His sniper outside would lay back and look for competition before taking up his position.

He expected the Zorro cartel to have about five to ten men and Gecko to have three in the Escalade, two in the semi, and three to four guys outside for perimeter security. Fluff had his own perimeter sniper who, on order, could take them all down in a few seconds.

Fluff could see that the Escalade and the semi were inside once the door had closed. Gecko's men had dismounted and stood facing the cartel's men. All of them were at the back of the truck, preparing to open the semi's back doors to check the cargo.

"Perimeter, what's happening outside?" Fluff asked on comms.

"Two men just ripped a woman out of a car. A cop pulled up to them and jumped out of his car with his weapon out."

A gunshot sounded outside, which made everyone duck and get their weapons ready.

"The woman with the bag over her head just shot one of her attackers," Perimeter said.

"Roger that, everyone's still got their backs to us," Fluff said on comms. "Kill 'em all, quickly, and no rounds into the engine block of the truck. Open fire."

∼

WHEN THE PERIMETER sniper got the green light to shoot, the situation changed rapidly: one woman dead or unconscious on the ground and one wounded man down. The other goon had just shot the cop and was running up to him, probably to finish him off.

He lined up his crosshairs on the head of the man who'd

just shot the cop, then pulled the trigger. The man took a hit to the back of the head and slumped forward. Following a tiny adjustment, the sniper took a headshot of the wounded goon on the ground to finish him off. After the final shot rang through the air, the goon stopped moving.

The sniper packed up his rifle and took off. No point in shooting the injured cop or the woman, who wasn't moving, just lying prone, the bag still on her head.

∽

PEDRO STOOD with everyone else at the back of the truck, waiting for the door to open. Once it did, he'd go inside and check a few boxes to make sure they were getting what they'd paid for.

Some sudden shots and loud pops echoed, and Pedro wondered what he heard. Then the men started falling. The Gecko crew lurched forward toward his men as they were hit from behind and dropped to the ground. His men fell to the other side, then went straight to the floor. The shots came quickly from at least two directions, and everyone went down fast.

Pedro dived to the floor when the first shot was fired. He crawled as fast as he could toward the back of the truck for protection. At first, he thought the other men on both sides were also ducking for cover, but then he realized they were all dead. It was just luck that he hadn't been one of the first people taken out by the shooters.

Pedro lay under the truck, breathing hard, trying to avoid making noise. Then a heavy quiet fell over the area. *My God, that was fast.*

Footsteps, a few random sounds, and some men murmuring. Pedro was afraid to speak on his phone, so he texted Rico: **Been attacked by third party. Everyone dead but me. May not get out.** He hit "send."

Bodies were dragged out of the truck's way. Someone had opened the cab and shut the door.

"Fluff, it's clean. No bugs. Low jack disabled," a voice said.

Pedro texted Rico: **Heard the name Fluff. Take care of my family.**

"Hey," a man said.

Pedro stopped typing. His heart dropped, and he raised his head. From his prone position, he saw a man crouched a few feet away, looking under the truck and pointing a pistol with a silencer at him. Pedro begged, "Please, don't kill me. I didn't see anything. I'll just disappear."

"Wish I could," the man said, shrugging. "You understand."

Pedro pushed "send" on his text, then shut his eyes and started praying.

The pistol fired.

∼

FLUFF GAVE NO ORDERS. Everyone knew what to do. They were gone before a siren could sound in the distance.

As they left, he saw the cop and the woman with the black bag on her head lying in the street with two bodies.

He regretted the collateral damage, but it was going well so far.

Fluff called up the two SUVs waiting a safe distance away. He and his men piled in and caught up to the semi hauling the weapons. They had no issues reaching Ellington Field in South Houston on the thirty-five-minute drive.

They drove into Ellington Field and then to the Air

Force Reserve Unit, the home of the 147th Attack Wing. Then they followed a military escort to the tarmac, where the US military's four-engine turboprop workhorse transport aircraft waited. The C-130 Hercules was lowering the back ramp as they pulled up. Armed military guards and some men to help with the loading hung around. The switch drones were quickly and efficiently loaded into the cargo hold of the aircraft and strapped down. The ramp lifted, and the aircraft taxied toward the runway.

As they drove away, the C-130 lifted off the ground.

"You know where they're going?" the driver asked Fluff.

"Nope. Above my pay grade, *and* I don't care."

Fluff left the SUVs where he'd been told, inside the secured area on the base with all their weapons. They were parked beside another SUV he'd been informed to look for. He unlocked it and found, for each operator, a bag of cash with their name on it. He re-locked the SUV. Everyone changed clothes and got into their private vehicles, then drove off in different directions. They'd be on call and offered missions they could accept or refuse. Fluff would be their point of contact and team leader.

10

THE HOTEL

Columbus, NM
Thursday Night

AFTER LEAVING THE RESTAURANT, Spike stood at the corner of the east-west New Mexico State Road 9 and the north-south New Mexico State Road 11. To the south, it was dark. He knew the border crossing was about three miles away. To the north were more lights, obviously into the heart of this village—Columbus. However, to his right, a block or two away, with only empty lots of desert surrounding it, was a beacon of light and color in a sea of darkness. Just like Lilly had said.

The hotel looked like a big rectangular house. The top half was bright pink with a balcony, while the bottom half was bright yellow, accentuated by lights everywhere.

Fear of a cop or border patrol agent driving by and stopping him seized Spike on the short walk. As Spike drew closer, he saw the lighted sign: La Rosa Hotel. It seemed too small to be a hotel.

A couple of cars were parked in front, but no people lingered inside beyond the front door. *Strange.* He opened the door, setting off bells to announce his arrival.

"Just a minute, please," said a female voice with a heavy Mexican accent.

The inside was as colorful as the outside. A few tables littered the area, and he spotted where the breakfast layout went, though no food or any trace of the mouthwatering aromas remained. Spike stood at the desk with the bag over his left arm and turned sideways to the counter.

A short, middle-aged Hispanic woman wearing a bright blue blouse and a red pleated skirt hurried around the corner. Her name tag read, "Lucia, Manager." Breathing a little hard, she showed a big, toothy smile and pushed out one accented word before taking a breath again: "Hello."

"Hello, Lucia." Spike gave her the biggest smile he could and dipped his head as he leaned forward. Before coming in, he'd scanned the street, then the area around the hotel lobby and desk. *No cameras? Not a safe place for her.*

"I'm sorry, sir. We have no rooms available."

Spike wanted to scream but didn't. Instead, he smiled. His expression was as sincere as if he were telling a couple that their baby was beautiful. *Always be smiling.* "Oh, that's too bad. I'm really tired. It's been a long day. You know, there are only two cars out front. Are you sure?"

"I'm so sorry. Really. You see, we have some parking in the back, so it's a little deceptive. We really have no rooms at all."

"I understand. It's not your fault." Spike reached out and touched her hand. "Do you know if there are other hotels close by?"

"I'm sorry. The closest would be in Deming. About thirty miles up Highway 11."

Spike kept that smile on his face. Behind it, exhaustion and pain overwhelmed him. Close behind was anger, followed by frustration. He stood there, thinking. "Could I have a glass of water?" *That'll give me a few minutes to think.*

"Of course, just a minute." She went back around the corner and out of sight.

As he waited, lights blazed into the hotel from the front parking lot. Spike walked to the window and saw a red pickup. A pretty young woman and a man, a little older, maybe mid-thirties, sporting some serious muscle, got out.

They entered, and the bell tingled. At the same time, Lucia came around the corner with the glass of water. She held it up. Spike took it, nodded with a "thank you," and stepped back to listen. *Could be my ride.*

The man did the talking but received the same news Spike did. No rooms.

The couple started for the door.

"Excuse me."

They stopped and turned. The man's stare was hard, with not an ounce of friendliness. The young woman stood behind him with a sweet smile.

"Whatever you're selling, I don't want any." The man walked out.

The woman followed. So did Spike.

"Excuse me, sir. I think we're all going to Deming, and I need a ride. I can make it worth your while."

The man turned and stuck his face into Spike's. His breath reeked. "I don't need your fucking money." His spit wasn't appreciated. "Beat it before you get hurt." The man glared and didn't move.

That smell. Dirty ass or pile of cow shit? Not sure. Spike leaned into him with a big smile. *Always be smiling.* "How about a thousand dollars cash?"

"Bullshit." The man's demeanor changed.

The young woman's eyes widened. She squeezed in closer to her boyfriend and whispered something.

Spike made sure the man saw the duct tape and blood on his arm as he reached into his bag and pulled out five hundred-dollar bills. He held them up, then offered them to the man. "You'll get the other five hundred when we get to Deming."

The man took the money. "You rob a bank or something?"

"Nope. It's a long story. I'll even pay for supper and your room if you can find a restaurant and hotel. If you get a room for me. I lost my ID."

The man stood in silence. Spike knew the man was planning to ask for more money or maybe even rob him. If the man tried anything at all, Spike would turn, back away from him, and pull his Glock 40 out of the bag. *Do it! Do it!*

"Let's make it a thousand now, a thousand when we get to Deming, plus supper and our room."

Spike laughed. "Sure." He handed over the cash.

"What happened to your arm?" The man dipped his head toward Spike's bloody, duct-taped wound.

"Cut it shaving." Spike didn't wait for an answer. He held out his hand. "Name's Spike."

The man shook his hand as he stuffed the bills in his pocket. "I'm Buck. This is Barbie."

She gave a little wave and smiled. "Hi."

Barbie got into the pickup through Buck's door and slid under the steering wheel to the center of the bench seat. Buck climbed in and settled behind the wheel. Spike eased in the passenger door. He wouldn't have minded pushing against Barbie's leg, but she snuggled up to her boyfriend. Buck backed up, turning to drive out of the little parking lot. As he was about to accelerate, his headlights illuminated a tall, big man.

"Hey! Spike!"

"Who's that?" Buck asked.

Spike couldn't think of anyone he knew who'd be in Columbus, but he'd known many people when he'd worked as a national sales manager. *Maybe that guy would be a better ride out of here than Buck and Barbie.* He opened the truck door and stood, remaining on the running board and speaking over the open door. "Do I know you?"

The man reached behind his back, pulled out a pistol, pointed, and shot.

A bullet hole appeared in the front windshield. Small shards of glass hit the interior of the cab.

"Punch it! Now!" Spike screamed, leaning below the dash and pulling Barbie down.

Buck sat there a second, stunned.

"Now!" Spike stretched over and used his hand to floor the accelerator. He heard the pickup throw gravel and lurch forward. Another shot rang out. It hit the windshield in front of Buck. He jerked backward. Spike waited for the thud of a body hitting the truck.

11

NO THUMP

Columbus, NM
Thursday Night

SPIKE WAS surprised there was no thump, and Buck still had the steering wheel.

"Let go of the gas! Move your hand! I got it!" Buck screamed. He ground his foot into Spike's hand, which held the accelerator to the floor.

"Damn! Ease up! My hand's pinned!" Spike yelled.

The truck hit the slightly elevated road so hard, the entire vehicle jolted and swerved.

Spike's bad arm hit something. "Damn!"

"What'll we do?" Barbie screamed.

"Shut up!" Buck grabbed Barbie by the hair and slammed the back of her head into the dash. She slumped down on the floor in a pile.

As he struggled to see out the back, Spike smiled. *Buck is a bad man.* He glimpsed the shooter limping into the empty street, his arm in a firing position, pointed at them. The man fired two more shots, one pinging as it hit the back of the truck. He then holstered his gun and limped to a parked car on the street.

~

DANTE TOOK two steps and fell. The pain was unbearable. He was sure his left leg was broken below the knee. When he jumped to avoid the pickup, he landed awkwardly on a concrete block.

He watched the pickup turn the corner, headed north on Highway 11. *Shit!* Shaking his head, he knew he had to make some calls.

Dante crawled to his car, which, to avoid cameras, he'd parked in a dark spot across the street from the hotel. Gingerly, he climbed into the passenger seat and called his lieutenant. "Jorge. Where are you?"

"Near Deming, coming from El Paso on I-10. Did you find him?"

"When you get to Deming, come south down Highway 11," Dante said, gritting his teeth with pain. "It'll be about thirty-five to forty miles to Columbus. Look for a red pickup going north with two men and a woman. Spike is one of the men. He's got a blue bag that we must get. They'll be passing you."

"You don't sound too good. You okay?"

"No! I'm not! I think I broke my leg. I can't drive, and I'm not having a lot of luck finding this guy. And we *have* to find him."

"Sorry, boss," Jorge said. "What if we miss them? It's dark."

"Don't miss them!" Dante tried to relax and deal with

the pain. "Look, there won't be much traffic. If you *have to*, turn around and chase someone down. Do *not* let them by you. And don't kill Spike. Kill the other two if you must, I don't care."

"Got it, boss. Oh, I got a hold of Gabriel, but he was on the other side of El Paso. He's coming down Highway 9 to your location. It'll be at least two hours before he gets there."

"Two hours ... damn!" He was breathing heavily. "Call me when you find them. I'm hanging up."

Then Dante made the call he dreaded.

"Boss, I think I found him."

"Really? Great! Where are you?" Rico asked.

Dante worried about the excitement in his boss's voice. "Sorry, boss, I didn't mean we have him yet," he said slowly and apologetically. Then, with more enthusiasm, he added, "But I think we found him."

Rico didn't scream. He didn't say anything. The words came out slowly and deliberately. "Tell me what happened."

Dante recounted finding the man who must have been Spike and how he'd gotten away. He finished with the fact that he'd probably broken his leg. Dante said he was sure they'd get Spike as he drove to Deming.

Rico listened, asking no questions.

Dante trembled with fear. He hated to break the silence but was afraid he'd lost the connection. "Boss ... you there?"

"Did you put a tracker on his truck? Or get the license plate number?" Rico didn't sound friendly. All business.

"I never got close enough to put a tracker on, and my leg hurt so bad, I couldn't even focus on the numbers."

Rico seemed to speak one word at a time. "Your leg hurt too bad to read a license plate?" An awkward pause ensued before he continued. "Find. Him. Get all the help you need from our other people ... and use any police contacts. Got it?"

"Okay, boss, I got it." Dante thought maybe he'd answered too fast. He'd already been informed about the "disloyal" people Rico had shot.

"Dante, use your head. If you find this guy, I'll owe you one."

"I'll do everything I can, boss."

"Let's hope that's enough." Rico hung up before Dante could reply.

~

SPIKE WONDERED how the gunshots would affect Buck, whose whitened hands gripped the steering wheel. Buck stared straight ahead, chewing his lip. Then he took the corner with a hard right onto Highway 11, headed north through Columbus and then to Deming.

The abrupt turn threw Spike into the space where Barbie would have been sitting had she not been on the floor. Based on the limited light available, Spike assumed some glass shards from the bullet had hit Buck in the forehead. Blood ran down his face and into his left eye.

Buck reached out and shoved Spike back to his side. Then the panicked questions started. "Who was that? Did you steal that money? How much you got? Is he going to follow us? How many are there? Are they going to follow us?"

"Calm down," Spike said.

"Calm down, my ass!" Buck pulled to the side of the road. "Get out!"

Barbie was moving, and Spike helped her back up on the seat. He felt a knot on her head.

"Just keep driving," Spike said.

"Fuck you! Get out!"

"Look, the guy was on foot. Just get me to Deming." Spike picked up his bag, unzipped it, pulled out a band of hundred-dollar bills, and threw it in Buck's lap. "That's ten thousand dollars. Just to drive me to Deming. Thirty miles, right?"

Barbie picked up the cash with her left hand while rubbing her head. "Jesus, Buck. Let's hurry before that guy catches up. Just drop him off in Deming, and then we'll keep driving."

Buck sat, shaking his head slowly, staring ahead, breathing deeply, not looking at Spike. His face betrayed his anger and confusion but mostly his fear. Buck wiped off the blood around his eye. The cuts were small and not bleeding badly.

He put the truck in park, opened his door, and got out. "Barbie, come here. I want to talk to you alone before we do this."

∽

BUCK SAW NO TRAFFIC. Once Barbie was standing outside the truck, he pushed her back. She was now out of Spike's sight. He took a step toward her so all Spike could see was Buck's left shoulder and back. Keeping one eye on Spike, Buck pulled out his phone and held it in front of him. Then he whispered to Barbie, "Get your phone out and turn it off."

"Why?" She frowned and furrowed her brow.

He stopped working on his own phone and jerked his eyes to hers. His eyebrows lowered, and his glare cut through her. In a loud whisper that threw spit on her, he said, "Because I fucking told you to!"

He did nothing until her phone was off. Then he took it away and put it in his pocket. Next, he turned off his phone and put it with hers. He made sure Spike couldn't tell what he was doing.

∽

Spike wondered what they were talking about. Maybe Buck was asking Barbie if they should try to get more money. He wasn't sure why Buck would ask her opinion on anything.

Finally, Buck stepped back and focused on Spike as he stood outside, next to the door. Too loud but not shouting, he said, "Alright! But no supper or any other bullshit. We drop you off, and that's it."

"Deal," Spike said. "Let's go."

Barbie hopped into the truck and slid to the middle, all smiles. "Thanks. The money will really help."

Buck climbed in behind the steering wheel and scowled at Barbie's comment. Shaking his head, he stepped on the gas and pulled back onto the highway. He didn't think Barbie saw his expression of disapproval.

Spike knew he could use his pistol to force Buck to do whatever he wanted. He knew he could take the truck, but he had no police record, and stealing the truck was stupid. *Just gotta get to Houston. These two are a means to an end.*

Barbie's touch startled Spike. Her left hand rested on Buck's blue-jeaned thigh, but with her right hand, shielded from Buck by her body, she extended a finger, touching Spike.

He looked up and smiled.

She side-eyed him with a "we have a secret" half-smile.

I'll be damned. She's a pretty little tramp. He snapped the rubber band on his wrist.

∽

DANTE worried that the cops would show up and find him, but his leg hurt too much to move the car. He stared at the rearview mirror. *Damn! My leg's killing me.* Finally, he checked it out closely. *Swollen, nasty color! Hurry up!* He sighed and gently ran his hand over the skin. *Hot! But thank God, no bone sticking out.*

A few cars went by, but Dante had a long wait until Gabriel showed up.

He called Gabriel on the phone. "Where are you?"

"I'm on the way, but I'm not even close yet. You okay?"

"No! You know my leg's probably broken, right?"

"Yeah, Jorge told me."

"Just hurry." Dante hung up.

12

WAKING UP

Houston, TX
Thursday Night

Ava Gunn, PI, opened her eyes. "Where am I?"

"Just relax. You took a pretty big bump to the head," the young woman next to her said.

Ava started to sit up, but the woman pushed her down. "Let go of me!" Ava screamed and pushed back, getting into a sitting position on a gurney. "What's this? An ambulance?" She started to stand in a crouch but got dizzy and fell sideways onto the cart.

"Officer! Officer, she's awake!" the woman yelled out the back. Then she turned to Ava and helped her sit down again. "Look, we're only trying to help you. You could easily have a concussion. You could have brain swelling."

"Okay, I get it. I'm sorry." Ava's head pounded hard. Her eyes pulsed outward in sync with her heartbeat.

"Miss Ava Gunn, I'm Detective Hank Gray. I need to ask

you a few questions." The man flashed his badge. "We can do it now, or I can meet you at the hospital after they examine you."

Ava raised her head and sized him up while squinting to help with the pounding. *Looks too young and good-looking to be a detective.* She put her head in her hands. "I'm not going to the hospital. Give me a second. I'll climb out of this thing."

The paramedic handed her a clipboard and a pen. "If you're getting out and refusing treatment, you need to sign this."

"Sure." Ava signed the form and handed it back.

"Here's a bottle of water. I'd drink it if I were you. Might help with the headache."

"Thanks. I'm sorry I was a bitch," Ava said. "I know you were only doing your job and trying to help."

"You were far from the worst patient I've had, but seriously, be careful about the bump on your head. If you don't see a doctor…"

"I know, don't go to sleep right away."

"No, you can sleep," the paramedic said. "That's a myth about staying awake after a concussion. I was going to say if you feel dizzy or off in any way, please see a doctor."

"Sure, I'll do that." Ava nodded.

"Ma'am," Detective Gray said. "If you're not going to the hospital, we need to talk for a few minutes."

With the paramedic's help, Ava moved slowly to the door.

"Wow. What are all the cops for?" Not far away but not at the building she'd been watching, Ava saw what looked like a disaster movie response to some catastrophe. Big lights illuminated the area, making it look like daylight, with cops scattered everywhere.

"Can't talk about it," he said.

"I see ATF, FBI, and covered bodies. What's going on?" She stumbled from dizziness.

Detective Gray grabbed her arm to steady her. "Would you like to sit down?" he asked, walking her to his car. He opened the front passenger side.

Ava sat while he squatted beside the door.

"Thanks, I'm sorry. Just hurts." She opened the water and sipped it.

"It's okay. Now, do you mind telling me what happened?" He held a small notepad and a pen.

"How did the cops get here so fast, and why?" she asked.

"A patrolman just happened to drive up on the scene, and he probably saved your life. He called for help before the shooting started. He saw everything. He also got shot by one of your assailants. You shot the other one."

"How's the policeman, and how do I thank him?" Ava knew the risk the officer had taken.

Gray touched his shoulder as he spoke. "He's in surgery. He got shot in his shoulder, but it went under his vest. He'll make it. I don't know much more about his condition."

"What about the two guys who attacked me?" Ava noticed Gray took a deep, long inhale. *Wonder what that's all about.*

"They're both dead." He tried to look serious.

"I killed the man I shot?" she asked without emotion.

"No, you shot him, but he was killed by a shot from where all the fireworks came. The same guy saved the policeman too."

She nodded. "I'd sure like to thank whoever that was." She reached up and touched her jaw as she moved it from side to side.

"Your jaw okay?"

"Yeah, I must have fallen on it, but it'll be fine." She lowered her hand. "What the hell was all this about? What were they up to? Why'd they attack me? And who were they?"

"Slow down," he said. "That's a lot of questions. Plus, I can't discuss much of anything right now. Let's just say they were part of a much bigger deal that went down about the same time you got knocked out." He looked at his notes with his pen in hand, ready to start interviewing her.

"Really? What kind of deal?"

"Can't discuss it." Gray was a little clipped now, frustrated.

"Oh. Since the policeman saw it all, I guess no charges for me shooting the guy, right?"

He didn't answer right away.

She saw he was staring at her, his mouth crooked. "What?"

"You know I'm supposed to be asking the questions." His left eyebrow rose, accompanying his upturned lip.

He likes me. "Sorry. I'll answer anything you want, of course, but could you answer my questions first ... pretty please?" She gave him an overly big smile that was goofy and playful, though she felt her pulse all over her body.

He sighed and smiled. "Okay, then, you do the talking."

"Yes, sir, Detective Gray." Her eyes waved a demure white flag.

He grinned and blushed, then gave her the names of the men who'd attacked her. "You know them?"

"Nope, never heard of 'em," she said. "So, I shouldn't be in any trouble, right?"

"Don't think so. We'll check with the DA, but I took a picture of your PI license. I'm sure there won't be charges, but you know we'll need to keep the gun for a few days.

When the evidence guys are done, you'll get it back." He paused. "This interview was all backward. I think you asked more questions than I did. Don't tell anyone. I'll get busted back into uniform."

"I'll bet you'd be handsome in a uniform."

He didn't acknowledge her comment. "So, the big question is, what were you doing here?"

"I was paid cash in advance to be here at this location and take pictures of what I saw."

"Who hired you?"

"A guy who says his name is Stanley Lawyer, but I'm sure it's not his real name. I think he gave me a burner number. He mailed me cash. I was told to take pictures and email them. Let me use your pen and paper."

"Sure." He passed off the notepad.

She wrote down Stanley Lawyer's phone number and the name of the man she was supposed to watch and photograph. Then she handed the pen and paper back to Gray. "I don't think it has anything to do with all of this. He wanted to know about this guy because he said the man wanted to invest millions of dollars. He was happy to take his money, but he didn't want trouble. So, he hired me to investigate. Of course, it could be, and probably is, bullshit."

"That's it?"

"Yep."

"Did you find anything yet?

"Nope. I got ripped out of my car and hit on the head. Then I woke up in the ambulance."

"Nothing about a big arms deal or drug cartel involved?"

Her eyes enlarged. Her jaw dropped, and her eyebrows lifted. "You're kidding, right?"

"Something happened. We've got a wounded cop, a lot of bodies, and a missing semi-truck. And you were here."

"Maybe I was, but when you're unconscious, you really aren't paying much attention."

"One more question. You ever heard of a guy called Fluff?"

"Really? That sounds more like a dog's name."

Gray's forehead dipped, and he stopped smiling. He punched the words out one at a time. "I'm serious."

"No, I've never heard of a guy named Fluff."

"Okay, I guess that's it." Detective Gray reviewed his notes one more time. "That's probably all I need for now, except any files you have. You can drop them off, or I'll come by and pick them up. Here's my card."

"I don't have any files."

"Well, I may need to talk to you some more."

"You have my address, right?"

"Yes, ma'am. From your driver's license."

"Call me Ava."

"Okay, Ava. I already told the Feds you were unconscious before all that happened, based on the officer's statement. I'll give them the statement you made to me, but no doubt they'll follow up with you."

"Sure, I'm easy to find."

He shook his head with a smile. "But seriously, you should get your head checked. It could be a concussion. Would you like me to have a patrol car take you home?"

"Nope, I'm fine."

"Be safe, then."

Ava turned to walk away. She twisted her head to throw a flirty glance over her shoulder and say something cute, but the maneuver made her dizzy and threw her off balance. She stumbled, and Detective Gray grabbed her. Ava fell into his arms, up against his chest. His eyes were a rich mahogany brown. She felt his heartbeat and his breath. *I could like this guy.* She lingered a second, then began pushing off slowly.

"You sure you're okay?" Detective Gray held her tightly before loosening his embrace.

"I'm fine. See you tomorrow, handsome."

"You will?"

"Sorry. Little loopy, but I'm okay." She made big, silly eyes with a clown-wide smile as she climbed into her car. Over her shoulder, she gave him a toodle-loo wave.

13

LONELY ROAD IN THE DESERT

Columbus, NM
Thursday Night

SPIKE NOTICED Buck constantly checked the rearview mirror. They were barely out of Columbus when he swerved onto a sandy dirt road heading east.

Spike jerked his head around. He expected to spot someone in pursuit, but no one was there. He glared at Buck. "What's going on?"

"Little detour. Relax, man. It's slightly longer and not smooth pavement, but it'll get us to Deming. We won't have to worry about that guy following or catching up to us," Buck said.

"You sure? Looks awfully dark."

"No sweat. I know the road, and I've got hunting lights mounted across the top of the cab. I'll turn them on when we need 'em." Buck didn't look at Spike.

Something's going on.

Spike was looking toward Buck, but Barbie was in his view. He gazed into her eyes. For a moment, she locked onto his, but then she turned away.

Spike unzipped his bag, discreetly put his hand inside it, and found his gun. "Hey, Buck, what do you do for a living?"

"Why?"

"Just curious."

"I was in the Army for a while, then mostly construction. I kind of move around chasing the hot markets. That's why I'm on my way to New Orleans. No family or kids, so nothing holding me down."

The occasional bump made everyone's voice skip a beat now and then.

"What were you doing in Columbus? There's no construction there."

"That's true. Nothing there, but I was working for a company that had a contract with the Border Patrol to work on the fence. Contract's over, need to move on."

"What about you, Barbie?" Spike asked.

"I've taken a few college courses, but my mom needed my help, so I had to quit. She's in bad shape. She just can't leave the booze alone, and she always picks the wrong men."

"I'm sorry, it must be hard on you," Spike said. But he couldn't care less. *Is she bad ... bad enough to die?* For a moment, Spike got lost in her eyes and his thoughts.

She smiled and secretly played with one finger on his leg. He was interested in her but not in the way she thought.

As Spike looked toward Barbie, he noticed Buck intently focused on the dark, rough side road. He seemed to be deep in thought and too quiet. *Is he up to something?*

I'm pretty sure he's bad enough to die. Did God put Buck in my path as he had the church? Lord knows I'm ready. Just might not be a good time. Maybe I'll come back to Buck.

Spike sighed. He was sure no one heard him over the sound of the truck and the bumpy road.

"Buck's going to help me finish school and take care of me," Barbie said.

"That's nice of Buck." They were getting farther from any light source except the stars.

Buck flipped on his hunting lights. The world in front of the truck lit up as he drove.

"You sure you know where you're going?" Spike asked.

"Yep, just a little farther and we'll turn north. We'll come into the east side of the city some twenty-five miles north of us."

Every time Buck talked about this shortcut, Barbie's face screwed up. Buck's every word had to be bullshit. Spike thought maybe God was giving him an opportunity to kill these two. He was ready.

Then Buck slowed down. "You see that up there? Something's up there. See it?"

So, this is it. Spike was a little anxious but excited. He'd accepted death a long time ago. He didn't want to die, but if it was time, so be it. He didn't look out the front window, just stared past Barbie at the side of Buck's head. "No, don't see anything." He held the gun firmly and prepared to aim it at Buck, but he'd have to make some kind of move. Barbie was in his line of sight. Spike didn't care if he hit her, but he knew a bullet that went through her didn't have much of a chance of hitting Buck.

"Up front, see it?" Buck glanced sideways at Spike. The truck was already slowing, and then it stopped. He put it in park. "You want to see what it is? Come on."

Buck got out quickly, leaving his door open. Barbie followed, shielding her boyfriend.

Damn! Spike stepped out but kept his hand in the bag, where he held the pistol. He walked to the front of the truck, looking in Buck's direction, but was blinded by the lights. Then he heard a gunshot, jerked, lost his balance, and stumbled forward, dropping the bag during his fall. The pistol was pulled out of his hand and stayed in the bag as it tumbled. Spike quickly checked himself. He hadn't been hit. *Thank God!*

"Don't move." Buck stepped into one of the strong light beams from his truck, just a few feet away, and pointed a pistol at Spike. "Gotcha! If you behave, I might not kill you."

Shit, I might die tonight. I didn't play this well at all. "How about taking some money and leaving me the rest?" *God, little help, please!*

Buck slowly took the strap of the blue gym bag, then dragged it into the light about ten feet from Spike. He unzipped it. "Jesus Christ, how much is there?"

"I haven't counted it precisely but about three hundred fifty thousand." *Maybe I can get out of this alive. If I do, I'll kill that asshole later. I know God approves. He must.*

"Why don't I take it all and leave you out here in the desert?" Buck asked. "Damn, here's a Glock and a switchblade too. You're a real badass son of a bitch, huh? But who's got the gun now?" Buck walked over and pressed the barrel against Spike's head.

He went for the gun in Buck's hand but missed.

Buck stepped back, then knocked him upside the head. "You asshole. I might have split the money with you but *not now*! I'm just gonna *kill you*!"

Spike looked up at the gun pointed at him, then into Buck's eyes. "Okay! Fuck it! Shoot me."

"You asked for it. Bye-bye. Thanks for the money." Buck waved goodbye with his left hand, then straightened his right arm, holding the pistol close enough that he couldn't miss.

So, this is how it ends. Damn! C'mon, God, give me some time. We've got work to do.

14

SAVED

Columbus, NM
Thursday Night

SPIKE WAITED for the bullet but felt God would save him. He didn't know how. *Maybe a lightning bolt. On a clear night? Why not? He is God! What the hell is Buck waiting on? Maybe God gave him a heart attack.*

Then he heard a strange sound. *Bong!* He saw Buck fly sideways into his peripheral vision. Turning quickly, Spike took in Barbie holding a tire iron and staring at Buck, who was stumbling.

Spike jumped on Buck and grabbed his hand, which still held the semi-automatic pistol. Buck was stronger and slowly turned the gun toward Spike's head. *Damn. At least it'll be quick, but I won't have a face. C'mon, God.* Spike bore down with everything he had, and the gun paused. It remained there for a few seconds, then started moving again.

Buck's hand lunged forward, followed by his body, and the gun went off.

Spike's ears rang. Dazed, he realized he was on the ground. The truck's hunting lights cast swaths of bright illumination with darkness in between, adding to his disorientation. Through his ringing ears and the fog in his head, a faint sound grew louder. Barbie was yelling, "Get the gun! Get the gun!"

Buck lay motionless on the ground. Barbie stood over him, again with the tire iron. The gun was right beside Spike, who grabbed it and stood. "Why'd you help me?"

"He's an asshole! You seem like a nice guy," she said.

"I saw rope in the back of the truck. Get it." Spike checked Buck for a pulse. *Alive. For now.*

Barbie had hit Buck so hard that blood oozed from his scalp.

"Here." Barbie handed the quarter-inch white nylon rope to Spike. It was still rolled up and had never been opened. "Here's some work gloves too."

"Thanks, Barbie."

She stood back, behind him. "I guess he's not dead, is he?"

"Not yet." Spike stuck Buck's pistol in his belt, at the small of his back, then opened the rope and tied Buck's hands behind him. Next, he removed the switchblade from his bag. With Buck on his stomach, hands tied behind him, Spike pulled his feet together and tied them too. Finally, he took some leftover rope and secured his knees together.

"Why are you tying him up so much?" Barbie asked.

"You'll see." Spike stood and smiled at Barbie. He had enough rope to tie up her too, but she didn't look as if she'd run. Where would she go anyway? *Is she an innocent?* He looked at Barbie. *Little help, God. Please? Some direction and guidance, maybe?*

Spike dragged Buck's tied-up body into the light of the truck. He was regaining consciousness. "Buck, you there, buddy?"

"What happened?" Buck asked groggily.

"Your girlfriend kicked your ass." After a good, loud laugh, Spike continued, "Good thing for me too. You're fuckin' strong. Too much time in the gym? Compensating for a little dick?"

"Fuck you."

"Really. You got bigger problems than that to worry about right now."

"Untie me! Untie me!" Buck struggled, twisting around on the ground. Then he got quiet. "Okay, okay, we'll just split the money. No hard feelings."

"I'm sure you'd love to split the money now. I thought you were going to shoot me in the head. Damn! That would have hurt. That was too close. Maybe I need to bulk up a little in case I get into an arm-wrestling match with a gun again. I thought I was dead. You know, I need some good training, so the next time, I can flip the gun out of the other guy's hands."

"What're you talking about, man? C'mon, keep the money. I'll still give you a ride anywhere you want to go."

"That's nice of you, but I don't think so. I'm going to kill you unless you talk me out of it." Spike felt so alive. Everything was going perfectly for him. *In the zone!* It seemed like he'd had close calls, but it was all meant to be. It was all going to go—just right.

Spike pushed Buck on his back and straddled him, sitting on his chest.

"What are you doing? Don't! Please!"

Spike was so juiced. He wanted to enjoy the moment. He remembered a Fyodor Dostoevsky quote and said it aloud. "Power is given only to those who dare to lower themselves and pick it up. Only one thing matters, one thing; to be able to dare!" Spike lifted the knife and brought it down fast. "Well, I dare!"

Buck screamed and shut his eyes. Spike felt Buck's entire body tense, anticipating the moment when the knife would be driven into his head.

Barbie said nothing at first, then yelped when the knife appeared to plunge into her boyfriend.

Spike drove the knife into the sand so close to Buck's head that he nicked his ear. Buck screamed one last burst, like he thought he'd been killed. Spike laughed so hard that he fell off Buck's chest.

"Oh, man, you should have seen your face. I wasn't sure if you thought you were dying or having an orgasm."

"Fuck you! Fuck you! You sick bastard! Okay, fun and games are over. Let me go. No hard feelings. I get it. I was kind of a dick. Please, let me go."

To Spike's surprise, Barbie was laughing too.

"Not so tough now, are you, Buck? Asshole!" she yelled.

"Barbie," Spike said. "You may not want to watch this. This is the main event. I'm really going to kill him now. He's a bad man, and God won't care. He'll be grateful if I kill Buck. He deserves to die."

"Can I watch?" she asked.

That surprised Spike. "Sure." *I've never left a witness alive. A little dilemma here unless she's not so innocent.*

"You can't kill me." Buck was trying to wiggle free. "Look, you don't know how this will affect you. It changes you, man!"

"Oh, you've killed before, Buck?"

"Yeah, a guy in a fight once. It was an accident, and no one ever found out it was me, but it *changed* me. I was never the same."

"You're so full of shit. But I'm glad you relaxed a little. I want you to save something for the final struggle."

"Bullshit!"

"I don't think so. I've killed over thirty people, so it won't change me. It'll make my day. To be precise, you'll be number thirty-six. You'll never really die as long as I live. I'll remember you as number thirty-six—forever."

"Bullshit! Enough! Untie me!"

Spike straddled Buck again. "You're going to die staring into my eyes, number thirty-six. I'll be the last thing you see in this world."

Buck struggled as if his life depended on it. It did, but there wasn't much he could do. Frantically, he turned his head from side to side. "Don't, man! Don't, man!" He kept repeating the words until, with both hands, Spike applied pressure to his neck. He lifted his body off Buck's chest and put all his weight into his arms, pushing with his hands. It didn't take long before the repeated, "Don't, man," faded and stopped.

Spike watched for as long as it took for Buck's dead eyes to stop staring at him.

His body was tense. A big sigh of release and euphoria washed over him.

Spike hadn't noticed Barbie was right there, not more than a foot from Buck's head, staring into her boyfriend's eyes.

Her own eyes twinkled with joy as she looked at Spike. "Oh, my God, that was incredible. I've wanted to do that for so long."

Spike had never been in a situation like this before. No one had ever seen him choke the life out of a person. And she was smiling like a kid. She must have enjoyed it. *Who is this woman? My kind?*

Spike remembered his first two kills. *Two at once.*

15

CHILDHOOD FLASHBACK

Harry "Spike" Hunter

HARRY'S FATHER WAS A CHARMER, handsome, and highly successful. But he was always a little different. It was subtle, and most people would never notice. Spike's mother knew something was a little off with her husband, but he seemed so loving most of the time. Then she watched a TV show about psychopaths among us. It gave her a chill, as parts of it reminded her of her husband, and she was five months pregnant with a boy. She cried all day but never mentioned it to her husband. She quietly read information on how to identify a psychopathic child and how to raise one.

Please, Lord. Let my baby be normal.

After Harry was born, she looked for the smallest thing to indicate that he'd be copying his father's behavior. She started to relax when he was three. But then, when he was five, he got a puppy.

Harry was in the backyard playing with his puppy. His mom heard a yelp and looked outside. "Harry, you have to be careful. He's just a baby. It's easy to hurt him."

"Okay."

Then Harry tied the little dog to a tree in the backyard, with some slack in the rope. The dog yelped again.

"Harry, be careful," his mom yelled out to him.

He came into the house. "He needs a drink. Can I have a bowl?"

"Sure, here you go." She gave him a bowl. From the kitchen window, Harry's mother watched as Harry put water in the bowl and set it in front of the puppy. Then she turned away to make lunch.

As the puppy enthusiastically drank the water, Harry reached over and petted him. Then Harry pushed the dog's head so his nose and mouth were underwater. The dog squirmed, got a breath, and yelped. Harry eased up on his head. His mom looked out and saw Harry stroking the puppy. Then Harry jerked the bowl away and ran into the house.

"Mom, can I have a bigger bowl? He's really thirsty."

"Okay." She gave him a larger bowl but made sure it was low enough that the little dog could get a drink. Harry's mom was happy he was showing so much attention to and playing with his new pet.

Harry filled the bowl to the top and put it down for the puppy, who lapped the water. This time, Harry grabbed the little guy's head firmly and held it under the water. Again, the puppy squirmed and twisted, but he never got his head out of the water. Soon, the puppy appeared lifeless. When Harry let go, the dog's head slid out of the bowl, and his body lay on the ground.

"Harry, oh, my God! What have you done?" his mother

said as she caught the end of Harry's deed. She knew he felt no remorse. Her biggest fears were being realized. She knew what he was, and it was overwhelming.

"Hi, Mom. Look," little Harry said. "I killed the puppy. He's dead."

His mother gaped. She didn't know if CPR worked on dogs, so she vigorously rubbed the puppy's back, pushing on his little body. Then she picked him up and kept rubbing, pushing on his chest. She had no idea what she was doing, but suddenly life jerked back into the puppy. He spat out water, coughed, and then whined. "Thank you, God," she whispered. Tears sprung to her eyes as she held the little dog tight against her body.

She was devastated and wondered how to react. Harry's mother decided to be direct and figure out how he felt. That way, eventually, she could help him.

"Harry, why did you do that? You almost killed the puppy."

"I know," he said, expressionless.

"Why?"

"I wanted to."

"Why?"

"I was curious, and it made me happy."

"Harry," his mother said. "You don't understand, but you should never kill any living creature. Can you try to understand that?"

"No. Why?" he answered, not looking at her.

"Because you want people to like you, and if people know you hurt or kill things, they will not like you. You will not get to have the things you want in life."

"Okay, I understand."

∼

He learned to never kill anything in front of others and to make sure they never knew he did it. Then they'd have no reason to not like him.

Harry had his mother to thank for his ability to act so normally and hide the monster. She'd watched him closely and explained to him from a young age that he was a little different than other people and that he must learn to make all those other people happy.

"Why?" he asked.

"Because if you are friendly and people like you, you'll be able to get the things you want from them," his mother said.

"But I don't care what other people think or if they like me."

"You must act like you care. If you pretend to like other people, pretend to think they are smart, or strong, or pretty, then they will do what you want more often," his mother said. "Do you understand me, son? Can you do that?"

"Yes, I can pretend to care about people."

"Good. Mommy will help you and always be there."

And she did. She watched him closely. Life was a laboratory, and his mother taught him well. He became a charmer on the surface, but underneath, in his mind and his private life, he was dangerous. This would lead to his first human kill and many more. Mommy never knew.

∼

Harry Hunter acquired his nickname in high school football. During games, he liked to step on opposing players' hands with the spikes on his shoes. From then on, he always introduced himself as Spike.

When he was a senior in high school, his mother and father died when their house burned down.

Spike was eighteen.

Spike needed money for college.

Spike made five hundred thousand dollars from life insurance that day.

College expenses were no longer an issue.

16

BARBIE'S FATE

Columbus, NM
Thursday Night

"He's a construction guy. See if he has a shovel in the back of the truck," Spike said.

Barbie ran to the pickup and climbed in. He heard her rummaging around. "What are we going to do with all his stuff? He was packed and moving to Louisiana for a while. There're some tools, a couple of bags, and a suitcase." She grew quiet for a second. "Got it. He's got four shovels that I see. A couple are flat, and a couple are curved on the end." She jumped off the back of the truck and ran around to Spike. "Can I dig a little?"

Again, Spike was amazed. *She wants to dig.* "Sure." He was exhausted, but Buck had to be buried. If his final resting spot was a hole in the desert, he might never be found. Spike took a shovel and used it to draw a rectangle on the soil. "Okay, this is where we dig. We need to go down as close to six feet as we can. We don't want animals digging him up."

Barbie took a scoop of sandy dirt and threw it over her shoulder.

"We gotta put the dirt back in the hole. Stack it up on the side," he said.

"Oh, yeah. Sorry." Barbie shrugged. "I didn't think about it."

Spike left for a minute and cleaned himself up as best he could with the Kleenex he found in the truck. He put the tissue in his pocket. Then he went back by Barbie and picked up a shovel.

They got into the rhythm of digging. The soil wasn't as hard as Spike had thought it would be. Barbie got tired easily and took a lot of breaks. She found a case of bottled water in the back of Buck's truck and brought a bottle to Spike.

Digging gave him time to think. He didn't want to kill Barbie, not now anyway. He snapped the rubber band. She seemed useful and provided company. She also seemed to have no problem with his need to kill. For the time being, he felt no desire to kill her. Buck had been his meal, scratched his itch, and filled his belly.

Barbie was interesting. While Spike didn't want to kill her, she might have to go sooner or later. She had seen him kill Buck. That couldn't be negotiable. Might as well talk to her.

"I thought you loved Buck," he said.

"Not even close. He was just a way to get out of a shithole."

They didn't talk much. It took about three hours to dig the grave. Spike was amazed at how hard she worked. When they were done, the grave plunged down about four feet.

"Deep enough," Spike said. *Room for two but not tonight.* He snapped the rubber band. He felt a little remorse about his decision to kill Barbie and his thought that she'd be in this hole with Buck.

It was still dark, and he glanced at his watch. Four in the morning.

Spike dragged Buck to the hole, then took his wallet, phone, and keys. He checked the driver's license. "Damn, his name is—was—William Nathanial Montague. No wonder he went by Buck."

"Wow. He never told me his whole name, just Buck Montague."

In another of Buck's pockets, Spike found Barbie's phone. "Why does he have this?" He held it up so she could see it.

"When he stopped and we got out of the pickup on the highway, he took my phone. Then he turned it off. He wouldn't tell me why. He just kept it."

"Here." Spike handed it back to her. "Don't turn it on unless you ask me. Someone might be able to track it. Got it?"

"Sure." She put it in her pocket. "I'll ask you before I turn it on again."

"It's just for a while, so we can be careful."

Buck's phone was off. Spike turned it on, then held the phone up to Buck's face. It opened, and Spike changed the password. Then he turned it off again and put it in his pocket. He and Barbie shoved Buck's body into the hole. It landed with a thud.

Barbie sat on the edge of the hole and looked inside, her back to the truck.

"I'll get us another bottle of water," Spike said.

"Okay, I'll wait," she responded. "I'll bet putting the dirt back in the hole's a lot easier and quicker."

Spike stood at the back of the truck by the tailgate and pulled Buck's pistol from his belt. He checked it—a round in the chamber and almost a full magazine. *I need only one bullet. This'll do.* He grabbed two bottles of water, then turned back toward Barbie and the open grave. He caught himself shaking his head. He really didn't want to kill her, not now. But...

He walked up behind Barbie, lifted the pistol, and pointed it at her head. *If anyone finds the bodies, they'll see that Buck's gun killed her. Irony.*

"Please, don't kill me," Barbie said. She didn't turn around. There was no begging in her tone. Just a request.

Damn! She keeps surprising me.

"I'll never tell anyone anything about you ... or what happened to Buck. I swear." Barbie sounded calm. "And it'll be easier if I help you fill the hole."

Spike remained silent. He became aware of his deep breathing as he worked himself up to pull the trigger. *God, do I kill her or not? I need a sign, or I need to kill her. She knows too much, God. You know it. I can't kill bad guys if the cops catch me.*

He took a deep breath and started squeezing the trigger. Then a shooting star, brighter than any he had ever seen, filled the sky of New Mexico.

A knot stuck in his throat, and his eyes watered. He had *never* felt an emotion this deep before. *Is God really there? Listening?* He lowered the gun and put it in his belt. Spike knew, on one level, this was probably just a coincidence, but maybe it wasn't. *God's answer felt real. Very confusing. She'll live for now.*

"Barbie, here's your water. Let's fill in the hole and get out of here."

For a moment, she stared into Spike's eyes. Then she picked up the shovel and threw dirt into the hole. Without looking at Spike, she said, "Thank you. I'll be loyal."

∼

WHEN JORGE and Pup got off I-10 at Deming, they made their way through town, looking at every car. Jorge was twenty-nine and had been part of Zorro's cartel since he was fifteen. He'd picked up a new guy to go with him—Gary or "Pup." He was eighteen and short, with a baby face topped by beach-boy blond hair. When Dante first met him, he'd ruffled his hair. "We'll call you Pup." Now that was the only thing anyone called him.

After getting off the highway, they started leaving the south side of town. It was a dark drive down Highway 11 south toward Columbus, but they didn't see any traffic at all.

"Look, the Columbus City Limits sign," Pup said.

"Shit!" Jorge called Dante on his cell.

"You find them?" Dante asked.

"Boss," Jorge said. "We just passed the Columbus City Limits sign, and we didn't see a single car since we left Deming. We're at a gas station/convenience store on what looks like the main drag on Highway 11."

"Spike must still be in this shithole. Keep going south a few blocks and turn left on Lima. I'm two blocks over on Main Street. You can't miss me. Oh, get two bags of ice and some painkillers, and hurry. I want you to look around town after you drop that off."

"We'll be there in a few minutes."

Within ten minutes, they saw Dante's car and pulled up

behind him. He was sitting in the passenger seat. Jorge tapped on the window. Dante opened the door.

Jorge saw Dante's swollen, purple leg. "Damn, boss."

"Put the ice on it, gently. Put the extra bag on the floor."

Jorge did as he was told, then reached back and took what Pup held. "Here's some aspirin and Excedrin and water."

"Good. I was afraid you'd forget the water." Dante put four of each of the pain pills in his hand and opened the water bottle.

"You think that's too much?" Jorge asked.

"I don't care. I may need more." He tossed the pills in his mouth and drank half a bottle of water. "Gabriel better get here soon."

"Should we take you somewhere?"

"No, go find Spike. We gotta find him. Look around Columbus. I don't think it's too big. If you see anyone, ask if they know who owns a red pickup. If you don't find him in an hour or so, call me and head back to Deming. Find a spot to watch the highway as it comes into Deming. Hopefully, if he's still here, he'll head that way. Or we may be fucked! Get going and keep me posted."

Jorge and Pup drove around Columbus, up and down the main streets. This late at night, there wasn't really anyone to ask. Finally, Jorge gave up and called Dante.

"Nothing, boss. We're headed to Deming now."

"Okay. Gabriel should be here soon, I hope. My leg is killing me and doesn't look too good."

17

SOUL SEARCHING IN THE DARKNESS

Columbus, NM
Thursday Night

BARBIE WAS grateful to be alive but had only one thing on her mind. She knew she'd ask when she got up the nerve. She switched between staring out the passenger's window and watching Spike drive. *Wow! I just watched him kill Buck. And I helped.* She sighed and shook her head. *Does Spike like me?*

He appeared deep in thought, with two hands on the wheel, bouncing around on the dark, dirt road. She took a breath and sheepishly asked, "Did you really kill *thirty-five* people before Buck?"

Spike didn't look at her or react to her question. The silence seemed to last forever. It was interrupted only by truck noises and the tools in the bed banging around whenever they hit a bump.

He slowed the truck. *He's going to kill me. I shouldn't have asked anything.* The truck came to a complete halt with a small jerk. *Should I run*? Her breathing deepened, and she looked outside.

Even in the dark, she could see dust rolling over the truck. Spike put the vehicle in park. In the distance, to the west, dim lights shone—probably a gas station along the highway that they were headed toward from their dirt road. Farther to the north was a glow of lights, which had to be Deming.

Nowhere to run. No one to hear my screams. Funny, Buck beat me but would never have killed me. She shut her eyes, then put her hands in her lap, sat up straight, and tried to calm herself.

"Yes, I have killed thirty-six people now."

She opened her eyes and looked at Spike. His hands were still on the wheel, and he leaned forward with his head on it.

Not gonna kill me. Thank you, God—again! "Were you in the military?"

"Nope, never in the military," he said. "You know, it's a long and complicated story. When I escaped the cartel tonight, which is another long story, and had supper in Columbus a few hours ago, I had a plan." Spike leaned back and lowered his arms. He took a breath and continued. "I wanted to reset my life. I needed to make a quick stop in Houston to pick up some stuff, and then I wanted to go somewhere quiet to get my life reorganized. Maybe the northeast or the northwest. Hell, I don't know where, just somewhere quiet. And then I met you guys, and Buck made me take a detour. Oh, and now I have company—*you*. Plus, it must be the cartel trying to kill me, and I don't know why for sure. It's probably the cash in my bag."

"Were you a secret agent or a hitman?" Barbie turned

sideways to face Spike and pulled her left leg up under her. She had lost her fear. The story could have been better only if she had some popcorn. She'd relaxed and again was thinking of a future with this man. He was exciting and confident, and he seemed so worldly.

"No, not a secret agent or hitman either." He paused. "I just like the sensation of killing people. It's a drive in me. I don't really have a choice. It's like how you have to eat."

"Really? How do you pick who to kill?" Barbie asked. She had scooched a little closer to Spike and taken his hand. "I really will never tell anyone anything you tell me. I promise."

∽

SPIKE REMEMBERED the feeling he had of not hiding his desire to kill when he was being held by Jeff Case and his team. *That felt great!* When Case had caught Spike trying to kill someone, he'd given Spike a choice—help Case find other serial killers or die. There was more to it than that, but that had essentially been the deal. It was an easy choice. Spike had even offered to help Case do the killing, but they hadn't trusted him that much. Of course, it was essentially a jail, no freedom, always guarded. But they'd treated him well. They'd even kept him locked in a custom bunker.

He could have that again, the great feeling of not carrying his secret alone. Of course, he had talked to Father Miguel and even had his phone number. But that was just in passing, and the padre couldn't tell anyone. Spike didn't know Barbie. *But give her a little slack. I can always kill her if it doesn't work out.*

"Okay, I'm going to tell you a lot more than anyone else

knows. I hate to threaten you, but I suppose you know what will happen to you if you tell anyone."

"I know, but I won't."

"Since I was a child, I have always had an urge to hurt and to control. I don't know why. And not all the time, just sometimes. It feels normal to me, but I know it's not, of course."

Barbie nodded.

"You asked how I pick who to kill. Until Jeff Case captured me, it was anyone who was an easy target. I was always on the lookout for hitchhikers, but I often hunted. When I found someone I liked, I researched them, followed them, and looked for a way to kill them and get away with it. At any time, if they seemed too hard to kill, I passed and moved on. After a kill, I wouldn't give it much thought for months, or even a year, but the desire would come back. My experience with Case changed me."

"How?"

"I had a lot of time, a whole lot of time, to read. Including the Bible. With the influence of Case, I could find bad people and kill to scratch my itch. I decided I wanted to be good. Buck was an accident. He attacked me, and I got your help. That was close."

"I'm glad he's dead, and I'm glad we met."

"One problem with killing bad men—they're a lot harder to kill. They'll likely be looking for possible attacks. They have experience fighting and won't hesitate to kill me first. To be honest, I need more training before I can safely go after really bad men."

"Can I help you get bad guys?" Barbie couldn't contain her excitement. "Can I get some training too—like guns, knives, karate, and that kind of stuff?" She did some fake judo chops on the dashboard. "Hi-yah! Hi-yah!"

"You're unbelievable." Spike smiled. She made him feel good.

"Can we be like Batman and Robin? No, no, no—I mean Batman and *Batgirl*."

"Yeah, maybe. How old are you?"

Barbie's expression turned serious. "Oh, I see where you're going. I'm twenty-two, but you think I'm too immature. I just like having fun. I'm not stupid. I'm not ditzy, and I can be serious when I have to be. I won't be a liability to you. Okay?"

"Sure."

Then she got silly again and quickly kissed Spike on the cheek. He jumped a little, as he hadn't expected the rapid move.

"But I also promise I'll try to keep you laughing and happy," she said.

"Wow. That is quite an offer. Let's see where it goes."

She did make him smile. But she also knew where Buck was buried and who had killed him. *Can't trust her.*

Spike put the truck into gear and stepped on the gas. He smiled and shook his head in disbelief as they continued into the darkness.

18

THE RED PICKUP

Deming, NM
Friday Morning

JORGE WAS DOING as Dante told him. Once in Deming again, he guarded Highway 11 coming north out of Columbus.

They parked on the southern edge of the town at a Circle K with four gas pumps covered by a tall red awning and nothing close but desert. The car pointed toward the highway, allowing them to see anyone headed to Deming.

Pup, sitting in the passenger seat, checked his weapon's magazine.

"Put it away. This guy, Spike, needs to be alive," Jorge said. "You still got that Ruger 22? I told you to get something with more punch."

"I know, I plan to. But about Spike, what if he shoots at us?" Pup asked.

"I don't give a shit what he does. Do ... not ... kill him."

"What about wounding him?"

"That's all you can do with that 22 anyway, but just shut the fuck up and watch the road. Look for a red pickup with three people in the cab."

~

Despite the pain in his arm, Spike was driving. He didn't want to give up control of anything. Besides, he wasn't sure about Barbie. It crossed his mind that she might drive into a telephone pole.

What do I do with her? Spike looked at Barbie. Her head was resting against the door, and her eyes were shut. He snapped the rubber band on his wrist. Then he did it one more time.

First, I need to get my arm sewn up. Get away from Deming. Find a place to sleep. Then get to Houston and get my shit out of the lockbox. Then ... think! What's next?

~

Jorge jumped.

"Look! There!" Pup yelled.

Jorge didn't see them right away. "I see 'em." He started the car. "We got 'em."

"Be cool." Pup put his hand on Jorge's arm.

"Get your fucking hand off me." Jorge glared at his subordinate. "You do anything like that again, I'll kill you. Understand!?"

"Sorry. I just meant you should pull out slowly. We can't lose 'em."

"More fucking advice."

"You know we might lose them."

"Damn, shut the fuck up." Jorge spun the car in the

gravel up to the highway, then cut off a car, which honked at him. The red truck had gone by them, headed north. On the highway, a car came between them. He sped up. As he passed the car, Jorge saw the red truck farther down the road.

He called Dante. "We got him." He couldn't contain his excitement.

"You sure?" Dante asked.

"Yeah, red pickup."

Then a different voice spoke up. "This is Gabriel. Dante's in a lot of pain. He probably broke his leg. We put some ice on it, but we're looking for a doctor in Deming."

"Okay. Should we grab this guy or wait for help?" Jorge asked.

"You'd better grab him if you get a chance, man. Rico wants him bad," Gabriel said.

"Okay. We're going after him the first chance we get."

After he finished passing the car between them and the red pickup, Jorge slowed down and settled in, looking for an opportunity to get Spike.

He wanted to impress Rico. *You never know. If something happens to Dante, or he falls out of favor, I'll be ready. Could be some movement in the ranks with a new capo.*

They followed the red pickup. When it pulled into the parking lot of a hotel, they followed and parked one row back.

"What do we do?" Pup asked.

"Let's go get him. Do *not* shoot him," Jorge said.

Pup opened the door. Jorge gripped his arm tightly and jerked him back. Pup's lips thinned, his brow lowered, and he glared at Jorge.

"What?" Pup asked.

"Did you hear me? Don't shoot him! You understand?"

"Got it!" Pup didn't jerk his arm away. Instead, he waited for Jorge to release him. "Sorry, man, I'm just a little excited."

Jorge saw two large men exit the red pickup.

"Where's the woman?" Pup asked.

"Still in the truck probably. Let's go before they get inside."

They jumped out of the car and walked quickly. Jorge put his hand on his gun to reassure himself but didn't pull it out. He'd likely need it to threaten Spike. He saw Pup had already pulled out his gun and was holding it at his side as he rushed forward.

"Which one's Spike?" Pup asked.

"We'll ask when we get closer."

The two men were walking away, but Jorge and Pup were gaining on them. Pup started to run.

"Hey, slow down," Jorge said in a low voice.

Pup pulled up behind his man first and shoved his gun in the guy's back. "Don't move, asshole."

Jorge stopped and kept about six feet away from the blue-shirted man.

The man spun on Pup so fast, he couldn't react. He punched Pup in the stomach, and Pup went down, dropping the gun. The man started for the gun at the same time as Blue Shirt lunged for Jorge.

Jorge lifted his gun. "Everyone stop! Now! Or someone's going to die."

Both the man who punched Pup and the man in the blue shirt froze.

"What is this, a fucking robbery?" Blue Shirt asked. "We got a few bucks. You're welcome to it if you need it that bad."

"Just relax, guys. This is not a robbery, and no one needs to get hurt. Which one of you is Spike?" Jorge asked.

"Who the fuck is Spike?" Blue Shirt asked.

Jorge and Pup glanced at each other.

Jorge wasn't sure what to do. He looked at the two guys, who weren't happy. However, they seemed to respect the guns and stood still.

"Look, we just need to ask Spike a few questions, and one of you guys is Spike. We have the license plate on your truck," Jorge lied. "We're special agents, and we just need to ask a few questions."

"By running up on us with guns?" Pup Puncher asked. "Look, this is my truck, and I'm not Spike. I'm Brian Howell. I'll get my driver's license for you if you'd like."

"Yeah, I'll show you my license too. I'm Roger Brown," Blue Shirt said.

"Stop fucking around. Spike's your nickname, right?" Jorge asked.

"Jesus Christ, man, we are *not* Spike. We *don't know* Spike. We *never heard* of Spike," said Pup Puncher.

Then Jorge remembered the blue bag and the girl in the truck. He looked at Pup. "Keep your gun on them." He said to the men, "I'm going to check your truck and talk to the girl…"

"What girl?" Blue Shirt asked.

"Unlock your truck!"

"Fine, if it'll settle this." Pup Puncher took out the fob and pointed it. The locks popped up.

Jorge took a few steps back and opened the door. *No woman but not a deal-killer.* He climbed inside and looked everywhere, under a jacket, behind the seat. *No blue bag.* He got out of the truck, stood on the runner, and looked into the bed of the truck. *Nothing … nothing at all.*

"Shit!" he yelled.

No one moved, but everyone seemed more relaxed.

Jorge called Dante, but Gabriel answered.

"Where's Dante?" Jorge asked.

"He broke his leg bad. We're at the hospital. They're putting a splint on it or something," Gabriel said.

"Do you know what Spike looks like? Was he a really tall guy?"

"No, he's average height, I think. I never saw him, but that's what Rico said."

Jorge holstered his gun and said to Pup, "Not our guys." He looked at Pup Puncher and Blue Shirt. "Sorry, guys, mistaken identity."

Puncher had the last words. "Yeah, fuck you too."

19

THAT DAMN CUT

Columbus, NM
Friday Morning

THEY'D FINALLY GOTTEN off the dirt road and back onto Highway 11, just south of Deming. The sky flirted with the sunrise. Spike's head spun with exhaustion, and his arm throbbed with pain. *I gotta get it looked at.*

"Where are we going?" Barbie asked.

"First, I need to get my arm sewed up and get some antibiotics," Spike said. "After all that shoveling, my arm is hurting so bad, it's almost unbearable. Then I need sleep. After that, we need to get to Houston. I have a set of IDs and some other stuff I need there. And we need to avoid whoever was shooting at us."

"Where will you go to get sewed up?"

"An emergency room. I've got Buck's ID and credit cards. I don't think anyone's going to look for us at an emergency room either."

Spike: 35 Kills and Smiling 105

A cell phone rang in the glove compartment. Barbie took it out. "A burner." She handed it to Spike.

"Please, be quiet, no matter what I say," he told her.

She nodded.

"Yeah." He lowered his voice.

"The timeline has been moved up. You must be here by Monday at noon. Is that a problem?" the man asked.

"Nope."

"Good. The address is the same one I texted you before. You have it?"

Spike checked. "Got it."

"Great. See you then. The whole team looks forward to meeting you."

"Me too."

The man hung up. Spike flipped the phone shut.

"What was that?" Barbie asked.

"I guess that was Buck's job. I'm going instead, and I have to be in Louisiana by Monday at noon."

"Lucky you're both about the same size and age," she said. "You both even got dark hair. I think you could pass for him if they don't look too close."

"That's good, but what'll I do with you?"

"I guess you can drop me off at my sister's. She's in Houston. It'll be a big surprise, but she won't care. You had to go to Houston anyway, right?"

"Yes, I did." *Wonder what in the hell this job is in Louisiana. Should be fun finding out. Test out my Buck identity.*

⁓

BARBIE WAS ON A TREMENDOUS ADVENTURE. To her, it was an exciting, bigger-than-life fairy tale like nothing she'd ever dreamed of. She thought she loved Spike, but she'd had those feelings before. She felt like she'd do anything for him, and right now, she would. But she knew things had changed. She wasn't sure why, but he seemed so powerful and always did exactly what he wanted. She was giddy. The ride might not last forever, but for now, she would just hold on.

When they passed a Circle K, she knew they were entering the outskirts of Deming. His injury would need a lot of stitches. She hoped it wasn't infected.

"Well, there it is, an emergency room," Spike said. It was a stand-alone, small, single-story building with a drive-through for ambulances.

"Good. Let's get you fixed." Barbie was tired but ramped up.

In the back parking lot, Spike parked as far from the entrance as he could. They were in the far back corner, with a few cars in between. Likely, whoever had shot at him in Columbus, probably Rico's men, would be looking for the pickup. On the long drive, Spike had told Barbie he hoped they hadn't gotten the license number. He would have locked the blue bag in the car, but he didn't want to take a chance. Spike took out the pistol and knife and put them behind the seat. He carried the bag tight to his body.

"I'm not looking forward to this." Spike held his arm. "A twelve-inch cut wrapped in duct tape for about fifteen hours. All the shoveling and dragging. It's gotta be bad."

"You'll be okay. Can I watch them sew it up?" Barbie asked.

"Damn, you are sick."

Barbie laughed. "No, I just think it'd be interesting."

"Okay, let's go see."

Spike and Barbie met at the front of the truck, then started toward the emergency room.

They walked with hats pulled down. In the early morning, the lobby was empty. Barbie stood beside Spike as he walked up to check in. He did the paperwork by showing Buck's ID and using Buck's insurance, telling the woman at the desk he'd cut his arm at a construction site. He had no problem getting checked in, and the receptionist barely looked up. They'd just sat down when "Buck" was called back into a treatment room.

The nurse stopped Barbie. "Are you immediate family?"

"I'm his wife," Barbie said. She felt proud, and the lie excited her. She wondered how Spike would feel but anticipated they might not let her go back with him if she wasn't related or his wife.

Spike looked over his shoulder, smiled, and shook his head slightly.

Nice! He likes it! Her smile grew even bigger.

"Oh, I'm sorry. If you two will follow me."

The nurse brought them into Exam Room A. The doctor was right behind them.

Spike set the blue bag beside Barbie as she took the only chair in the small exam room. After a little chit-chat, the doc cut off the duct tape.

Barbie looked at his name tag. "What do you think, Dr. Welby?"

"Your husband is lucky with the tape. Whose idea was that?" Dr. Welby asked.

"Mine," Spike said.

"Wow, this is a long cut, but you made my job a lot easier by getting the duct tape on right away and tightly." He looked the wound over. "Good job."

"Thanks."

"The nurse will clean the wound, and then I'll be right back to stitch it up."

∾

Dante was relieved when Gabriel finally showed up. Immediately, they headed to Deming, looking for a place to get Dante's leg looked at. They passed a Circle K. "Where's a doctor?"

"Up there, boss, an emergency room," Gabriel said.

Dante looked up. "Oh, thank God."

Gabriel pulled into the front of the emergency room and waved for help. An orderly in white scrubs came out, pushing a wheelchair.

Dante got rolled in, checked in, and taken to Exam Room B. He waited a few minutes, and then the doctor came in, "Hi, I'm Dr. Welby. It looks like you may have hurt your leg."

"No shit!"

The doctor didn't back down. He raised his eyebrows and crossed his arms.

"I'm sorry, Doc, it just hurts like a son of a bitch. And it's all bruised and swollen like it's going to burst. It looks like hell."

"It's okay, I've heard worse. Pain doesn't bring out the best in us, and I know it hurts." He looked at the leg closely, squeezing it a little here and there. "This is caused mostly by blood escaping from the capillaries where the tissue is damaged. So, the bad news won't surprise you, but it's probably broken. The good news is that I'm sure it's nothing we can't fix. We just need to get some X-rays to see exactly what we're working with. The nurse will give you something for the pain. I suggest you take it. Then she'll escort you to radiology. I'll see you back here in a few minutes."

"Thanks, Doc. How long will I be here?"

"We'll get you out as quick as we can, probably an hour or two. Not many people are here right now, just you and a wicked laceration in the next room."

20

THAT'S IT

Columbus, NM
Friday Morning

SPIKE WATCHED the nurse clean the wound. Mostly, he watched the thirty-ish nurse lean over and show a little too much cleavage. *Is the nurse a bad person? Or maybe an angel of mercy? Could a nurse be bad enough to deserve being killed? Probably not.* He looked at the rubber band on his right arm. He didn't need to snap it.

There was a light double tap, and Dr. Welby came back into the room. "Mr. Montague, your wound cleaned up nicely."

"Just call me Buck," Spike said.

"Okay, Buck. Well, your wound cleaned up well." The doctor turned Spike's arm and examined it from different angles. "I see no signs of infection, but you'll still need to take antibiotics."

Barbie's breath came hot on Spike's neck as she watched the doctor.

"Your wife is very interested in this," the doc said.

"She's a sponge for knowledge." Spike glanced at the floor under the chair. The bag was still there. No one could get out with it.

"Are you a nurse?" the doc asked her.

"No, sir, but I'm thinking of going to nursing school."

"Well, good luck. It's a noble profession."

The nurse rolled her eyes, smiling at Spike.

The doc numbed Spike's arm, then left. He returned a few minutes later. As he stitched Spike's arm, he explained what he was doing. Because the cut was so long, the doctor sutured its middle first, then halved the distance between sutures, evening out the skin so it wouldn't bunch up.

When the doctor was done, he stood. "Well, there you go. Good as new in a few weeks, except you'll have a real nice scar as a souvenir."

"Thanks, Doc. It looks like you did a great job."

"Thank you for that duct tape," the doc said. "The nurse will wrap it up and give you some oral antibiotics. Take them all. It's a five-day regimen. Don't get the wound wet for at least forty-eight hours if the sutures look good, which means no redness or swelling. Otherwise, you'll need to come back in about a week to get the sutures removed. And be sure to change the bandage daily."

"Thanks again," Spike said.

"And try not to cut yourself again." The doctor gently shook Spike's right hand and left.

Spike moved the bag so it was next to him on the table. The nurse gave him an odd look but said nothing and started wrapping his arm.

∼

Dante was watching Dr. Price wrap a splint on his lower leg when Dr. Welby walked into the room.

Dr. Price looked up. "Hope you don't mind. I got back when X-rays were done, and you were busy with the laceration. I'm almost done with the splint. I told him it's too swollen to cast, so he should use crutches and stay off it before seeing a doctor in a few days. Then it'll likely get casted."

"All good and accurate information," Dr. Welby said. "Thanks for helping."

"No problem. I'm almost done."

Both doctors chatted with Dante for a few minutes. They let him try the crutches for a few steps. Then they gave him final instructions and a prescription and told him to make sure he saw a doctor in a few days. The orderly pushed a wheelchair in and rolled Dante to the checkout desk. Gabriel was waiting.

Wheelchair-bound Dante pointed out the floor-to-ceiling glass front of the emergency room. "Look! A red truck!"

"Where?" Gabriel asked.

"Damn! There!" He pointed frantically.

Everyone in the waiting room stared at him as if he'd yelled, "Fire!"

"I think that's the truck!" In his excitement, he slipped on his crutches and put weight on his splinted leg, then screamed as he fell and sprawled on the floor, crutches going in two directions. "Goddammit." He got up on his elbow. "Go after him! Now!"

"Language! There are children here!" An older gray-haired woman stood and wagged her finger.

"Fuck you, lady!" Dante screamed and flipped her the bird.

No one else did anything except look away.

Gabriel glanced at his boss, hesitated, then ran for their car.

Dante, sitting on the floor, saw him stop halfway, turn, and walk back into the emergency room.

Dante shook his head but had no more outbursts.

"Boss, I never saw him. I didn't even see which way he turned."

Dante shook his head again, then was helped into the wheelchair. The pickup was gone. *I'm fucked!*

∽

OUT ON THE HIGHWAY, Spike stepped on the gas. He tried to keep his hands firm on the wheel, but his grip tightened in protest against the nerves coursing through him. *What if the cartel finds us? If we could just get out of Deming, we'd be in the clear. Maybe forever.* He was pretty sure that Rico and his men didn't know his real name. They knew him only as Spike. He checked Google Maps on Buck's phone and decided to take New Mexico State Highway 26. All they had to do was go out of Deming to the north, go under I-10, and turn right. It was a secondary road, and he didn't think they'd have the manpower to cover it. It would take a little longer to get to Houston, but this route was much safer.

They grabbed some food at a McDonald's drive-through, then drove another four hours to Carlsbad, New Mexico. As exhausted as Spike was, he wanted to make sure they had gotten away from whoever was trying to shoot him.

21

WE LOST HIM

Columbus, NM
Friday Morning

JORGE GOT BACK in the car with Pup and drove away from the wrong red truck.

"What now?" Pup asked.

"I don't know. Just drive up and down Main Street. We'll look for a red pickup."

"Not a very good plan, is it?"

"Nope." They were quiet for a while, and then Jorge spoke again. "Dante found them at the Rosa Hotel. Maybe the person who waited on them knew one of the people. Not Spike but the man and woman with the red truck."

"You think so?"

"Better than just looking for a red pickup." An ounce of hope brimmed in Jorge. "We have no idea where they are, and there are a lot of red trucks. But we could get a name this way."

Spike: 35 Kills and Smiling 115

"Let's go for it." Pup was excited, like a kid. He was a kid. Jorge called Dante.

∼

WITH GABRIEL'S HELP, Dante had just gotten settled into the passenger seat of his car. They were still in the parking lot of the emergency room.

"What the hell am I going to do?" Dante muttered to himself. Then his phone rang. He saw it was Jorge. "God, I hope he found the guy." *Bail my ass out! Please!* "Jorge, tell me you found the son of a bitch."

"We found a red pickup, followed them, and confronted them. But it wasn't him. Sorry, boss," Jorge said. "How's your leg?"

"I saw a doc, and it's splinted. It still hurts like hell. Where are you?"

"In Deming. But I think we need to go back to that hotel where you first found him in Columbus, then figure out who waited on them last night and see if they know who they are. If we find them, we might find Spike."

"Good idea. We're at the emergency room as you come into town from the south, by a Circle K. Come to us. You can follow us back to Columbus. I gotta go. I need to call Rico and update him."

Dante hung up and sat there for a moment. *I don't want to make this call.* Then he did. He explained that while they hadn't found Spike, they thought they had seen his truck in Deming going north. Dante also told Rico about his leg.

Rico's response was curt. "We had a deal that really went south at a warehouse in Houston, and everyone we have there may be dead. I'm on the way there now. I need you and your men in Houston. Make a run through Columbus.

Someone must know who the people with Spike were. Get a lead, you hear me! Find Spike! Then get your ass to Houston. Keep me posted." He hung up.

Dante and Gabriel took the lead, with Jorge and Pup following.

∼

BOTH CARS PULLED into the Rosa Hotel parking lot after a short drive back to Columbus. Jorge walked to Dante's car, and Dante put down the window.

"Can you handle it?" Dante asked. "My leg's throbbing so badly, I feel it in my eyes."

"Okay, boss," Jorge said.

Inside, the doorbell went off, and a Hispanic woman came to the counter.

"Were you working last night?" Jorge asked.

"I was here last night, and I'm just getting ready to leave now."

He looked at her name tag. "Lucia. Do you remember last night when a couple came in and another man? They had a red pickup."

"That's not much of a description." Lucia picked up her purse. "Really, I'm off now, and I don't think I can help you."

"Just before the shooting last night … I think someone may have shot a gun about when they left."

"Oh, my God, the shooting. Yes, I remember. It must have been the Jackson girl, but there weren't three of them together. A man came in alone, then the couple, but they all left about the same time."

"You knew the woman?"

"Of course, she's lived here for a long time with her mom and … well, she's had a dad and a few stepdads too."

"What was her name again?"

"Barbie Jackson. She lives with her mom in a mobile home trailer."

"You know the address or how to get there?"

Lucia slowly backed behind the counter. "Why don't you leave your name and number, and I'll get it to her?"

"I'm sorry, we're in sort of a hurry. You know where she lives, right?"

She didn't answer. Her eyes darted around.

"Look, lady, you scream, and I'll kill you." Jorge pulled out his pistol, a Ruger Security 9.

Lucia started to run, her mouth about to open. Jorge grabbed her hair and hit the side of her head with the butt of the gun. No real scream escaped, and she fell limp. He scooped her up. Lucia never had a chance to yell, and no one was in the lobby. They went out to their car, and Jorge put her in the back seat.

He shrugged at Dante and jumped into his car. "Drive!" Dante told Pup. "Go! Just out of town."

Jorge and Gabriel followed. They were on the south side of this small town near the city limits, so they had to go only the equivalent of a few city blocks.

"Pull down that side road," Jorge said.

Gabriel, with Jorge watching the woman, pulled in behind Dante.

Jorge's phone buzzed. It was Dante, but he had to do a few things first, so he didn't answer.

He checked her pulse. "She's alive. Give me your water." Jorge removed the water and a zip-tie from the glove box. He slid in the back seat and zip-tied Lucia's hands while she was still unconscious. He opened the plastic bottle and squeezed it. The water hit her face like a firehose. Then he quickly got out of the car and shut the back door.

Jorge saw her cough as the water entered her throat. Then she struggled to sit up. The fact that her hands were tied behind her back added to her disorientation. Now conscious, Lucia screamed and yelled in Spanish as she frantically wiggled and thrashed.

His phone kept buzzing. Jorge looked up and saw Dante turning red and screaming. Gabriel had opened his door and stepped out, yelling at Jorge, "What the fuck's wrong with you?"

Jorge knew Dante would be pissed. *So fucking what? Maybe I'll promote myself and pop both Dante and Gabriel.* He walked back to Dante, who sat in his car with his window down. Jorge was ready to take the wrath that was coming.

"What the hell? When I call you ... *you* answer! You moron. And are you stupid or what? Kidnapping that woman!" Dante screamed.

"Boss, no one saw it."

"Now what?"

"She told me the woman was Barbie Jackson, and she knows where her mother lives," Jorge said.

"Really?" Dante's breathing evened out.

Now they both heard Lucia screaming.

"Okay, see what you can do. We'll follow you, but I don't want her to see me. Got it?"

"Got it."

Jorge walked back to his car and spoke loudly to Lucia through the closed window. With a level voice, he kept repeating in Spanish, "Lucia, I'm sorry. We're not going to hurt you. Please, calm down."

Finally, she stopped. Lucia lay on her back, her hair tousled and her dress partially pulled up from jerking about. She sweated profusely, her makeup ran, and her chest heaved as she sucked in deep breaths from her exertion.

"My head hurts. Are you going to rape me, then kill me?" she asked in English with squinted eyes and a red face. "Please. Don't kill me. I have a family."

22

LITTLE HELP

Columbus, NM
Friday Morning

THE MEN LAUGHED. "NO, NO," Jorge said. "All we want to know is where Barbie lives. That's it."

She glared at them.

"Look, you sit in the back seat and behave yourself. My friend here will drive, and you just tell us where to go. Take us to Barbie's house. I'll go in and talk to her or her mom for a minute, and then we'll let you go. Or if you give us trouble —" He flipped a switchblade out and showed her. "Let's just say it would be very bad for you."

She continued to glare at them.

"Say you understand," Jorge said.

"I understand." Lucia sat back in the seat and stared straight ahead. "Get back on the highway."

"Good, that's better. Just help us out, and we'll let you go. No harm will come to you, Lucia."

She directed them to Barbie's mom's trailer. It was a short trip.

"You sure this is it?" Jorge asked.

"Positive," she said. "Please, let me go now."

"In a minute. Do they have a car?"

"I don't know."

He put on rubber gloves. "Stay with her. I'll have a look around," he told Pup as he opened the door and stepped out of the car.

"Please, don't hurt me. I won't tell anyone anything. Please."

Jorge put his finger to his lips and shushed her.

Tears sprung to Lucia's eyes and rolled down her cheeks.

"Be patient. We won't hurt you." *I guess she's figured out that we may have to dispose of her.* He shut the car door, walked up to the trailer, and tried the door. *It's open. I'll be damned.*

Cool air hit him as he cracked the unlocked door. A window A/C unit hummed. It was dark, with the curtains closed on all the windows. *What a mess. It smells. Overflowing ashtrays, dirty clothes everywhere, empty liquor bottles sitting around and in the trash baskets. Wow! But no address books. The mail is all junk and bills.*

He walked down the narrow hall. The first room was neat, with a pink bedspread and a bookshelf containing some books. The closet held a young woman's clothing. Barbie's room. And there was her senior picture. *We know what she looks like now.*

He continued looking around the trailer but found nothing useful.

Jorge went outside and stood in the shade of the trailer as he waved for Pup to join him.

Pup walked up to him. "Find anything?"

They stood in the shade. The only relief was a warm breeze.

"Not much, but I got a picture of her." He showed it to Pup.

"She's pretty," Pup said. "Now what? And what about the *señora* in the car?"

Jorge chewed his lip and stared into space. "I hope Barbie's mom knows where she might go and who she's with. Also, if we get Barbie's phone number, we might be able to track her. I hope that if we find her, we'll find Spike. But that's all a big maybe." He chewed his lips some more. "As far as the *señora*—"

Pup interrupted. "We're not going to kill her, are we? I mean, we don't live around here. She hasn't seen us do anything bad. She doesn't know our names. We just need to make sure she doesn't see our license number."

"I'm not sure yet." Jorge sighed and shook his head. "We gotta find Spike."

~

THEY SAT in the car where they could see the trailer's driveway. It took a while, but she showed up.

Jorge pulled open the screen door, knocked on the metal door, and stood there. He knew the door was probably unlocked, but people tended to get pissed and were less cooperative when someone just walked into their house.

"Just a minute!" she yelled, then opened the door. The transition from sunlight to relative darkness in the older mobile home made it hard to see her.

"Ma'am, I'm Detective Gonzales," Jorge lied. "Excuse my appearance, but I've been pulled in from an undercover assignment to help on the shooting at the Rosa

Hotel last night. I need to ask, is Barbie Jackson your daughter?"

"Oh, my God! Yes! Yes! Is Barbie hurt?" She flung open the door. "Please, come in, Detective." Her face wrinkled in disbelief. Clearly, she feared hearing that her daughter was hurt or dead.

"Ma'am, we think she was kidnapped during the shooting, and we're doing everything we can to find her. Have you heard from her?"

"No." She looked like she was about to lose her sanity. "Is she alright?"

"We just don't know yet."

"What do you know?"

"We know she was at the Rosa Hotel, but she didn't get a room. She was with two men in a red pickup, and someone fired at them."

"That's Buck's truck."

"Who's Buck?"

"That's her boyfriend. She left with him, moved out yesterday, late in the day. They were going to Louisiana. He had a construction job offer. But I don't know who the other guy was." She was on the edge of her chair. "Who shot at them? Why? You never told me. Is she okay?" Alcohol reeked on her breath, but she didn't act drunk or slur any words.

"We don't know who he is or why the man shot at them. As far as we know, she's fine, but we have to find her to be sure," Jorge said.

He was patient. He guessed she would tell him anything he asked, so he kept probing with simple questions like a cop would. He found out she didn't know Buck's last name, where he worked, if he had any family, or where he was from. She thought he had lived in Deming and did construction on the border fence, but the contract had run out.

Then her eyes brightened. "Oh, Barbie has a sister in Houston. She was in the FBI and is a private investigator now. She might stop there, but they haven't spoken in a while."

She provided Jorge with the name of the sister, Ava Gunn, as well as Ava's phone and address and Barbie's phone number.

"Thank you. This will help." He stood.

"Oh, I forgot. You can track her phone." She slurred her speech a little. "If it's on, I mean, because her phone is on a family plan. It'll pinpoint its exact location, but it has to be on. If it's off, it'll just show you where it was last on."

She typed something into her phone, then handed it to him.

"It says her phone is on the highway on the north side of Columbus. Let's go check on her," Jorge said.

She jumped up, staggered a little, and grabbed her purse.

"Ma'am, please, let us check this out first. I'll call you as soon as I find out anything."

She wrote down the website, her ID, and the password and handed the information to Jorge. "Okay, please find her. I really need her. I mean ... you know, I hope she's alright."

He returned the phone. "You've been a great help, thank you. I'll call you soon."

She stood at the door and leaned against the frame as she waved goodbye.

Jorge was grateful Pup had Lucia lie down in the back seat. If Barbie's mother had seen Lucia, it might have complicated things, and someone would have had to die.

He got in the car. "Stay down, *señora*. It looks pretty good for you. You might be able to go home soon." He looked at Pup. "Let's go." He'd already pulled up the tracker website. "This is where we're going. But I don't want to discuss it now." He flicked his eyes toward the back seat.

With a nod and a smile, Pup indicated he understood.

The site was close. They drove to where the phone should have been and pulled over. "*Señora*, just behave. We'll let you go soon." Jorge motioned with his head for Pup to get out, and then they started looking for the phone, walking to the exact spot where it should have been. They searched in a wider circle, but there was nothing—just highway. *Shit! Need to call Rico.*

23

A GRAY AREA

Houston, TX
Early Friday Morning

DETECTIVE GRAY WAS FEELING GOOD. *Ava Gunn. What a great name. Beautiful, short blond hair, and a great smile.* The woman of his dreams had just entered his life. She was smart, a kickass private investigator, and she had a great sense of humor. *I really like her.* He couldn't stop thinking of her. He was smitten.

By the time he left the crime scene, it was late, but he wanted to drive by Ava Gunn's address. *Just because!* He slowed as the street numbers got closer. Then there it was. He drove past it, turned around, and slowly approached her condo. Trees hanging partially over the road shrouded the neighborhood in thick darkness. He found an open parking spot close enough to see her place. A three-story condo in Rice Village. On the third floor, the lights were on. *Must be the bedroom.*

Being a PI must pay well. Rice Village was upscale, a great location. It was close to Rice University, near downtown, and centrally located in the city. It was one of those areas where an old shithouse sat right beside a brand-new expensive house or, in Ava's case, a set of six condos. Back at the ambulance, he'd snapped a few pictures of her on his phone without her knowing, before and after he'd talked to her. He pulled out his phone and admired the new Mrs. Gray. *Or maybe Gray-Gunn. She must keep Gunn in her name.*

Gray threw a kiss at Ava's place as he drove home. Then he cleaned up and went right to bed. The red numbers on his clock read six minutes after one a.m. He didn't get much sleep because he kept thinking of Ava Gunn. Lying in bed, he decided to see her again as soon as he could. He'd say he was checking on her because she had a concussion. He knew he shouldn't. He'd just taken a statement from her, but she was barely involved in the case. *Fuck it! I want to see her. If she complains, I'm sure the excuse of checking on her will get me off the hook. Besides, she did flirt with me, I'm sure.* Somewhere in the middle of thinking of Ava, he fell asleep with a smile.

The alarm was set for six a.m., but he woke up about five minutes before.

Gray called his partner, Detective Peter Hannigan.

"What's going on?" Peter asked.

"If you don't need me, I'm going to take a sick day," Gray said.

"I think I'll survive. Hot date or something?"

"You know I got in late last night. I thought I'd sleep in and get a head start on the weekend." Gray wondered if he should have made his excuse simpler.

"Damn, you goin' soft on me?" the older partner asked.

"No, just fuckin' lazy, and I thought I'd visit a friend in

Dallas for the weekend." *If I'm out of town, it's less likely that they'll expect me to be available.*

"Have fun. I'll tell the Lieutenant. See you Monday."

Gray slowly got ready, thinking that he'd go to her place about mid-morning and knock on the door, play it by ear, maybe invite her to supper and a movie. *Something innocent.*

Then he remembered that she owned a PI firm. *Shit, it's Friday. She could leave for her office at any time.*

He dressed quickly, got in his car, and drove as fast as he could but not so fast that he'd be stopped by a cop. They'd let him go, but it would kill even more time. He wanted to catch her at home. It'd be much more intimate and relaxed. When Gray turned onto her street, his legs shook, and his hands gripped the wheel tightly. *Maybe she's already left.* He found a parking spot where he could see her condo. It was daylight, so he couldn't tell if her lights were on.

He saw her double garage doors, small windows across the tops, next to the red door. He walked past the windows and shined a flashlight in. The classic red BMW she'd had at the stakeout was parked inside. *She's home.*

He suppressed a giddy laugh. *Better catch her now, before she tries to drive out.*

Gray walked to the door and wrung his hands, then ran his hand through his hair and a finger over his teeth. *My God, my heart is beating fast. Calm down!* He took a few deep breaths, then rang the doorbell. He felt like a teenager on a date.

Some rustling came from inside, and then the speaker at the side of the door came alive with her voice. "Can I help you?"

"Miss Gunn, this is Detective Gray from last night. Can I talk to you for a few minutes?"

"Sure. Is everything alright?"

"To be honest, I just wanted to make sure you were okay, with the concussion and all. May I come in for a minute?"

"Give me a second to put a robe on."

"Okay." He wasn't sure if she heard his last comment. She must have been naked or at least in her underwear. He sighed and smiled.

The door opened. "Sorry to keep you waiting."

"No problem. I was just worried about you."

"Well, come in, please." She stepped back in her baby blue silk robe and held the door fully open. "I have a Keurig and lots of choices of coffee and hot chocolate."

He followed her to the second floor. At the top of the stairs was a kitchen with a high table and four bar stools. They took up about thirty percent of that end of the second floor. Gray saw four other chairs pushed back against the wall in different places. A sunken living room took up the rest of the space.

They had coffee while sitting next to each other on adjoining sides of the square table. After a little chit-chat about the weather and a few other things that didn't matter, Ava asked, "So, is this official?"

"Not sure how I should answer that," Gray said. He was breathing hard and hoped she didn't notice. He loved her robe and how suggestive it was. *Damn!* She was wearing make-up and had probably been getting ready to go to work when he showed up.

"I think you just answered it. Not official? Right?"

"Is that bad?" Gray's face flushed.

She touched his hand. "No, it's not bad. I like you too."

He smiled and relaxed.

"Look, Detective Gray."

"Please, call me Hank or just Gray. Everyone calls me Gray."

"Okay, Gray, I do like you too. But I have to get ready and go to work. I have an engagement tonight, business. And I have a stakeout tomorrow night, but Sunday is open. Maybe brunch, and we make it a day around town?"

"That'd be great!"

Ava leaned over and kissed Gray on the cheek. "You gotta go, and I gotta get dressed, but I'll see you Sunday. Can you find the front door?"

"Sure. I can't wait."

"Me either," she said over her shoulder as she walked toward the steps to the third floor.

Gray walked outside. "Oh, my God. Thank you, God. She's perfect." Then he quietly sang "Oh What a Beautiful Mornin'."

He called his partner. "Peter, hope you're having a great day."

"Yeah, I guess so. I thought you were sick."

"Feeling better. Feeling *great*. Look forward to seeing you soon," Gray said over-enthusiastically.

"What, did you just get laid?"

"Not yet but soon."

24

THINGS HAPPENING FAST

Chihuahua, Mexico
Friday Late Morning

RICO HAD BEEN the new Zorro cartel boss for a day, and it was one shit storm after another. He had to hold onto power while a big arms deal fell apart in Houston. It had cost him not only money but also leadership, and many of his men were dead. This would not go unnoticed by the other cartels. And Spike had gotten away with sixteen million dollars in bitcoin. *That's too much to blow off.*

Rico got a call from Dante.

"Where are you, and what's happening?" Rico's voice was dry. *Maybe I can salvage the bitcoin money.*

"Boss, the young woman with Spike, her name is Barbie. The mother told us how to track her daughter's phone, but it has to be on. So, we drove to the spot where the tracker showed the phone was located, but it's not there. That means she turned it off at this location. When she turns it back on, we'll have her."

"What if she doesn't turn it back on?"

"We found out the boyfriend was driving, a guy named Buck but no last name known yet. He apparently is going to Louisiana for a job, and Barbie has a sister in Houston named Ava Gunn. She's ex-FBI and currently a private investigator."

"That's fucking great!" There was silence as Rico thought. "Start driving toward Houston and keep checking the tracker. If she turns on the phone, that should put you closer to her. But no matter where she turns on the phone, we should be able to find someone close to her, even a few cops here and there."

"Okay. We'll go to Deming, get on I-10, and head toward Houston. I've got Jorge and Pup with me."

"Take 'em with you. I may need everyone we can get in Houston. We had a big deal go sour. Pedro's dead. There's no leadership there, so someone may be making a move on us. I'm flying to Houston soon," Rico said. "I'll be there in a few hours. You should get in late tonight. Get some sleep and plan to meet me at our office there."

"Got it, boss. I'll keep you posted."

Rico hung up.

He was about to get on his private jet. Based on Pedro's last message, he knew Pedro had to be dead. *Damn.*

"Toro, call down the list of our guys until you get a live one."

"Yes, sir." Toro did as he was told. He was seven people deep before he got an answer. "It's Sebastian on the phone." Most cartels were highly decentralized to protect the leadership.

Rico took the phone and held his hand over the receiver. "You know him?"

Toro shook his head as he pursed his lips.

Many larger cartels had a horizontal structure with informally communicated responsibilities and operating procedures. So, it was no surprise that neither Rico nor Toro knew Sebastian.

"Sebastian, do you know who this is?" Rico asked.

"*Sí, Jefe*," his passive voice quivered. Toro had told him.

"You are now in charge of Houston until I get there. I'll arrange my transportation, so don't worry about meeting my plane."

"*Sí.*"

"Do you know what happened with Pedro and the deal?"

"No, *Jefe*, but one of the men knew where the deal was supposed to happen. I went by and looked. It's covered with cops, FBI, ATF, and maybe others too. I couldn't get close."

"Call everyone to meet at our stash house on the east side of Houston tomorrow morning at eight a.m. You know where it is?"

"*Sí.*"

"Good. I also need someone at Ava Gunn's house. She's a PI. Find her and call us with updates. There's too much to tell you now, but we'll be there soon. I'm giving you back to Toro." He handed Toro the phone and told him what to say. "Explain to him about Ava Gunn and why we're watching her. We're really looking for her sister Barbie, and we hope Spike is with her."

Toro nodded to Rico and explained to Sebastian what was happening.

Less than two days earlier, Rico had been number two behind Zorro and had seen Spike for the first time.

So much has happened. So fast.

Just a day and a half ago, Zorro, Rico, and his other men had freed Spike from Jeff Case's ranch. Case had been holding Spike in an upscale, underground bomb shelter structure—but still a jail. He'd installed it specifically to keep Spike in confinement. But now, Spike was free, had a ton of Rico's money, and was a pain in the ass.

Toro finished briefing Sebastian and hung up. "He sounds young, boss."

"We were all young once, but someone from El Paso will need to take charge, probably Dante. I hope they get their asses to Houston as soon as they can. What a shit storm." Rico shook his head. "Have we heard from the seller yet?"

"Nothing and they won't answer our calls," Toro said. "I've heard rumors that someone took them out. That the US government didn't like them stealing Switchblade drones that were on the way to Ukraine, and they came down hard."

Rico made a fist and punched his open palm. "Damn!" Then he grew quiet before continuing. "Check into this and make sure it wasn't another cartel. Sounds like we may have to cut our losses and distance ourselves from the whole deal."

"Tomorrow morning, we'll have everyone together and figure this out, boss, including Spike."

I wonder if someone will shoot me in the back of the head.

I wonder if any of the competition will move on my guys. Or me.

Rico pulled out his Sig Sauer P320 and checked it. *Round in the chamber.* He set it on his leg as he zoned out for a few seconds.

Perilous times! Trust no one. No one!

He looked at Toro. *Not even you. Maybe especially you, just one step from being the boss. Very tempting.* He nodded, unaware that he was doing it.

"You okay, boss?"

Rico zoned back in and focused on Toro's face. He saw the concern and smiled at Toro. "Couldn't be better. I'm depending on you." *Julius Caesar could trust no one. "Et tu, Brute?" Neither can I.*

25

SEBASTIAN

Houston, TX
Friday Late Morning

Sebastian hung up from the call with Rico and Toro. Then he returned to his table at a Starbucks where he'd met his girlfriend for coffee.

"What's that all about?" she asked. She was just out of high school and didn't speak Spanish.

He didn't look up at her. "Business, give me a minute." He entered "Ava Gunn" in a search engine on his smartphone. There she was, a private investigator, with her office address. It was about twenty minutes away.

He stood, looking at the map to her office. "Sorry, we gotta go. Business." He took a step toward the door and glanced at her. She hadn't moved. "I'm serious, this is important. C'mon. Now."

She picked up her drink and started toward the door. As he walked her out, he wanted to drag her. He had things to do for the boss, and she was moving too slowly. *This is important!*

"Will I see you tonight?" she asked.

"Doubt it." He walked past her to her car door and stood until she caught up. Then he kissed her and said, "I really gotta go. I'm gonna be really busy the next few days. Don't call me, but I'll text you later."

Sebastian ran to his car. He knew where he was going. He called one of the men in his crew. "Call all the guys and get them together at your place. Text me when they're all there. Got it?"

"I'm on it now."

Sebastian didn't want to wait to find someone, explain what he needed, and then let them take their time getting to Ava Gunn's office. He had to catch her at her office and follow her home. He knew what she looked like. He'd check out her office building when he got there. *Maybe I'll call and ask for her, to see if she's in her office.*

He had been with the Zorro cartel for about three years but had met Zorro only once. Now Rico was in charge of the cartel, and Pedro, his Houston boss, was dead. Sebastian ran his territory well, but he had no idea how to run Houston and didn't even know all the other territory bosses. He'd contact the ones he knew and tell them to spread the word about the meeting with Rico tomorrow morning. *How can I be the senior man in Houston?* But he'd just talked to the new head of the cartel and been given instructions. *I'm the Houston boss for now. Pretty damn cool! Maybe the new permanent boss if I play it right.* This was a great opportunity. A once-in-a-lifetime chance, and he was only twenty-one.

Sebastian pulled up by Ava's office in a one-story complex. *Harder to hide.* Because the suites were all side by side, with some interior ones, it was hard to tell how many of the cars in front of her office belonged to those who worked there. He parked so he could see her front door. The sign beside it read: Ava Gunn, PI. *Love that name, so cool. Ava Gunn.* He had to find Ava and then the gold prize, which was Barbie, and the promotion prize, which was Spike.

Shit! I could be here a long time, and she may not even be here.

So, he waited. *Now I gotta piss. And I'm thirsty. Shit!* But just fuckin' find Spike. *Promote immediately!*

Then, there she was. Walking out of her office.

She got into a late-model silver Corolla and drove off. Sebastian gave her as much distance as he could, then started to follow her.

After about fifteen minutes, she pulled into a garage of what must have been her condo. It was three stories and connected to five others facing the street.

Easy access. Sebastian looked at the address as he drove by. In his rearview mirror, he saw her garage door descend. He also noticed a red sports car in Ava's two-car garage. *Nice!*

He parked about five car lengths from her condo. Lots of trees, a narrow street, cars up and down both sides. He blended right in.

"So, now I wait." *Damn! Still gotta pee, still thirsty.*

26

SLEEP AT LAST

Carlsbad, NM
Friday Noon to Night

SPIKE CHECKED IN AS BUCK. He was exhausted and planned to get some sleep as soon as he got in the room and cleaned up. Whenever he woke up, they'd drive on to Houston. Driving at night would be cooler anyway, and they'd encounter less traffic. The sun was bright at noon. The small motel had rooms lined up facing the road. Spike took their stuff into their room. Barbie had everything she needed because she'd packed to leave with Buck. Spike had only what he was wearing, but he was too tired to care.

Once in the room, he looked at Barbie sitting on the bed. Then she let herself fall backward and lay on her back with her legs over the edge. "This feels great, like I died and went to Heaven."

Spike snapped the rubber band, then lifted it higher and watched as he let it go. The first one stung, but the second time it hurt. *Is this gonna help?* But he didn't need to snap the rubber band to know he wouldn't hurt Barbie. For that matter, he'd hardly even noticed her so far that night. She was young and beautiful. He'd shower with a plastic bag over his arm, then go to bed and sleep for as long as possible.

"Can I ask you more about the people you've killed?" Barbie asked.

He hadn't expected that question. "Not now. I don't feel like talking at all. I'm going to shower and then go to sleep." After brushing his teeth, Spike stepped into the shower. He heard Barbie come in and start brushing her teeth. Spike ignored her and quickly washed, then stood in the water and enjoyed it while making sure his bandaged arm remained dry. With his eyes shut, he let the water run over him. *Oh, God, that feels good.*

A warm body against his back made him jump. He didn't expect it, and he hadn't heard Barbie get into the shower. She reached around and took his growing member. Spike turned to face her and fell into a deep "forget where you're at" sexual kiss. He was fully erect now.

He turned her a little roughly. She caught herself with both hands against the back wall of the shower. He spread her legs with no resistance from her. It had been a long time. He made sure she was ready by sliding it in once gently. Then he started thrusting. The bag on his arm made an odd rustling sound with every stroke, but he didn't give a shit. Barbie didn't seem to care either. He thrust as hard as he could, and it didn't take long. Once spent, he leaned into Barbie and held her from behind.

She feels so good. Their hearts beat loudly, and they were breathless.

Over Barbie's shoulder, he said into her ear, "My God, that was unbelievable. Thank you."

"Anything for you, baby," Barbie said. "I'm your girl."

"I gotta get some sleep," Spike said. He turned to face the showerhead and rinsed off. "You shower. I'm going to bed." He was getting out when she stuck her lips up for a kiss, so he obliged.

Fuck, I hope she didn't get the wrong idea.

He dried off and got into bed naked, then glanced at the clock. One p.m. He was asleep as soon as his head hit the pillow.

Barbie spooning him awakened him. Her warm body felt so good. He hadn't had a woman for quite a while. *That was good. Best shower I've had in a long time.* Her breasts rested soft against his back as her naked body snuggled against him. His member reacted, strong and erect again. *Too tired.* He looked at the clock. Five p.m. Then he shut his eyes.

~

Barbie woke up and glanced at the clock. It was six p.m. She smelled Spike's hair and the soap he'd used. Both good, comforting aromas. *I love feeling him next to me.* Without moving, she stared at the back of his head. *What's going to happen to me? Spike seems so nice. Killing Buck was self-defense. Is he dangerous? Don't think so, and I'm not tired.* She didn't want to wake Spike, so she moved away slowly to avoid disturbing him. He seemed to be in a deep sleep anyway.

She stood naked, watching Spike sleep. *He feels like an opportunity. Don't push too hard.*

Barbie wanted a snack, a drink, and to walk around. *Maybe check on Mom too.* Getting dressed without light was no problem. She'd had lots of practice sneaking out. Keeping an eye on Spike, she quietly dressed. The light snore and lack of movement confirmed he was out.

Barbie sat on the smelly carpet beside Spike's blue bag. *Chemicals, yuck!* After unzipping the bag, one tooth at a time, she pulled it open. *So much money.* Barbie took two one-hundred-dollar bills out of one band, then put the banded stack on top to show Spike later if he wanted to see it. *I'm not stealing from him. I want to be his partner. His lover ... maybe his wife.*

Her phone was still in her pocket. *Off.* She took the room key and opened the door an inch at a time, then closed it the same way. It let out a little click when it shut. Barbie waited a few minutes but heard nothing.

Barbie turned and walked down a hallway that led to the back of the motel. She sat on the concrete slab edge with woods in front of her and her feet in the grass. Looking around and seeing no one, she got out a joint and a match, lit up, and took a hit. She held it, feeling the comfortable, familiar warmth. Pulling out her phone, Barbie powered it up and called her mom. It went to voicemail. "Mom, it's me. I'm sorry. Don't worry about me. I may go to Ava's. Not sure where I'm going eventually, but I'll let you know. I love you. I just needed a change. I gotta go. Oh, I think I found a really good man. Love ya again. Bye."

The big Pilot Truckstop sign was easy to see when she came out of the room. After a few more hits, Barbie walked to the front of the motel. The truck stop was beside it. She wasn't sure what Spike liked, so she bought chips, candy, a couple of sandwiches, a few Cokes, a six-pack of beer, and a couple of bottles of water. She also bought two burner phones. *Shit! I didn't turn off my phone.* Shaking her head, she took it out, turned it off, and put it back in her pocket. *It wasn't on for long. Shouldn't be a problem. I hope. Better not tell Spike. Shit!*

Sauntering back to the motel room, she felt good but worried about her phone being on. She figured they'd probably be out of there tomorrow morning before anyone could track them.

It was hot out, even at night, but the joint had relaxed her. The heat didn't bother her. Barbie opened a beer before going into the room so she wouldn't wake Spike, then snuck back in and found he hadn't moved. Spotting a cushy chair in the corner, she pulled it slowly across the carpet so she could watch him sleep. Then she sat back, relaxed, and sipped her beer quietly. *I think you're my future.* She felt content. *Thanks, Buck. Without you, I'd never have met Mr. Wonderful.*

27

COKE MACHINE

Carlsbad, NM
Friday Night

WHEN SPIKE OPENED HIS EYES, the clock said nine-thirteen p.m. Barbie sat in a big chair, sipping a beer, staring at him with a smile.

"Hi, Sleepyhead. I picked up a few groceries. I bought us a couple of prepaid burner phones too, just in case we need them." She walked over and kissed him on the cheek, then hugged him as best she could.

"Burner phones. Good idea, I guess ... if we need them." Without moving his head, he looked at his blue bag. It was right where he'd left it. He'd open it the first chance he got to make sure everything was still there.

"Don't worry," Barbie said. "Everything's there except the two hundred dollars I took to buy us some groceries and the phones. I took it out of that top stack. Hope that's okay."

Spike smiled. "Sure, no problem." He got up, feeling

refreshed. His arm ached a little, but at least it was stitched and healing.

Barbie pulled back the curtain. The hotel lights shined in the parking lot. The highway running through the city was just down a little hill.

Then Spike saw a state cop pull into the parking lot. He jumped up, pulled the curtain shut, and turned out the lights.

"What's the matter?" Barbie asked.

"Be quiet."

He peeked out from the corner of the blinds. The state trooper slowed behind Spike's red truck and stopped. "Grab all your stuff. We're leaving. Now. Hurry."

"Why?"

"Do it!"

Spike got dressed fast, then grabbed the blue bag. He didn't want to confront the cop. It would be the end of anonymity. Quickly, he checked the window in the bathroom. *Too fucking small!*

He peeked out the front window again. The cop had gotten out of the running car, blocking the pickup. Then the cop turned and walked over to the office.

"Get ready to go." Spike placed his bag on his shoulder. He moved the knife, Rosa, to his pocket and the Glock 40 to his belt in the small of his back.

"We gonna kill the cop?" Barbie asked.

"Not if we can help it. The goal is to not get caught. To not even let people know we've been here ... *but*, if we have to, we will."

Spike saw the cop step into the motel office. "Let's go." He ran out the door, feeling Barbie right behind him. After a short distance to a hallway, Spike rounded the corner. He saw the ice machine and a Coke machine, and then the hall opened to the back. It was dark, but he thought it might be a wooded area.

"Hey! Stop! Police!"

Damn, he must have caught a glimpse of Barbie.

"Go up there and lay down, hold your ankle, and do not look back at the cop no matter what. Now," Spike quietly barked.

Spike backed in behind the Coke machine. He set down his bag and took out Rosa. *Ear to ear if I have to slit his throat.* He planned to cut the cop and shove him forward to keep the blood off him. But if things went wrong, he'd use the Glock.

Barbie ran just off the concrete onto the grass and sat sideways. She held her ankle and moaned, sitting with her back to where the cop would approach.

The cop came running around the corner, then stopped suddenly, short of the Coke machine. "Ma'am, put your hands up! Now!"

Spike didn't want to make a sound. He didn't move and tried to breathe quietly. He heard the cop pull out a gun. The cop's flashlight shone on Barbie's back.

"Oh, oh," she moaned, writhing in pain convincingly. "My ankle. I think it's broken." Slowly, the cop walked toward her, passing Spike hiding behind the Coke machine. "Let me see your hands! Now!"

Spike was ready to cut the cop's throat. Anticipation and worry gripped and twisted his gut. He looked at Rosa in his hand, imagined the blood dripping off it. Then he saw the rubber band on his wrist. *Fuck! The cop's probably a good guy.* He switched Rosa to his left hand, then rushed the cop from behind and hit him in the head with the butt of his pistol. The cop collapsed. Spike checked his pulse. *Still alive. Thank you, God. That should be worth a few karma points.*

"Let's go! Good acting." Spike grabbed Barbie's hand.

They darted behind the motel until they got to another passageway and ran up to the front. They were about six units away from the other one, where the cop was hopefully still unconscious at the back of the motel. Spike peeked out and to his left, where their room was located.

Holy shit! He couldn't believe what he saw. A running car with its doors open sat beside the cop car. Two Hispanic men got out, shut the doors, pulled out weapons, and started looking closely at the red pickup.

"Should've killed the fucking cop. He's dirty." Spike leaned back into Barbie. "We got a couple of Hispanics with guns too. It's gotta be the cartel. Must be working with the cop. That's bad." He shook his head. "That cop's gonna wake up soon with a headache and be pissed. I think they're tracking Buck's identity or his truck. We gotta get out of here."

Spike looked out. The two men had their backs to him. Bent over and dragging Barbie by the hand, he scurried four feet to get behind a parked SUV for cover.

He considered hotwiring it but knew he could never get it done and escape without getting killed. The SUV shielded them as they ran away from the motel.

Spike planned to get them a ride—by gunpoint, most likely—if he could find one. Next door was a fast-food place and a truck stop beside that. He knew the clock was ticking. Spike's blue bag blended in, but Barbie's suitcase didn't. They'd lose Barbie's suitcase soon if they didn't find a ride. They walked fast and looked over their shoulders through the parking lot of the fast-food restaurant.

"Look! They're getting in their cars. The cop too," Barbie said.

"Hurry!" Spike pulled her harder, and they broke into a

run as they crossed into the truck stop's lot. Spike got between some trucks and tried their doors. One lane over, a truck started. He let go of Barbie and took off at a dead run as the truck moved twenty or thirty yards ahead. Spike ran at a dead sprint. He saw through the trucks that the cop car had pulled into the other side of the lot. Spike jumped up on the running board. The door was locked. He pulled out his pistol and tapped the window.

The old, overweight driver's eyes widened as he reached under his seat and pulled out a revolver. Then he pointed the gun at Spike. "Get the fuck off my truck! I'm counting to three, then shooting! Self-defense! One! Two!"

28

TIMING

Carlsbad, NM
Friday Night

"Stop! Stop! We just need a ride. I'll pay you." Spike stuck the pistol in his belt. "No gun! See! Please! Ten thousand dollars."

The driver lowered his gun but didn't say anything. The truck was still moving.

"We just need a ride. Please, please!"

The truck slowed but didn't stop. "Is the money stolen?"

"No!" Spike yelled. He saw the police car slowly making its way around the trucks.

"Why ya running?" the truck driver asked.

"It's nothing illegal! We aren't in trouble with the cops."

"You got the money in cash?"

"Yes!"

The truck continued to slow. The driver put the gun in his lap but kept his hand on it, and the big rig stopped with a small jerk. The doors unlocked. Spike opened the door and waited for Barbie. He threw her suitcase inside, helped her up, then climbed in and shut the door.

"I need to see the cash now. Or I stop and yell at the cop."

Spike stuck his gun back in the bag and pulled out ten thousand dollars, banded. He handed it to the driver.

"Okay, we're going to Lubbock. No debate." The driver stashed his revolver back under the seat, put the truck in gear, and started out again.

"Anywhere. I don't care. We'll get out at Lubbock," Spike said.

"Good. Just relax. It'll take us about three hours." The driver eased back and scratched his unshaven chin.

Spike found himself looking at Barbie off and on for the next three hours. He was trying to decide who she was and what she was like. But she also knew too much. The big question was: Should he keep her for a while? And then what? Nothing lasted forever.

∼

SEBASTIAN SURVEYED AVA'S HOUSE. She'd gone nowhere since he'd watched her pull into her garage. He called one of his guys. Ted was new, about six months, and spoke no Spanish. *A new gringo. Perfect. No competition for me to move up.* Sebastian had to pee so badly that he couldn't stand up straight. *It hurts!* He'd let Ted keep an eye on Ava while he took care of business and got some food to go.

He hated to leave for any reason. *I want to be the one to see Barbie and Spike first and tell Rico.* He knew it would score big points. *Is it possible I might be left in charge of Houston?*

There were no empty parking spots on this residential,

tree-lined street. He pulled out and motioned for Ted to take his spot. Sebastian left his car double parked while he walked back and hunched over to talk to Ted through his driver's window.

"You okay?" Ted asked.

"No. I've gotta piss so bad, it hurts. Get your phone out."

Ted held his phone so Sebastian could see it. "Okay."

Sebastian had Ted pull up the website with Ava's picture, so he knew what she looked like. He messaged Ted a copy of Barbie's picture, which Dante had forwarded to him. But there was no picture of Spike.

"We're looking for a guy named Spike," Sebastian explained, "but we don't have a picture. He's fortyish, white, in good shape, average height, and has a long cut on his left arm, probably bandaged. See any activity at all, call me. I'll be back as soon as I can."

"No problem. I've never been on a stakeout," Ted said with a childlike smile.

Sebastian didn't answer. He hobbled back to his car and then drove off, texting Ted every five minutes and getting the same answer each time.

Sebastian: **Anything happen?**

Ted: **Nothing!**

Twenty minutes later, Sebastian was back and took Ted's parking spot. He texted Ted to be available, and he'd text or call him if he needed him.

When Ted left, Sebastian settled down to eat a cheeseburger, fries, and a Coke. He planned on peeing in the cup when he needed to go next. *I'll be here when the time comes.*

Oh, shit! He remembered the eight-a.m. meeting with Rico and everyone in the area. *How can I do both?* He sighed, then texted Ted.

Sebastian: **Be here at 7 AM to relieve me. I'm going to**

Rico's meeting. Don't leave until I relieve you. It could be many hours or all day.

Ted: **I'll be there, 7 AM.**

Sebastian: **Good!**

He smiled and felt a little relief. *I could use some face time with Rico.*

～

Toro had overseen their Texas and Arizona regions, so he was familiar with their operations in Houston. He called ahead while still in the air and arranged their hotel rooms. Toro had the hotel send a limo to meet their jet at a private airport on the west side.

Rico had really surprised him—more like gut-wrenchingly shocked him—when he'd killed Mateo. Toro had shut his eyes, thinking Rico was going to shoot him next. But Rico only reaffirmed Toro was the second in command. Toro had no time to process this or dwell on it. He'd accepted that Rico would execute a few mid- and low-level men after he'd explained to Toro and Mateo that a statement needed to be made to send enough fear for everyone at all ranks to stay focused.

Toro had not agreed and had told Rico so in front of Mateo. He remembered Rico's words.

"I appreciate your honesty. Never be afraid to tell me the truth as you see it, but never challenge me in front of anyone. If you must tell me something right away, and we're not alone, then call me to the side. Do you understand?"

"*Sí, Jefe,*" Toro had said. He remembered that this had felt good, like he planned to use real management. He remembered looking at Mateo's pained expression and thinking Mateo might have thought he'd missed a chance to shine. He might have been right.

Toro had never seen Rico exhibit that kind of violence against his own men before, but on the other hand, he felt an extra comfort knowing that the ranks couldn't be thinned anymore. He knew they'd be hiring, so to speak. Especially after what had happened in Houston.

Then he thought the unthinkable.

Maybe Rico is too brutal. Maybe I should just put a bullet in the back of his head. Embrace those who are left and start over. But I need his code first.

29

BIG MEETING

Houston
Saturday Morning

Rico wondered how all of this would play out. He had no desire to go to Houston, but he needed to let everyone see him and know he was in control. He looked at his watch. Seven-forty-five a.m. He and Toro had gotten some sleep at a nice hotel on the west side of Houston. Dante had arrived late last night with Gabriel.

He knew Dante was in a lot of pain, but he trusted him. He made good decisions and had experience, so Rico would probably leave him in charge of Houston. He'd arranged for a retired doctor to come by the morning meeting and look at Dante's broken leg.

Jorge and Pup were on their way from Carlsbad, but he knew they were coming straight with no stops. They'd texted about seven-thirty, saying they expected to arrive around eight and would come straight to the meeting.

The good and bad news was that Barbie had turned on her phone yesterday, and Jorge and Pup had almost caught them. Jorge had made the motel owner back up the surveillance footage after he'd seen that Spike was with her. Rico was sure Spike and Barbie were on their way to Houston, and Jorge had lost them again at about eleven p.m. If they drove straight to Houston with no stops, it might take nine hours. That would be about eight a.m. at the earliest.

He knew his new leadership, or at least those representing their territory, would be there. He also knew his only way to Spike was through Barbie if she visited Ava or turned on her phone again.

As Rico walked through the door of their warehouse office, it crossed his mind that Spike might not even know he was carrying around sixteen million in the bitcoin wallet.

Inside, there were chairs and couches. At the end of the long office was a desk where Dante stood on crutches, Jorge beside him. Rico's two senior people entered the room after him and Toro. He noticed a lot of faces he'd seen only a few times, along with many he'd never seen. These types of meetings were rare but necessary.

Rico maintained a stern look while nodding to one side and then the other. As he passed them, walking the length of the office to reach Dante and the only desk in the room, everyone said, "*Jefe*," in greeting and respect. The effect was almost like that of the wave at a football game.

"As you all know, Pedro and others were killed in the big fuck-up where we got screwed over two days ago on Thursday. The details aren't important, but tell your people to be aware of new faces. Others may try to take advantage of us having a misstep. This will pass quickly, so report anything unusual. Obviously, we'll need a new man in charge in Houston. That announcement will come soon. Do your jobs. That's all I ask." Rico stood, making eye-to-eye contact with everyone. "Get to work." He turned to his number two. "Toro, have someone go outside and get the doctor. He's sitting in his car."

A few minutes later, the gray-haired, slightly overweight older man walked in with a box and his black bag.

"Dr. Hoover, this is Dante," Rico said.

Dante stood up with the help of a crutch and shook the doctor's hand. "Thank you, Doctor, for coming in."

"Always happy to help. Please, sit down," Dr. Hoover said.

"Doctor," Rico said. "Take care of him. He's important to me, but I must go."

The doctor nodded.

Rico turned to Dante. "I'm leaving, but I'll still be in town. Call me with any news."

"*Sí, Jefe*," Dante said.

Rico and Toro left.

∽

DANTE HAD BEEN WAITING for a chance to talk to Sebastian. "Why aren't you at Barbie's sister's place?"

"I'm splitting the surveillance with Ted. He's there now."

Dante wondered who Ted was. He didn't know him, but at least it was covered. His leg hurt, but the pain meds helped. He was more comfortable with his position in the cartel and his relationship with Rico, but nothing was solid yet. Still, opportunity was on Dante's doorstep, and he would fight through any pain to avoid disappointing Rico or giving anyone else a chance to outshine him.

Dante noticed a box of stuff Dr. Hoover had brought. "You're going to cast my leg?"

"I have what I need to do it, but I need to make sure the swelling has gone down." The doctor asked a couple of guys to help Dante into a better chair. He got his leg up on a coffee table, then removed the splint. "It looks pretty good. I can cast it now."

He went to work.

"Thanks, Doc," Dante said.

"No problem. It's been a while since I put a cast on. It'll start to dry right away, but it'll take twenty-four to forty-eight hours to be completely dry. Take it easy until then." The doctor handed a card to Dante. "I should be able to remove the cast in six to twelve weeks. I'll check in on you, or you can call me for any reason. Try to stay off it, today at least."

"Can I put weight on it if I have to?"

"Yeah, you *can*. It depends on your threshold of pain. It probably won't do any long-term damage, but it'll hurt like hell."

"I'll try to stay off it, but I'm very busy right now. Thanks again, Doc," Dante said.

The doctor nodded and left.

Gotta wait and see if anything turns up. Relax for a day, maybe. Damn, my leg hurts.

~

Ted had relieved Sebastian at seven. Then he watched. He placed a novel on the steering wheel so he could read and see the front of Ava's place over the top of his book. Out of the corner of his eye, he caught her garage door move.

He checked his watch. Nine-fifteen a.m. He texted Sebastian.

Ted: **Garage opening. She's going somewhere. I'll follow her and keep you posted.**

Sebastian: **Don't lose her.**

Ava pulled out in a red BMW, and Ted followed. She made a stop at a La Madeleine restaurant, where she walked out with coffee and a bag. Then she parked at an office park, unlocked a door, and went into one of the offices.

Ava had food delivered at about one-fifteen p.m. She didn't leave the office until about six p.m.

Throughout the day, Ted got a couple of breaks from Sebastian. At six, he followed her home. He found a place to park and settled in. It was close to where he'd been before, and he saw an old lady look out her window at him. Again. *Mind your own business, lady!*

30

ROAD TRIP

Lubbock to Houston
Saturday Noon to Night

The truck driver told Spike about a truck stop where he could drop them off. Spike called a limo service fifteen minutes ahead of time.

While they were waiting, they bought snacks and several magazines. Spike purchased two novels.

They grabbed some food to go and got into the limo.

"My name's Jim, and welcome. Mr. and Mrs. Buck, is that right?"

"That's me," Spike said.

"We're not married," Barbie said. "Wow, this is really nice. Smells like leather."

"Just cleaned up for you, ma'am," the driver said.

"I like it." Barbie acted like she'd never been in a nice car.

"Fifteen hundred to Houston, right?" Spike asked.

"Yes, sir."

Spike handed the man cash. "You get us there safe, and I'll give you a two-hundred-dollar tip."

"That would be great, sir. Ready to go?"

"Let's get the show on the road," Spike said.

"No problem." The driver drove out of the truck stop. Without looking back, he kept talking. "Just to let you folks know, I'll need to stop for gas once. It'll take us about eight hours without any other stops to get to Houston. But I'll make it as quick as I can, and, of course, we can stop as often as you want—restrooms, stretch your legs, eat, or drink. Do you have a hotel I should take you to, or an address?"

"Maybe, but for now, just point us toward Houston," Spike said.

"I have an address," Barbie said. "It's in Rice Village. You know where that's at?"

"Sure. Really nice area, right by Rice University. Great shops, a younger crowd."

"Exactly." She gave him an address, and he put it into the car as the destination.

"Does she know we're coming in late?" Spike asked.

"No, just that we're coming."

"Take out a burner phone and text her." Spike handed the bag to Barbie. "They come with a charge and ready to go."

"Sure." She opened a phone and went to work typing. "I just texted her."

"Good." Spike was looking out the window.

"I just got an answer. She's at her office now and has to go on a stakeout tonight. But she said she'd leave a key with the neighbor if she's not home," Barbie said.

"She's a cop?"

"No, she's a private investigator."

"Was she a cop?"

"She was in the FBI for two years, but something happened, and she left. Then she got hired by a PI firm owned by a woman in Houston to do some investigations. She got her license and just kept doing it. She's partners with her old boss now."

"Huh. How old is your sister?" Spike didn't know what to think of this.

"She's thirty-four—twelve years older than me."

"Can't wait to meet her."

For a while, Barbie talked to the driver about nothing in particular. Then she perused the magazines and a crossword puzzle book before putting them down and diving into a romance novel.

Spike worried this was a bad idea, showing up to this job as Buck. *What the hell? Should be exciting.* Besides, if he didn't like what they were doing, he'd just leave. He had to be in the New Orleans area by noon tomorrow, and it was about a six-hour drive from Houston. *What should I do with the bag of money, including the gun and knife? Too much to trust Barbie with. Take it to Louisiana, maybe.* He'd try to figure out what to do when he got closer.

∽

WHEN THEY ARRIVED, it wasn't dark yet. Spike looked around.

A nice neighborhood with a college-town atmosphere occupied the middle of Houston. The apartment where Barbie's sister lived looked brand new.

What happened to Barbie living in that shithole in New Mexico ... and in a trailer?

Barbie rang the doorbell. No answer.

She got the key from the neighbor and let them in just as she got a text. "Ava told me she's on her way home now."

They had just gotten to the top of the steps on the second floor when they heard the garage door open.

"There she is," Spike said.

Barbie ran down the steps while Spike followed at a walk. The double garage took up the space where a large first-floor room might have been if not for the parking area. The door from the garage opened into a small hallway that led to a back room one way and the front door the other. The steps were against the outside wall.

The door opened, and Barbie ran into her sister. Spike stood a polite distance back as they embraced.

Ava took Spike's breath away. *My God, I want her.*

She was so friendly, tall, maybe five foot six, and so pretty. She grabbed Barbie and pulled her into a bear hug, pinning her arms to her sides. Being taller, she lifted her younger sister off the ground, then put her down and kissed her on the cheek.

"I'm so happy to see you. I'm glad you decided to come. You know I'd do anything to help you. You just never say yes."

"I know. But I guess I'm ready now. I want to make something of myself." Barbie smiled and continued holding her older sister.

What the fuck? Spike wondered what was going on. He'd thought Barbie would stay with her sister until he got back. *Fuck it! I don't care about Barbie that much—but damn, the older sister.* He snapped the rubber band on his arm.

"I'm sorry. I'm Ava Gunn." Ava didn't let go of her sister as she put out her hand to greet Spike.

"Hi, I'm Spike," he said.

"Spike. There must be a story with that name."

Spike gave her a big smile and tried to act unassuming. "There is. It goes back to my football days. I was a hard tackler." *And the rest of the story is that I liked to step on the other team's fingers with the spikes on my shoes.*

"Tell me more about that later, but I'm going to have to go soon. Barbie told you that I have a stakeout tonight?"

"She did tell me. But I'm going to have to leave soon too. I have a job in the New Orleans area that I have to report to by noon tomorrow. We were hoping Barbie could stay with you a few days until the job is over."

Ava looked at Barbie. "Sure, of course, but I thought you wanted to stay longer, maybe go to school, find a career path."

Barbie frowned and shifted her weight. She pulled back from her sister's hold a little. "Where's the bathroom?"

"I'm sorry. Let's go upstairs and get comfortable. There's a bathroom up there."

They went to the second of three floors. This was the main living area. Barbie went to the bathroom.

"You must be proud of her trying to find some direction," Spike said.

"Maybe." Ava rolled her eyes. "God, I hope so. Sit down. Can I get you a drink?"

"A beer?"

"Sure." She handed Spike a beer a moment later. "Bottled water for me. I'm working tonight," Ava said as they sat at the table in the small dining room area next to the tiny kitchen. "About Barbie. We tried this after I joined the FBI and went to Quantico. I offered to give her a stable place to live and told her I'd make sure she got through college. She was eleven, in the sixth grade, and headed nowhere. Our mom and her dad were both drunk most of the time. She agreed, and I flew down and picked her up. It was late summer. I enrolled her in school, as her guardian, and she did great. From Cs and Ds to straight As."

"That's very impressive." Spike looked compassionately into her eyes. *I wonder if Barbie can keep her mouth shut about me killing Buck.*

"I thought things were great," Ava said. "We went to the movies, went bowling, and took short trips as much as my time allowed, given I was still new at the FBI. Then I let her go back home one Thanksgiving, and she wouldn't come back. I didn't know her dad had left our mother. Barbie said Mom needed her."

"I'll bet that was tough on you." Spike broke eye contact so it wouldn't get uncomfortable but kept looking in her direction to show interest. He snapped the rubber band. Twice.

31

ALONE TIME

Houston
Saturday Night

"Rubber band snapping?" Ava asked. "What's that all about?"

"Sorry, just a habit," Spike said. "Please, keep going."

"Well, I flew back to New Mexico and tried to reason with them both. Mom was the problem. If she'd told Barbie to go with me, Barbie would have. Mom was lonely, feeling sorry for herself, at the expense of Barbie's future. I told them both, as Barbie's guardian, that I'd force her to come with me. Barbie ran away, or at least went missing, until my plane left. Then I found her note: 'I'll keep running away. Let me go.'"

Spike heard Ava but listened only enough to respond. He leaned forward, kept a serious look, and nodded his head sympathetically. "Wow, you have such a big heart."

Spike sat beside her and squeezed her hand. *Wonder why she left the FBI? Can Barbie keep her mouth shut?*

"Maybe. Just trying to do what's right."

The bathroom door opened at the far end of the second floor. "I *really* had to pee." Barbie took a seat at the table, a bottle of water in front of her chair. "I'm back." Barbie leaned over and kissed Spike on the cheek, then looked at her big sister. "Can we get the tour?"

"Sure. Not much to see, but come on." Ava led them upstairs to the third floor, where there were two bedrooms. The bigger, front one was her bedroom with a master bathroom, and the one in the back was used as a study with a desk. They went back down to the second floor. The front two-thirds consisted of the living room, while a kitchen and small dining area occupied the back. Downstairs was a small bedroom she used as a junk room in the back and the two-car garage in front. "That's it."

"Really nice," Spike said.

"I love it," Barbie said

Ava led them back to the second floor.

"What kind of job is it you're going for, and what do you do for a living?" Ava asked.

"This is a special job ... a construction job. I'm helping a friend. But as a profession, I've always been in high-end sales and consulting. I know you're worried about Barbie, and yes, I am older, but you can be confident I won't hurt her or take advantage of her. She was in a bad place with her boyfriend, and I offered to help. She wanted to come see you. So, here we are."

Ava looked at Spike. "Okay, Spike. Can I trust you in my house alone?"

"Not going to steal your silverware," Spike said.

Ava chuckled. "Okay. I'm sorry, but I have to go. A

stakeout waits for no one. Spike, you stay as long as you want. Staying overnight on the couch and leaving early in the morning might be a good idea, but it's up to you." As she talked, she picked up her things, put on a shoulder holster, and slid a Glock into it. "I'll be back late. If I'm not here, you can just lock the door when you leave. Barbie, you can take the guest bedroom. Help yourself to my clothes if you want. Or ... you can come with me. We can catch up, but you might get bored."

"Can I come, really?" Barbie's eyes glowed, like a kid going to camp.

"You're not tired?" Ava asked.

"For a freaking stakeout like the cops? Nope! I'm ready to go." Barbie paced in front of Ava. "C'mon, sis."

"Sure. Spike, you'll be okay alone?"

"I'll be okay. You know I'll be arranging transportation and be out of here early tomorrow. If I don't see you before I go, thanks for everything."

"No problem. We'll get to know each other when you get back. Towels are in the bathroom. Linens are in the closet. Help yourself to the fridge. Oh, just a minute." Ava wrote her phone number on a sticky note and put it on the back of her door. "Can I get your number?"

Barbie kissed Spike on the cheek. "Sorry, but this will be fun. You're okay with me going?"

"Of course," Spike said.

"Miss you. Bye-bye." Barbie threw Spike a bunch of kisses and walked out the door.

"You wanted my number, right?" Spike looked at his burner and told Ava the number.

She put it into her phone.

"Be careful tonight," Spike said.

"No danger, just a cheating husband stakeout. What

could go wrong? Well, it's nice to meet you. Gotta go." Ava waved.

Spike lifted his hand in a wave.

∼

TED HAD BEEN WATCHING Ava all day and saw her pulling out again. He texted Sebastian: **She just got home and is going out again, not in the Beamer but an old silver Toyota.**

Sebastian: **Follow her.**

∼

SPIKE WAS STILL free and alone. He went to the fridge. It had some food and a few beers—Shiner Bock. *A good Texas beer and a woman after my own heart. Just one more thing to love about you, Ava.* He opened the beer and held it in the air. "To you, Ava." He took a long pull. "My God, that's good."

The cold beer tasted like an old friend.

Spike's shower was soul-cleansing. The new underwear he'd picked up at a truck stop on the way to Houston made him think of his childhood. Of how his mom used to remind him to have clean underwear. "You never know if you might get hurt and have to go to the hospital." He smiled and shook his head. Then he remembered how much effort she'd put into giving him the tools to survive, especially the phrase "Always be smiling." He regretted what he'd done to her.

As he got dressed, he looked at his blue bag. *I can't leave it here. Might be too much temptation for Barbie.* He would soon walk into a situation where he didn't know what to expect, dealing with unknown people. He didn't want to take his bag. On his burner, he texted a message to the number he had memorized: **Magic, it's Spike. I'm going to call you on this number in a second.**

He waited. The burner buzzed. Spike answered playfully with a long, dragged-out, "Magic, man, long time." He smiled. This was a person he trusted, and it had been a while since he'd talked to him.

"Spike, long time, but you know I'm still taking care of you."

"I have no doubt. Look, I need to drop a bag off with you to hold for me for a few days. Is that okay?"

"Of course. You coming over now?" Magic seemed eager to see him.

"No, I'll be by early tomorrow, a little after five a.m. Is that okay?"

"Yeah, but I'm not dressing up for you."

"No problem." Spike laughed. "I'll be gone a few days."

"Take as long as you want."

"Great. When I pick it up, we'll spend some time talking. Maybe you can buy me a drink."

"What if I just put it on your tab?"

"Deal. Not to be rude, but I gotta go to bed."

"Sweet dreams. See you in the morning."

Good. It'll be safe with Magic. Spike put a sheet and blanket on the couch and arranged a limo for a five-a.m. pick-up. He lay on his side, fluffed his pillow, and shut his eyes, but he didn't go right to sleep.

It bothered him that Barbie was a loose end. Without opening his eyes, he snapped the rubber band. She wasn't a pure soul. She'd tried to kill Buck. *Is she bad or just fucked up? Did fucked up count as being bad? God would probably understand when the time came. Maybe I'll ask for a sign again. That was amazing when I got a sign for Barbie. A shooting star. Real or coincidence? Not sure.*

God, give me the strength to channel my needs into removing only bad people from the earth. Let tomorrow give me more opportunities to serve you. Spike had read more than a few things about being grateful.

God, I am grateful for the superior intellect I have been blessed with and all that you have provided to me to bring me to this place in time. He drifted off.

32

STAKEOUT

H ouston, TX
Saturday Night

BARBIE KEPT SNEAKING peeks at Ava as they pulled up along the curb a block away. The streetlights created a yellow hue in places.

Barbie wondered why Ava had parked. "Is this the stakeout?"

"No, I just need a little insurance." Ava didn't look at Barbie as she talked. She was busy scanning the area outside the car. "I'll tell you in a minute. Stay here. I'll be right back." Ava got out and walked casually down the sidewalk, looking around discreetly.

Barbie watched Ava turn into a parking lot and walk up to a parking spot next to a building with a man's name on a sign in front. Ava seemed to do something to the car parked there and then came back.

As soon as she got in the car, Barbie pounced on her with excitement. "What'd you do? C'mon, tell me."

"Just a minute. Thank God I got the A/C fixed." Ava leaned into it and flapped her blouse to cool herself. Even at night, it was hot in Texas.

"C'mon!" Barbie waved her hands.

"Sorry, I need the cool air first. Okay, okay, I put a tracker on his car. It's illegal in Texas, so don't tell anyone, but who'll know? I'll still try to tail him, but I can't lose him for long with the tracker. That's my insurance."

"That's cool. It's like we're secret agents."

"Yeah, I guess so." Ava smiled.

Expecting the man to leave soon, and wanting to keep the car cool, she left the vehicle running. They could see the parking lot's exit. Ava told Barbie that she knew whom to follow. She had the type of car he drove, his license number, and a photo of him as well as a file with a lot more information.

"What's this guy's name?" Barbie asked.

"We'll just call him Bob."

"Where's Bob going?"

"I think he's going to meet his girlfriend. At least that's what his wife thinks." Ava stared ahead, focused. "Barbie, you've got brains. It's not too late to choose a career. And I think you could do almost anything you wanted. Hold on." Ava straightened up and put the car in gear but kept her foot on the brake. "I want to talk some more, but there's our guy." She waited for him to leave the parking lot and allowed a gap between them, then pulled out slowly. "Sorry, but I need to pay attention now. We'll chat again soon. Okay?"

"Sure." Barbie looked at her sister with awe. She kept sneaking stares, looking at her as they started moving.

When Ava mentioned a stakeout, it had seemed exciting at first, but Barbie quickly realized she didn't care about it. Instead, sitting beside her sister, just the two of them for a few hours, was like an exclusive, private, one-on-one with her hero. A real hero, who'd climbed out of a potentially shitty life to become smart and important.

Why did I leave her years ago when she offered me a new life?

"I love you, sister," Barbie said.

"I love you too ... and I do want to talk some more, but I gotta pay attention."

"Sorry, I'll be quiet. Just wanted you to know."

He was easy to follow. It took about forty-five minutes to arrive where he was going. He pulled into a motel's parking lot on the outskirts of Houston, then remained in the car.

"What's he doing? Waiting for her?" Barbie asked.

"Maybe. I don't know. Maybe she stood him up." Ava picked up a camera with a telephoto lens.

Barbie watched with interest. "Is this enough? Pictures of him sitting in his car in the parking lot of a motel late at night?"

"Well, it's not proof of an affair. It'd never stand up in court. But I think it'd be hard to explain to a wife. And it may be all we can get."

"So, we just sit here?"

"If he sits in the car all night, then we will too."

"Great. Can I go get us some snacks at the convenience store across the street?"

"No. We'd better sit tight for a while and see what happens."

"Okay." Barbie pulled up her knees and sat on her legs as if she were having girl talk on the couch. "Can we talk now?" She bounced in the seat, her eyes lit up.

Ava looked at her sister and touched her hand. "I know Mom always picked men who drank too much, and no woman or person deserved to get beat as much as she did. She has a disease. She's an alcoholic. I'm sorry I couldn't get you away from that. I was blessed Aunt Gertie took me when I was young."

"You know I'm proud of you." Barbie started to cry, though she tried to hold it back. "I feel so bad for Mom. It breaks my heart. I feel I've made some bad choices, and you were always there, but I never let you help me. That was stupid, but I felt Mom needed me too." She shrugged and looked down in shame. "And I just left her two days ago. I really feel bad, like I deserted her." She looked out the window, away from Ava. "Mom's all alone. Hope she's okay."

∽

TED FOLLOWED Ava to some office building and then to a parking lot in front of a motel. He found a parking spot with a good vantage point. He'd relayed all the details to Sebastian, including the fact that he was sure two women were in the car.

He'd been sitting there for an hour when he got a call.

"Sebastian," Ted said.

"Ted, good job! I told Dante everything you told me, and he's sending two of our guys to take your place. You don't know them, but they'll find you. They'll look for your car. When they get there, go back to the surveillance on Ava's house."

The men showed up about thirty minutes later, and Ted went back to watch Ava's house. He always took the same spot because it was open. His car covered a small portion of an unused driveway. As soon as he parked, the curtain moved back. *Damn! Mind your own business!*

∼

"Mom will survive," Ava said. "And she knows how to lay on the guilt. You need to get your life together and live for yourself." She paused. "Look, our guy finally got out of his car. It's been over an hour. It's two a.m. Damn!"

"He's going into the motel office," Barbie said.

"Showtime," Ava said. "Stay here." She got out and half-ran to catch up, keeping cars in between them. She arrived near the office but didn't see him. Ava stood and walked in like she didn't have a care in the world. Once in the office, she didn't see him. She approached the counter.

A young man behind the check-in desk smiled. "Good morning. We're sold out. I'm sorry."

"Oh, that's fine. Did you see a man just walk in here?"

"Oh, yeah, he asked to use the restroom. It's right over there."

"Thanks. I'll just wait for him in the car." Ava turned and left as fast as she could, then scurried to her car.

"You see him?" Barbie asked.

"No, he's in the restroom. Very strange," Ava said. "I've never seen anything like this."

"Here he comes."

"Damn, back in his car and still sitting there. Might as well relax. He doesn't seem to be going anywhere yet. So, is Spike your boyfriend?"

"I hope so, but I'm not sure. I mean, we just met, but he seems to care about me, and we've had sex," Barbie said.

"Wow! Too much information. I wasn't asking if you'd had sex. I guess I don't know who he is to you, why you're with him, and why he'd bring you to me to drop you off. Not that I'm complaining. I'm happy you're here. Also, he is quite a bit older than you. Oh, and where's he going to? Sorry, too many questions, I guess?"

"No, it's fine. I met Spike in Columbus. He was really nice. We sort of bonded over an unusual date. He took me to the desert away from the lights. We saw a shooting star. That touched me."

"That does sound romantic."

"Yeah, I guess it was. I felt close to him and explained what was happening with Mom. I told him about how successful you are and that you were in Houston. He said I needed to do the obvious thing and get closer to you."

"Wow, he said that?"

"Yes, he did. And he had a job to do in Louisiana and offered to give me a ride. He's got money, too, and he's very ambitious. He used to be a very successful salesman."

Time passed. The conversation ebbed and flowed.

"Can I buy us some coffee now?" Barbie asked. "There's an all-night diner about a block back on the corner."

"You mean walk?"

"Why not? It's right there."

Ava chewed her lip. "He's got to go soon." She looked at the car clock. It was three minutes after four a.m. "And what the hell's he doing anyway?"

"It could be a couple more hours. Besides, I have to pee too. Please. I'll hurry." Barbie put her hands together like she was praying as she begged. "Worst case, if you have to follow him, I'll just wait for you to come back or Uber to your place. You gave me a key."

"Hurry, then. Get there and get back."

"Bye!" Barbie jumped out quickly and jogged toward the diner.

Ava watched as her little sister ran around the corner and out of sight.

She kept checking her watch. *Fifteen minutes.* Then a car pulled up beside the man's car. Both drivers got out. She checked her watch. Four-twenty. Her sister wasn't back yet. *Come on!* The men talked for a few minutes. It looked like the man whom they were following had handed a package to the other man. *Wonder what's in the package? And why so late at night? And where's my sister?*

The man who had shown up was holding the package now. Then he walked around the car, waving something. He stopped and pulled off the tracker. After showing it to Bob, he dropped it on the ground and stomped on it. It went offline. *Damn it!*

The man started waving his arms. He shoved Bob.

Ava was busy taking long-distance photos. *Can't get his license plate. Something very weird is going on. Can't be an affair unless he's gay.* Both men got into their cars. The visitor pulled up beside the man whom Ava was following. Then two shots rang out. They were accompanied by the flash of a gun firing. *Shit, he shot him.* As the shooter pulled away, Ava got a picture of his license plate when it hit a patch of light. *Gotcha!*

33

SURPRISE

Houston, TX
Sunday Early Morning

"DAMN!" Ava said. The gunman drove off quickly. *Where's Barbie?* She kept glancing toward the diner. *She should be back. Tracker's gone, but gotta check this guy. May need an ambulance.*

Ava drove over to the car she was following, pulled up alongside it, and shined her flashlight into it. Head back, eyes open and staring at nothing, mouth open, and blood everywhere. *Definitely dead.*

She called 911 with a quick message, no discussion, and hung up. She knew they'd come. After she found her sister, she'd call them back or talk to the responding officer. *Please, let her be there.* Ava drove to the diner, taking less than a minute, then parked and ran inside. Her heart beat like a runaway train.

Standing just inside the doorway, Ava could see the

entire interior. She scanned every booth and seat. *She's not here.* She yelled, "I'm looking for a young woman who came in here twenty minutes ago. She's wearing blue jeans and a white top. Long blond hair. Pretty girl, little skinny, five foot six."

"Yeah, she was here. Left with some Hispanic guy a few minutes ago," said an old man on one of the red stools at the bar. "She was a hottie too."

Rushing up to the man, Ava opened her phone to pull up a picture of Barbie. "You sure?" She held out the phone.

The man slipped glasses on and leaned forward. "That's her."

"Did he force her to go with him?"

"No, I don't think so. I mean, it didn't look like it. He walked in and told her something, and then she ran out. He was right behind her."

Ava called 911 again. She explained she was the one who had called in the shooting. Then she reported her sister had been kidnapped. She told them the two events may be related.

"Stay on the line, please," the operator said.

"Sorry, I can't. Send the police."

Next call. She knew at this hour she'd wake up Detective Hank Gray.

"Hello." He sounded groggy.

Yup. I woke him up. Should I even be calling him? "I'm sorry to call you. This is Ava Gunn."

"Ava, something wrong?"

"I know you must be off duty, of course, but I trust you, and I need help. I just saw a man shot and killed in front of me. I had him under surveillance. He was a suspected cheating husband. And my sister just got kidnapped. I don't know if the two events are related or not. Will you help me? Please?"

"What? My God! Call 911!"

"I did, but I'm worried about her. No, I'm frantic! She should *not* be gone! There are no cops here yet, and nothing ever happens fast. They don't know me, but you do!"

"Of course, I'll help," Gray said. He sounded like he was still waking up.

"Something very bad has happened," she said. "I'm afraid the police may put their focus in the wrong direction since this is my second shooting in just a little over twenty-four hours."

"I got it. I understand. Where are you?"

"By the diner and the motel, on the outskirts of Houston. It's called Motel X."

"It'll take me about thirty minutes to get there. Just tell the cops what happened. Tell them to call me too."

"Please, hurry. I'm scared."

∼

UNIFORMED POLICE WERE TAKING statements when Detective Gray arrived. The officers told him more detectives were on the way. He took Ava to review the security cameras. It all happened the way Ava and the old man had said, but there were no real leads. A man walked into the diner and talked to Barbie. She left with him and got in his car, and they drove away. *Weird!* And no cameras caught the man who murdered the man Ava was following. The security cameras didn't show the license on the Hispanic man's car.

"There's nothing else you can do here," Detective Gray said.

"Well, I'm not doing nothing. My sister's life may be in

jeopardy. Something weird is going on. Who'd want to kidnap her anyway? And walking out with some Hispanic guy ... what's that all about? I should have called her sooner. I'm going to go see the woman who hired me, see if she knows what's going on. It has to be tied to what happened the other day, when I got knocked out."

∼

Barbie woke up slowly, disoriented. A black cloth covered her head, and her hands and feet were restrained. "Hey! Let me go!" She jerked at the restraints but realized she was in a chair and almost knocked it over. "Help! Help! I'm being held captive!" She stopped jerking as her head swam. She had a horrible headache, and her mouth was desert dry.

"Spike!" she screamed loudly, dragging it out. Then she did it again, "Spike! What the fuck is going on?"

She stopped struggling and listened. *Nothing. I wonder if someone is just quietly watching and listening to me.* Her breathing was heavy, and the bag held moisture from her breath when she yelled. It was uncomfortable. If she inhaled too deeply, the bag restricted her airflow.

She tried to relax and figure out how she was restrained. *I might be alone. Maybe I can escape.*

"Is anyone there?" she said in a normal tone. "What do you want?" *Am I alone?* "Can I please get a drink? I'm very thirsty." *Shit!* It was quiet except for the whisper of an air conditioner.

This has to be about Spike or maybe something to do with Ava. I gotta get loose before they come back.

She sat in a straight-backed chair with no arms. Her arms hung straight down, and each hand was tied to a back leg. *Feels like one of those plastic ties.* It cut into her wrists as she pulled and twisted. *Damn!* Her feet were secured to the chair legs. She couldn't move them either.

Barbie twisted her head, shrugged, and rocked her upper body. *That bag is going nowhere.*

Then a door opened, like it was in a separate room.

"Hey! Let me go!"

"She's awake," said a man with a Hispanic accent.

A door closed, and men muttered in Spanish. Their voices sounded muffled, like they were in another room.

"Tell me what's going on!" she screamed. "Get me a drink, and please take this bag off my head!"

∼

RICO WAS HAVING breakfast with Toro when they got the call.

"We got Barbie."

"How?" Rico asked.

"We took over for Ted watching Ava on her stakeout. Then a younger woman got out of the passenger side of Ava's car. We saw her go into a diner, and we recognized her. We snatched her, thinking she could tell us Spike's location.

"Snatched her?"

"I went into the diner with a hat down and told her that her sister was hurt. I said her sister had asked me to get her. I told her they'd called for an ambulance, and we needed to hurry. I drugged her as she passed our car, and then I shoved her inside. Then bagged her. No fight and no one noticed."

"Good, good. What about Spike?"

"No Spike. She was with her sister when we grabbed her."

"What?" Rico barked at him. "Never mind. Where is she now?"

"In the interrogation room at the warehouse office. We tied her to a chair, but she's come around since then, screaming off and on."

Fuckin' idiot! Rico took a few deep breaths, then asked, with no emotion, "Why didn't you call me sooner?"

"Don't know," he said. There was a long pause. "Sorry, boss."

Rico shook his head repeatedly. "Okay, don't hurt her. Did she see your face?"

"No. We put a bag over her head from behind."

"Good. Don't take it off. She sees us, and it could be fatal for her. Understand? Don't give her a drink or food and don't say anything around her. Leave her alone."

"*Sí, Jefe.*"

∽

About thirty minutes later, Rico and Toro showed up. Rico pulled up the curtain on the two-way mirror, and there she was, quiet with a bag over her head.

"Did you question her?" Rico asked.

"No, we didn't ask her anything at all."

"Good." Rico walked to the refrigerator and took out a bottled water. "Everyone be quiet. Toro, you can come in if you want, but stay behind her and say nothing."

"Okay, boss."

Rico opened the door.

Barbie sprang to life, at least as much as possible in her position. "Who's there? Please, don't hurt me. Just let me go. I won't tell anyone."

"Barbie, I just need some information from you. Tell us what you know. You won't be hurt, and we'll let you go."

"You know my name? That's creepy, but I'll tell you

anything you want. Just let me pee and drink something. I'm thirsty."

"I have a few questions first. Where is Spike?"

"I have to pee—now, please."

"Sorry, but I need to know where Spike is. Then you can pee."

"We left him at my sister's condo. He had a job to do in Louisiana, and he was leaving early tomorrow, or I guess today."

Rico nodded toward the exit. He and Toro went into the other room and closed the door. "Dante, are you good to get around?" Rico asked.

"I'm good," Dante said.

"Have we heard from our guy watching her place?" Rico asked.

"I don't think so." Dante looked over his shoulder. "Sebastian, you heard from your guy watching Ava's place?"

"No, sir. No activity, I'm sure."

Rico nodded and looked at Dante. "Okay, take a couple of guys and Sebastian to her sister's place. Be careful. He's armed if he's there, and her sister's a PI, so she's probably armed too. I need him alive. Go. Hurry. Call me as soon as you know if he's there."

Dante, on crutches and with his new cast, turned and headed toward the door with Sebastian and Gabriel.

"Wait," Rico said. "If he isn't there, his blue bag and the thumb drive might be. You'll need to search the place and contend with Ava Gunn even if he's not there." Rico held up his finger for a second, holding them in place as he thought. "Take another guy and the van too. Call me when you get there and tell me what it looks like."

"Okay, boss," Dante said. "I'll let you know as soon as we get there."

They took off and Rico returned to the interrogation room.

"Do you know what's in his blue bag?" he asked Barbie.

"Yes, a gun, a knife, and some cash."

"That's all?"

"I think so."

Rico went back into the entrance office. He had a couple of men take care of Barbie, then locked her in another room. He needed to wait and see what Dante found.

C'mon, Dante, don't let me down.

34

JUST MISSED THEM

Houston, TX
Sunday Morning

TED LOOKED AT HIS WATCH. It was four in the morning and still dark when a police car pulled up to his rear but remained in the street.

Shit. He'd smoked a joint a couple of hours ago. He couldn't get out if he wanted to. His pulse quickened. *What do the cops want?*

He put all the windows down, trying to get the smell out.

A cop walked up with a flashlight and shined it into the car but didn't say anything.

Ted was breathing hard but tried to relax and give his biggest smile into the darkness as the flashlight hit his face for a moment and moved away.

Ted's voice cracked. "Is there a problem, Officer?"

A deep, no-shit, emotionless voice came from the dark. "License and registration, please."

"I'm just sitting here. I didn't do anything."

"Sir, some neighbors have noticed you sitting here or close to here for the last few days. Can you tell me why?"

"I ... I ... oh, I'm waiting on my sister," Ted said. "She lives around here." The lie sounded bad even to him.

Officer Nelson sighed in annoyance. It was almost a growl. "I'm not asking again. License and registration," the cop said, more forcefully this time.

"Okay, okay." Ted leaned over to open the glove box.

∽

OFFICER NELSON FELT that something was off. Cops tended to have a sixth sense. Especially those who'd been on the job for a while and kept their warrior's edge sharpened. He knew the man had been smoking marijuana. The smell hung in the air as it wafted out of the window, and the idiot had put all four windows down as Nelson walked up. And "waiting on my sister" was the worst lie ever. When the driver stretched to open the glove box, Nelson shined his flashlight on the man's back and saw a gun stuck in his pants.

Quickly, he pulled out his pistol as his body tensed up. "Freeze! Do not move! Do *not* move!" He waited a second to make sure the man complied.

The man froze like an ice statue. "What is it?"

"Sir, I have a weapon trained on you, so do not move. I'm going to reach in and lift the pistol out of the back of your pants. Do not resist, or you will be shot. Do you understand?"

The officer heard the man sigh and drop his chin as he shook his head. He seemed to submit. *But I've been fooled before. Never again.*

Officer Nelson reached in, took out the gun, and put it on Ted's roof while he awaited backup.

"Do you have any other weapons in the car?" he asked.

"Nope. Well, maybe under the seat too ... but it's legal to have a weapon, no license required. Right?"

"Not when you're smoking marijuana." The cop was all business.

Once backup arrived, Ted was handcuffed and put in the officer's cruiser for possession of marijuana and possession of a firearm while in possession of a controlled dangerous substance. Arrangements were made for the car to be towed. As Officer Nelson drove off to take Ted in to be booked, Ted realized he'd dropped his phone on the floor of his car.

"Officer, I forgot my phone."

"I inventoried it with the car's contents. You'll get it back after you're released."

"Damn! When do I get my call?"

"After you're booked, you'll be able to make as many calls as you'd like, sir, but it'll be at least an hour, I imagine."

"Shit! Please, I need to make a call!"

Officer Nelson ignored Ted and glanced at the clock on the dash. Four-thirty-five a.m. "You know, if you were on some kind of stakeout, you really screwed up."

∽

Spike's alarm went off. It was four-thirty a.m. He woke up disoriented from a deep, sound sleep. The sisters hadn't returned. He got dressed in his new clothes from the truck stop: jeans and a red cowboy-style shirt. Then he picked up his blue bag. It felt good. It was still dark when he walked out the door, which he locked behind him. At five a.m., he got into the limo for New Orleans.

He made the one stop he'd arranged, which was on the way.

Magic opened the door in an open bathrobe, the older man exposing his boxer shorts, which were bedecked with dollar signs. Spike shook his hand with a smile, then handed the bag to Magic.

"Too damn early," Magic said.

"I know." The handshake and exchange were brief. Spike was already backing away to return to the limo.

"You don't need to ask," Magic said. "I'll keep it safe, and I won't look in the bag."

"I never had a doubt."

Spike sat back in the limo. "Find me some coffee."

"Got it, boss."

Spike liked the smell of the leather interior. He relaxed in the comfortable seats, anticipating the quiet ride. *Wonder what's waiting for me in Louisiana. I'm ready.*

35

UNINVITED GUESTS

Houston, TX
Sunday Morning

AVA WALKED INTO HER CONDO, revved to kick ass and hurt someone to get her baby sister back. *But who?*

She called Spike. No answer. *What the hell is he doing?* "Answer the phone!"

Ava showered and sat in front of the mirror. *Bags under my eyes.* Exhausted, she fell forward from dozing off. *No leads. I gotta rest, just a couple of hours.* Setting the alarm for two hours, she crawled between the cool, smooth sheets. Sleep came immediately.

Then the alarm went off mid-morning. Before doing anything, Ava called the detective in charge of Barbie's case. The response didn't surprise her.

"Sorry, ma'am, it's been only a few hours. We're working on it, and we'll call you as soon as we have anything."

"Thanks." She tried to make her voice sound pleasant but knew she was a little short. *Asshole.*

She called Detective Gray.

"Hi, Ava. Did you get any news on your sister yet?"

"No. I just called the detective on the case. He said they're doing everything they can and to be patient." She paused. "Is there anything you can do?"

"It's not my case. I'll just piss people off if I ask questions. They'll get all territorial, and they'll feel I'm wasting their time."

"What about the cheating husband I was staking out who got shot and killed?"

"I can't discuss the case, but you should read the news. Someone got a scoop on that. It alleges that the man you were staking out wasn't a cheating husband but was blackmailing someone who decided to kill him."

"Damn, I'm glad I got my fee in advance. Well, I'm sorry for the wife, my client, of course. But about my sister, please, help me. I'll do anything if you help me." She thought she might mean it too.

"I'm really sorry, but I'm sure you understand. Even if I knew anything, I couldn't discuss an ongoing case. Plus, as I said, it's not even my case." There was a long pause, with no one speaking. "Promise not to call back and tell them anything?"

"What?" She couldn't hide the excitement in her voice.

"Promise!" he stated a little too strongly.

"Yes, yes, yes."

"I shouldn't be doing this, but to give you a little comfort, I'll tell you that they do have some leads they're following up on. There were a lot of bodies in the warehouse by where you were assaulted, and they've started identifying some of them."

"What? The other detectives told me they didn't have anything. Assholes."

"They're just trying to do their job."

"I know, I know. Look, if you're free, why don't you come over, and I'll fix you a little brunch?"

"I'd love to, but are you sure?" His voice was hesitant. "I mean, with everything going on..."

"Yeah, I know, but yes, I'm sure. I'm going crazy all alone with no leads. Chatting with you might give me some ideas. I've got tons of energy and no way to focus it. I don't know what to do."

"Oh, I get it. You feed me, then pump me for information."

"Maybe," she said in an innocent voice.

"You win. Of course, I'll help you. Not sure what we can do, but I'm on my way. Be there in about thirty minutes."

She hung up and headed to the kitchen to prepare brunch.

"We're here," Dante said. "Someone's in there, but we can't tell who. Should we go in?"

"Yes," Rico answered. "Be careful. Call me when you're inside. If she has to see a face, let it be the new guy."

"Relax, boss, I got this." Dante looked at the condo. It was one of six facing the street. Ava Gunn's unit was on the end to his left as he looked at it. A gate with no lock led to a small yard that offered access to the back of the unit and the utilities. The ground floor was a two-car garage, and on its left was the condo's entrance, a bright red front door trimmed in white. He assumed the rest of the ground floor was likely one room in the back. The second floor was likely the kitchen and living room, while the third floor would be a couple of bedrooms. He had a plan.

Dante saw no one on the street. Sunday mornings were usually quiet for traffic. "Stay here." He got out with a cap pulled down and limped over to the gate with his cast and one crutch. The gate opened easily, and he entered the yard smoothly, with no noise. There were no useful windows on the side, but when he got to the back of the unit, he heard activity and saw light coming from the second floor. The six-foot-deep backyard ended at a fence—just enough room for the A/C unit and a small concrete slab. The patio had a sliding glass door that opened into a dark room. The lock was easy to pick. Dante held his breath as he slid the door open a few inches. *No alarm, or at least it's not on.* Then he pushed it a full two feet. *Still no alarm.* He limped into the room and listened. He thought he heard a man's voice. *Spike!* But the TV was on, so he couldn't be sure. He couldn't even tell how many people were there.

The activity was on the second floor, and the kitchen appeared to be above him. *Bright lights.* He'd bring in the guys, and they'd quietly sneak up the dark stairs. They could be on top of everyone there before they could react.

Counting Dante, there were four men. He'd tell them to go for the closest person, put the gun to their head, and subdue them. The men had to quickly clear the upstairs and subdue anyone before they went for a gun or another weapon or made a 911 call.

Dante knew this had the potential to be a shitstorm, but it was the best plan given the available information. He went back into the side yard and waved his men over from the van across the street. His leg was killing him, but he didn't trust his guys to handle what they found.

Ready to return to the back room on the first floor, he

checked to make sure everyone was gloved up. They didn't have to get anyone to open the door, so they put on their black ski masks. Everyone also had a pistol.

"Don't shoot unless you have to," Dante whispered.

They nodded.

As they moved out of the room and down a short hall, the men found a staircase against the outside wall. Dante took each step one at a time, which was easier than walking with the cast. He squatted on the steps just below the second floor. Slowly raising his eyes so they were level with the hardwood floor, he peeked at the area. To his left was the kitchen, with a table and high chairs that could seat two on each side. A mid-size TV hung on the wall. Someone was working a knife on a cutting board.

Two-thirds of the second floor consisted of a big sunken living room with a large-screen TV set to the news channel. He saw a couple of stuffed chairs with their backs to him. *Someone could be seated there. Spike?* An empty couch sat perpendicular to the chairs. *No more than two people on this floor.*

Dante went down a couple of steps so his men could see him. With his fingers, he indicated he'd take the kitchen. Gabriel was to check the upstairs because Dante trusted him, while Sebastian with his guy would secure the living room so he could keep an eye on them. Dante mouthed "on three" and showed them his fingers. They all nodded.

Getting back in front of his guys at the top of the steps, Dante held his hand where they could see it and started a finger countdown. "Three." *The chopping stopped.* "Two. One."

Dante sprang forward, but his back foot, covered by the cast, caught on the top step. As he fell, he glimpsed a determined woman with a long knife. *She could kill me.*

36

STAND YOUR GROUND

Houston, TX
Sunday Morning

AVA THOUGHT she heard someone on the steps. She'd thrown her gun and shoulder holster in the first chair in the living room. It wasn't close enough, and she'd have to run by the steps to get it. But she held an eight-inch stainless-steel chef knife and knew how to use it. Slowly, she backed up and flattened herself against the wall with the knife firmly in hand, extended toward the sound. She inched closer to the edge so she couldn't be seen around the corner to the steps.

If he was bigger and had a gun, she'd have to go for a death blow. Otherwise, the advantage would shift immediately to whoever was on the steps in her house. The Texas "Stand Your Ground" law gave her the right to kill the bastard. Her heartbeat was in her ears, and her breathing was deep. *Stay quiet.* She listened. Nothing happened, and she started to relax. *Maybe no one's there.*

Then a man stumbled and fell right in front of her. He hit the floor hard. Ava saw he grasped a semi-automatic pistol. She planned to kick the gun out of his hand and threaten him with her knife. Her body had started to move forward, focused on the gun, when a second man ran into her. They both fell to the floor.

On her back, with this man on top, Ava was nearing panic. She saw the first guy, the one who had tripped, trying to get up while one or two other men ran past them into the apartment. She ripped off the man's mask with her left hand and slit his throat deeply with her right. She was sprayed with blood—lots of blood. Ava closed her eyes to keep the blood out of them as she threw him off and grabbed his gun.

She pointed at whatever was in her line of sight, which was another man on the bottom of the steps going to the third floor. Ava fired three times. She saw him twist and go down as lead tore into him. The man who'd tripped had fallen into the living room and was at her eye level. He pushed his gun to her head.

"Drop it! Or I'll fucking kill you," he said.

She didn't drop the gun. The man reached up with his left hand and took it out of her hand.

She saw a fourth man come down the steps from the third floor with a pistol aimed at her.

"Goddammit, lady!" said the man with the gun to her head. "Why didn't you just come with us?"

So, they want me alive.

The man at the bottom of the steps checked the pulse of the man she'd shot. "He's dead. You okay, boss?"

"Yeah. What about the upstairs?"

"It's clear."

Ava saw the man with the gun to her head turn his eyes toward the man at the bottom of the stairs. The latter man lowered his gun as he checked the dead man.

Hope they want me unharmed too.

Ava dropped flat on the floor and turned into the cast man as she threw her arm up to push aside the pistol. Then she launched herself up with the full force of everything she could muster. The man fell onto his back, and she drove her knee into his groin. With a loud curse, he curled into a fetal position while she picked up his Beretta 9M and swung around to shoot the man at the bottom of the steps.

"Stop! You pull that trigger, and I will kill you! I don't give a shit if we're supposed to take you alive or not." The man was a few feet away, close enough that he wouldn't miss and far enough away that she couldn't move on him.

"Damn!" She lowered the Beretta to her side. "Who are you guys, and what the hell do you want from me?"

"Drop the magazine out and clear it. Now!" said the man at the bottom of the steps.

The man she'd kneed in the groin reached around Ava and took the gun out of her hand. "Never mind, I got it. Put your hands behind your back."

She did it slowly. He put zip-ties on her hands and jerked them tight.

"Damn!" Then he hit her on the head, and she went down.

∽

Dante bent over and checked her eyes. "She's out." Then her pulse. "She's alive. Check for the blue bag, hurry! You know the cops could be here in a few minutes. Hurry!"

"Damn, you could have killed her," Gabriel said.

Dante was already moving down the steps, slowly, hopping on his good leg as much as he could, with Ava over his shoulder. His balls hurt, and his leg was killing him. He opened the front door of her condo, left it open, and, seeing no cars or people, limped across the narrow street as fast as he could with her dead weight. He reminded himself of what the doctor had told him: There would be no permanent damage if he walked on it. It was more of what his threshold for pain was. Sliding the van door open, he flopped her in. Then he zip-tied her feet and slammed the door. Dante limped as fast as he could, ignoring his surroundings, and burst through the door, then went up the steps to the second floor.

"Gabriel! We gotta go! I got Sebastian! Get the other guy!" Dante ignored the tremendous amount of blood. He slipped a little, which sent a stabbing pain through his leg, but he gritted his teeth and tried to ignore it. He threw Sebastian on his shoulder, got to the top of the stairs, and started down. "Now! Right now!"

"Right behind you," Gabriel said.

Dante didn't look over his shoulder. He struggled down the steps as fast as he could. "Shut the door behind you." As he limped across the street, he heard a siren in the distance, so he threw Sebastian in the van. Then Gabriel tossed in his man. Both bodies were partially on top of Ava. Dante and Gabriel jumped into the van, pulled off their masks, and drove out slowly.

After stopping at the corner, Gabriel looked in his side mirror. "Cops."

In his own mirror, Dante saw the flashing lights of a police cruiser around the corner a few blocks back. "I see them. Just drive normal. They have no idea it's us."

Gabriel turned right, and they were quickly out of sight. "That was close."

"Too close." Dante kept watch in the side mirror.

"I think we made it, but that was a trainwreck," Gabriel said. "What about all the blood?"

"Unless they have Sebastian and the new guy's DNA on file, they can't identify them. I'm not bleeding. What about you?"

"Nope."

"What was the new guy's name?" Gabriel asked.

"I'm not sure. Mauricio, I think."

"Too bad. Mauricio didn't even get started," Gabriel said. "And Sebastian, I liked him."

"Yeah, we're losing too many guys," Dante said. "Back to the bloody mess at her place. We should be good. We wore gloves, so no fingerprints. I didn't see any cameras, and we wore masks just in case."

Dante kept checking the side mirror, but he knew he was safe unless they got pulled over for a traffic violation. *Need to be extra careful. Hope the taillights don't burn out.*

"Shouldn't we call Rico?" Gabriel asked.

"Be careful with the names. Not sure when she'll wake up. I'll text him." At the next light, Dante quickly sent a text: **Got the package, back in about fifteen minutes. No bag.**

As Detective Gray approached Ava's condo, he spotted two guys running across the street, carrying something. One guy was limping. It looked as if they came out of Ava's condo, but he wasn't sure. He'd have to get a little closer. Then a white van pulled out from the row of cars parked on the side of the street. *Odd.*

A police cruiser came around the corner with its lights blazing. As Gray pulled over, he noticed the white van turn right on the next street. He let the cruiser go by, then pulled out, following it but not rushing. The cruiser stopped in front of a row of condos. As Gray drove by, he saw it was Ava's. He was in his private car, so he'd never heard the police radio call.

Gray stepped on the gas. He had a hunch and would circle back if he was wrong. As he rounded the corner, he saw the white van take another right, maybe three to four blocks away. He called police dispatch, gave his badge number and Ava's address, and asked what had happened.

"It was a response to shots fired," the dispatcher said.

Gray hit the gas, driving too fast with no lights or siren on his car. There wasn't much traffic, which was a big help. When he got to the intersection where the van had turned, the light turned red. Gray saw a car coming, but he punched the gas and turned in front of it. The car laid on its horn, which he couldn't care less about. What he did care about was what he didn't see: the white van. *Please, let her be okay.*

37

THINGS GOT GRAY

Houston, TX
Sunday Morning

"Someone is driving pretty wild behind us and closing the gap," Dante said, checking the side mirror. With no windows in the back of the van, Dante knew Gabriel had only the side mirrors. Dante turned to see if Ava was still unconscious. She apparently was, as she was still lying beneath his two dead compatriots. *Sorry, guys, I didn't think anyone would die.* "After we take this corner, take the first right and see if he turns."

Gabriel turned before he saw the blue car do likewise onto the sleepy residential street.

"Shit, this is a dead end with a cul-de-sac," Dante said. He looked in his side mirror. "There he is, going really slow. Damn! He must have seen us. He's backing up to turn."

"What'll we do? Think he can identify us?"

"Shut up!" Dante said. "Pull the van over and park it in

an open space. Stay here." He grabbed his mask, opened the passenger door, and limped to the front of the van as Gabriel gripped the steering wheel. Looking around, Dante saw no one walking on the street. Then he peeked and saw the car inching carefully toward the van.

When the blue car was parallel to him, Dante pulled down his mask and limped a step or two so he was level with the passenger window. "Stop! Or I'll shoot!" He held his pistol against the window, pointing it at the driver. "Don't try going for a gun or hitting the gas. You won't make it." He saw the man tense up, his eyes darting around. Dante knew he was thinking of stepping on the gas. "Don't do it. I won't miss from here. Not worth dying for. Put the window down and put it in park."

The man scowled and gave a small shake of his head, giving up. He parked the car and rolled down the window.

Reaching in, Dante opened the door and slid into the passenger seat. He scooched down in the seat, keeping his gun on the man. He didn't want to take off his mask, but he knew if anyone saw a masked person, it would raise suspicions. "Open your jacket carefully so I can see if you have a gun."

The man opened his jacket. *A badge on his belt and gun.* "Fuck, you're a cop!" Dante glanced at the road. Still no traffic. *Might not be any traffic for an hour with the cul-de-sac.* "Okay, with your thumb and one finger, pull your gun out and put it on the seat."

The cop did.

Dante quickly picked up the weapon and stuck it in his belt. "Let's get the gun on your leg too. Be very careful with that."

The cop unholstered his throwaway gun and put it on the seat.

Dante picked it up and stuck it beside the other gun. "You got a third gun?"

"No."

There was an open parking spot two spaces in front of the van. "Pull up into that open space, then show me your ID." Dante never took his gun off the cop or got too close.

The cop pulled in and put the car in park again. "I'm getting my ID." He pinched his jacket between two fingers and, in an exaggerated move, pulled it away from his body. Then he slowly pulled out an ID and handed it to Dante.

"Detective Gray," Dante said with a little huff. "I'll be damned. Anything you want to tell me?"

"Like what?"

"Zorro cartel ring a bell?"

"Maybe. Who're you?"

In the rearview mirror, Dante saw that Gabriel, brow furrowed, had stepped out of the van from the sliding door. Dante opened the door and looked back at Gabriel. "Get back in the van! I'll be there in a minute!"

Gabriel waved in an understanding gesture and got back into the van. Dante watched until the door slid shut.

He leaned back into the car and pulled the door closed. After looking straight ahead for a moment, he turned his head to Detective Gray. "I'm the guy who knows you're on Zorro's payroll. Who could fuck up your life or have you and any family you have killed in any number of ways." He gave Detective Gray his guns back. "So, forget all of this. I gotta go."

"Wait! What's going on? You got Ava Gunn in there?"

"Why do you care?"

"She was a witness in something I'm investigating."

"Well, then you're out of luck. Whatever you're investigating, I think that witness just went missing. She's the key to getting back a thumb drive with sixteen million on it. That trumps anything you're working on. Beat it. Go give someone a ticket." Dante jumped out and hobbled back to his van.

∼

DETECTIVE GRAY GRABBED a tracker from his glove box and jumped in front of the van with his hands out.

Dante put down his window. "You're starting to piss me off."

"What happened to Pedro?" Detective Gray asked. He knew Pedro was dead, but he couldn't think of any other excuse to stop the van. "I always worked with him."

"You won't be working with him anymore. Someone will get in touch with you." Dante rolled up his window and inched forward.

Detective Gray cupped his hand on the tire as the van started to move. The magnet latched to the van. He watched to make sure it didn't fall off, then glanced at the side mirror. He didn't see Dante looking back at him. *I wonder if they have Barbie too.*

He wasn't sure what was going on, but that was a lot of money. *Sixteen million dollars.* Plus, he'd hardly gotten to know Ava. He sighed. But he wanted to. *I like her. What would I risk for her? What would I risk for sixteen million? Two birds with one stone, maybe.*

He watched the old Zorro cartel man, who hadn't given his name, turn around in the cul-de-sac. As he drove by, Detective Gray waved.

The man didn't wave back. Gray saw him start to remove his mask as he passed him.

What an asshole.

38

THE GUYS

New Orleans Area
Sunday Noon

Spike got out of the limo, walked up to the front door, and knocked.

The door opened, revealing a man with a buzz cut. The man reminded him of Arnold Schwarzenegger, complete with a camouflage wife beater shirt.

"You Buck?" the man asked with a French accent.

"Yeah."

"Roman, Buck's here!" the big man yelled.

"Great!" yelled a man in what sounded like a Russian-accented voice. "Love it! I really love it when a plan comes together! I'm cooking! Come say hi!"

"He's a happy guy," said the Schwarzenegger man. "I'm Pierre." He offered his hand and stepped back so Spike could enter the house. "What happened to your arm?"

"Cat scratched me."

"Damn. Based on that bandage, was it a lion or a tiger?"

"A lioness as I remember." Spike smiled, then winked. "If you know what I mean."

"I *do*." Pierre winked back. "Roman loves to cook. Always cooks us what we call the last supper before a job."

"Smells good," Spike said. "You're French, and he's, what ... Russian?"

"Ukrainian. Follow me to the kitchen." Pierre started walking but kept talking. "You know, you come with a great reference. Tommy loved you, man. He said we could depend on you if we ever needed to, and you were available."

"Yeah, well, here I am." Spike wondered how long he could keep this up. *And what are we going to do? A robbery, maybe?*

"Really too bad Tommy didn't make it back from the last job. But we all know the risks. That's how he came to offer your name. The boss asks for a suggested replacement from all of us in case we don't make it. Of course, that's after you prove yourself."

"Of course, but it was too bad about Tommy."

"Welcome," Roman said, wearing an apron over a black utility uniform. "Nice to meet you, Buck." He was fixing pasta and some side dish. Spike couldn't miss the aroma of the bread in the oven. "You named after Buck Rogers or something?"

"I wish. My mom loved *Call of the Wild*. I'm named after Buck the dog. He's a half St. Bernard, half Scotch Shepherd mix. He's kidnapped and becomes a powerful sled dog in Canada." This was one of the books Spike had read in captivity just a few days ago. Who wouldn't believe that story? *I like it.*

"No shit," Roman said. "You got fleas?"

Roman and Pierre laughed.

"I would never have guessed that," Pierre said. "I was thinking Davy Crockett or some frontier man ... or a redneck."

"Nope, a fucking dog," Spike said. This wasn't what he'd expected. *These guys are friendly and funny.* "I could get used to hanging around you guys. Where are we going again?" *Call me crazy, but fuck, this is exciting.*

"Need-to-know basis," Pierre said. "Only Fluff, the boss, knows right now. He'll fill us all in at the briefing. It's not always like this, but there were last-minute changes. Fluff had to do a quick recon. He just got back in the country a couple of hours ago."

"We don't know where it's at?" Spike asked.

"Not yet. There've been a few times we never found out," Roman said. "We flew or boated in, executed the op, and left."

"Really. That secret?" Spike asked.

"Better we don't know sometimes," Pierre said. "He did tell us this'll be a little on the fly. There's a time crunch. That's why the bonus. He should be here soon."

"There he is. Hear the plane? That's the boss. We have a dirt strip out back," Roman said. "Show him his gear. He needs to change," he told Pierre.

Pierre must be second in command.

"This way," Pierre said. "You're the last piece of our little team. All your gear is in that bedroom. It's mostly Tommy's stuff, but the clothes are your size. Get dressed. We'll eat when the boss gets here, then get briefed. I'm sure we'll be airborne a couple of hours after that." Pierre pulled the door shut. Then, a few seconds later, before Spike could assess the gear, Pierre cracked the door open. "Oh, I forgot to tell you. There's a safe on the closet floor, like the hotels. Put your own code in and put all your identification and personal stuff in the safe, as well as any personal weapon. We go in with no ID and all standardized equipment. They're always black ops. Don't get killed. I hear it sucks."

"You leave the bodies?"

"We'll try to bring them out, but, occasionally, it's just not possible." Pierre pulled the door shut again.

Spike looked in the closet and found a black utility uniform with boots, like the other guys wore. He pulled open a chest of drawers full of black underwear.

Spike changed his clothes and came back out. He walked into the kitchen at the same time a man with a deep, pensive look came in the back door. He had to be Fluff and was dressed in Florida casual—a golf shirt and shorts with sneakers. Over his shoulder, he carried a small bag.

As he entered, he said, "Smells good. Ready to eat?"

"Hey, Fluff, we missed you," Roman said with too much enthusiasm.

"Yeah, right."

"But, yes, we're ready to eat. I'll serve it up," Roman said. "Did you get what we needed on your recon?"

"Yeah. I'm still thinking, so I don't need any conversation. Start getting your head right. Let's eat." Fluff hung the bag on the back of his chair at the head of the small table.

Spike stood a little to the side.

"I guess you're Buck," Fluff said. "Hope you know what you're doing. Don't eat too much. It'll make you sluggish."

"Sure," Spike said. *What a fuckin' asshole!* "Can you pass the Parmesan cheese, please?" *Maybe I should just get the hell out of here the first chance I get.* "Can I ask exactly what we're going to do?"

All three men laughed. Roman laughed so hard, he choked on a mouthful of food.

"What do you think we're doing? You don't get the big

bucks to go on a picnic," Fluff said. They all thought that was pretty damn funny.

I hate Fluff! Hate him!

Anger boiled in Spike at being the brunt of the joke. He wasn't sure if this was a rhetorical question, but he chose not to answer. Instead, he laughed with everyone else. He patted the knife in his pocket.

Fluff was already done eating. In fact, Pierre and Roman were almost done. Spike had just gotten started. *Shit, slow down, guys! Never seen food before?*

"We've got an elimination order," Fluff said as he stood.

Roman and Pierre followed as they pushed away from the table. Fluff was the shortest, probably an inch or two under six feet, fiftyish but ridden hard, with lots of sun patches and wrinkles. His bald head was naturally shiny or waxed. It was odd he was bald. Thick, coarse, gray hair stuck out of his collar. The effect was topped off by a sizable scar on his cheek.

But the best description of him so far seemed to be "asshole."

Everyone placed their dishes in the sink.

"You two, take a shit, take a piss, get a drink, and say your prayers. We take off in thirty minutes. Buck, come with me," Fluff said without looking at Spike. He turned and walked out of the kitchen into an empty room.

Spike walked past him, and Fluff shut the door.

"Tommy liked you, said good things about you. We talked to three guys who all knew you from different Merc jobs. I know you were in the army and that you do Merc jobs a few times a year. When you're waiting on a job with a gun, you do construction. Is that correct?"

"Yup, that's me." Spike didn't know how far to go with the lie, but it seemed too late to turn back. Fluff's eyes were dark brown but appeared almost black. Spike had never looked into colder, more emotionless eyes. He wasn't sure this was a good man. He felt like Fluff could kill anyone without remorse. *Little scary.*

"Is there anything else I should know?"

"Don't think so," Spike said. *Fuck, this could end up very badly.*

"We would have vetted you more and done a run-through of the op as many times as needed, but the timeline got moved up. This is a four-man job, or we wouldn't be taking you."

"Okay." Spike felt weird. Out of control, which he hated, but this was still more exciting than anything he'd done before—except his hobby. This was a different class of excitement.

"Don't fuck up." Fluff leaned forward and growled into his face. "Any questions?"

"I have no real idea of any of the specifics of what I'm supposed to do."

"I know. You'll get a full brief on the plane, and we'll gear up at the safe house."

"Where's the safe house?"

"Panama."

39

TELL ME NOW!

Houston, TX
Sunday Afternoon

AVA FELT HERSELF WAKING SLOWLY. *Weird dream. Damn. What a headache. I need to get up gently.* She opened her eyes and tried to roll over. Momentary panic hit her hard with everything restrained and then—reality.

"C'mon, a black bag, *again*! And stop hitting me on the head. *Damn*! And tied up? What the hell do you want?" she yelled. All her screaming made her head pound as if she were hitting a base drum. She wanted to squeeze her temples, but she couldn't get free, so her head pulsed.

"Ava, you okay?" Barbie asked. Her voice sounded muffled.

"Barbie! I'm fine. You alright? They hurt you at all?" Her voice sounded stilted inside the bag.

"Yeah, I'm okay."

"You tied and bagged too?"

"Yup."

"What do you know?"

Before Barbie could answer, a door opened and shut. Someone was in the room.

"Ladies, I'll answer a few of your questions," said a man with a Hispanic accent. "But let me just say, if you don't see any of us, and if you tell us how to find Spike, you can both still get out of here in time for a good supper and maybe go to a movie tonight. That's why you have the bags on your heads."

"This is about Spike? Why?" Ava asked. "Hey, first, how about finding some way to take these bags off our heads? Like maybe face us close to the opposite wall from the door and then stay behind us. Or maybe you could put on a ski mask when you come in to see us. Or do both?"

"You'll cooperate, then?"

"Why not? I barely know the guy," Ava said.

"And your sister?"

Barbie answered, "Sure."

"Okay, wait a minute," the man said.

The door opened and closed again. The sounds of a conversation in Spanish came from the other room. The door again. By the sound of it, two men were picking up her chair, tipping her back with one man on each side, and moving her. Ava could tell she was being turned around. Then her chair was set down and moved forward until her feet hit something. *Probably the wall.* The bag was loosened at her neck and pulled off from behind. When the bag came off, she reflexively shut her eyes. When she opened them to bright light, she closed them again. Squinting, she slowly opened her eyes and turned to look at her sister. "Barbie, wow." She smiled lovingly, and her sister did the same.

"I'm sorry," Barbie said. "This is my fault, I guess. They want Spike, and I'm not sure why. I told them what I know."

Though Ava was looking at her sister, she noted, in her peripheral vision, a man standing ten feet behind them. She couldn't see any features and didn't want to. Apparently, the other men had left the room. This man seemed to be letting them talk as they wanted to, probably hoping to get something useful.

"Don't worry about it," Ava said. "We'll get out of this. Whatever they want to know about Spike, give him up. You barely know him. These guys aren't playing. And don't look at them."

"You guys done?" the man asked.

"Yes, but I don't have much to tell you," Ava said. "Spike met Barbie just a day or two ago in Columbus, New Mexico. He dropped her off at my place and left this morning to go on a job in Louisiana."

"Do you have an address for the job, name of the company, anything?"

"Nope. That's all I know," Ava said.

"Did he leave anything with you?"

"Yeah, he gave me his number. It's in my phone. He also said that's the only way we could talk to him. It goes to his burner."

"Did he leave you a bag of any kind?"

"No, but he showed up with a blue bag. I don't think it ever left his sight."

"Barbie, do you know what's in this blue bag?" the man asked.

"A bunch of cash, a gun, and a knife," she said with no hesitation.

"So, that's it. He has a bag of your cash," Ava said.

"Did either of you ever see a thumb drive?"

They answered, "No."

The man reached around and held Ava's phone in front of her. It recognized her face and opened. "We took this out of your purse. Guess it's yours since it opened."

"No kidding," Ava said.

"I'll need your security code too."

"010195. That's J. Edgar Hoover's birthday."

"Cute. I want you to call Spike. Talk to him. Try to find out where he is or at least when he's coming back."

"Sure, why not?"

"You must make it natural. It may be least suspicious to just find out when he's coming back. And make sure he's coming back to your condo."

The man moved close to her right side and went down on one knee. He did it so quickly that Ava was startled. She began turning away when she noticed he wore the same black three-hole ski mask as the other men.

"Glad you're wearing the mask." Ava smiled with relief. She could see him smile back. *I know those eyes. Nice eyelashes for a guy.* This was the man at her condo. He cut the zip-tie securing her right hand and handed her a bottle of water.

"Thanks," Ava said. She was sure this guy liked her, but she knew he'd still kill her if he needed to.

The man walked over and cut Barbie's right hand loose, then handed her a bottle of water. *A kind man or just playing us. Maybe wants us to have to pee for more interrogation later. I don't care. I'm thirsty.*

"Thanks," Barbie said.

The man returned to Ava's right side and again went down on one knee. "I don't have to remind you that if you do something stupid, your sister will pay for it first. You get to watch. You understand?"

Spike: 35 Kills and Smiling

"Look, this guy is nothing to me. If he stole from you, I guess he deserves what he gets."

"Okay, good. Put it on speaker. You ready?" he asked Ava.

"Ready." *I guess.* She still had a killer headache, so the extra stress of calling Spike under duress made her head feel like a balloon about to burst.

The man handed her the phone. She moved her right hand over to her left, which was still zip-tied, then pushed "send" and the speaker.

It rang once. *Answer it.* Twice. *Answer it.* Three times. *Answer it.*

"Leave a message," the man said as fast as he could as the fourth ring started. Then it went to voicemail.

"Spike, this is Ava. Do you know when you'll be back? I'd like to have a nice home-cooked meal ready for you. Give me a call and let me know. Oh, Barbie says hi. Have a good day. Bye."

The man took the phone from her and ended the call. "Damn!"

"Sorry. You can let us go if you want. I'll let you know if he calls me back."

"Yeah, right," the man said. He wasn't smiling now. "When do you think he's coming back?"

"It could be a day, a week, or a month. He said he didn't know. He had to be somewhere at noon today in Louisiana."

40

DANTE'S DAY

Houston, TX
Sunday Afternoon

Dante went back into the main office space.

"Did you get rid of the bodies?" he asked Gabriel.

"They're on their way to an incinerator, and we already cleaned out the van."

"Good."

Rico had two local men waiting there in case they were needed. Dante's own men from El Paso—Gabriel, Jorge, and Pup—were there too. They all looked to Dante for information. He didn't give them any.

They didn't know they were looking for sixteen million dollars' worth of bitcoin on a thumb drive that would give the owner anonymous access to all the money. He thought only Rico knew, and maybe Toro too. Dante knew this because he'd been involved with the thumb drive from the start. He knew Rosa had it on her.

Sixteen million wasn't enough money for Rico, a cartel head, to take a chance on getting sideways of the law in the US. Other than the first meeting in Houston to see how things were going, he didn't plan on hanging around. Rico had told Dante that he'd be at the hotel for a couple of days, maybe, and then go back to Mexico.

Dante stepped outside, away from everyone, and called Rico.

"Did you find out where the thumb drive or Spike is?" Rico asked.

Dante recounted what he knew.

"Okay, I'm going back to Mexico now," Rico said. "You take care of this, but don't forget Houston. You've got Houston now. If you need more men, tell me, but find Spike and my money so you can focus on our business. Can Gabriel handle El Paso?"

"Yes, sir."

"Does he need your other two guys right away to help him in El Paso?"

"I don't think so."

"Ask him, but if he doesn't, then keep them as long as you need or want them. Tell Gabriel to leave now and to call me or Toro when he's back in El Paso."

"Okay, boss. What if I can't recover the money from Spike?"

"I don't want to hear that shit! Find it! You understand?"

"Yes, sir."

"Hurry up, then get our business running smoothly in Houston again. Another shipment's coming in a week, very pure. If you can't handle it all, tell me. If you need more help, tell me. We can replace the men we lost. Let me know. I'll send you more help."

"Okay, boss. I think I'll be alright. But should I do anything about the messed-up arms deal?"

"Stay away from it. Too many bodies. The cops will be all over it. Something is very wrong with how that deal blew up. I've heard that the seller and his organization have been taken out. It was a simultaneous hit at about the same time as our fucked-up deal. Maybe Uncle Sam didn't like someone fuckin' with the Switchblade drones destined for Ukraine. Black ops. No arrests that I heard of. Just a lot of dead people all the way to Europe and the Middle East."

"I'll keep Houston running smoothly. You can count on me."

"I know that." There was silence. "Find Spike and my *damn money!*" Rico hung up.

Dante held the phone in his hand as he digested the message. *This could go very badly for me.* Then he turned to the men in the room. "Gabriel, you're in charge of El Paso. Congratulations. Take off now and call Rico or Toro when you get back."

"Yes, sir."

"Jorge, you've been to the country house?"

"*Sí.*"

"Good. Take Pup and one of the other guys. Move the women to the country house. There's a secure retaining room, kind of like a comfortable jail with a toilet. Put them in there, feed them. But be very careful. The older one already killed two of our guys."

Jorge waited a few seconds to be sure that was all Dante would say.

Dante considered telling Jorge that he was keeping the burner phone and that he should be ready to get Ava back as soon as he could but decided not to. He'd let Spike call first. He wouldn't answer it but would have Ava call back.

"When should we do that?"
"Now!"

∽

Detective Gray pulled out a few minutes after the white van left. He could hang back significantly and let the tracker do the work. Then the tracker stopped moving. He was about ten minutes away. Gray pulled into a long parking lot in front of a row of small warehouses with roll-up truck doors between them. The doors weren't loading platforms but more like garage doors that let the vehicles enter.

The beeping signal was in front of him, beside him as he passed the warehouse, and then behind him. He didn't see a white van. Detective Gray circled the complex to look for a back entrance. He saw none, just a small loading dock in the back. As he passed the front entrance a second time, he kept going and parked far away, in a spot no one would notice but where he could still see the front of the warehouse.

What should I do? Just wait, I guess. He sighed and chewed his lips. *What am I trying to do anyway? Save Ava? See if I can make a run at the sixteen million dollars? I've made some bad decisions. Time for a change of luck, maybe.* He glanced at his watch. *Forty minutes.*

He started the car. *Just leave, just leave. Less complicated. Safer.*

He put the car in gear, took his foot off the brake, and started for the gas pedal. Then he hit the brake, jerking the car from the slight roll.

"I'll be *damned*. It's all about timing." The car-type garage door had started to open from the bottom up. Gray put his car back into park. He didn't want to follow so closely that they noticed him. *What if Ava isn't in the van? A* man ran to the back door of the van and opened it for a second. The light came on in the van, and Gray caught a glimpse of two people on their backs, tied to chairs. *Damn! That's gotta be Ava and Barbie.*

He let the white van roll out of the lot. Then he left and stopped at a McDonald's, went to the restroom, got some food and a cold drink, and returned to his car. He checked the tracker. "Yep, there they are." He pulled out.

Sixteen million dollars. My God, that's a lot of money. It'd take care of all my problems.

41

MOVE OUT

Near New Orleans, LA
Sunday Afternoon

PIERRE AND ROMAN TALKED, laughed, and joked the whole short drive to a small airport. Fluff said almost nothing. They boarded a private jet. Fluff chatted with the pilot in the cockpit for a few minutes, then sat down for an immediate takeoff. In just less than three hours, they landed. There were no passport checks. They loaded into another van and drove about an hour to a small facility with a fence and guards. The guards looked at Fluff, opened the gate, and waved them through.

None of their group talked to anyone. The van was parked inside a garage. When everyone got out, Spike hung back so he would be last, then followed the group down some steps until they came to a door with a keypad. Fluff entered a code, and the heavy door popped open. They all went in, and Roman held back to secure the door.

As soon as they were inside, a casually dressed man walked up to Fluff. "Everything's ready, sir, according to your instructions. It's all in the Green Room down the hall. Uniforms, weapons. As I said, everything you asked for."

"Thank you, Wilson."

"Yes, sir. I'll be in ops."

"We'll be there in a second." Fluff had already turned and was walking toward the Green Room.

"We'll be ready," Wilson said to Fluff's back.

Spike saw Fluff a few feet behind him. Then he walked into the Green Room, right behind Roman and Pierre. Each of their names was on a card affixed to one of the four sets of gear—for clothing size, probably, as everyone seemed to have the same set of weapons and equipment. They each picked up an automatic rifle and cocked it before looking it over. Fluff came in behind Spike and started the same routine. Quickly, each man did a cursory check by touching or lifting everything and looking at the rest of his gear. A pistol, a knife, some night vision goggles, and other equipment. They then stripped down, including underwear, and redressed.

"Let's test-fire them before we get geared up," Fluff said.

They walked a short distance to an underground firing range. Roman was the first in. He hit a switch, and the ventilation fans started. There were two shooting spots. Roman and Pierre stepped up and started shooting—a few rounds through the rifle and a few rounds through the pistol.

"Mine works," Roman said.

"Mine too," Pierre said.

Both men cleared their weapons, said, "Clear," and stepped back from their firing positions.

"Next," Roman said.

Spike had been watching them closely. In the past, he'd

fired his Glock 40 but no other pistols or a rifle. He noticed Fluff kept a constant watch on him.

Without a word, Fluff test-fired his weapons in what seemed like seconds. Then he stood and watched Spike.

Spike was smooth and got off a few rounds with the pistol. He heard them talking and knew this was a Sig Sauer P320. It was a 9 mm and had less kick than his 40 cal.

"Nice." He ejected the magazine and smiled. He set the pistol on the shooting table in front of him, looking down range.

No one said anything, but all three were watching him.

Fuck, no pressure!

Spike put a full magazine in his rifle and tapped the bottom as he saw the others do. He lifted it to his shoulder and pulled the trigger. It didn't fire.

"Oh, damn, I forgot the safety." Then he tried to fire it again. It didn't fire. He fumbled around, looking for the safety.

Spike glanced up. Three sets of eyes were staring at him in disbelief.

Fluff moved fast. He jerked the M4 out of Spike's hands. Spike didn't resist. He knew it was about to get ugly.

Without taking his eyes off Spike, Fluff handed the M4 back blindly to one of the guys. Pierre took it. Then Fluff picked up the Sig and handed it back blindly. Roman took it.

"You know it's got a round in the chamber," Fluff said.

"Got it, boss." Roman cleared it and said, "Clear."

Fluff shoved Spike so his back was against the wall. "Buck, or whoever the fuck you are, based on how you handled that M4, you don't know what the fuck you're doing."

Spike sighed and tried not to roll his eyes.

Fluff's hot breath was in Spike's face. "You'd better take a second and think very carefully before you answer. I'm goddamn serious. If I think you're lying your way out of this, there's a jungle just outside. I'll kill you and throw your fucking body out there, and no one but us will ever know. If you tell me the truth, you may survive this. Do you understand?"

Spike nodded slowly. *Fight or flight?* He smiled. *Maybe neither. I could be screwed. What was I thinking?*

"Who the fuck are you?" Fluff asked. "When you're ready, we're listening."

Tell the truth. I'll tell the truth, mostly. They don't need to know about all the people I've killed. They might not understand, even though I'm sure they've all killed people. Hypocrites?

"Okay, my name is Spike."

"Your real name, asshole." Fluff shoved Spike in the chest, causing him to gently bounce against the wall and back in Fluff's face.

Spike kept the smile on, but he knew it faded for a moment. He was trying hard not to show an attitude.

"Harry Hunter, but I go by Spike."

"Okay, Spike, what are you doing here? Skip nothing."

Spike told them a version of the truth—how he'd gone to Mexico with a friend to help rescue his family from the cartel. *Not exactly true.* How he had been separated and had to escape Mexico on his own. *Kind of true.* How he'd killed three cartel soldiers. *True.* How he'd killed the cartel boss's wife during his escape through a drug tunnel. *Half true.* And how he'd climbed out of the tunnel in Columbus, New Mexico. *True.*

He continued with, "That's where I met Buck. He tried to kill me and steal my money. But I killed Buck instead. Then I got your call on Buck's burner. It sounded like a profitable adventure, and here I am." *That's all true.*

"I'll be goddamned. You killed Zorro's wife, Rosa. We heard about the upset in that cartel." Fluff gaped. He took a step back, his demeanor less intimidating. "You came on this trip knowing you were going into an assassination with a kill team of highly trained operators. You that stupid, or sowing your oats because you escaped the cartel and killed a couple of people?"

"Nope. I thought it was a robbery, and I was looking for excitement."

All three shook their heads, speechless.

Fluff pointed at a pad of paper with a pen beside it. "Write down your real full name, your Social Security number, your last address, and maybe your job. You married?"

"No."

"Okay, write that stuff down and wait here," Fluff said. "We need to discuss this."

All three walked out of the room and into the room next door.

Spike sat down. *Good sign. They're discussing it. Still fuckin' hate Fluff.* Spike heard them whispering but couldn't make out a word. *If they let me go, maybe I'll accidentally shoot Fluff in the head ... if someone shows me how to use the damn thing.*

They came back a short while later, and the three men stood shoulder to shoulder.

Spike handed Fluff the paper. He looked at it briefly. "A couple of questions first. You ever been in the military?"

"No."

"What have you done?"

"Mostly sales and computers. But I've always kept myself in great shape." Spike paused. *Let's spin a half-lie. I did help Jeff Case find serial killers while he kept me captive.* "I guess I can tell you guys. I was also on a special task force hunting serial killers. But it was a secret agency, and you won't find it anywhere."

"Really?" Fluff said. "Maybe we'll talk about that later. For now, we don't have much time. You don't know what you're fucking doing. That makes you a liability. We're all impressed that you went on a rescue mission. That shows you're not a coward. We're also impressed that you escaped the cartel, regardless of how it really happened. That shows resourcefulness. But we know you're holding something back."

Spike thought it best to not comment yet.

"This is a four-man job. We need the fourth man as a lookout while we take care of the two bodyguards and the target. We don't have time to find a replacement. If you are who you say you are, then you're in. Roman, give this to Jonesy in ops. Tell him to find out everything he can about Harry Hunter and do it now. Whatever he gets, bring it back to me in about ten minutes. With a picture of Harry, if he can find one."

"On it." Roman jogged about twenty paces down the hall and ducked into a room, then came back.

The team kept getting ready. Spike sat and waited.

In about ten minutes, a man walked up and handed Fluff a few printed papers. "Here it is."

"Thanks." Fluff took the papers. "Well, Harry, there's your picture. Looks like a lot of sales experience. Nothing related to the cartel or hunting serial killers."

"You think that shit would be on a resume?" Spike got up, walked over to Fluff, and glared. "And do not call me Harry again. It's Spike."

"Okay, Spike." Fluff poked him in the chest.

Spike fumed but didn't react.

"Don't fuck up. Our lives depend on you. Do you understand?"

"Yes, sir."

∽

FLUFF HAD BEEN surprised when he'd gotten the call offering him the chance to get the arms dealer who had been behind the stealing of the Switchblade drones from the United States. Much of the man's organization had gotten rolled up when they'd taken back the drones. However, within the last forty-eight hours, they'd found out the name and location of the head of the arms operation. One of his men had given him up. Fluff had wanted the mission. He'd had a different one lined up but opted out to take this one instead. He'd already set up three men to go with him. Spike wasn't one of them.

During the briefing, Fluff watched Spike. He seemed to pay close attention. The rest of the team had gotten this briefing before, minus the updates about last-minute changes. It was all new to Spike, who asked no questions.

Who lies to become part of a special op with no training or skills? The guy must be crazy. Fluff was extremely worried about Spike. If Spike ended up wigging out, Fluff would just drop him. No IDs on any of them, and Spike didn't even have a military record. *No problem leaving his body behind.*

As soon as they cleared the briefing room, Fluff gathered the four of them in a tight circle. "We leave in two hours. Set your watches."

Everyone did.

"We need this guy alive. They'll probably hide him at some black ops prison and squeeze every bit of info they can out of him. The briefers expect our target to be alone with his bodyguards. But if he's not, we don't compromise the mission. We'll take down everyone who's with him. We don't need anyone raising the alarm any sooner than need be. Everyone got it?"

Roman, Pierre, and Spike nodded.

"Pierre, help Spike get geared up. Run him back to the range and give him a quick course on the M4 and the Sig. Just show him how to shoot, reload, clear it—the basics. Don't worry about how to break the weapons down. We don't have time."

"Got it, boss," Pierre said. "Let's go, Spike."

Spike nodded with a smile.

"Pierre says you have a big cut on your arm. How serious is it?" Fluff asked Spike.

"It's long, not deep. It happened a couple of days ago, and it's stitched up."

"Is it going to be a problem?"

"No. It will not." Spike was afraid they'd leave him behind.

"Okay. Pierre, put duct tape over his bandage. That should keep the stitches from pulling."

"Can do, boss," Pierre said.

Fluff waited for them to round the corner, then spoke to Roman. "We have to use him, but don't completely rely on him, and watch the slang, as he may not get it. I'll keep him on my hip until he has to take his lookout post. Let's try to bring him back alive, but don't risk your own life. Tell Pierre when you're alone."

~

What the hell am I doing? Don't know ... but I like it.

Spike was dressed in camouflage and geared up, thanks

to Pierre. He felt more comfortable with his M4 with a silencer and his Sig. They'd even painted a camouflage design on his face. His stomach roiled. He'd hunted, stalked, and killed, but this was clearly different—frightening and exhilarating. The prey would have guns too. *Shit!* He wasn't sure he'd ever want to do this again—but maybe.

Not afraid to die. Feels kind of important.

I wonder how Ava and Barbie are doing. Doesn't matter. Wonder if I'll see them again. Not a big deal.

They loaded up on a prop plane and took off into the dark.

Spike looked at the rubber band on his arm. He'd had no reason to snap it since meeting these guys.

Maybe I'll see life depart from one of our team's eyes, or maybe someone we shoot or stab. What if I kill the whole team? Surprise! Maybe as I walk behind them. They wouldn't even have time to react ... but then how the hell would I get home?

42

COUNTRY HOUSE

Outside Houston, TX
Sunday Afternoon

"I'M A LITTLE SCARED." Barbie looked at Ava.

The man questioning them had left the room a few minutes earlier.

"We'll be fine. Never lose hope," Ava said.

Barbie saw the confidence and resolve in her sister's eyes. It was comforting. "I won't lose hope as long as you're with me, big sister. I love you." She smiled at Ava, but she knew these guys might kill them. *I don't wanna die. I think I have a future with Spike ... if I live through this. If he wants me.*

"I love you too." Ava stopped struggling for a second and looked at Barbie again. "Keep trying to get loose. Give it everything you've got." Ava was jerking and twisting all the ties until droplets of blood fell to the floor at the back of the chair. "It could take just one more pull, twist, or tug."

"I'm trying. But what the hell do they want with Spike?

The cash?" Sweat beaded along Barbie's hairline, and her hands felt clammy.

"I don't know. I'm guessing they're more interested in the thumb drive they asked about. There must be something on it they want really badly. Spike must not know he has it."

"Maybe. They don't seem to care about the cash." Barbie pulled at her restraints and looked at her sister. Ava's wrists were bleeding.

"Yeah, that's strange. Where the hell did he go, and how long until he's back?"

"I don't know." Barbie slowed her struggling. Her eyes watered, but she couldn't wipe them because her hands were constrained. Tears ran down her cheeks.

Then someone came into the room. Barbie knew she couldn't hide the tears. She was embarrassed, ashamed. She looked at Ava and knew she'd see no tears there, just resolve. Their eyes met. Barbie smiled, then lowered her head. *I'm so proud of Ava. If I have to die, I'm glad it'll be with her. I love her so much. I wish I were better. Give me another chance, God.*

"We're going to move you somewhere more comfortable until we hear from Spike," said the same man with the mask. "You won't be hurt. I won't be talking to you for a while, but some of my men will take good care of you." The man left.

"Help! Help!" Barbie screamed. "Help!" *If the only thing I can do is call for help, I will.*

She looked at Ava, who didn't scream, just twisted her ties and bled more.

Barbie kept screaming for help, crying as she did.

Two men walked into the room. Barbie's screams abruptly stopped when a ball gag was pulled into her mouth. Her eyes widened, and the bag was placed over her head again. She assumed the same thing was happening to Ava. Her chair was picked up, and she was carried away. *This is not good.* She said the Lord's Prayer over and over, surprised she remembered it. She hadn't said it in years.

～

Jorge moved the women to the country house with no problems. The men didn't take their prisoners out of the chairs. They laid them side by side on their backs, still tied, with bags on their heads, in the back of the white van. Jorge and Pup sat in the back and watched the women while the new guy drove, as per Jorge's instructions.

"The hotel woman was something else," Pup said.

"Shut up." Jorge gave Pup a scolding look as he nodded at the bound and hooded women.

"Oh, yeah. I just wonder if she got home," Pup said.

Jorge shook his head as he leaned in and whispered to Pup, "Who the fuck cares? She didn't see anything and doesn't know anything except we'll kill her and her whole family if she talks. Now shut up. Not another word."

Pup nodded.

Jorge leaned over and whispered again, "And we'll never be going back there."

"What're you guys talking about?" the driver asked.

"Just drive," Jorge told him.

The remainder of the one-hour long drive was quiet. The location was remote—no neighbors in sight. They carried the women one at a time into what they called the guest room, then set their chairs down just inside the room, facing away from the door.

"Ladies, we'll let you loose within this room in a few minutes if you cooperate," Jorge said. "There will be food, a restroom with a shower, a TV, and even some cots with bedding. There's no way out of the room. You'll have a phone to talk to us if you need to. You must not look at us. If you never see our faces, we'll let you go when we're done. It may be a day or two or a week. But, again, you cooperate, you won't be hurt. If you understand and agree, nod."

Both women nodded.

"Good. One man will cut your zip-ties. The rest of us will be pointing our weapons at you. Don't try to get up or take the bags off your heads until I instruct you to do so. Do you understand? Nod."

Both women nodded.

"Good. After we leave, you can take the bags off your heads and do whatever you want in this room. When we come into the room again, you must put the bags back on and sit in your chairs right where they are now. Nod if you understand."

They nodded.

"Okay, cut their ties."

∾

AVA FELT her bindings being cut. She knew it was a horrible time to make a move. Blinded by the bag and disoriented, she heard one voice. There had to be at least two men, probably three. *Fuck it! They want me alive, I think. Go for it!*

She turned and ran toward the voice with her arms out, trying to grab someone. With her shoulder, she slammed into a body, latched onto him with two arms, and kept driving him backward like a linebacker tackling a quarterback. He yelled something in Spanish.

As she pushed backward, Ava felt him stumbling, and she fell with him, landing on top of him hard. She heard the air forced out of him as he lay there, not moving. She ran her hands down his arms until she found a hand limply holding a pistol and grabbed it. With her other hand, she tried to pull off the bag as she jumped up and ran forward blindly to get some space between her and her captors.

Going at full speed, Ava hit a wall and fell, losing her weapon. She sat on the floor, a little dazed. She had just started to jump up when she felt hard metal pressed to her head.

"Please, I don't want to shoot you." This was the man who'd been talking before.

Ava thought she'd tackled him, but it must have been one of the other men.

He took her by the arm and led her into the room. "Stay here."

Ava heard the door close. Then, from a speaker, she heard, "Ladies, you may take your hoods off now. Please, get comfortable and please cooperate. As you can see, we have cameras on you, but you do have privacy in the restroom and shower. If you need us, pick up the phone, and we'll talk to you. Please, relax as best you can."

~

Barbie, still sitting in her chair, pulled off her hood, then looked at Ava, who stood to her right and behind her chair. Ava was breathing hard, and her face was red. "What happened?"

"I tried to escape," Ava said.

"With a hood on?"

"Yeah, it didn't go too well. But I think they're supposed to keep us alive, so I thought I had nothing to lose."

"You're fucking crazy." Barbie walked over to Ava and

hugged her long and tight. "I'm scared," she said with her head on Ava's shoulder. Then she pushed back a little. "I love you. Thanks for being you."

Ava hugged her back. "I love you too. Don't worry. We'll get out of this."

∽

DETECTIVE GRAY SIPPED on his Coke as he casually followed the tracker. He saw he was getting close, so he pulled into a gas station, went in, and gave the cashier fifty dollars in cash for gas. No credit cards, just in case he needed to deny being in this area. He went to the restroom and got another cold drink. At the gas pump, he filled the tank almost entirely. Then, after throwing away his trash, he hit the road. It was only a few miles away, off the main road.

On a small, paved state highway, Gray looked to his left as he drove by the tracker and saw where they had to be. It looked like an older farmhouse with a barn. He slowed. Puffy white clouds decorated the bright afternoon sky.

He found a place to pull off the road where he could still see the house. *Gotta wait until dark for my next decision point. Go home or rescue Ava. My door to the money.* His stomach was upset. He felt wired.

Just not sure what I'm going to do yet. But sixteen million dollars is a lot of money.

His phone rang. It was Lou Whitaker. *Damn!* He answered, "I'm working on it."

"Look, shithead, you owe me money. I've been a patient man," Whitaker said. Gray knew the man had hurt people, but Whitaker was more interested in getting his money. The last time Gray had run up a big tab, he'd been sold to the cartel. Pedro paid his debt, and they owned him. They continued paying him a monthly fee, but he had to be available whenever they needed him. *I hate, hate, hate being a dirty cop.*

"Float me for one more bet. Double or nothing. I can get myself out of this," Gray said.

"It's too much money. Can't do it. Ask your friends for more money. Sell your house, rob a bank. I don't give a shit. You got one week, and then I'm going to get serious about collecting. Understand?"

"Yeah, I understand." Gray felt he at least had an out. *I gotta get that flash drive. At all costs. A new life.*

43

CAREFUL

Somewhere in South America
Sunday Night

SPIKE HAD no idea where they were. He'd been in a van and on a plane and had just gotten off a helicopter. He was now squatting in tall, damp grass with his weapon pointed outward, in an opening big enough for the helicopter to drop them off. Pitch-black jungle surrounded him. The helicopter's chop-chop faded quickly.

Pierre moved past him, and then Fluff followed Pierre. Both were headed toward the jungle, crouched forward, weapons ready, on a small trail.

Roman squatted beside Spike and checked Spike's safety. Then he whispered, "Keep the safety on until you're ready to fire, but remember to take it off. Follow Fluff. Keep your distance, but don't lose sight of him, or we're both screwed. If he stops, you stop, and say nothing. I'll be behind you. Go. Catch up." He patted Spike twice on the shoulder.

Excited. Not scared yet but nervous. All Spike could think of was doing his job and not letting the team down. *Fuckin' weird. I feel an odd bond with these guys. Even Fluffy.*

As Spike walked, he concentrated on keeping his eyes on Fluff. In the dense darkness, he couldn't even see Pierre, who was in front of Fluff. The walk was one foot in front of the other until Fluff went down on one knee. He motioned for them to close in. Spike saw the big house, more like a small mansion, and the lights illuminating it, just past the edge of the jungle on the other side of a private drive.

Fluff looked at Spike and whispered, "You stay on my hip. I'll tell you when to break off and where to go. Don't shoot me in the back. Roman, Pierre, you know what to do. Try not to use the comms until we have to. Meet at the rally point on the other side of the mansion. Good luck."

Roman and Pierre went to the edge of the jungle, then sprinted to the mansion and split, going around it in opposite directions.

Fluff turned to Spike. "We've got an inside guy. He'll turn off the security systems, and the lights will go down. You know how to switch your night vision goggles on, right?"

"Yeah, I know how." *I think.*

"Good. I'll be going into the mansion to take care of the target. Roman and Pierre are going in the only other two entrances, so he'll have no way out. You stay here. Anyone comes up this road, let them get close and then take them out. You hold this position. It's our way out, and our lives depend on it. Got it?"

"Got it." *I hope this goes smoothly. I barely know what's going on. I feel like Rambo.* Spike glanced at the rubber band on his wrist. *Whole different world.*

∽

FLUFF WAS RUNNING up on the mansion. *Spike better hold his position. Could be a shit show.* The intel had said two bodyguards, one walking around and one within a room or hallway from the target. *Three total. All to be eliminated.*

He was moving quietly and low along some hedges when he saw someone light a cigarette to the left, at the bottom of the front steps. Then he spotted another guard on the porch.

Shit, many more men than we planned for. Can't abort. Fuck! He keyed his mic to warn everyone, but then he heard shooting from the back of the house. *Pierre or Roman?* Not M4s with silencers but loud automatic fire from many places on the other side and the back of the mansion.

Fluff shot the guy with the cigarette, who was farthest away, and then shot the man close to him. Charging the front steps in a crouch, weapon pointed forward, he put another round into each of the men as he passed. *Lights are still on. Damn!*

"This is Romeo One, report," Fluff said.

Roman responded, "Romeo Two, took fire, put two down, and breached the back of the house. I'm under fire from down the main hall, maybe three. I saw the target duck into a room off the hallway as I came in. Had no shot."

"Romeo Two, this is one, on the way, about to breach the front." *Hang in there, Roman.*

Three did not report. *Shit, Pierre's down.*

"Romeo Four, you there?"

"Roger, this is Four. What should I do?"

"Romeo One to Four, just watch the road."

∽

Spike's breathing deepened as Fluff took off running for the mansion. *A few seconds and the lights will go out. I'll flip down my night vision goggles. A quick raid by the crew, and they kill the target. I get a call. So, fifteen minutes or so. I'll get a call, meet everyone at the chopper at the back of the secured mansion, and fly out. Piece of cake.*

Spike looked at his watch. He stared down the private road. He imagined people in the shadows, but it was nothing. Fluff had told him if he saw anything, it'd be a vehicle with lights.

Then the shooting began. Then the radio calls.

His heart was about to explode. *Shit! No response from Pierre. Must be dead. Shooting everywhere. The lights are still on. A firefight! We're all going to die!* Spike's hands started to shake. He had never been so scared in his life, but he was armed to the teeth, and there were people to kill. *Fuck it! No one's coming, and I couldn't stop them anyway.*

Spike jumped up and started running along the path Fluff had taken toward the front steps of the mansion. He saw the body of the first bodyguard Fluff had killed. He didn't know why, but he pulled out his knife and slit the dead man's throat. *No squirting blood. Of course. The asshole's already dead. No fun!*

He sheathed his knife and didn't slow down for the second body. The firing raged. The guards' unsuppressed weapons were loud, while the team's were muted pops.

Spike was coming up behind Fluff, who was shooting down the main hall. Spike keyed his mic. "Coming up behind you, boss. Don't shoot me. I'm charging them."

∽

FLUFF WAS SHOCKED. Spike ran right past him, then started shooting on full auto.

"Romeo Two, Four is charging. Cover him on your right. I'll try to cover him on the left," Fluff said.

"Got it."

There was one wide, long main hall. Fluff and Roman each took a side and covered Spike, firing as fast as they could, just short of full auto. This was the push that would determine their success.

What the fuck? He's not shooting!

∼

SPIKE WANTED to get close and open up on the bodyguards with full auto. He wanted to see their bodies explode, their blood squirt everywhere, and their bodies flail. He felt protected.

As he passed Fluff, the situation seemed surreal. Slow motion. He smiled, expecting to get shot at least once or more, but he knew it wouldn't stop him. It wouldn't kill him.

This was meant to be. He was right where he was supposed to be at just the right time. He'd had these episodes before when he knew everything would go perfectly. Spike didn't fear death, and he wouldn't die tonight.

He smiled as he approached the intersection. Four men, one at each corner, shot down the hall toward Fluff and Roman. They'd all pulled back out of the rain of fire, no doubt expecting to return fire when a lull came. *But here I am.*

Spike, on full auto, spun around and hit the first guy in the chest. The second guy's head exploded, and the third guy twisted around from the burst. He didn't know where he'd hit him. And the fourth guy—*Shit!*

Out of bullets.

Spike saw the fourth man clearly. He had scared eyes and a beard. He fumbled with his weapon. Scared he couldn't change the magazine in time and get a shot off, Spike pulled out his knife and lunged at the close man. The man stumbled over backward due to Spike's weight. With no hesitation, Spike thrust the knife under the man's chin and into his brain. Warm blood hit Spike's face. He licked it off his lips. *Salty and warm.*

"Un-fuckin-believable!" Fluff paused for a second to take in the carnage. "Make sure they're all dead." He ran into the room.

"Dammit! The target went into a panic room," Spike heard Roman say from inside the room.

He heard Fluff tell Roman, "You know what to do. Hurry up!"

～

SPIKE DIDN'T HAVE to be told twice to make sure everyone was dead. No doubt the guy he'd knifed under the chin was dead, and so was the guy he'd shot in the head. They were on the same side. The two on the other side he wasn't sure about, so he walked across the hall to check. First, Spike went to the guy moaning. He'd caught the man across the chest with at least two to three hits. The man was weak, and Spike was surprised he was alive. Spike rolled him onto his back and straddled him across the wounds.

I can't believe all this. Kid in a candy store. Spike slapped the man a few times until he opened his eyes. Then Spike smiled, put his hands on the man's neck, and squeezed as hard as he could. *Don't have all day.* The man suddenly found some strength but not enough. The first reaction was a jerk of the body, and then he grabbed Spike's arms. However, the man's grip quickly grew weaker, and he succumbed to death. His eyes glassed over.

The other man might have been alive, but he was dead now. *Too bad.* Spike kicked the corpse. *Fuck, I just killed four guys ... no cops. It's okay.* He smiled. *Fucking strange.*

44

BIG DECISION

Houston, TX
Sunday Night

DETECTIVE GRAY WAITED until it was dark. He'd had all afternoon and early evening to think of what he was going to do. That would be his way in. He'd save the women and, eventually, they'd lead him to the money. He hoped.

The white van sat behind the house. It hadn't moved since Gray first drove up. He hadn't seen them when they went into the house, so he didn't know how many people were guarding the women. *Two probably, maybe three?* There had been no activity all day, except one man who came out every hour on the hour and smoked a cigarette.

Gray knew rescuing Ava meant he would have to deal with her guards. They worked for the Zorro cartel, and so did he. *Part-time anyway.* He would have to kill them so no one would know it was him. *They're bad guys anyway. Big decision.*

He pulled out his ankle gun, a small revolver. Gray flicked it open, spun the chamber, and flipped his wrist to close it. He put it back, then pulled out his Glock 17 and made sure a round was chambered. He had three extra magazines. From the glove box, Gray took out a pair of rubber gloves he used at crime scenes and put them on.

With the glove compartment still open, he removed his hunting knife, a top-of-the-line Buck Frontiersman with a six-and-a-quarter-inch blade. He opened the sheath, pulled it out, and looked at it before returning it to his belt. He hoped he could get a weapon from one of the men and use it on the others.

Ready as I'll ever be.

Gray opened the door and got out quickly to prevent the interior light from remaining on for too long. He wanted to be there in plenty of time to be ready for the smoker.

He'd made the walk overland earlier but hadn't gotten too close. It took him twenty minutes and would take a little longer in the dark. He'd picked a place where he could hide. If the smoker sat on the same lawn chair at the back of the house by the van, Gray would be close to him and behind him. *Cut his throat, take his gun, and then check out the house.* If Ava was there, he'd go in shooting. They were in the country. The noise likely wouldn't attract attention.

When he got there, Gray stood behind the corner of the barn, then checked his watch. If the man was on time, he'd be out in the next ten to fifteen minutes. Gray could barely see the lights of the neighbors over the next little hill with trees around it. *Not close at all. Probably won't hear gunshots.*

It seemed like he checked his watch every minute. *It's time. Where's he at?* The smoker was five minutes late, then ten minutes. *Damn!* He stood and peeked in the window. Suddenly, the smoker flung open the door, causing light to shine right on Detective Gray. *Shit!* He squatted down and froze. It was too far to run back to the barn, his closest cover. The door shut, and darkness descended again. Then Gray saw a lighter flick a few times. The sparks were followed by a flame. The man must have been messing with his cigarettes when the light hit Gray. He stopped to take a drag, bright red on the tip, then sauntered over and sat in the lawn chair.

Given the darkness, Gray was sure that even if someone was looking, they wouldn't see him. *No point in waiting.* Bent over, with no hesitation, he moved quickly and grabbed the smoker's hair with his left hand. Then he jerked the man's head back and sliced deeply, ear to ear, across his neck. The smoker grabbed his throat. The only sound he made was a gurgle as he dropped to his knees and fell over on his side. The man wiggled as death throes overtook him. Then he stopped moving, and his hands fell loosely from his neck.

This wasn't Gray's first kill. He'd had to kill a man to pay off the debt with the cartel. He wiped his bloody blade on the dead smoker's shirt, then put it back in the sheath on his belt. Gray pulled the man's pistol from his waistband and checked to see if a round was chambered. Its magazine was full.

Seeing shadows at the kitchen window, he had to act quickly. He turned the doorknob and pushed. It was unlocked, but it creaked.

"Hey, Pup, you done already? You shouldn't smoke, you know. It'll kill you," said the man in the kitchen.

Detective Gray walked into the kitchen, Glock up. The man stood at the stove, his back to Gray.

"Ready to eat something?" the man asked.

Gray walked right up behind the man and pushed the pistol into his back. "Don't fucking move or say a word. Turn the stove off. How many other men are here besides the smoker?"

The man didn't answer.

Gray jammed the gun harder into his back. "Answer me and you might live."

"One."

"Call him. Be convincing and no one gets hurt. Or I can just kill you both. Understand?"

He nodded.

"Now."

"Jorge, come here a second. Try the food," the cook said. Then the cook grabbed the skillet and started to swing it as he yelled, "Gun! Gun! Man with a gun!"

45

DUCK!

Houston, TX
Sunday Night

Detective Gray ducked beneath the frying pan. The man swung with a backhand as he moved forward into Gray. Given the strength of the cook's arm and the weight of the skillet, the swing had some momentum. However, the man missed, exposing his ribs. Gray fired one round. The man released the pan and dropped to his knees, holding his side as blood poured between his fingers. Gray took a step to the side and raised the gun, then put a round into the man's forehead. The cook's head whipped backward, and his body fell to the floor. *One more to go!*

As soon as Gray pulled the trigger, he took off running toward the hallway. He assumed Jorge would walk through the door from the dining room, the most direct route. Gray was two steps down the hallway when Jorge emerged at the other end and started shooting. Gray dropped to the floor and shot three or four times, hitting Jorge in the chest. He stumbled backward, losing his weapon.

Gray stood and looked down at Jorge, who was slowly moving his arms and legs with bloody hands clutching his chest. His eyes were wide in disbelief, and he moved his lips as if to say something. However, nothing came out, and his eyes lost the brightness of life.

Mesmerized, Gray stared at Jorge for a second. *Damn! I just killed three men, and I think I'll get away with it.* He'd heard screaming for a while, but only now did it register. *Ava is here.*

Gray put Pup's pistol in his belt and followed the screams. There was a hallway with doors open on both sides, except one. He stood in front of the door, which had four video monitors along its side. Gray could see Ava standing by the door to the side, apparently ready to attack anyone who came into the room. Barbie was there too. Gray recognized her from the picture Ava had shown him. He wasn't surprised. Barbie screamed for help for a while, then stopped and got behind Ava.

It wasn't hard to break into the room from his side. The door had been hinged, so it opened into the hallway and had a low-tech but effective locking device—a two-by-four sitting in a metal cradle on either side. It seemed nearly impossible to break out.

"It's Detective Gray. Relax. I'm opening the door." He took off the wooden board, set it beside the door, and turned the knob.

Barbie, now standing behind Ava, ran around her and hugged him. "Thank you, thank you!" She jumped around and smiled.

While Barbie was all over him, Ava stepped around him

and looked down the hall. "I thought the police were here. Is it just you?"

"Yeah, just me."

Barbie ran down the hall, then stopped. Her hands flew to her face as she screamed for a second, then calmed herself. "Oh, shit! He's dead!"

"We gotta get out of here!" Gray walked toward Barbie and the way out.

"Where is everyone? Why are you by yourself?" Ava asked.

He didn't want to answer any questions now. "Please, let's get out of here. I'll explain everything as soon as I can."

He led the two women far enough away that they didn't notice Pup on the ground with his throat cut open. Only the dim moonlight illuminated their way. Gray continued behind the barn about fifty feet down the path back to his car.

Stopping, he turned to face the two women following him. "Wait here. I'll just be a few minutes. I forgot something."

"What are we doing?" asked Ava.

"Please, be patient. We need to get away from here." He walked past them, back to the house.

Ava grabbed his arm. In a firm voice, showing her impatience at not getting an explanation, she asked, "Why didn't you call 911? What's going on?"

He knew he could break her grip, but he didn't want to do that. "Look, I risked my life to save you and your sister. You did ask for my help. Please, just give me a little slack."

She stared at him for a moment in silence. "Okay, for now." As she spoke, she relaxed her grip on his arm. "Hurry."

Gray jogged back and ran into the house. Using a cloth

in the corner, he started a little fire in the room where the girls had been. Then he stopped in the kitchen and turned on the stove's gas without lighting it. As he emerged from the back, he stopped at the body on the ground, put Pup's pistol in his hand, and fired it once to put some gunshot residue on Pup and confuse any investigators.

"Let's go," he said as he approached the women. He moved past them, so he was in front again. "Let's try to jog a little. Pick your feet up and follow me." *Damn thing should blow up at any minute. Should I tell them? They'll know soon.*

When no blast came, Gray began to wonder if something was wrong. *Maybe the house wouldn't explode. Did the fire go out?*

Just as they got to the car, a huge boom echoed behind them. The structure must have been filled to its fullest before it ignited. Instinctively, he ducked. So did both women.

"Jesus!" Ava said.

"Fuck, what was that?" Barbie asked.

"Get in the car! Let's get out of here," Detective Gray said.

Ava climbed into the front passenger seat, and Barbie got in the back. They drove down the state highway and saw the house burning off to their right.

"Holy shit!" Barbie yelled. "Unreal! Thanks again for saving us. You're like a superhero or something."

"I told your sister I'd help save you," Detective Gray said to Barbie, but he felt disappointed about Ava. *A little lie. I wanted to save Ava and find out how to get that sixteen million.*

He looked at the house. Just parts of the first floor were there, fully ablaze. He saw Ava staring at the fire, shaking her head. She didn't turn to look at him but asked, "How many men did you kill?"

He wasn't sure if he should give the number. Or admit he'd killed anyone. *No one saw me kill anyone. Ava wasn't as happy to see him or as grateful as he thought she'd be. Maybe not love after all. Maybe I should focus on the money. Boy, I fucked up! She knows I killed those men, and she's former FBI.*

They'd passed the burning house. He sighed loudly. Ava must have heard it.

She turned to look at him. "What's going on?"

"Well, I was on my way to see you when I saw a suspicious van. I followed them all the way to a warehouse. I thought they might be the same people who took Barbie. I sat and watched but figured there were too many people to do anything."

"Okay, why not call 911?"

"I didn't know what was going on. I was afraid that if there were a lot of cops or maybe SWAT, you'd be held hostage or even get killed in all the confusion. So, I followed the van when it left, hoping for a better opportunity to save you. Then I found the farm. You're both safe now."

"Well, I really do appreciate what you've done for us. I understand the risk you took." Ava leaned over and kissed him on the cheek. "But what now? We go to the police station and give our statements?"

"Not yet," he said. *And hopefully never.* "You're still in danger. I heard them say they were holding you because you knew how to get back their sixteen million dollars."

"Sixteen million dollars!" Barbie screamed. "Damn!"

"Wow, that's a lot of money. That explains why they wanted the thumb drive," Ava said.

"You didn't know it was that much?" Detective Gray asked.

"No idea," Ava replied. "But I've never seen it. I just heard about it today."

"Really?"

"Spike might have it," Barbie said. "But they aren't sure."

"Who's Spike?"

Barbie jumped in and explained how Spike had escaped from Mexico and had a blue bag with cash in it. She went on, "The cartel wants to see if Spike has the thumb drive. But Spike's out of town, and we don't know when he's coming back. Plus, they have Ava's phone with Spike's number in it, and he's not answering."

"So, that's why Ava might be their way to find that money."

"Yup," Barbie said.

Detective Gray wrinkled his lips and shook his head. *Wow, I fucked up. How do I get out of this?* He looked at them individually. "Can't go to your place," he told Ava. "Probably still a crime scene, plus it will be watched. Can't go to my place either. I'm sure it'll be watched too."

"By who, the police?" Ava asked.

"Never mind. We need to get a room, just for tonight. Get some rest and make a plan tomorrow."

"I want to know what's going on. Now! Or I'll call the cops," Ava demanded.

"The truth is, I'm afraid they have some cops on their payroll," he said. "Please, just one night, okay? We'll figure out what to do tomorrow."

"Cops on the take? Really?" Ava asked.

No one spoke for a few seconds.

"Okay, we'll think about it tonight." Ava looked at Barbie, who nodded.

Detective Gray glanced back at the road, feeling grateful he had more time. *Gotta find a way to get that flash drive.*

46

PANIC OR NOT

South America
   Sunday Night
   "Damn!" Fluff screamed. He ran to the panic room's door. "Our guy has to be in there." He pounded on the door a few times and shook his head.

"What do you think?" Roman asked.

"Looks amateurish and homemade. The door hinges are even on the outside. This'll hardly slow us down." Fluff looked at Roman. "C-4 on the hinges ... and hurry!"

Then a man was screaming in Spanish at them. They turned quickly, but their weapons were down. The man kept screaming, motioning for them to drop their weapons. Fluff knew all this guy had to do was pull the trigger. They'd be dead before they lifted their M4s. The only chance for one of them to survive was for them to jump in opposite directions. One of them would be shot, but the other would have a chance to lift his weapon and shoot the man.

"You know what we gotta do?" Fluff asked Roman.

His talking made the man yell louder and wave the rifle more.

"I know," Roman answered. "Good luck, man."

"You too. Count to three in your head on my mark ... now."

One ... two.

FROM AROUND THE CORNER, Spike heard a man yelling. He eased to the edge of the hallway and peeked around. A man in a bodyguard uniform stood screaming just inside the doorway, his automatic rifle pointed into the room. The scene reminded Spike of a cop trying to intimidate a suspect.

Gently, Spike laid down his M4 and pulled out his knife. Then, quickly and quietly, he moved to the side of the doorway. The man was still yelling and jabbing his weapon toward where Fluff and Roman must have been.

Spike swiftly stepped behind the man. Then, with his left hand, he jerked the man's head up and pulled back tightly with all his strength. Spike's right hand sliced deep into the man's throat from ear to ear. The man went limp, but Spike held on and slumped down with him. He wanted to feel the weight of the man's body and watch the blood pump and spray from his neck.

Finally, Spike let him go. The man lurched forward, face down. Spike rolled him on his back and looked into his face. The gaping cut still squirted blood in rhythm with his dying heart, slowing as the pressure dropped. Spike stared at the dead man's empty eyes and smiled again.

... THREE.

In a flash, Fluff saw the man about to kill them. Then the man dropped his weapon as blood gushed from his neck. Roman had jumped out of the line of fire, as had Fluff, but both had the presence of mind to not start shooting.

"Cutting it kind of close, aren't you?" Fluff asked.

"Thank you. A sight for sore eyes." Roman gave Spike a quick thumbs-up as he rushed back to set the C-4 and caps on the hinges.

While Roman worked on the top hinge, Fluff worked on the lower one. Fluff saw Spike lingering over the body and staring at the corpse's face. Over his shoulder, Fluff yelled, "Get over it. You had to kill the man. You'll get used to it. Guard the door."

Slowly, Spike got up and walked to the door.

"Hallway clear?" Fluff yelled.

Spike stepped into the hallway. "Clear."

Fluff ran into the hallway, emerging beyond the wall standing between them and the coming explosion.

Roman followed and put the wires in the clicker. "Fire in the hole!"

The explosion was ear-shattering. The pressure of the blast wave screamed out the doorway.

"Stay on the door," Fluff yelled at Spike.

The explosion ripped the door off the amateur panic room, leaving it stuck at a weird angle where it cut into the wall.

Fluff and Roman rushed through the smoke and into the dust-filled room. Grabbing the man roughly, Fluff looked at his face to ID him, then flipped him on his stomach with a knee in his back. The man did not resist and was zip-tied.

Also in the room were a woman and two children. Everyone was moving slowly, coughing and covered in dust. They looked stunned, with blood coming out of their ears.

Roman didn't wait for orders but quickly checked them and zip-tied their hands.

"No one's hurt bad. No big cuts or broken bones," Roman said.

"Good. We'll leave 'em. Someone'll be here soon."

Fluff dragged their prisoner out of the panic room. Roman ran to the door, looked both ways, and said, "Nothing."

Spike stood there, unsure of what to do.

"Go help Fluff. I'll take point." Roman ran to the back door, hesitated, weapon ready, and then slipped out into the dark.

Spike took a few steps back to Fluff.

"Hold this guy a second," Fluff said.

Spike grabbed the prisoner's arm. Fluff ducked back into the smoky panic room and turned just out of sight, where the prisoner's tied family was located.

What the fuck? Spike thought he heard some muffled sounds.

Fluff came out quickly while buttoning a big side pocket on his pants. He grabbed the prisoner's arm and moved out of the room. "Cover the rear."

Spike ran to the door and into the hallway. Then he jogged up and fell in behind Fluff, who was dragging the prisoner. Spike watched their backs while looking down the hall.

Fluff started a radio call for their ride home. "Raven One, this is Romeo One. Immediate extraction at LZ Alpha."

"Romeo, this is Raven, ten minutes out."

"Roger out."

"How's he going to get here that quick?" Roman asked.

"They've been waiting in a secure zone a few miles out for our call."

They ran down the steps and into the dark, following Roman somewhere in front of them, heading for the helicopter.

Spike was hooked on this special op stuff.

∽

THE HELICOPTER SET DOWN. This ride was a much longer one than the insertion. When they got off the chopper, a black SUV was waiting. Two men took their prize—who was still wearing a black bag on his head—and they drove away. Pierre's body lay in the helicopter in a body bag.

Spike just stood there, waiting to be told what to do. He took a deep breath. He was ready to get back to the real world. He snapped the rubber band on his wrist. Funny he thought of that, but he felt more alive than he'd ever felt before. *I definitely want more of this.*

Fluff elbowed Spike on his cut arm.

"Ouch," Spike said. Then he saw why he got the nudge, as everyone stood at attention, saluting as they took Pierre's body bag off the helicopter. Spike did the best salute he could.

Fluff elbowed him again, and Spike lowered the salute.

"Show me where the cut is," Fluff said.

Spike ran his hand along his left sleeve on the top outside of his forearm.

Fluff cut Spike's sleeve, then turned his arm over and cut the duct tape on the opposite side of the stitched wound. Gently, he pulled off the tape. "Well, look at that. No blood on your bandage. Probably not even one stitch pulled. Duct tape is fuckin' magic."

"Thanks. That could have been a mess without it."

"Let's make things a lot easier," Fluff said. "Just

remember you're Buck. Do not mention your real name. We'll talk about that more when we get back to the States."

They all got debriefed. Spike told them what happened, making sure he said nothing to make him look bad. He was even commended for his bravery. *Not bad!* Someone came in and rewrapped his cut. It looked pretty good, with no infection.

~

NEW ORLEANS AREA
Monday Mid-Morning

THEY LANDED BACK IN LOUISIANA. Spike followed Fluff and Roman as they walked through their safe house to the front door. Four bags lay on the floor.

Spike zipped open his bag. "Cash?"

"Even crypto can be traced, but not cash," Fluff said.

"The fourth bag is for Pierre?" Spike asked.

"Yeah, I'll get it to his family," Fluff said.

"What if I hadn't made it?"

"Then whoever Buck wanted it to go to would have gotten the money."

"Oh ... that would have been okay, but I prefer it to be me."

Roman took his bag and shook Spike's hand. "Damn, that was crazy, Wildman."

"Wildman? Please, no more nicknames."

"Okay, Spike. You're pretty rough ... but you saved my life. For that, I owe you. Thanks. I wish you had some training. But anyway, goodbye, new friend."

Spike smiled. "Thanks for being patient with me. I hope I see you again soon."

Fluff and Roman looked at each other without comment. Roman turned to Fluff and shook his hand. "We made it again. Let me know when we have another op?"

"I will. Be safe," Fluff said.

Roman opened the door, left, and pulled the door behind him, leaving Fluff and Spike alone.

"Hey, who was that guy we snatched?" Spike asked.

"You don't wanna know," Fluff said.

"Okay, but I don't suppose you'll tell me who we were working for?"

"I don't really know. I assume it's some off-the-books secret US organization that wants to make sure whatever they do can never be put back on the US. I'm always contacted, and it's not always by the same person. It pays better than anything else I could ever do. I get to pick my own team, and I usually have only a couple of ops a year, though one year was pretty packed. You don't need to know about that."

"Damn!" Spike said. "This is incredible. Am I part of your team now? I loved it. I mean, really loved it. I'm ready to go again."

"You have no idea how lucky you got on this op. But you're fearless, and, as Roman said, you actually saved our lives. That counts for something. However, you're just a liability to us now and very dangerous."

"Yeah, I figured that." Spike nodded. His smile faded to downturned lips. *Fuck! Damn! Oh, well! Back to looking for people to fulfill my hobby.*

"But damn, you are fearless." Fluff handed Spike a card. "It's not cheap, it's not easy, and it's not quick. The guy on that card, John Wild, is an ex-Navy SEAL who can train you well enough to maybe join my team. He has a camp where he gives people the extreme SEAL experience. Tell him Fluff sent you and that you need the Fluff package."

"If I do that, you'd take me on your team?"

"Maybe, but if he clears you to me, that doesn't mean you're ready. I'll arrange for you to do some more training with me. That will determine if we let you join our team."

"Fair enough." Spike shook hands with him. "Can I get a ride to somewhere I can get a cab?"

"Where you going after you get a cab?"

"Houston," Spike said.

"I'm going to Houston and could take you, but I have a detour first. Sorry. How about New Orleans International? You can fly back or rent a car if you want to drive. Driving is probably the better option instead of trying to explain a bag full of cash to the TSA."

"The airport rental cars will work fine. I appreciate it."

"Alright, then, let's go."

They climbed into Fluff's blue Ford F-150 pickup.

"Nice ride," Spike said. But nothing compared to the ride of the last twenty-four hours. *Fluff probably isn't the only game in town, but how do you find these contract ops guys?* Spike smiled wide and did a small head shake. *I need some more of that. Feels good to be back in control.* Spike looked at the rubber band on his arm. He didn't snap it.

∽

When they arrived at the car rental, Spike thanked Fluff, who made sure he had Spike's contact information. With Buck's ID and credit cards, getting a car was pretty easy. They never seemed to look closely at the picture. Besides, there was some resemblance. Spike rented a shiny Atlantablue Mustang with thirty-three miles on it. He inhaled the leather and the newness. He'd have it for a week, and then he'd return it in Houston.

Driving alone, he was as giddy as a kid. *Feeling my freedom again.* He sped for short distances. *Feel the power!* But he never got in front of the traffic. He didn't want to get pulled over.

After Jeff Case had captured him, Case had shown Spike how he'd deleted him. Case had closed and paid off Spike's bank accounts and credit cards and had papers drawn to make it look like Spike had donated his house to charity. *Case was an asshole! But I really respect him. I expected, when I ran out of leads on serial killers, it'd end with him killing me, unless ... maybe I joined their team. That's crazy. He'd never trust me.*

Need to get back to Houston to talk to Magic. Maybe crack open my secret stash.

47

NEED A FEW THINGS

Houston, Arriving at the Motel
Sunday Night

ONCE THEY GOT some distance between them and the burning house, Detective Gray stopped at a restaurant. They couldn't discuss anything there, and when Ava tried to ask questions, he deflected.

"Let's get a room and some rest. Try to figure out the next course of action."

"We need to go to the police," Ava said.

"Please, give me a little time to think. The police department wouldn't be happy about how I rescued you guys, and it's not safe as long as the cartel sees you two as a negotiation piece for that thumb drive. The cartel may even want to kill us all in retaliation. We need to lay low."

After they left the restaurant, he pulled into a cheap motel on the edge of Houston.

"We all need to stay in the same room. It's the safest thing to do. I'll be a gentleman."

No one disagreed.

Gray pulled the heavy curtains closed. He and Ava each took a chair. Barbie turned on the TV and hopped on the first bed.

"I'll take that one. Closer to the door," he said.

"Okay," Barbie said as she jumped to the second bed.

Gray noticed Barbie seemed fine, but Ava, as ex-FBI and a PI, wouldn't let things go.

The atmosphere was serious and tense. Ava started pushing for answers.

"We need to just call 911 or maybe your partner," Ava said. "Or someone in law enforcement. I know an FBI agent in the Houston office. I'd trust him with my life. We could call him."

"Why?"

Barbie had tuned them out while clicking through the TV. She was startled when Ava jumped up and blasted Gray again. "I appreciate your saving us, but something is fuckin' off here. You'd better fess up now, or I'm going to the motel office and calling the police."

"Okay, okay! Just calm down, please. You guys are still in danger. Look, you asked how I knew where you were. I didn't want to say. I just wanted to leave my informant out of this, but that's how I knew where you guys were. I got to your condo, and it was a mess, and you were gone. Later that day, I got a call. He knew where you were located at the country house, and I saw an opportunity to free you guys."

"Okay, but why didn't you call the police instead of coming by yourself?" Ava seemed to have calmed down.

"I came alone because I was afraid if I called it in, some dirty cops would warn the cartel. I've heard there's at least one cop passing info back to them. Even if that didn't happen, I was worried SWAT might get too aggressive and get you guys killed. Ava, I haven't known you long, but I care about you—*a lot*—and, of course, your sister too."

Ava had listened intently with a scowl on her face. "It seems like a big risk for you to take. And you said you wanted to talk to Spike before we called the police. Why?"

"I'm just worried about you guys. If Spike agrees to give the thumb drive to the cartel, they'll have no more reason to want to hold or hurt the two of you."

That was when Ava surprised Gray and Barbie. "Let's call him. I memorized his burner number."

"You've known all along?" Gray asked. His heart started beating fast. He had no idea what his next move would be, but to have a chance at getting the sixteen million dollars, he needed to see Spike. *I hope Spike has the thumb drive and codes.*

"Let's just call," Ava said.

They called.

Gray was relieved when no one answered, but he didn't have a plan yet. To give himself a chance, he just had to stay in the game. *What would I do for sixteen million? Kill the girls? Kill Spike? Maybe. Could I blame it on the cartel and tie it into something about the house burning down and the bodies there? Don't know what my story would be yet.*

~

MONDAY MORNING

BARBIE WOKE UP FIRST. The heavy curtains were doing their job, as the motel room was dark. Slowly, Barbie climbed out of the bed she'd shared with her sister. The red letters of the clock showed it was eight-fifteen a.m. Her movement didn't wake Ava, and Barbie cast a look at Detective Gray in the other bed. He lay on his back with his mouth open. *Not real attractive, but he'd do. Spike's my guy for now, though.*

Barbie noticed Gray's keys, wallet, and badge on the nightstand between the two double beds. She'd seen him put his bigger pistol under his pillow, but she didn't know what he'd done with the smaller one. That question hadn't crossed her mind last night, but now she wondered. Maybe he didn't trust them. *Why? Maybe, being a cop, he doesn't trust anyone. Respect!* She had always respected the police. *Tough job. And he risked his life for us, with no backup. A real fuckin' hero.*

Careful not to wake anyone, Barbie picked up her clothes as quietly as possible, then sneaked into the bathroom and carefully shut the door. The mirror didn't lie. *God, I look bad. My hair is horrible.* She looked at her clothes, then picked them up and smelled them. She sat on the vanity chair with her lower lip stuck out. Then she found a solution. If she could sneak out, she'd run to her sister's condo. *That's stupid!* But thinking of the condo and her shoes made her recall something else.

Oh, my God! The money! She realized Spike may have hidden his money there until he came back. When Ava had given them the guest tour of her condo, Barbie had wondered why Spike seemed to be looking in all the nooks and crannies. She remembered him going back into the walk-in shoe closet under the steps from the first floor to the second. He'd even tapped the wood where it tapered off with a paneled front about two feet high. *I'll bet he pulled that wood off and nailed it back on after he put the bag of money behind it.*

Barbie's pulse quickened. She really needed to sneak out. This was a chance for her to grab the money and maybe hide it somewhere else. *All for me.*

She put on her stinky clothes and picked up Detective Gray's keys, which were on the same nightstand. Ava had told Barbie where she hid a key outside, but there was always the old lady next door, who had a key too. Barbie took slow, long steps. She didn't want to wake up Gray, who might grab his gun and start shooting if startled. She turned the handle slowly, opening the door just enough to squeeze out. Fortunately, the light that came in hit only the wall.

Once out, Barbie eased the door shut to the point just before it latched. She knew the door would make a little noise when it closed. *Click. That wasn't too bad.* She waited a few minutes to see if anyone woke up and came storming out. *Nope!*

She turned and faced the sun. *Feels good!* It felt liberating. Barbie drove out of the parking lot, knowing she'd be at Ava's condo in a few minutes. *Starbucks! Great! I forgot, no money, just keys.* A big, exaggerated frown crossed her face. *Oh, well, I can grab some juice from Ava's fridge.*

Feeling good! She was hoping to get all this solved soon. Maybe go somewhere and start over. Her life had been exciting since she'd met him. In the desert, after Spike had killed Buck and stood behind her with a gun, she'd expected to die. *Wow! I cheated death. And in the last twenty-four hours, I did it again.*

It bothered her that everything was out of her control. She wanted some control in her life. Then she turned onto the street where Ava's condo was located. As she drove, she didn't see anyone sitting in a car. *I'll be careful.* Passing Ava's condo, Barbie didn't slow down. The door was closed, with yellow police tape over it. The police tape was a surprise, but, based on what Ava had told her about the capture, she should have known it would be there. Barbie made another pass in the opposite direction.

No one. I'll hurry.

Barbie pulled into a space on the opposite side of the street. After looking both ways for cars, she ran to the side of the condo where the key was hidden. She grabbed it from a fake rock, then darted to the front door. There, she fumbled with the key, trying to get it to slide into the lock.

The roar of a car blared from the next block over. A sense of urgency gripped her gut and twisted. Finally, the key slid into the lock, but it didn't open the door. Barbie didn't want to break it off in the lock, so she slowed down and gently jiggled it. The car was getting closer. It was the only one on the street. *C'mon! C'mon! C'mon!*

The car was almost upon her.

C'mon! She kept jiggling the key.

The car pulled up in front of the condo. A man jumped out and ran right at her. The key finally turned the lock, and she pushed the door inward. In a panic, Barbie jumped into the house and tried to slam the door shut as she fought to pull out the key. It was stuck again. Then the door flew back and hit her in the face. The man must have kicked it. Dazed, Barbie was hit again in the face with something and grew even woozier. The man picked her up and carried her to the car, where she was thrown in the back. Landing on her back, she rolled onto her stomach so her face was pushed into the floor. She felt something hard against her head as the door slammed shut and the car took off.

The man's knee was in her back, and his weight was on her. He had a Hispanic accent. "Feel the gun." He poked her with it a few times. "This is a gun. Relax and you won't be hurt."

"My nose is bleeding," Barbie said. *Good thing my head's down. Fucked up again. Whatever! Damn, so stupid. Should have listened.*

"Shut up. You'll be alright," the man said.

Then she heard the driver on the phone. "Yeah, we got her. The dumb bitch came back. Can you believe it?"

There was a pause.

"*Sí*, I don't know. Okay, just a minute," he said to whoever was on the other end of the line. Then he yelled at her, "Hey, are you Ava or Barbie?"

"Barbie."

He passed the news on. She heard him say he knew where to take her.

Barbie sighed. She wasn't scared this time, just pissed. *God, please let my sister figure out how to save me again. I'll be better, I promise.*

48

WHERE YOU BEEN?

New Orleans to Houston
Monday Noon

BEFORE HE HIT THE ROAD, Spike stopped at a mall in New Orleans. There, he went on a shopping spree, picking up a MacBook and some extra stuff he'd need to enhance his security when he got online. He also bought some thumb drives. *Feels good to go shopping.* The anticipation of getting online, surfing the dark web, and engaging with people who shared his hobby was exciting. He knew right where to go and that there had to be places he hadn't discovered yet. He already had some contacts. They were just screen names, but he could flush them out. Those would be *righteous* kills for God. So many evil people were online and would die if he found them. *This feels better than killing just anyone. Kill the bad for God. I'm like a crusader.*

With his arms full, he put his purchases in the Mustang,

then headed to Houston. He was happy to be on the road. *I'm feeling really, really good.*

He had so much to think about. His mind wandered and jumped around.

Fluff. That was another first. I swore I'd kill you, but I changed my mind. I never forget a wrong done to me, and no one yells at me, but this was different.

Feels like I need to hunt. I can hunt without killing. He snapped the rubber band. *A truck stop coming up. The car is full of gas, but let's take a look. Maybe just give someone a ride.*

If not for the fact that he'd left his blue bag at Magic's, Spike wondered if he'd even go back to Houston.

Spike took the next exit. He saw two truck stops, one on either side. He'd hoped to see someone walking on the road near the entrance with a backpack. That would be perfect but no such luck, so he drove slowly around the first truck stop. *Nothing.* No obvious hitchhikers. He drove across the street and did the same thing at the other truck stop. He didn't want to waste a lot of time, but the air was hot. He'd make a quick walk-through, maybe buy a bottle of iced tea.

There she was, maybe in her twenties. Hiking boots, a shade hat, and a backpack. *Just offer a ride. Won't hurt her.* He snapped the rubber band.

"Pretty hot out there, isn't it?" Spike said with a smile, turning on the charm.

"Yes, it is."

That was all it took to lead to some small talk. She was going to Houston. He offered her a ride in his new Mustang for some conversation. Then he saw her take out her phone. He overheard her conversation.

"Hi, Mom. I know, I know. I'm being safe. I should be home in about three hours. A nice guy in a blue Mustang offered me a ride."

Then she listened.

"He seems nice. His name is Spike. His license, just a minute." The girl walked behind the car and read it to her mother.

Spike waited until she hung up. Then he took her backpack out of his car and set it on the ground. "I'm sorry, I forgot something back in New Orleans. I have to run back and get it. Be safe."

He waved and backed out.

"Fuck you, asshole." She flipped him the bird.

He smiled at her and waved again. *Shit! Oh, well, waste of time anyway. I wasn't going to hurt her, just going to give her a ride.* He snapped the rubber band on his arm. The mileage markers went by fast, and he drove well above the speed limit but always behind the traffic. Then he saw an exit that made him think of an "online hunting acquaintance." After meeting him, Spike had realized the guy was sick. *The world would be better without him.* Spike made a hard right off the interstate highway onto the exit, almost missing it.

He'd been to Bubba Smith Williams' place once, about a year ago. One visit was enough. The man liked to humiliate and torture young women. *Not my style.* Spike also remembered that Bubba seemed too careless, and Spike didn't want to get caught.

Spike didn't have Bubba's phone number. He'd never had it. They'd met on the dark web, and, after a lot of warm-up conversations, they'd met at a truck stop near Bubba's home. Bubba had gotten comfortable too quickly—carelessly, in Spike's opinion—and invited Spike to follow his pickup back to his country home. Spike had done so, not sure what to expect but very curious.

He'd brought a knife, just in case, because he didn't trust Bubba. Once at his house, Bubba shared a beer with Spike as they talked about the weather and sports. Then Bubba took Spike behind the house. They walked a hundred yards, just past the tree line and twenty feet or so into the woods, where Spike saw an old trailer sitting on blocks. After they stepped into the trailer, he saw an elaborate dungeon built into it.

"Sorry," Bubba said. "No guests right now, but I'm looking. Won't take long to find one. A few days, maybe. I go out looking every day. I'll let you know, and I do hope you'll come back."

"Sure, that would be exciting. Let me know," Spike said with a smile. *No fucking way am I coming back here!* Spike was glad there was no guest. He didn't want to see a young woman tortured. *There's no respect in how Bubba treats women.* Spike remembered Bubba had offered to tell him a secret, which he thought was odd. *This whole damn thing is a secret.*

"Oh, you told me you were going to tell me a secret. Is this it?"

Bubba leaned in so close Spike could smell his beer breath. For some reason, even though no one else was close by, Bubba whispered his response: "The trailer is rigged to explode."

"What? Really?" Spike asked. *This asshole's crazy!* "Any chance it'll accidentally explode?"

Bubba shrugged. "It shouldn't."

Spike smiled and acted as if Bubba were the greatest guy ever. He'd then promised to come back when Bubba had a guest.

Within a week, Bubba had sent him a message on the dark web. "Got a guest. Wanna come and play with me and my new friend?"

Spike hadn't answered and never expected to see the

man again. But for different reasons, the time had come to re-visit Bubba. He was a bad man, a very, very bad man. Spike was still riding high on the adrenaline of the combat mission and feeling self-confident.

I've killed many times, but I've always respected the life I took. I've killed innocents, but I didn't know any better then. I regret that now. But God's shown me a way to serve his desires and God's will. I know what I have to do. This is God's plan.

After getting off the exit at breakneck speed, Spike slowed down. He knew right where Bubba lived. *Easy to find.* Even once was enough to remember the way. Miles separated the houses out here, and Bubba's rundown two-story farmhouse was barely visible from the road. But there it was, baby-shit yellow. *How could anyone forget that?* Bubba had told Spike that the land and house had been willed to him by his parents. He made money working at a feedstore in a small town.

Spike drove up the driveway, then knocked on the door.

The door opened, and a big man filled the frame. Bubba stood there with a big smile. "I'll be damned," he said. "Spike, where have you been? It's been a while. You didn't answer me on the message board."

"I know, sorry." Spike stuck out his hand with a big smile. "Missed you, man. It's just been crazy. I've had a lot of out-of-state work, you know?"

"Sure, brother." Bubba grabbed his hand and pulled him into a bear hug. "Just good to see you."

Bubba backed off a little and waved Spike into the house. He looked over Spike's shoulder. "Damn, nice car."

"Thanks," Spike said. "It's a rental. And again, I'm sorry I didn't reach out sooner."

"No problem, really. You wanna beer? And what happened to your arm?"

"I'd love a beer. And the arm ... eh ... I cut it cooking."

"Damn!" Bubba scratched his back and set a beer on the table in front of a chair. "There you go." He fell into a chair at the head of a red metal kitchen table and took a drink. His legs were open wide because he was so big. "So, why come see me now?"

Spike took a seat where the beer sat and lifted the beverage to his lips. "Damn, that's good." He leaned forward but still held the beer. "Well, I could say I just missed you, but the truth is, I'm really sorry I never got to meet one of your guests." Spike smiled, then winked. "You know what I mean?"

"I know what you mean, but why now? Can you lift your shirt?"

"What? C'mon, man."

"You can never be too careful, and I haven't seen you in a long time."

"Fair enough." Spike stood, lifted his shirt, and turned around. "Good enough?"

"Yeah, we're all good."

As Spike spun, he saw a faded yellow wall phone in the kitchen. "Does that work?"

"What?"

"The wall phone. I didn't think anyone had a landline anymore."

"Everyone I know since I was a kid has that number, and it doesn't cost much. Of course, I've got a cell phone." He showed Spike his cell. "But I keep the house phone too."

"That's good. How about your playroom? Still have that too?"

"Yes, I do! And it's fucking great!" Bubba leaned into Spike and said softly, "I've even got a playmate right now." He winked. "Wanna see?"

Spike knew this would be an innocent girl. He snapped the rubber band. "You still let them go?"

"Usually, I do. You know, I go a long way off to find them, then keep them drugged up. When I'm done, I drop them off a long way in the other direction."

"A blonde, right?" It surprised Spike that he had no fantasy thoughts about the girl. He was now focused on how he'd kill this very bad man. It was a new type of excitement. *This man's a formidable foe. He won't go down easily.*

"Always a blonde. What can I say? I like them."

Spike was, for the first time, looking at Bubba differently. Before, Bubba had been an interesting person who Spike knew would let him watch as Bubba took a new young woman, undressed her, played with her, and defiled her, first slowly and then aggressively. Spike now dreamed of wrapping his hands around Bubba's neck and choking *him* to death. Maybe his neck was too big to strangle him. *So be it. I'll stab him until he dies or bleeds out.* To him, Bubba was a killer of the innocent.

"How long you keep them?" Spike sipped his beer.

"Oh, always at least a few weeks. Sometimes longer. I guess until I get bored."

Bubba had told Spike he'd do anything he could think of to the women, short of killing them. Unless he had to. He always tried to push them to the limit and then give them time to recover. He wanted to use them and return them. Again, Spike thought Bubba was a little reckless and cruel.

"They've never seen you?" Spike asked.

"A few times and that's too bad. Then they gotta be disposed of. I planted them outside beside the playroom. But when I snatch them, it's always from behind when they're alone somewhere outside. A quick sedative and they're out. When I get them here, I control them with chains and tie-downs. I tell them if they ever see my face, I'll have to kill them. It's not that I want to. I just don't have a choice. You understand, right?"

"Sure," Spike said, nodding. *He's fucking crazy.*

"I also leave the TV on when I'm gone to keep them happy."

How considerate. In the past, Spike hadn't been judgmental of others who felt the need to kill. *Odd how God gave me a yardstick of good and bad I don't fully understand. But Bubba is a bad man!* He snapped the rubber band.

It was a short walk out the back and into the woods. Bubba undid the locks and held the door of the small trailer to let Spike go in first. There she was, with her legs spread in stirrups like in a doctor's office and her arms tied to bedposts. A blanket was haphazardly thrown over her. She wasn't drugged. In fact, the way she jumped when they came in made her seem fully alert, even with a black sleeping mask over her eyes.

Spike stood still for a second. *Wow! Like showing a steak to a hungry lion.* He shut his eyes and felt his pulse and breathing quicken. It was a rush. The pull was strong. He snapped the rubber band again. *I want to do the right thing. I will do the right thing.*

49

WHAT TO DO?

New Orleans to Houston
Monday Noon

SPIKE OPENED HIS EYES. *God help me. Another test? Give me strength!*

"Sandy, I brought a friend," Bubba said to the young woman.

"No! No!" She started crying. "Please, whoever you are, help me get out of here."

"Funny, you showing up. I'd planned to play with Sandy this afternoon. I got her ready and covered her with a blanket to keep her warm. I treat you nice, don't I, Sandy?"

"Please. Let me go," she begged, tears streaking down her cheeks as she trembled. "Please! Please, help me!"

Bubba ignored her cries and pleas. "I get her ready while she's more pliable, you know, after a little something to relax her, but I make sure she's alert for the fun."

This wasn't how I expected to feel. No more thoughts of the girl, only of killing Bubba.

"If you want her alert," Spike asked, "what are the two syringes for? And why two?"

"One will knock her out. Then she'll start coming back loopy for an hour or more. The second one is insurance. If she somehow got out of control, the second one would kill her." Bubba jerked the blanket off Sandy. "You ready for some fun?" he asked her. "Here I come, sweetheart."

Sandy, blindfolded, jerked when the blanket was removed. Then she started pleading and crying again.

Spike had no reason to wait. He'd forced his thoughts away from the girl. Bubba was lustfully focused on Sandy, with his back to Spike. Spike stepped forward, picked up the two syringes, and jammed them both in as deep as he could, one on each side of Bubba's neck. He pushed hard and fast, expelling the drugs completely into the big man's neck.

"Ahhhhh! What the fuck!" Bubba grabbed both syringes, then jerked them out of his neck and threw them. Sandy had gone quiet. Not a sound.

Spike jumped back and out of the way, picked up a piece of chain, and wrapped it around his right hand. He was ready to deliver a blow.

"Why?" Bubba's deep brow furrowed as he slowly stood up straight, but he made no move toward Spike. His head tilted. His hands touched his face. The next "Why?" was much softer as Bubba dropped to his knees. His glazed-over eyes were no longer focused as he fell forward to the floor. His face hit hard.

Sandy broke the quiet. "What happened? What happened? Is anyone there?"

"You'll be home soon, Sandy. I'm here to help you. Just be quiet for now." Spike looked around and found a dull machete. He tried to roll Bubba over, but the man must have weighed over three hundred pounds, and there wasn't much floor space. He couldn't do it. He had planned to hack Bubba's throat until he was dead or at least crush his windpipe.

Fuck!

"What's happening?" Sandy asked.

"Be patient! Please. I promise you'll be out of here soon."

"Can you take off my blindfold?"

"No, sorry ... I don't want you to see me. Look, just relax. I promise you'll be rescued and have a hell of a story to tell people. Oh, and don't forget to mention how a nice guy saved your ass. You know what I mean." That made Spike chuckle. *I am a nice guy.*

"Will you cover me, please?"

"Sure." Spike picked up the blanket and threw it over her.

"Thanks ... and thanks for helping me."

"You're welcome," Spike said in the most pleasant, upbeat voice he could muster.

Now, how do I kill this big bastard?

Then the door flew open and red-fingernailed fingers on a right hand grabbed the side of the doorframe to pull whoever they were attached to into the trailer. Spike grabbed the chain again and held it low in his right hand at the side of the door. The woman, in her early forties, with a few extra pounds and a weathered farm face, came unglued when she saw Bubba on the floor. With her left hand, she pulled a shotgun from outside the door. "Bubba!" Then she saw Spike at the side of the door. "What happened to Bubba? And who the hell are you?" She pulled the shotgun into a shooting position. Spike's chain was already in motion with a lot of momentum halfway to her face.

The chain caught her by surprise and hit her solidly. The shotgun went off as her finger caught on the trigger, Then the gun fell to the floor. The heavy chain hitting her face sent the woman off balance and backward against some cabinets and to the floor.

The young woman screamed, as she had likely been hit by the shotgun. Her ear-piercing cries continued.

Spike went for the shotgun, landing on his stomach. He lifted himself onto his elbows, raised the gun a few inches, pumped a shell into the chamber, and pulled the trigger. The woman was trying to get up, but her face caught the full blast from only inches away. Her head disintegrated. She was a headless corpse in a red pleated skirt, sprawled on the floor. Spike sighed. *She had to be bad.* He knew he was holding a twelve-gauge, pump-action shotgun, as his dad had one and used to take Spike hunting with it. He could also tell, from the shot pattern, that it was buckshot packed into a shotgun shell and not a solid lead slug.

Now he knew what to do with Bubba. Bending over, he started to pull Bubba's phone out of his back pocket, but then he stopped. *The house phone would be better.* Straightening and looking at the shotgun, which was about a foot above Bubba's head, Spike hesitated. *Blood splatter.* Then he turned. "Sorry, Sandy, I need your blanket for a minute."

"What? I've been shot too!"

"Hang on." Spike moved next to her.

She jerked. "What are you doing?"

"Looking at your wounds." Quiet hung heavy in the air, broken only by Bubba's heavy breathing. "You'll live. One buckshot single pellet just under your skin. It's about one-third of an inch in diameter. You're lucky. The full impact hit the ceiling, or it would have caused a lot more damage. No crisis. It must have been a ricochet. When help comes, it's an easy fix. Not even bleeding. You're real lucky."

No doubt how Bubba will die now. Think! What have you touched? No doorknobs. I'll get the glass in the kitchen when I leave. The syringes. He looked around, found the two syringes, and slipped them into his pocket. *I'll take the chain and shotgun. Time to finish up.*

"I'll bet your horrible experience got weird when I showed up." Spike held the blanket between him and Bubba and pulled the trigger. This was the first time he was aware of the noise, which was deafening in the small confines of the trailer. His ears rang. Spike lowered the blanket slightly and saw what looked like a caved-in watermelon, full of bloody goop. He dropped the blanket so the side with the gore on it fell over Bubba.

"What's happening? Please, let me go!"

"Gotta go, but I'll dial 911. Someone will be here soon."

"Don't go! Please, wait for them! Cover me at least! Cover me!"

Spike stepped around the headless woman. *No blood on the floor right here.* The gunshot had thrown the woman's blood splatter behind her. The blanket he held up had contained Bubba's blood splatter to his side of the trailer. This left a clear, bloodless path for Spike. As he left, he saw two clean blankets folded on the counter to his right, on the unblemished side of the trailer. He grabbed one, took a step toward Sandy, flicked the blanket open, and watched it float and settle to cover her nakedness.

"Thank you. Please, tell them to hurry. Oh, and God bless you for saving me. I'll never forget you did this."

"You're welcome." *Hey, look at me, getting a "God bless you" again.* With his elbow, Spike pushed the unclosed door open wider so he could get out. He turned to kick the door shut so he wouldn't have to touch it, while also holding the shotgun and the chain. "You know God sent me!" he yelled at the girl with a smile. Then he kicked the door shut.

Using his shirt to turn the knob, Spike opened the back door to Bubba's house. Again, with his shirt, he lifted the phone off the hook and picked up a pencil from the counter to dial 911.

"This is 911. What is your emergency, please?"

Spike held a kitchen towel over the phone and tried to disguise his voice. "There are two dead serial killers here and a young woman being held hostage in a trailer behind the house in the woods. It might be hard to find, but she's a little frantic about being rescued, so please hurry. Oh, I think it's wired with explosives too, so tell them to be careful."

Spike dropped the phone and left it off the hook, then exited out the open back door.

When he got to his car, he opened the trunk and laid the shotgun, chain, and syringes inside it. A few miles down I-10 headed to Houston, he got off onto a side road, then took a couple of other roads until he came to a small bridge over a swamp. *No cars in sight.* He wiped down everything and threw it into the water. *Even if someone finds that stuff, no ties to me.*

50

MAGIC

Houston, TX
Monday Night

Spike enjoyed a few hours of interstate driving with no radio—just quiet time and thinking. *That was nice.* Coming in late to Houston after traffic had thinned was nice too.

Spike had a problem he'd been mulling over and that needed action and a decision. *Who could I be? Who should I be? Where should I live? Not Houston. A change of scenery will be good anyway. What should I do? Should I set a goal of killing all the bad people I can without getting caught? How many in a year? Or maybe it doesn't matter. And this special operations stuff. More missions? More training? What a rush.*

The burner phone buzzed again. He'd turned it on when he got back to Louisiana and seen he'd gotten many calls from Ava, as well as a voicemail. She was the only possible caller. He turned it off. He hadn't listened to the voicemail yet. *I don't want to talk to her now. I'm not even sure I'll see them again. Except Barbie is a problem. Not now.*

The immediate problem was: Who was he going to be?

What name should he live under? He hoped James Poole "The Magician" or "Magic" could help. Magic was waiting for him now at his house. Few people in the gray world knew Spike's real name. That took time and trust.

Spike had come to know Magic about ten years ago, when they'd met for coffee. By day, Magic was an accountant with his own practice, so he was detail-oriented. In his free time, he was an artist, a hacker, and a geek. Magic's phone number was one of the few Spike had memorized.

Since meeting Magic, Spike had been using his alternate identity, Michael Smith, which Magic had created for him and then updated every year. Magic had picked Michael Smith because it was the second most common first and last name combination in the United States. Then he'd found a Michael Smith who had died at around the age that Spike had been at the time Magic had created the new persona for Spike. Magic even made some posts on Twitter and a few other places to create a deeper background.

Spike had options. He'd been a very successful sales executive and always had a plan to carry out if his hobby of killing people were discovered. Magic had already created a whole alternate identity for him. Spike also had, in a safe deposit box, some documents as well as cash, trophies, and a thumb drive with pictures taken before Case captured him.

He needed more information, and Magic was the man to help him decide. After parking the car, Spike trotted up the steps to Magic's place.

The doorbell rang. Magic answered and offered his hand.

"Magic, great to see you. Thanks for letting me come over so late," Spike said.

"Of course. It's never too late for friends." Magic shook

his hand with a firm grip and jumped around, grinning like he'd come home to his dog after a week. "Come in, please. Can I get you a drink? A glass of wine? Anything?"

"A glass of wine would be great. Anything red if you have it."

Magic was half-bald with a comb-over. He wore a light blue polo shirt and dark blue shorts that showed his hairy legs.

"Sure. We can talk in there." Magic pointed to the living room. "I'll get a couple of glasses and open a bottle." Then he stopped. "Let me get your bag first."

"Thanks." Spike walked into the living room but didn't sit down.

Magic came back and handed the blue bag to Spike. Then he turned, left, and re-emerged with two glasses of dark red wine. "Cabernet okay?"

"Sure." Spike sipped his wine. He'd heard soft music when he entered the house, but it was a little louder here coming from surround sound. The big flat-screen TV had stunning pictures of scenery from around the world. Beside it was some audio equipment with lights blinking in sync with the music. When he glanced around, he saw modern, white leather furniture. But what attracted him most were several abstract paintings on the wall, all illuminated with art lights. "Damn, your paintings are really good. I love how they're so bright. This isn't what I'd think an accountant would paint."

"We're all complicated souls with many layers. You should have seen my paintings before my divorce two years ago." Magic frowned and shook his head as he looked at the floor. "I should have burned them, but I didn't. I just hid 'em."

"I didn't know about your divorce." *Look sincere, sad.* "Magic, I'm really sorry."

"You kidding? That was the best hundred and forty pounds I ever lost. Loved her at first, but we grew apart." He was all smiles. Then he held up his glass. "To her. May she be happy anywhere but with me." Magic took a drink of his wine.

"Yeah, I understand." Spike wasn't listening and didn't care. *Hard to change subjects and be polite sometimes.* "Do you sell your art?"

"No. Take one if you like."

Neither man had sat down.

"Really? Well, maybe I will. Thanks. I love art. I studied art as a minor in college. I used to paint. The feeling of creating art, seeing your finished work ... it's special. I think I'll take up painting again. You know, I even started writing a couple of books. I like the creation of a story too."

"I knew you were in sales but an artist and a writer too? Another Renaissance man. You still in sales?" Magic must have been ready to get down to business.

"That's a long story. But not for now. I have no job, no house, no nothing. Except I do have enough cash to make it for a while."

"Oh, that's interesting." Magic sipped his wine and then set it down. "Well, is there anything else I can do for you? You know I'm keeping your IDs up to date and a little social media, though nothing to raise any flags or label you as anything."

"Everything stays with you, right?"

"Of course. Let it rip."

Both men sat down.

"I was kidnapped about six months ago. The guy was crazy. He locked me up, sold my house, canceled all my credit cards, even sold my clothes and threw away my books. He threw away everything. He said he'd erased me. Of course, he couldn't completely make me disappear, but he sure screwed up a lot of my personal stuff."

"Oh, my God." Magic leaned forward. His stare became intense. In a lower tone, he asked, "Did he do anything to you? I mean, sexually?"

Spike laughed. "No, but the asshole was fucking crazy." *Not really crazy. More like bold and driven.* "I don't really know what he wanted." *Can't tell you he wanted me to find serial killers for him so he could kill them. You just wouldn't understand.*

"Did you go to the police?" Magic rubbed his hands together and readjusted his position—crossing his legs one way, then the other.

"I can't. He told me he'd planted some false evidence that would make me look guilty of murder if I told the police. And if I somehow got away and he found me before the police ... he'd kill me."

"Damn!"

"The guy is rich and may have friends in the police department."

Magic nodded. He chewed his lip and rubbed his hands again. "Okay, let's think about this for a second."

Spike sat back and sipped his wine.

"So, you have no police record, not even a speeding ticket. Unless you got one in the last year or so."

"Nope."

"You still have no fingerprints anywhere, right? You know, the military, the police, any licenses requiring fingerprints?"

"Nope."

"Still have your Louisiana driver's license? No fingerprints required from Louisiana?"

"Yup."

"Okay, good. So, if you want to keep using your real name, as long as you don't use your credit cards or Social Security number, you should be fine. And, of course, don't post anything on the internet."

"Besides my real name and the alternate identity that you created for me, I have another option."

"You're full of surprises. Tell me."

"I have all the identities of a man about my size, a few years younger than me, but he kind of looks like me. I mean, credit cards, driver's license, passport. I even have his computer, but I haven't dug into it yet."

"Does he have family?" Magic asked with a wrinkled forehead. He turned away to refill his wine glass and held the bottle toward Spike.

Spike held out his glass for a top-off. "I don't think so. That's what I've been told by someone who knew him well."

"And he won't pop up and claim his identity?"

"He will never pop up again. Let's just say he's kind of like a doornail if you get my drift." Spike did an exaggerated wink. In all his dealings with Magic, he'd never had to admit he'd killed someone, and he still hadn't.

"You mean dead as a doornail?" Magic asked tentatively, scrunching up his face.

"I never said that." Spike did another exaggerated wink.

"Oh. Got it. You know where the phrase comes from?" Magic paused, waiting for a response.

"Nope." *And I don't care.* Spike caught his sarcastic attitude and tried to turn it around with a big smile and a better response. "But please tell me. I love fun facts. And how do you know those kinds of things?"

"Oh, I read a lot. It's from the 1300s. When someone hit a nail all the way when securing a door hinge, the nail was very hard to retrieve. It was considered a dead nail because it could never be used again. So, dead as a doornail."

"That's very interesting. Now back to my problem. Could I—should I—use this guy's identity?"

"Well, it would take some thought and a little research. If you can just step into his life, it might be something to consider. But he may have fingerprints on file, and that could be a problem if you're ever arrested. Your prints wouldn't match his."

"Yeah, I thought of that."

Magic jumped up so quickly, he spilled his wine. "Damn, fuck it." He set down his glass and looked back at Spike. "Hey, you can be all three. Have some fun. Mix 'em up. Use a different personality for each one. A little different clothing preference ... make every day a play day."

"I never really thought of that. I'm not sure it's practical. I could fuck with Case—that's the guy who held me—and leave some breadcrumb trails for him someplace I'll never go back to. I need to give this some thought. It could be fun."

"Maybe so," Magic said.

"Maybe I set up a life around Buck, then use the other two now and then, for trips, maybe. Or I could travel as Buck, then do shit as the fake. The possibilities are endless. One other thing to consider is to see an attorney. Not my specialty, but he could probably hold property with some untraceable corporation, maybe in the Cayman Islands."

"You do have an imagination. Of course, I'll help you with anything you need." Magic still sat forward, appearing interested.

"One other thing. Do you have the contacts and resources to retrieve his pickup from Carlsbad, New Mexico, and destroy it? Crushing would be good."

"I can arrange that. Is it hot for any reason?"

"Nope, except I left it parked in a motel parking lot. It may have been towed."

"You have the details?"

"Here's all the info you need." Spike grabbed a small pad sitting on the end table and wrote down the name of the hotel and what he knew about the truck as well as Buck's driver's license information.

"Good. I'll take care of it and charge you something reasonable. I just don't know what it'll cost yet."

"I really appreciate you hanging onto my bag for me. You're the only person in the world I trust." Spike kind of meant it but said it mostly because he knew it would make Magic feel good. And maybe it would tilt the scales in his favor if Magic were ever tempted to act against him. "Well, it's been fun. I'll talk to you soon." Spike stood to leave.

A strong handshake and good eye contact were the last things Spike left Magic with as he turned at the door to leave.

51

TWO BAGS

Houston, TX
Monday Late Night

SPIKE HAD LEFT Magic's house in the Heights of Houston, inside the inner loop, about thirty minutes earlier. With his black ops payoff, he had two bags of money in the trunk. *That's a lot of cash.*

By now, it was dark except for the streetlights. He'd gotten a cheap motel room for cash before entering Houston under a fake name. He didn't even need an ID. His plan had been to see Magic, then go back and spend the night in his motel room. Tomorrow, he'd swing by Ava's and see if Barbie was up for moving to a different city with him. Maybe he'd circle back for Ava someday, but for now, he needed to keep Barbie close. She knew too much. He thought she'd go with him. *Can't leave her here, and I don't want to kill an innocent. If she is, in fact, an innocent. That's not for sure. Anyway, I couldn't do it here, now, and get away with it.*

He snapped the rubber band on his wrist three times in rapid succession.

If she didn't want to go with him, that would complicate things.

He was starting to feel he had less freedom than when he'd climbed out of the tunnel. *Barbie saw me kill Buck, and, oddly, she enjoyed it. Should've put her in that hole with him.*

He shook his head, then smiled. *Don't mention a move to her. Just a fun trip. She'll do that. We get out of Houston, maybe go camping in some remote area. Colorado, Montana, Wyoming.* The smile widened. *Yeah, why not? I'm not on a schedule. I like that. Camping. Need to learn how to do that. It'll be fun.*

His burner rang. *Ava's number again.* He put on a fake smile. *Always be smiling.*

"Hello, Ava." Spike gave her his upbeat, happy voice. "Sorry, I've been indisposed. You guys doin' okay?"

"Spike," said a man with an accent. "It's so good to talk to you again. You've been a hard man to find."

"I guess this isn't Ava, is it?"

"What gave it away? The accent or the deeper voice?"

"I'm guessing this is Rico, my old buddy from south of the border?"

"Good guess, but no. This is Dante. I speak for Rico."

"I suppose you want your bag of cash back. I didn't really steal it. Rosa gave it to me." *A lie.* "I'm surprised you're trying so hard to get it back. It's just three hundred thousand dollars or so. Won't break the bank, will it?"

"Rico said you can keep the cash." Dante was quiet for a few moments. "What else did you find in the bag?"

"Nothing. I mean, except a Glock 40."

"You sure?"

"What are you looking for?" Spike was perplexed and intrigued.

"You have a thumb drive that was in the blue bag. I'd like it back. A simple swap. You get Barbie back unharmed. Well, she has a bloody nose but no serious damage. I get our thumb drive back."

"Barbie? What are you talking about? She's with her sister."

"You mean her sister Ava Gunn? No, she *was* with her sister, but I have her now."

Spike started laughing, then caught himself. "Sorry, it's just that you have a mistaken idea about how much I care about her. What's on the thumb drive anyway?"

"You aren't worried about Barbie? You know I'm very serious. I have no qualms about torturing her, giving her to my men, or even killing her."

"Hey, you do what you gotta do but answer my question. What's on this thumb drive?"

"It's just accounting stuff, but it will take a lot of time for us to reconstruct. We just need it—"

"Bullshit!" Spike cut him off. He felt emboldened. In his mind, he had all the cards. "You shot at me, chased me down, and kidnapped someone you *think* I care about—it's more than some files. Tell me the truth, or I'll disappear, and you can keep Barbie."

The silence screamed for someone to say something. Spike's experience as a very high-end salesman in his previous life had taught him that the first one to talk would lose. He'd wait all day if he had to, but he knew Dante would be the first to talk.

Dante started with a big sigh, then spit out his words. "You must be *crazy*. You know who you're fucking with, right?"

"Yeah, yeah. You'll kill everyone I know. Just tell me the truth. What's on the drive?"

DANTE HATED THIS PRICK, showing him no respect. When this was all over, he'd find and kill Spike. However, he felt he had to tell Spike about some of the money on the drive, for credibility. Plus, Spike was already getting the three hundred and fifty thousand dollars in cash in the bag.

"Okay, all the accounting stuff was true, but there's also about a million dollars in bitcoin," Dante answered. "But it doesn't matter. It's of no use to you. You need a secret code to access the money, and it's impossible to hack."

Nothing is impossible to hack, right? There has to be more than a million too. Magic might know someone.

"You do have it, right?" Dante asked. "It's not very big, and it's in the blue bag."

"I haven't seen it. I'm driving. Wait a minute, I'll pull over and check." Spike pulled to the side of the street. He got out and popped the trunk. Then he unzipped the blue bag and searched in the corners. *Nothing! Nothing! Nothing!* In the last corner of the bag, he felt something. *I'll be damned.* He knew he had it before he pulled it out to look. *Bingo!* Then he looked at it more closely. *Bingo again!* Just a small black thumb drive. *Fuckin' A. A million dollars. Plus millions more, I'll bet. Wonder how much?* He picked the phone back up and took a breath. "Dante, I thought it was in the truck, but I left the bag I brought from Mexico at the hotel on the floor. I never looked closely in the corners. I just took the cash out and put it into a smaller bag. And I just checked the smaller bag. I thought maybe I moved it without noticing, but it wasn't there. You want me to go check the blue bag?"

There was a long pause from Dante. Spike sat by the side of the road. This was an intense moment, so the driving could wait. He'd wait as long as necessary for Dante to answer. He knew Dante was thinking, and Spike was giving him space.

After what seemed like a long time, Dante sighed, then spoke deliberately, with some anger. "When will you be back to your motel and be able to check the bag for the thumb drive?"

"Yeah, I'm not sure," Spike said as nonchalantly as he could. "But I'll call you as soon as I know."

"Don't fuck with me! Do it now!" Dante screamed. "You know I have Barbie, and it could be very bad for her."

"Hey, I have no doubt you're a badass guy. And you guys don't play. But I guess I really don't know if you got her or not, do I? Or maybe you did take her, and she's already dead."

Dante spoke slowly, probably not used to disrespect. "You're playing a dangerous game, my friend." He had calmed down, likely seeing he could accomplish nothing by shouting. "I'll go get her."

Spike hadn't expected any of this. Then her voice came on the phone. "Spike! Spike! It's Barbie. I'm scared. Please, help me." She sounded pitiful.

Always be smiling. Nobody could see his smile, but that was what he always thought when he didn't have any real feelings about a situation. Spike didn't love Barbie. He didn't love anyone. *But she saw me kill Buck. And she's fun, sort of.*

"Barbie, don't worry. Are you okay?" Spike asked.

"Yes."

"Don't worry. I'll save you," Spike said in an upbeat and confident tone. *Why did I say "save"? It did feel good when I got all the thanks for saving that old man from choking. But no money was involved.*

Spike was still thinking when Dante came back on the phone. "How long will it take to get to your motel?"

"Three to four hours," Spike lied, only five minutes away.

"Three to four hours? Seriously? Where are you, in Dallas? You could piss me off enough that I just kill her and go back to Mexico."

Again, Spike said nothing, just waited for a reply. He knew if Dante wanted to kill Barbie, she'd be dead already.

Dante's voice became friendlier. "Okay, Spike. Three hours. But if you don't call me on this number within the next three hours, maybe I start cutting body parts off her. If we finally kill her, we'll find you and kill you and everyone you know too. You'll always be looking over your shoulder. We have a big reach. Do you understand, my friend?"

"Sure, that's a deal," Spike said cheerfully. "Talk to you later." Spike hung up. *Control! Feels good.* He wondered if Dante felt that was abrupt. *I hope so, and I hope if he kills someone, it's Barbie. Then that problem would be solved.*

He glanced in the rearview mirror. *No hurry. Five minutes to the hotel. I'll bet Dante hates not having any control.* "Yeah, we're having fun now," Spike yelled to himself, not completely sure he meant it.

He held up the thumb drive and rolled it between the fingers on his right hand. In his best impersonation of Gollum from *The Lord of the Rings*, he said, "My precious. Yes. My precious."

I wonder how much money is on this thing. And how can I keep it?

Ten minutes later, Spike picked up a six-pack of beer

and walked into his motel room with his bags and the thumb drive. *Maybe I have some options.*

Spike had to think about what he wanted to do. He opened a can of beer, sipped it, and then turned the TV onto the news channel before flopping down in a cushy chair. *No rush.*

He set down the beer and put both hands on top of his head. He knew the easy thing to do.

He sighed, stood, and paced the room. *How do I keep from getting killed if I trade anything for the woman? If I trade for her, maybe I can get a finder's fee ... if I don't die.*

He shook his head, stopped by his beer, picked it up, took a big drink, crushed the can, and made a jump shot at the small trashcan in the bathroom.

But she's with a bunch of crooks. The fuckin' cartel. What if they get caught? What if she tells the cops I killed Buck?

"Fuck!"

He knew he could just leave. Go to California, Florida, or perhaps Montana. *Who knows? Maybe just get my ass out of here. Maybe Seattle.* He took the thumb drive out of his pocket, then grabbed another beer and snapped it open. He studied the thumb drive as he sipped. Spike shut his eyes, holding the beer in his mouth. The taste was cold, familiar. Slowly, he opened his eyes and held up the drive in his hand.

Wonder how much money is on this.

Then he called Fluff.

52

IS IT POSSIBLE?

Houston, TX
Monday Late Night

Spike was comfortable in the chair. He muted the TV and put his phone on speaker.

Two rings and Fluff picked up. "Yeah."

"Fluff, this is Spike."

"Spike. Damn, did you forget something? I didn't expect to hear from you already. Oh, maybe you got lost driving to Houston?"

Spike chuckled lightly. "No, I made it alright. But I was hoping you could help me."

"What'dya need?"

"I have a friend who has been kidnapped. They let me talk to her. She sounded alright. They're holding her and threatening to do bad things to her and eventually kill her if I don't give them a thumb drive with some bitcoin on it they think I have."

"What?" Fluff barked, then laughed. "Someone is kidnapped? Bitcoin? You have something that someone else wants." He laughed some more. "What the fuck? You drunk or pranking me?"

Fluff's laugh was infectious. Spike was half-laughing just because of Fluff. "Hey! I'm serious."

Fluff's laughter trailed off. "Okay, who are we talking about? Who are the kidnappers? And who's your friend? Just tell me what's going on. I'll help if I can, brother. We've been in the shit together, and that counts for something, even though you ain't too good. Yet."

Spike was deciding which question to answer first and where to start.

Fluff continued, "And what's this about some bitcoin? Have you looked at it? How much is it worth? And whose is it?"

"I'll answer all your questions, but first, do you know anyone who could hack this bitcoin?"

"I don't think they're hackable. Find a computer and plug it in, then tell me what the public number is. I can tell you how much is on it."

"Okay, stay on the line. I'll go see if they'll let me use their computer at the office." Spike had a new computer in the box in his car, but he didn't know how long it would take for him to set it up. He walked out the door, then saw a young man sitting by the pool, working on his computer.

"Excuse me. May I use your computer just a second for a hundred dollars?" Spike waved the bill around. "I need to open the file on this thumb drive."

"Okay. Just for a minute, right?" The young man handed his laptop to Spike as he took the hundred-dollar bill. He sat beside Spike on a lounge chair and nervously hovered.

Spike opened the thumb drive. He was still on the phone

with Fluff. "It's a Word doc with two numbers on it. One is called a public key, and the other is a private key."

"Holy shit," Fluff said. "You got all you need to cash out. Just a minute ... okay. I can tell you how much is in it. Just slowly read me the public key number."

Spike read the number.

"At the last closing, it's worth ... $16,351,556."

"What! Sixteen million dollars!" Spike yelled. "Oh, my God, that's a lot of money. Wait a minute. Let me go back to my room." Spike handed the computer back to the young man and double-checked to make sure nothing was saved to the laptop. He'd just opened and closed the file. "Thanks."

"You're crazy, man," the boy said.

"You don't know how right you are," Spike replied, still holding the phone. He made some crazy sounds for fun before jogging back to his room. There, he got a cold beer. "Fluff, you still there?"

"Still here."

"Good. Sorry, I forgot you were on the phone." Spike explained the rest of the story and tried to answer all of Fluff's questions.

"Are you really thinking of fuckin' over a cartel, stealing their money, and still somehow getting this Barbie back?"

"Yeah. Can we do that?"

"The cartel? Shit. That's a whole different thing. Which cartel is it? Not that it matters."

"The Zorro cartel, but it has new leadership." Spike couldn't stop thinking about the money.

"Jesus Christ. You know, when you first asked, I thought you wanted help moving furniture or something. But rescuing your girlfriend while stealing money from the fuckin' cartel? That may be too much."

"She's not my girlfriend."

"Yeah, whatever. Trading the bitcoin for her ... there's at least a chance we could do that. But it seems like you and I are too early in our relationship for that kind of ask. Don't you think?"

"If we figure out a way to keep the bitcoin on the thumb drive and save Barbie, I'll split it with you."

Spike could hear Fluff's breathing, but it took a moment before he spoke. "It has to be a three-way split. We need Roman. If he agrees, I know he'll be in for five mil."

"I can live with five million dollars and change," Spike said. "I don't think I have the necessary skills to do the trade by myself and not get killed. I'm open to ideas. Will you help me?"

"I'll help you save the woman, but I don't want to walk away empty-handed. I'll be honest, I'm a little worried about stealing from the cartel. Besides, that money won't be easy to cash. I mean, you need to find a buyer or use a broker. A broker will make you fill out a lot of paperwork and require some proof of who you are to prevent money laundering. Plus, you lose those numbers or type one in wrong, and the money is gone, or if somebody gets them from you, they can get the money. The bottom line is, you'll die if you fuck over the cartel and they find out. They won't let that much money go without payback. Again, you'll die, and it doesn't sound like you care, but your friends and family might die too."

"I don't have any friends or family," Spike said. "So, that's not a problem." He chewed his lip and sipped his beer. *Damn! I got about eight hundred thousand cash between the job with Fluff and the blue bag. What's another five million? A lot. I'll figure out a way.*

"What if I or Roman have people we care about and don't want dead?" Fluff asked.

"Relax. This part is my world. I'll find a way to smile at them while keeping the money, and they won't come after us. Trust me."

"Fine."

"So, you need to concentrate on saving Barbie. What do we do now? Oh, and I have to get back to the cartel guy, Dante, in about three hours. Otherwise, he'll start fucking her up."

"Get back to Dante and tell him what?"

"I'm not sure. What should I say? He doesn't know if I have the thumb drive or not. And he acted like he didn't know if I had the private key and could cash it out. I need to call and tell him I got it and then arrange for an exchange. Either they don't know I can cash it out or they're trying to bluff me into thinking I can't."

"Good. Let them sweat a little. I'll pick the place, make a plan, and get Roman started. Sit tight."

Spike sat there thinking about the sixteen million dollars. He got his new computer, still in the box, out of his rental car. After setting it up, he copied the two bitcoin keys off the thumb drive. He'd trade the thumb drive for Barbie, maybe, but he wanted options. He also picked up two empty drives and labeled them with tape, "sixteen million." *How do I get that money and stay alive?*

He called Magic and explained in detail what was going on. "Any ideas?"

"I can easily split the money," Magic said. "I'll just put it on three separate thumbs or send the new amounts through secured email to wherever you want. You know, the value fluctuates every day all the time, like stock. How many coins do you have?"

"I think it was nine hundred."

"That's what we'll split up." Magic went on to give Spike a few ideas.

"I like it. If we pull this off, keep ten percent for yourself."

"That seems fair. Oh, I took care of that pickup too. If it hasn't been crushed yet, it will be within the next day."

"Great. I'll be calling you back soon."

53

NO PROMISES

Houston, TX
Monday Late Night

SPIKE'S PHONE RANG. He thought it was Dante again but saw it was a different number. It had been calling at least every hour since earlier in the day. *Who the hell is that?* "Hello?"

"Spike! Thank God. It's Ava."

"Ava, what the hell's going on? Dante has the phone I gave you, and he said he's got Barbie."

"We assumed they got her. Now we know for sure. She snuck out this morning, took our car, and never came back. We grabbed an Uber and found our car at my condo without her. My house keys were still wedged in the front door. Damn, a lot has happened since you left. You have the thumb drive he wants, right?"

"Yeah, I have it," Spike said. "Tell me what you know."

"Not much. Dante kidnapped Barbie and me at different times. He wants that thumb drive back with the sixteen million dollars on it. We got away, rescued actually, but then they just grabbed Barbie again. That's all I know. Oh, the man who saved us—his name is Gray—is with me. It was a hell of a rescue too, involving a shootout between him and some of Dante's men."

"Are the police involved?"

"No, not as far as I know."

"And how'd you get away again?"

Ava explained in more detail how Gray had followed and saved them. Now they were waiting to talk to Spike before they did anything else. "We haven't even told the police Barbie and I got free and that she's recaptured. We weren't sure if getting the police involved would hinder your trading the thumb drive for Barbie."

"I get it."

"Gray is concerned it would put us at risk," Ava said. "There could be cops on the cartel's payroll. Plus, I guess the money puts a potential target on many people's backs."

Spike waited a few seconds, then said, "Dante, the cartel guy, has talked to me. He doesn't know if I have the thumb drive or not, but he thinks I might. I have a couple of hours before I have to call him. Can I reach you on this number?"

"Yes, it's Gray's cell. You want to talk to him?"

"No. Where are you guys?" Spike wasn't sure what to do yet.

"A motel on the south side of Houston."

"Let me think about this. I'll call you back soon. One way or the other, this will be over soon." *If Barbie were safe or silenced, I could just leave with the money. But I'd still be looking over my shoulder.*

"Wait!" she yelled.

"What?"

"I want to be involved in getting Barbie back. You know I have skills."

"No promises. But I'll call you back before I do anything."

"Please, let me help," Ava said. There was a long pause, then she added, "I'll wait for your call."

"Wait!" Spike yelled before she hung up. "Okay, we could use the help, I guess, or the backup. Start driving this way. I'm maybe thirty minutes away." He gave her the motel address.

"On the way. And thanks." She hung up.

54

MOTEL MEET

Houston, TX
Monday Late Night

SPIKE FELT A NERVOUS ENERGY. He was wired, spring-loaded for action, ready to be Rambo again, like he was with Fluff. This was the feeling he used to get before a football game, when he couldn't wait for that first violent hit. It was so different from when he found an unsuspecting person to stalk and kill.

He was now deep in things he never would have expected to be involved in. He could quietly get in the car and drive off with sixteen million dollars. But the cartel would try to find and kill him, and he needed to save Barbie to make sure she didn't talk. *It's so fuckin' exciting!*

The operation he'd been on with Fluff had been unbelievably exhilarating.

Spike paced the small motel room, waiting for Fluff or Ava to show up. It was getting late, so he figured Fluff would recommend tomorrow. That would give them more time to get ready.

He had picked up his phone to call Fluff when he heard a knock at his door.

He opened it, expecting Ava.

It was Fluff. "Let's talk this out." He walked right past Spike, then turned to face him. "After we chat and agree, you need to call Dante. After that, you tell him where we're meeting and when. Then we need to take off as soon as possible."

"What if he doesn't agree?"

Fluff wrinkled his forehead. "I thought you didn't care about Barbie, right?"

Another knock sounded on the door. Fluff jumped, then went into a crouch as, in one fluid motion, he pulled out a Sig and aimed it at the door. "Who the fuck is that?"

Spike peeked out the curtain. "It's a friend, Barbie's sister. Relax. Put the gun away."

"You're shitting me. You didn't tell me she was coming."

Spike raised his eyebrows and shrugged as he yelled at the door, "Coming!" Then he looked at Fluff. "Relax."

Spike turned the knob and pulled the door open. Ava and a man in a suit stepped around him.

"I'm out of here," said Fluff and the man in unison. Both took a step toward the door.

Spike stepped in front of the suited man, who was closest to the door, and held his hands up with his palms facing the man and Fluff. "Gentlemen, please. Just a minute. Everyone's here. Let's just talk a minute. No harm done. Right?"

Fluff was deeper in the room and stopped, though he kept an eye on the man with Ava.

The man got into Spike's face and, in what he must have

thought was an intimidating growl, said, "Get out of my way."

Spike didn't move. Instead, he smiled. In as nice a voice as he could muster, and with a quizzical air, he asked, "And who are you?" *Wonder if that pisses him off.*

Ava put a hand on the man's shoulder. "Gray, please. Just relax and hear him out." She took the man's hand. "Sit here on the bed with me? Okay?"

Gray stared Spike down, and his mouth was set in a deep frown, but he kept it shut and let Ava lead him back a couple of steps. They sat on the bed. She continued to hold his hand.

Fluff took a chair in the back of the room and waited for Spike to talk.

"So, you're Gray," Spike said. "*Why* are you here?" Out of the corner of his eye, he saw Fluff sit back in his chair, cross his arms, and shake his head. Apparently, Fluff wanted to hear the answer to that question too.

"I know Ava and Barbie and just want to help," Gray said.

"But why? Don't you wonder why we haven't called the cops?" Spike asked.

"I figure you're afraid she'll get hurt and that just doing a trade for her is the safest thing."

"I assume you're up to speed with what's going on?"

"You plan to trade a thumb drive with some bitcoin on it for Barbie."

"Yeah, that's it. To get her back, we may do some things the police would frown upon."

"Look, I'm all in to help get her back."

"And what do you do for a living?"

"Personal security and I'm armed," Gray said.

"You know this guy personally?" Spike asked Ava.

Ava answered without hesitation. "Yes. I'll vouch for him." She knew Gray had lied about his job, but she also remembered he wanted to keep the police out of it, as he was concerned about dirty cops. She really wasn't sure what was up, but she played along with Gray. She was concerned she'd gotten herself too deep into this with too many people. But it was her sister.

"And who's Ava?" Fluff asked.

Ava answered. "I'm Barbie's sister, former FBI, and currently a PI. And to respond before you ask, I'll do what I have to do to get my sister back, and I'll never tell." She paused. "And I'm going to need a weapon."

She planned to watch everything carefully. Ava was wholly committed to getting her sister back but not so much to this group of strangers.

***

Spike asked Fluff, "We gonna have a gun for her?"

"We'll have plenty of weapons," Fluff said. "You both know how to use an AR-15?" He posed the question to Gray and Ava.

They nodded.

"Okay, good." Fluff stood and spoke as he walked to and opened the door. "Spike, I need to talk to you outside for a second."

Spike stepped out. Fluff got close and whispered angrily, "I didn't agree to extra help, and there's no more splitting."

"No one knows about our deal. Just you, me, and Roman."

Fluff glared at Spike, almost nose to nose. "They listen to you and me, and just know they could become collateral damage."

"I can live with that." Spike nodded.

"Okay, then."

They stepped back into the room.

"Sorry." Spike looked at Ava and Gray. "Fluff wanted to make sure it was okay for his friend to help us. I agreed."

"Time to call Dante," Fluff said. "Spike, tell him you have the thumb drive. The meeting will be at nine a.m. tomorrow, and you'll call with the address in the morning. Don't negotiate at all. If he argues, ignore him. Tell him to take it or leave it. You've looked at the thumb drive and know you can cash it out if you want. Tell him you just want a clean trade. No trouble, no drama. If he argues, hang up."

Spike took the burner out of his pocket.

"Wait!" Ava jumped up. "What if he argues about the location and time? They might hurt Barbie."

"It's Fluff's call," Spike said. "He has a lot of experience with this kind of thing. That's why he's here."

"Bullshit! It's my sister's life. When you talk to him, you may need to give him something, depending on how it goes. And what're your qualifications?"

"Spike asked me for help. This is not a fuckin' democracy. Spike brought me in to coordinate and run this—"

"So what?" Ava screamed.

Fluff didn't respond. He looked at Spike.

"Fluff is running this. Ava, you and your friend are welcome to leave. If you stay and go with us, you will do what Fluff tells you. Do you both understand?"

Ava grit her teeth so hard, the others in the room could see the muscles in her jaw. Gray seemed indifferent.

"Fine!" Ava said. "Make the call!"

As Spike was about to press send, Fluff said to Ava, "Keep your mouth shut. No noise in the background." Spike saw her face was red, and she was breathing hard, but she nodded.

Spike put it on speakerphone.

"Spike, an hour and a half early. Good. Did you find it?" Dante asked.

"Yup, I got it."

"Good. Let's meet in an hour at—"

Spike cut Dante off. "Hey, hey, just a minute. If you don't mind, it's getting late. Let's meet tomorrow, about nine a.m."

"What? No! We do it tonight!"

"I'll call you in the morning. Have a good night." Spike hung up.

"What'd you do that for?" Ava screamed. "Jesus."

"Relax," Fluff said as he laughed. "That was great. Perfect."

"Give me the phone." Ava yanked it out of Spike's hand.

Spike grabbed her hand, the one that was holding the phone, and squeezed hard. The phone started to ring, and he smiled. "See?"

Ava winced as Spike reached with his other hand and took the ringing phone out of hers. He let it ring again. Then he answered, putting it on speaker.

"Yes, Dante," Spike said in a friendly voice.

"You know we can hurt her."

"Do what you want, but I could just take the sixteen million and never show up. That secret code you mentioned, I guess you knew it's on the thumb drive too. So, be nice to me and no discussion. I'll call you tomorrow at nine a.m. If I get Barbie, you get your money. Can we play nice?"

"Sure, see you tomorrow." Dante hung up.

"Let's go," Fluff said.

Fluff went out the door with Ava and Gray behind him.

Spike waited behind until they'd all climbed into a black Yukon. "Fluff, come here just a second."

Fluff walked back to Spike. They were out of hearing range of the other two.

"Should we be taking them?" Spike asked.

"Might need them. If they get killed in the action, you don't really care, do you?"

"I kind of like Ava, but she's a little bitchy. I guess the only two people I really care about are you and me." He smiled.

"Then why don't we just split the money and not do all of this?"

"Did you forget it's the *cartel*, and they'll come after *us*? Plus, I need Barbie back. Trust me, we'll have our cake and eat it too."

55

THE FACTORY

Outside of Houston
Tuesday Early Morning

Spike looked at his watch. It was three a.m. and very dark, with some stars. They were well outside of Houston, to the northeast, and had pulled off a two-lane state highway. Now they were traveling down a gravel road. The scenery opened up, and they saw big metal buildings with an open graveled area where trucks could turn around or park.

"These were warehouses for a manufacturing company that made parts and machinery for the oil business. Long ago abandoned," Fluff said.

"The way we came in is the only entrance?" Spike asked.

"Yeah, for a vehicle. We're backed up to some woods and marsh area. Someone could approach with an ATV or on foot, but it wouldn't be easy. That's why we don't give them a lot of time. If we call them at seven-thirty, they should make it without a lot of time left."

"Good." Spike nodded.

This had the feel of his unbelievable and exciting mission to South America. On that excursion, he'd learned that Fluff was a former Army Special Forces officer. Given that, Spike wasn't surprised at his ability to take charge. But he was surprised Fluff had probably murdered the wife and children of the target. This didn't upset Spike so much, as it allowed him to classify Fluff as a bad man if he ever decided to kill him. But for now, Fluff was an asset and a window into another world.

Fluff wore a small smile. "When they come in, they'll have to do it the same way we did. We'll be ready." He drove behind the biggest building to a smaller, rectangular metal building about the size of a comfortable house.

"How are we going to get ready?" Ava asked.

"Be patient. Roman's waiting for us. He has everything we need," Fluff said.

He pulled up as the door ascended. Roman pushed it up, revealing that the SUV was already parked. Fluff drove his SUV forward, making sure to straddle the grease pit.

"This had to be a repair facility for the vehicles the plant used. We use it when we train here. It's exactly what we need to stage out of. That's why it looks lived in."

Roman walked back to Fluff, who shook his hand and asked, "Got everything, brother?"

"I got it all laid out for us."

"Go say hi to the new guys," Fluff said.

Roman walked to the front of the SUV and shook Spike's hand. "I'm not sure I expected to see you again, *ever*, and definitely not so soon."

"As you know, I had something come up. I can't thank you enough for helping."

"No problem, we owed you," Roman told Spike. He

turned to Ava. "Hi, my name's Roman. We'll get your sister back, don't worry."

"Thanks. I appreciate what you guys are doing," Ava said.

"Me too." Gray reached around her and shook Roman's hand. "My name's Gray."

"Over here, please," Fluff said to everyone. He stood by an undetailed mockup of the buildings and the area. Everything was represented by different-sized wooden blocks.

Spike walked over and stood beside Fluff. Everyone else moved toward a repurposed ping pong table. Spike looked around at the old, cleaned-up garage. It felt more like a big clubhouse, with a refrigerator, a stove, some cabinets, a couch, and other beat-up furniture, including a dartboard. He could hear the two window A/C units straining to keep the interior cool.

Fluff picked up a pointer and held it as if he were General Patton. "First, the general plan, then make sure you two can use the weapons. We'll try to get this done in an hour or less. Then we all get some shuteye. We have sleeping bags. If we can go to sleep by about four or sooner and get up at six-thirty, we'll get at least two and a half hours. Not much, but better than nothing."

As Fluff talked, Spike looked at everyone. They all seemed to be paying attention.

With his pointer, Fluff showed where their SUV would be parked: in the open area, not far from the large building behind them. Then he said to Spike, "Being close to the building won't let them park behind or even beside you. It will force Dante to park in front of your vehicle with just open ground behind them. You can sit in the SUV until they drive up." Fluff pointed to two locations to the right and left of the SUV at either end of the building and higher.

"Roman will be here, and I'll be there, with sniper rifles. We'll have them in an interlocking fire, and the sun will be to our backs. From this distance, we don't miss often. Ava, you'll be behind Spike in the building but high. Your job is to give him direct cover if he needs it. Gray, you'll be in this building that'll be behind them once they pull in. If the shit hits the fan, the only cover they'll have is behind their vehicle, but from your position, they'll be totally exposed. In summary, Dante and his men will have virtually nowhere to hide."

56

GRID COORDINATES

Houston, TX
Tuesday Morning

DANTE WAS SO angry over how Spike was treating him, he decided that, after he got the thumb drive and verified the money was there, he'd kill Spike, Barbie, and anyone else whom Spike might have brought along. If Spike had been respectful, they could have met at a Starbucks. *Fuckin' idiot.* Besides, in trying to get back this thumb drive, he'd lost five people. *That deserves payback.*

The burner phone buzzed as Dante received a text with a set of GPS coordinates and a time, nine a.m. He looked at his watch. It was seven-thirty. He put the coordinates in his phone. It said it would take sixty-three minutes. He did some checking on the coordinates and saw it was an old steel factory. *Fuck! This isn't good. What's he planning?*

"You ever been to this place?" Dante showed his phone to his new number two.

"No, sir."

"How many men do we have?" He thought Spike must be planning to rescue Barbie and keep the thumb drive.

"Seven and you with three vehicles. Everyone's here and armed."

Dante put the GPS coordinates into Google Maps on a computer with a bigger screen so they could see it better. "Everyone, come here. We're going after a guy named Spike. He has something of ours. The woman we have is supposed to be for a trade, but I don't trust him. I'm going in the front along with one other vehicle. I want you…" He looked at one of his men. "What's your name?"

"Tomas, sir."

"Tomas, take two men who are in good shape and can run. I want you to leave right now, as soon as you pick up your two men. Then haul ass to this location, get as close as you can in the SUV, park it, and run so you're coming in from the back. Do you understand what 'run' means?"

"Yes, sir."

"Text me when you park and then when you get to the back of the building. Take pistols and extra magazines. It'll be easier to run. Be very careful. I think this is a trap, but I don't think they'll expect you to come from the back. You gotta be there by nine. This is very important, Tomas." Dante took him by the shoulders and looked him in the eyes. "I'm depending on you."

"We'll be there, boss."

Dante nodded. "I know you will. Go."

Tomas took off and pointed to two guys, who fell in behind him. Dante assumed he knew them. They were out the door within seconds.

Tomas may have some promise.

Houston had a lot of losses at mid-level management.

Dante was from El Paso and didn't know many men in Houston. Most had been killed in the last few days. He turned to the only man he knew, Alex, who'd been with the Zorro cartel for about a year. Dante had met him once on a trip to Houston.

"Alex, is the woman in my SUV?"

"Yes, sir, already zip-tied and bagged in the cargo area behind the middle seats."

"Good. You ride with me. The rest of you, follow us." Dante got into the passenger's seat and glanced back to see Barbie on her side in the far back. The driver got in, and Alex slipped into the seat behind the driver. The other two men were in the SUV following Dante. Everyone was armed and ready.

~

Tomas was excited to prove himself. He had the driver go as fast as they could without getting pulled over. They got as close to the back side of the abandoned manufacturing plant as they felt comfortable doing, then pulled off the road. The ground was soft where they parked behind some brush. They saw a stretch of wilderness between them and where they had to go.

He texted Dante: **We're here and running. Should make it easily.**

He got a short reply: **Good. Text me when at the building. NRN**

He glanced at his watch. "We've got about thirty minutes. We should make it." They couldn't see the building because of the brush obscuring it. Tomas took out his phone and looked at the building's location again based on the

GPS coordinates Dante had given him. He knew where to go and started running. "Come on."

The three men dashed through wispy grass about eighteen inches high, but they could see trees and thicker brush ahead. After about a hundred yards, they were about to enter a denser area.

"Wait, wait!" his two men said from behind.

Tomas turned and saw both bent over with their hands on their knees.

"Winded already? C'mon, let's go!" Tomas said. He was suddenly worried they wouldn't make it in time. If he had to leave them, he would.

"Just a second," one man said as he gulped air.

"We have to keep moving," Tomas said. "The boss will have our asses if we aren't there. If you can't run, then walk as fast as you can. I think we can still make it there in time." He turned and took off at a jog.

The other men followed, but sometimes they'd go just one step at a time as the brush grabbed their feet, occasionally causing them to fall. Tomas was still constantly stopping and encouraging his men. Their hands were scratched up, their pants were covered in weedy stickers, and their shoes were muddy. It had been fifteen minutes, and they weren't even halfway. He knew what he had to do.

He took a few steps back to face his men. "We're going too slow. We aren't going to make it. Keep going, follow your phone. I'm taking off. When you get there, you know our guys, but everyone else is a target." He looked at them. With ninety-five-degree weather and humidity, their clothes were wet from sweat, and perspiration ran off their faces. He knew he must look just as bad. "Look for me, but use common sense. Good luck!"

I'll make it. Tomas took off at breakneck speed.

He stumbled into a tree and got a cut on the forehead. He was breathing extremely hard, but he kept pushing himself. After struggling through the dense thicket, he saw the building. It was much bigger than he'd imagined, with a smaller building right behind it. He crouched at the edge of the wild area and looked at his watch. Eight-fifty-five. *I made it.*

Tomas texted Dante: **I'm here but alone. Brush was very thick. Other two delayed, may not make it.**

Dante replied: **Move into the building, look around. Report anything unusual.**

Tomas replied: **Will do!**

He knew the boss thought he was at the big building. *Shit! Should have been clearer.*

He moved up to the small building and peeked through a window. He saw nobody, but it wasn't abandoned. People had been there, as evidenced by the refrigerator and stuff lying around. With his pistol leading him, Tomas opened the door. *Gotta hurry!* The cold air hit him like an Arctic blast. *My God, that feels good.* He looked around. It was an open area. One parked SUV, some furniture, and a kitchen. *No one here.* Quickly, he opened the fridge. It contained several bottles of water.

Thank God! He took three bottles and sat on the floor with his back to a cabinet, facing the door. As quickly as he could, while never letting go of his gun, he drank the first bottle. He poured the second one over his head and put the third one in his pocket. The cold air and water felt so good that he hated to move, but he had to hurry. It was worth it. The break had reinvigorated him.

As he sped to the door, Tomas hesitated and glanced out the back window for his two men, but they were nowhere in sight. It was a little after nine. He wondered if Dante was sitting on the other side of the building in his SUV. Tomas ran as fast as he could while crouching until he was beside a door leading to the back of the big building. It was unlocked and it opened without a creak. He saw some steps and started climbing them, trying to see if anyone was aiming down at Dante. *Playing it by ear.*

∼

"Stop. Pull onto the shoulder," Dante said. He sat there, thinking, and looked at his watch. *Just a few minutes before nine o'clock.* The turnoff was thirty yards ahead. They sat on a paved but remote stretch of road. No houses in this section, just dense trees and heavy underbrush on both sides. *Verify the thumb drive. Kill them all.*

Do I dare keep it? Sixteen million dollars ... better give it to Rico. Brownie points and safer in the long run. Kill everyone and disappear? Depends on how this plays out. Always an option.

He looked at his watch. Five minutes after nine. *If Spike tries to leave, he has to pass me on that narrow gravel road. Make him wait a few minutes!*

57

ACCIDENT

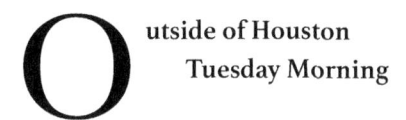

Outside of Houston
Tuesday Morning

SPIKE SAT ALONE in the Escalade, in the driver's seat, facing the parking lot. Behind him was a deserted three-story brick manufacturing building. In front was a big open parking area where he could see the entrance. Tall, wild vegetation and short trees encased the whole area, buildings, and parking. Fluff had picked the location.

Spike knew he'd have to get out to make the deal. Butterflies fluttered in his stomach as he looked at the clock on the dash. The meeting was set for nine. It was a few minutes after the deadline. *They're late. Assholes!*

Fluff and Roman were in overwatch positions with the sun on their backs. They knew this area well. Any gunfire, if necessary, would go unreported. They'd fired weapons here before.

Behind Spike was Ava, ready to cover and defend Spike

and Barbie. Gray was in his position where the narrow gravel road opened to the large area in front of the factory. Most likely, it had been used for parking in the past. In the early hours of the morning, everyone had gotten checked out on the weapons. They'd also learned how to use their comms and put on a bulletproof vest. Then they'd gotten a little rest and eaten breakfast. Now they were in position, waiting.

With Spike parking in the open area first, it was almost certain that Dante would park facing Spike's vehicle. If he did so, he'd be in the exact position Fluff wanted.

Spike sat and waited. Then he saw dust on the road leading up to the old facility. "Here they come."

"Just passed me," Gray said on the comms, though everyone could see the two SUVs pull into the large open graveled area.

As expected, the first SUV pulled up facing dead-on to Spike's vehicle, about talking distance away. The second SUV pulled up to the right of the first, about ten feet behind it. The windows were dark, and no one got out.

"What the fuck. I'll go first," Spike said on comms and climbed out of the Escalade. He walked about halfway between the vehicles, held up his hands, and yelled, "Dante! Hey, buddy! Come on out!"

The doors opened on both vehicles. Dante got out but stood halfway behind the door to support himself. He knew Spike could see his white cast. Two more guys got out of Dante's SUV. From the second SUV, two more men got out, both with AR-15s.

"Spike, nice to meet you," Dante said as he held onto his door. "But why here? Pretty melodramatic, isn't it?"

"Yeah, maybe. You got a bum leg?"

"Thanks to you. Remember the motel in Columbus?"

"Damn, that was you?"

"It was a rough night."

"Why all the firepower? And where's Barbie?" Spike asked. His Glock 40 was in his belt, under his vest. *Could be a tough fast draw. Looks like they plan to kill me. Maybe Barbie's already dead.*

"She's in there." Dante pointed at the other SUV. "She's a little rattled but unharmed. And the firepower is just for safety. No one has to get hurt, but I need the thumb drive now. We'll check it to make sure the bitcoin is on it. Then we give you Barbie, and we leave." Dante motioned with his head, and his driver started walking toward Spike.

"Wait!" Spike held out his hand at the man. "I need to see her first. Release her. You can see there's no way I can run."

"Why don't I just take the thumb drive and then kill both of you?"

"Look at your shirt."

Based on the shit-eating grin on his face, Dante seemed to know what he was going to see. He didn't look right away. Then he slowly dipped his chin and stared at his chest for a few seconds.

Spike wondered what he thought when he saw the two red dots. He would wait as long as it took for Dante to say something.

"I must admit, I'm surprised." Dante held out his hands and mockingly clapped, using his elbow through the door window to hold himself up. "Well played, my friend. You got two friends with red laser pointers?"

"I got a few friends with sniper rifles, among other things. If I die, you'll also die, Dante, and all your men." Clearly, all of Dante's men were listening, as they shifted, getting more at the ready. Each of them moved a little more behind his door, and all eyes started scanning the building. "Get Barbie, now, and send her over to me."

Dante looked over his right shoulder and spoke to his men at the second vehicle. "Get her!"

Spike saw the two men walk to the back of their SUV, out of his sight. The back opened, and then they brought her around. One pulled her by the elbow while the other was behind with an AR-15, still scanning the building. Each of the men held one of Barbie's arms as they walked her toward Dante. Her hands were still zip-tied in front.

One man took Barbie to the right side, just behind Dante. His AR-15 was slung on his shoulder. The second man, with his AR-15, was at the ready just behind them.

Fluff came on the comms to everyone. "Dante's men look super tense. Spike, get Barbie next to you. Do not give Dante the thumb drive until you get Barbie. Play hardball. If he sends her over, tell her to keep going and get into your SUV. Then hand it to him, and hopefully, they'll just leave. Roman, if they start shooting, you take the guy with the AR-15 closest to you first. I'll take the other one. Ava, take out Dante. Then everyone fires at will. Gray, if we get an exchange without gunfire, let them go. If not, kill anyone trying to leave. Stay alert."

"Let her go," Spike said. "Let her come to me."

"Show me the thumb drive."

Spike pulled it out and held it up.

Dante turned to his man and said something. That man cut the zip-ties on Barbie's hands. "Go ahead."

Barbie took off, running to Spike. She ran into him and hugged him so hard that they spun around. He muttered into her ear, "No questions or discussion. Run to the SUV and get in as fast as you can." When the spin was complete, it felt like a dance, and he released Barbie. She kept in motion, as she was told, and ran toward the SUV close behind them.

***

Tomas hadn't seen anyone hiding in the building so far, but it was big. He was trying to be extra quiet. He sat back in the shadows, his pistol in one hand and an extra magazine in the other so he could reload quickly if necessary.

Wonder if the two losers turned back or are still lost in the woods and scruff. Fuckin' idiots. What an opportunity to impress Dante! Maybe even save his life.

The space inside seemed huge. It reminded him of a train station. Because of the dampness and the sunlight shining in through the broken windows, it was a vibrant green, with vines everywhere. It was beautiful, like nature had reclaimed it. The open space traveled the length of the interior. There were three floors with walkways and some space along all the levels. He knew he didn't have time to check it all.

Tomas went up to the second-floor walkway that traveled along the back of the building. There, he scanned for anyone on the front walkway. *Maybe no one's in here.* Then he heard Dante's SUVs and saw them through the gigantic windows and openings. The men got out of their vehicles. Dante hung on his door and started talking to a man who seemed to be alone. The man must have been Spike.

Tomas moved slowly, looking across the open area, trying to see movement on the front walkway. He stumbled once, then froze. No one seemed to hear him.

From out the front windows, he saw they'd brought out Barbie. When he noticed movement to his left front, he froze again. He tried to take one more step to get a better look around a post but stumbled. This time, he fell on the walkway with his arm pinned under him, forcing his finger to pull the trigger. The gun went off in the open building. Loud echoes followed.

~

AVA WAS on the second floor of the building, on the front walkway, lying down with an AR-15 aimed at Dante. He stood a couple of car lengths in front of Spike. If she had to take a shot, it would be from about fifteen feet up, coming behind Spike and passing on his right side before hitting Dante.

A loud echoing gunshot made her jump. It struck on the right line but well above her. Gunfire erupted on Dante's side, spraying the building.

They were firing and running.

Ava reflexively ducked, then glanced outside. Her hesitation had allowed Dante to drop down and head for his SUV. People ran for cover. The two men with AR-15s were dropped with headshots where they stood. No doubt Fluff got one and Roman the other. The shot in the building had distracted her. Ava saw Spike grab Barbie from his SUV and pull her toward the building. She knew she had to deal with the shooter in the building and behind them. Quickly, she flipped one hundred and eighty degrees, into a prone shooting position, and scanned for motion on the walkways. *It had to be the second or third floor.*

A lot of shooting was going on behind her now, but she ignored it and focused on the inside. She saw movement and adjusted her aim. Only a few seconds later, she saw a forehead raised about five feet from where she thought she saw movement. When the man's eyes were above the rail, she squeezed the trigger. The shot lifted the man, and he flew backward, making a thud. *Asshole.*

She flipped back to examine the scene and saw Spike's SUV sitting in the same place. Directly in front of the building was the SUV with Barbie in it. Two dead men lay in front of it. In front of the other SUV sprawled one body, but Dante's SUV was headed toward the exit. She figured he was getting away with one of his guys.

"Barbie, you here?" she screamed. Her voice echoed through the gutted building.

"Right here!" Barbie yelled. She ran into the center and looked up. Spike probably told her where to look.

"Up here! I'll be right down!"

～

When all the firing started, Spike got Barbie into the building and told her where to find Ava. "Stay here."

He ran out and jumped into his SUV to chase Dante. As he started to drive away, Spike heard yelling. Fluff was running from one side and Roman from the other. He waited, and they got in, Fluff in the front and Roman in the back.

"What was the gunshot in the building?" Spike asked.

"It wasn't us," Roman said. "I hope Ava can handle it."

On comms, Fluff said, "Gray, fire them up when they're close enough. Ava, what's going on?"

Gray replied, "I'm ready."

Ava answered, "I'm looking for a shooter who's behind us."

"Stop!" Fluff yelled.

Spike hit the brakes hard. They slid to a stop on the gravel.

"Roman, go and make sure she's okay. If she is, come help us."

"Got it, boss. Be careful." Roman jumped out and started running back to the building.

"Hit it!" Fluff said.

On comms, Fluff said, "Ava, Roman's coming to help you."

"What a shit storm," Spike said.

"What do you want us to do with Dante if we have a choice? Alive or dead?" Fluff asked.

"Alive!" Spike yelled. "I've got an idea."

"Let's hope Gray doesn't kill Dante first." Fluff put down his sniper rifle and pulled out his pistol.

58

BRICK HOUSE

Outside of Houston
Tuesday Morning

"Hot damn!" Gray yelled. He knew no one could hear him. He had just seen something go really wrong with the exchange, and his target grew closer with each second. He'd shoot the driver. The car would probably get wrecked. Maybe that would kill anyone else in the vehicle. If not, he'd run up and finish them off.

"Shit!" He saw Spike's SUV take off, following his target. *It's not all bad. I'll have help if I need it.*

Gray was on the lower floor of a smaller two-story brick administration building. He sat in a chair and steadied his rifle on the windowsill. He was positive they didn't expect or see him.

The SUV wasn't weaving, just coming closer. It would pass right by him, but he wanted to give himself time for a second burst if he needed it.

Gray's heart was in his throat. He was sweating from the heat and maybe the pressure, so his trigger finger was wet. He squeezed. A burst of shots hit the window in the area in front of the driver, but the vehicle didn't swerve in the least. He had one more chance, and then they'd fly by him. He squeezed the trigger again, not letting up until the magazine was empty. He riddled the windshield. It didn't swerve dramatically or flip. It just changed course a little and came right at him.

He jumped up and ran back, away from the wall. A collision would happen in a matter of seconds. He looked over his shoulder. He was only a few steps away when the brick wall exploded inward. Gray saw the front of the vehicle, the tires turning, and then felt himself being lifted off the floor. Something hit him on the head, and everything went black.

~

Spike pulled up outside the building out of which the back of the SUV stuck. He and Fluff roared from the stopped vehicle, then ran over the loose bricks and through the hole in the wall. With his pistol ready, Spike approached the driver's side from the rear. The driver was dead. A piece of metal pipe had pierced the windshield and hit him in the throat. It had almost decapitated him. Spike looked past the dead man and saw the passenger door was open, but there was no passenger. Just Fluff shaking his head.

They met in front of the smashed radiator. "Dante's alive," Spike whispered. "What happened to Gray?"

"Over here," Gray said. They saw a hand rise above the rubble. "I'm banged up but okay. I saw a guy limp off into that room."

"Thanks. Hang in there. We'll be back," Spike said.

Fluff started toward the door, but Spike quickly grabbed his left upper arm to stop him.

Fluff crouched back down. "What?" He kept his eye and gun focused on the door.

"We need Dante alive. He could be our best bet to keep the cartel from chasing us."

"What? You crazy? He won't help us. He'll kill us if he can," Fluff said.

"Seriously, if we don't have to kill him, then don't."

"We'll see."

Each ran to one side of the framed doorway, which held no door. They peeked into the next room and saw nothing. The small building was little more than a box divided into four rooms. This one had an open side door to the outside. Spike covered Fluff as he checked the doorway to the room to their left.

"Clear," Fluff said.

Spike ran up to the window and looked out. He waved Fluff to him and whispered, "I don't see anything. He couldn't go far with his leg in a cast."

Fluff motioned for Spike to follow him away from the window to the back of the room. He whispered, "He's out there. It's all open. Could be lying outside the door against the wall, ready to pop us. You stay here. I'll go out and circle the building. Stay alert. He could just pop up and take a shot."

Fluff left.

Spike glanced around the room, looking for cover, but he saw no furniture. *Nothing. Just empty rooms.* He moved back through the door where they'd entered the room and used it for cover. He peeked around the frame, pointing his Glock at the door that led outside.

Spike soon heard a gunshot that seemed to come from right outside the window.

Then Fluff yelled, "The asshole's at the corner of the building! Took a shot at me! Fuck! Be careful. He can cover both walls and could hit you if you come out."

Knowing where Dante was, Spike moved up to the window. He couldn't see anything without sticking his head out. *Not going to do that!*

"Dante, can you hear me?" Spike yelled.

There was no answer.

"I've got a plan where we all walk away richer. No one else dies," Spike yelled.

There was still no answer.

Then Dante yelled, "Fuck you! If you kill me, someone else will come and kill you!" Then, a few seconds later, he yelled, "Okay! What's your plan?"

"Throw your gun away from you, and we'll talk," Spike said.

"Dante, you don't know me," Fluff said. "I'm the sniper who dropped your guys with the AR-15s before they could lift them. With headshots. All I have to do is get in the SUV and drive a little way down the road, out of your pistol range, then put a bullet in your head. Or you throw your gun away, and we all talk like friends."

"You'll kill me anyway. You opened fire on us."

"Dante, that was your guy. He was in the building and started shooting at my people from behind. Then the men with you got spooked and started shooting. We were the last ones to start shooting. So, your guy started it."

There was no answer.

"You'll let me walk after we talk?" Dante asked.

"Dante, I give you my word," Spike said. *Always be nice!* "I swear on everything sacred. We won't hurt you. This whole thing got out of hand by accident. You lived up to your end of the deal. I've got Barbie back unharmed. I'll complete the bargain and give you the drive after we talk. Fair enough?"

"Okay. I just threw my gun away from me."

Spike saw the gun fly into the open and land on the ground.

"You got a second gun?" Fluff yelled.

"Nope, take a look. I have my open hands up too."

Spike peeked out the open door. Dante sat at the corner of the building with his hands held up about halfway. He grimaced in pain. Fluff was all over him as Spike approached. Fluff pushed Dante from a sitting position onto his back.

"Please! Don't roll me over! Broken leg!" Dante raised both hands to his face. "Please, I've got no guns, no knives. I'll behave."

Fluff hesitated. Then he patted Dante down and stepped back, leaving him on his back.

"Thanks again for the broken leg," Dante said.

"Yeah, sorry about that. Can you walk?" Spike asked.

"With crutches, or I can hop. I may have rebroken it when we ran into the wall of the building."

Spike apologized but still zip-tied Dante in their SUV while they got Gray out of the rubble. Gray's legs were pinned by a wood frame. Spike and Fluff lifted it off him. Luckily, his legs weren't broken. The four of them then made the short drive across the parking area and pulled in behind the big building next to their smaller, staging building, "The Hut."

59

THE NEW DEAL

Houston, TX
Tuesday Late Morning

"I'm really sorry," Spike said, being as nice as he could. He'd even elevated Dante's broken leg to make him more comfortable. He also put his phone on "record" and set it behind Dante, as close as possible to him.

"Nice place," Dante said.

"It'll do. We call it The Hut," Spike said. "Ava and Barbie will watch you while we clean up the mess in front of the factory building. Two of our guys have already started." Dante had been given a cold drink and some Excedrin. Both women sat at the table with cold drinks.

Ava lifted her pistol. "I know how to use this."

"I know you do," Dante said. "I'm zip-tied to this chair. I don't think I'll give you much trouble."

"We'll hurry," Spike said as he climbed into their SUV,

parked in The Hut. Fluff drove and backed out. Then Ava walked to the door and pulled it down.

"You know someone who'll come remove all these bodies and the extra vehicles?" Spike asked as they drove around to the front of the main factory.

"Yup, he's already been called. He said it'll take him about two hours to get here," Fluff said.

"I've got a plan coming together," Spike said.

"You know," Fluff said, "if Gray and Ava are aware that we have the sixteen million, that's two more people that the cartel could beat our identities out of. We're gonna have to kill them or split it some more. And if we split it, it's still two more people who know we have it. Plus, I don't think Ava would take it. So, bottom line, if they know, they die. And you'll have to deal with Barbie if I ice her older sister."

"Chill out," Spike said. *Fluff is willing to kill Ava and Gray. Does that make him a bad guy? Not for thinking it, only if it happens.* "I'm trying to make this so they don't have to be killed. Just keep Dante talking when we get back to The Hut."

"What?" Fluff's forehead was wrinkled in confusion.

"Just keep him talking. Tell Roman when you're alone with him too," Spike said. "Okay, looks like Roman and Gray are almost done picking bodies up." He saw no bodies, and the SUV was parked by the one that had crashed into the building. "That one's going to be messy. The windshield tore up the driver pretty badly. Your cleanup guy who's coming, he knows that he has an SUV to tow away too?"

"Yup. He'll take care of it." Fluff nodded. "He'll take it to a chop shop or crush it."

"Good."

They pulled up and stopped.

"That's all of them, four bodies," Roman said.

"What about the guy in the warehouse who took a shot at Ava?" Spike asked.

"Shit!" Roman smacked his forehead. "Forgot him. We'll get his body. You two can go back to The Hut."

"Okay. When you get to The Hut, we'll discuss what we're going to do," Spike said.

Fluff and Spike parked in The Hut. Roman and Gray parked outside and immediately went into the factory to look for the body.

Barbie ran over and hugged Spike, then kissed him. He tried to give her a peck, but she held on. *Always be smiling.*

"Done already?" Ava asked.

"Sweetie, not now." Spike pushed Barbie back gently, restraining his real feelings. *Damn!* Then he looked at Ava. "Roman and Gray did all the work. We just drove out and back."

"So, what's the big plan?" Dante asked. "You going to give me the thumb drive?"

Spike talked as he walked with his hands interlocked on top of his head. "I was going to, but with all the shooting, I think we have more options."

"More options!" Dante screamed. "You're all going to fuckin' die and get me killed too."

No one reacted except Barbie. She moved her chair back a little and looked away from Dante. Everyone else just glared at him. He was a chained animal that would kill if he could.

Spike got a beer out of the fridge and held it up to show Fluff.

"Hit me!" Fluff held up his hands, and Spike tossed the beer at him. Fluff caught it, popped the cap, and took a drink. "That is sooo good." He went to the table and took a chair next to Ava and Barbie. They all faced Dante and the door.

"Want one?" Spike asked Dante.

"C'mon, this is no game! What options? What are you talking about?" Dante yelled.

Spike just smiled and held a beer toward Dante. "Like a beer?"

"How?" He strained at the zip-ties holding his hands to the arms of the chair, then looked at them for a second and back at Spike.

Spike grabbed an extra beer and walked to Dante.

"No more screaming, please." Spike cut the zip-tie on Dante's right hand and handed him the beer. "I'd cut you loose, but I'm not sure you understand that we both have the same interests. So, I need to wait a little longer."

"Well, tell me. What's going on?" Dante asked.

"We'll wait for Roman and Gray." Spike sipped his beer and took a seat on the couch facing Dante but about ten feet away, against the wall.

After a few minutes, Roman and Gray walked in the door beside the back of the two vehicles parked in The Hut.

"Done," Roman said. "We had to put him in the back seat. It was getting too crowded in the back."

"Actually," Gray added, "both of the back seats have a body, but we slumped them over to the middle so no one can see their silhouettes from the outside."

They each got a beer and sat beside Spike on the couch.

"Who are you guys?" Dante asked.

No one answered.

Spike stood. "I called this meeting to decide what to do with the sixteen million dollars and how we avoid the cartel chasing us and trying to kill us all."

"That's crazy!" Dante yelled. "It's not possible. They'll find and kill you all."

"Thanks for your input, sunshine." Spike laughed. He was in his sales mode and thought this could be an opportunity to keep the money. He walked around like he was giving a presentation. "But let's assume there's a way. Let's start, of course, with all of us splitting it." He pointed as he said each person's name. "Fluff, Roman, Gray, Ava, Dante..."

"I won't take any of it!" Dante yelled.

"You don't want to split the sixteen million dollars?" Spike asked.

"No, I don't want any part of the money."

Spike heard Dante say, embedded in his answer, "I want part of the money."

"And you don't want to keep it?"

"No, I don't want to keep it."

Spike heard Dante say the words "I want to keep it." *Good words for him to look guilty.*

"Yeah, yeah, okay," Spike said. "Look, just listen for a while, unless you have something to add that's helpful. And you don't need to yell. Agreed?"

Dante nodded with pursed lips.

"Good and thank you." Spike nodded and pointed to Dante. Then he clapped his hands. "Okay, to finish my thought, not counting Dante, there are six of us. That, my friends, old and new, would be about two and a half million dollars each."

"I don't want any part of it," Ava said. "For many reasons. I say let's just wrap up this chapter of our lives, give Dante the drive, and let him go. That is, if Dante tells us they won't come back and try to kill us."

"I just need the thumb drive. We have no other interest in any of you. Just the money," Dante said.

Spike twisted his lips. "Maybe. Barbie, any comments?"

"It is a lot of money, but whatever you decide." She watched and listened.

"How can we trust him?" Gray asked. "He'd say anything to get free and get the drive." He stood up from the couch.

Spike continued. "My idea is that Dante calls Rico and tells him—"

"Shut up!" Gray said. "Shit! On and on and on. Just shut up." Everyone stopped what they were doing and looked at Gray, who was waving his AR-15.

60

SIDEWAYS

Houston, TX
Tuesday Late Morning

"What're you doing?" Spike yelled as he stared at Gray. For a split second, Spike considered going for the gun in his belt. However, he knew he'd never get a shot off before Gray killed him and maybe everyone else. Spike was sure everyone else was making the same calculations. He hoped no one made a move.

"What is it about the phrase *shut up* that you don't understand?" Gray asked.

For a second, a pissed look crossed Spike's face. Then he broke into a smile. However, before he could say anything, Dante spoke.

"I wondered when you'd make a move. Cut me loose," Dante said. "C'mon! Hurry up!"

"What?" Ava yelled.

Everyone's jaws dropped.

"Gray works for me," Dante said, smiling broadly.

"Everyone, throw your weapons on the floor and kick them away from you," Gray said.

They moved slowly, pitching their weapons.

"You didn't know?" Dante said. "Gray is on our payroll. I'm surprised nobody figured it out. My ace in the hole." He looked at Gray. "C'mon, undo me."

"I don't think so. Fuck the cartel and all of you." Gray slowly waved the rifle back and forth in a small arc, covering everyone.

Ava stood from her chair at the table. "Why? You risked your life to save us. I thought you cared about me."

As she spoke, Gray went into a crouch and raised the gun slightly, pointing it at her. "Yeah, well, things could have been different," he said. "But I had two reasons to rescue you. One was to find Spike and have a shot at the sixteen million. I wasn't sure if it would materialize, but I figured why not try. And you're right. The second reason was I really liked you."

"I like you too. Take me with you."

"Is that the FBI training kicking in? Just shut the fuck up! The opportunity showed up, so it's payday! Sixteen million dollars is a lot of money. I can't see anyone suspecting me. Cash it in and just keep protecting and serving. More likely, I'll change my name and move to some tropical island. I'll decide later. Spike, throw me the thumb drive. I gotta get going."

"Hey! Cut me loose! Now!" Dante yelled.

Gray walked over to Dante and hit him on the head with the butt of his rifle. Dante's head whipped back, then slumped forward. He was unconscious and bleeding from the forehead. Quickly, Gray turned the rifle back, pointing it at everyone else. His movement had led Spike, Ava, Fluff, and Roman to make a move for their guns, but they froze when the AR-15 was pointed in their direction.

Gray laughed. "That looked like freeze tag. Pretty damn funny. Everyone moved about six inches and froze again." He stopped laughing, "C'mon, Spike. The thumb drive. Now! Throw it over."

"You plan to kill us all? You'll never get away with it," Spike said.

"I didn't say I was going to kill you all," Gray said.

Spike knew that was bullshit. Soon, he'd have to go for his gun. He hoped everyone would too.

Spike took out the thumb drive and held it up. "You know there's nothing on this. It's blank. I hid the real one. You didn't think I was going to take the real drive to the exchange?"

"Fucking asshole. You're kidding me!" Gray said. "Where's it at? I'll start shooting arms and legs until you tell me." He raised the rifle and aimed at Spike.

"No, wait! It's real!" Spike yelled.

"What the fuck? I'll just kill you all and pick it up off the floor," Gray said.

The door beside the parked SUVs burst open.

Two dirty, sweaty, slim men with muddy shoes ran in. They were gasping for breath and hesitated with their guns up, but they weren't aiming at anyone. Gray swung his weapon at them, and they both opened on him. A few rounds hit his chest and one entered his head. As soon as the first shot rang out, everyone went for their guns and started shooting. The two men were riddled with bullets.

The echoes died down, though adrenaline pumped

through Spike's veins. "A couple of Dante's guys, I guess, who got lost."

"Anyone hit?" Fluff yelled.

A quick check confirmed everyone was okay.

"Who were they?" Barbie asked.

"Don't know." Spike wet a wash rag to put on Dante's head.

"We'll look around outside for more guys," Fluff said.

Roman followed. Fluff checked the first guy for a pulse. He turned and gave a thumbs-down. Roman ran around him and out of sight outside. Fluff moved just outside the door and checked the second man. He gave a so-so hand wave and headed out after Roman.

Ava was already checking Gray. "He's dead."

Spike handed the wet rag to Ava. "Check on Dante, will you?" he said. "I'll look at the guy Fluff gave a so-so on."

Spike saw Ava go to Dante, who was still unconscious, and gently wipe the blood away from the wound on his forehead.

Spike got excited. If Fluff and Roman were out of sight, maybe the second attacker who was just out of sight beyond the door, was alive enough that Spike could choke him out. He started breathing hard. *Kill the guy, watch the life leave his eyes, with Ava and Barbie next door, and right under Fluff's and Roman's noses.* He hurried. He sprinted. *Don't die yet!*

"Be careful," Ava yelled to Spike. "He's probably not going to make it anyway."

Spike went to the door. He saw the man on his back, with two or three gunshots in the chest. The man was wheezing. Spike quickly looked, then ran to the corner to get another look. Fluff and Roman were checking the area for anyone else. Spike knew he didn't have much time.

He sat on the man's bloody chest and whispered to him, "You're a bad man and deserve to die."

The man's eyes sprang open. They were still full of life and hanging on. "Help me," the man said in a soft, gurgling voice as blood foamed out of his mouth.

"Let me help you along. Death awaits you," Spike said as he softly put his hands on the man's throat.

The man reached up and took Spike's hands gently. Then Spike threw all his weight into strangling the man. The man gripped Spike's hands with a strength that surprised Spike, and he started to twist and turn. The man's eyes bugged, showing panic. He was trying to say something, but it was barely audible, maybe "No. No." However, the man's strength was the last burst. As fast as it started, the man went completely limp. His hands fell away, and his eyes stared lifelessly ahead. *That was my kill ... the bullets slowed him down, but I took his life. Number forty-four. Seems like a special number.*

Spike stood, examining his work. He smiled. *Similar to Buck but oh so different.*

As he stood there, Fluff came back and said they couldn't find anyone. Then he looked at the dead man covered in blood. "Too bad, but I didn't think he'd make it. You were wasting your time trying to help him."

"I did what I could," Spike said. He showed a sad face while feeling smug. It was a little hard to pretend to be sad, but he was smiling on the inside. He wondered if other people felt that way when they lied. Like someone at a funeral who hated someone and was glad they were dead, but when they talked to the relatives, they feigned sadness, looking them in the eyes and saying the asshole was really a great guy.

Spike: 35 Kills and Smiling

He was lost in thought when Fluff patted him on the shoulder. "Don't feel bad."

Spike loved pretending. He pursed his lips and nodded. He tried to give sad eyes to Fluff. "Thanks, I'm okay. We'd better get inside and decide what to do."

Roman had shown up. "I can't find any more bodies. I think we got all of them."

"How's the plan coming?" Fluff asked Spike.

Roman leaned in, obviously interested.

"If it goes the way I hope, you'll hear me say some weird stuff. I may say some things that surprise you. It's all acting. When I tell you to, take Dante out of The Hut and kill him. Don't let him be found." Spike was getting his instructions out as fast as possible, afraid someone would come out of The Hut. "Fluff needs to take the girls and me back to my room. Then go somewhere and wait for my call. Roman can coordinate the clean-up here. When Ava leaves, I'll meet you and Roman somewhere with my tech guy, who'll then split the bitcoin so we can each have our share. Got it?"

"Why are we doing this?" Fluff asked.

"So we don't have to kill Ava and Barbie when we split the money," Spike said.

"I hope you know what you're doing." Fluff picked up the dead man's feet. "Let's just put the bodies over there beside the building and cover them. We have that canvas in The Hut." He was already dragging the man whom Spike had just hurried along to death.

Roman started to go inside. "I'll get Gray."

"Leave his gun, his badge if he has one, and his ID in The Hut. He needs to just disappear."

"Got it," Roman said.

Spike followed Roman back inside and saw Ava finish

putting a bandage on Dante's cut. "Is he gonna make it?" Spike asked.

"He'll live," Ava said.

Roman put Gray's stuff in a pile and dragged his body by his feet out the door.

Spike looked at Gray's body as his head bounced on the floor. He shook his head. "Dirty cop asshole."

61

THE HUT

Houston, TX
Tuesday Late Morning

SPIKE SAT on the couch and took a breath, watching Ava work on Dante.

"He probably has a concussion," Ava said. "There's a nice cut on his forehead that'll need stitches."

"Still unconscious?" Spike asked.

"He's coming around."

Spike was on a bigger high than anyone could have imagined. He was realizing that he loved all of this, having been on the edge more in the last few days than ever before. *Alive and untouchable! God's protection?* He'd always been so careful. He'd felt maybe he wasn't living to his fullest, but lately—*damn!* He'd still be extra careful when he pursued his hobby, but he needed to get the hell out of Houston as soon as possible.

Fluff and Roman came back into The Hut. They said

they'd taken care of the bodies for now. The corpses were out of sight, waiting for the clean-up crew.

Everyone was now in The Hut, and Dante was conscious.

Spike addressed everyone. "Okay, we all agree the goal is to stay alive now and not be chased by the cartel, and we'll give the money back?"

They all agreed. He noticed Fluff and Roman nodding too but not enthusiastically.

Spike turned to Dante. "What's going to happen to us if we give you the thumb drive?"

"We all leave and go our own ways," Dante said. "No one will ever come after you."

"Convince us, please," Spike said. He thought he had enough, but he wanted Dante to talk more, just to make sure.

"Why would we? You're not our competition, and we'll have our money back."

"What about all of your men who were killed chasing the thumb drive?" Spike asked.

"The people killed today were a mistake, started by our own man. It's hard to hold you responsible for that. The men killed taking Ava ... again, she was just protecting herself from what she perceived were men attacking her."

"What about the men killed where you were holding Ava and Barbie?"

"That was Gray," Ava said.

Dante said, "Gray's actions were a big surprise. Hard to find good people."

Spike had made up his mind about what he'd do. He kept asking questions about different things, then encouraged everyone to ask Dante a few questions. He was confident no one knew what he was up to.

"I got what I need," Spike said.

Everyone, including Dante, looked at him, perplexed. He picked up the phone, showed Dante it had been recording, and then turned it off. He played just a little so Dante could hear his own voice.

"You ever hear of deep fakes?"

"No," Dante said.

"I've recorded enough of your voice that I can run this through a sophisticated software program," Spike said. "Then, when I speak into a microphone, the voice coming out won't be mine but yours. And no one will be able to tell the difference. So, I'll record a deeply damning message and send it to Rico. Maybe, in my message, you tell someone there was really twenty million on the drive, that you kept four and gave Rico the sixteen he was expecting. Maybe you'll even say what a fool you think Rico is."

Dante scowled deeply.

"Look, that never needs to happen. Do you have your phone on you, and can you reach Rico on the phone?"

"Yes and probably."

Spike walked over to their SUV and got his laptop. He plugged in the thumb drive and pulled up a page to show Dante the sixteen million. The code to access it was there. "There it is. Satisfied?"

"Yes." Dante sighed and nodded. "We have a deal. Cut me loose now."

Spike twisted his face. "Almost. I just need one more thing."

"What?"

"I want you to call Rico and put it on speaker. Tell him what we discussed and that you have the drive and the money is on it. And how you've lost some men, and it wasn't our fault. You say what you need to say, but when you hang up, I want us all to be convinced Rico isn't coming after us. Don't tell him we're here. Do you understand?"

"May I have both hands?"

"Sure." Spike cut the zip-tie on Dante's left wrist. Now only Dante's legs were zip-tied. "Make the call good, and I'll cut the ties on your legs and wish you well as you leave."

He took his phone out of his hip pocket, got it ready, and set it on the arm of his chair. He pushed "call," then "speaker."

Rico picked up immediately. "Did you get it?"

"I got it, boss, and I've looked at it on a computer. The money's there, and so is the code we need to get it out."

"Good job, Dante! Seriously! Just one more thing I don't have to worry about. Was there any trouble?"

"Not with Spike, but one of our guys started shooting. I don't have a clue why. Some of our guys got killed. It was their own damn fault, but Spike and I calmed everyone else down."

"Okay. I'm busy. Call me back later. We have a shipment coming into Houston soon. You need to get ready," Rico said. "So, we're done with Spike?"

"Yeah, poor bastard didn't even know he had it. Rosa must have dropped it in his bag."

"Good job again, Dante. I knew I could depend on you. Build Houston back up."

"*Sí, Jefe.*"

Rico hung up.

Dante put away his phone and asked Spike, "How was that?"

Spike called everyone to the corner of the room.

"I think we're okay. I can live with that," Ava said.

"Me too," Barbie said.

"That deep fake stuff was great. Can you really do that?" Fluff asked.

"Absolutely," Spike said with confidence, as he was relying on Magic's earlier assurance.

"Good to know. I think this is the end of it," Fluff said.

"Me too," Roman said.

"Then that's it," Spike said.

They all walked over to Dante. Spike handed him the thumb drive and cut the last zip-tie. He handed Dante his crutches. "Thought you might need these." He also offered his hand.

Dante shook it. "This has been the strangest thing that has ever happened to me. I'll go to the grave with our deal. Thank you. I feel like I cheated death." Then, Dante shook everyone's hand. "Can you call your clean-up crew off? I have my own clean-up people. In particular, I need to know the cop is disposed of correctly and permanently."

"I can do that. The cop's gun, badge, and ID are on the table," Fluff said. "Just lock the door on your way out. Oh, the cop's private car is parked at Spike's motel."

"Write down the name of the motel and call me back with the license number on the burner. We'll take care of that too," Dante said. "Well, I have a lot of work to do. You guys should leave now. I've got to call for some help."

Roman said, "Before you call, let me show you where the bodies and your vehicles are located."

"Yeah, that's good. I want to get something out of my SUV anyway."

Everyone else piled into Fluff's Yukon to head back to Spike's motel room.

～

"Follow me," Roman said.

"Damn, what a day," Dante said. "Such a relief to have this all settled. You guys did the right thing." He used his crutches to swing each step out the door, which Roman held for him.

Roman watched Fluff drive away with everyone. Within seconds, the vehicle rounded the corner and was out of sight. Spike hadn't mentioned it, but he assumed Roman would retrieve the thumb drive from Dante after killing him.

Dante, on his crutches, followed Roman as they walked away from The Hut. Roman pulled out his pistol, trying to use his body to shield the action. He lifted the gun to his chest and swung around to shoot Dante but was hit in the face with a crutch.

Roman made a loud, unintelligible sound and dropped his pistol. His hands flew to his mouth as he staggered backward and went down on one knee. He lost teeth. Blood gushed out of his mouth, and he felt jagged edges. Dante kept coming at him.

Roman composed himself and had started to stand when he saw Dante lunge at him. Dante jabbed the end of his crutch into Roman's throat, pushing him off balance. Roman's blood-covered hands flew from his mouth to his throat. He fell backward to the ground. He saw Dante crawling, dragging his casted leg away from him. Then he saw Dante was about to pick up Roman's dropped pistol.

Roman, still on his back, knew he had seconds before experiencing a very surprising death. *Is this how I die?* He reached to his boot top, and his bloody hand fumbled.

Dante grabbed the gun.

Roman got a slippery grip and pulled the knife out of his boot.

Dante, still half on the ground, swung the pistol around.

With Dante on his back and raised only slightly, Roman worried the target was too small. Plus, he had a loose grip. Still, he pulled back his arm and let the knife fly.

Dante fired but missed. Before he could fire a second shot, the knife hit its mark, the soft spot under Dante's chin. The weapon drove into his skull through his mouth. Dante didn't even release the gun or make a noise. He just fell backward. Dead.

Roman moved over and took the drive out of Dante's pocket. Then, sitting beside Dante's body, he tried to pull out his knife. It was stuck, and he had to use his foot as leverage to remove it.

He rubbed his throat. It throbbed with pain, but there was probably no damage. He was afraid to look at his teeth. His mouth was still a bleeding mess. Roman threw Dante's body where the rest were and then went back into The Hut to look in a mirror. This wouldn't be the first time he needed dental work.

He texted Fluff and Spike: **Job done, retrieved thumb drive, waiting on clean-up crew.**

∽

BACK AT THE MOTEL, Fluff said his goodbyes and left. Spike followed Ava and Barbie into the motel room. He needed to wrap things up in Houston, take care of the bank and bitcoin, and leave. *Maybe the Northwest.*

62

RELAXING

Houston, TX
Tuesday Early Afternoon

SPIKE WALKED INTO THE MOTEL, excited to move on. *Get rid of Ava, maybe take Barbie with me. Ready to go! Anywhere but Houston.* He opened the curtains to let light flood the room. Then he got a cold bottle of water and sat in a chair by the window, waiting until Ava and Barbie both used the restroom and got a cold drink.

Ava sat down first in the other chair in the room, also by the window. A small table separated it from Spike's chair.

"That was unbelievable," Ava said. "My condo has blood everywhere, and the cops never clean up a crime scene. May I use your phone? They took my purse."

"Sure." Spike handed her the burner. "I guess you need to get going to coordinate all of that. I'll drop you off. I'm ready to go as soon as you are."

"Good. You're right, I want to get it cleaned up right away

and check on the office. So, you think we're done with all of that?"

"They got their money. No need to chase us anymore. Over. Done. Finished. Get on with our lives," Spike said.

"Good." Ava called her office. She told her assistant to call the police and make sure they'd released her house, then to get Bio-One, a crime scene cleaning service, over to her condo. She told her assistant that she was going to swing by her condo to get her car, then come to work. She was asking her assistant to book her a reservation at a nice hotel near her house when she stopped and put her hand over the phone. "Barbie, you staying with me? You're welcome to. Like we discussed, I'll get you on your feet, pay for your education if you want. I love you, and I want to help you."

"Thank you, sis. I love you so much. You feel like Superwoman to me." Then Barbie looked at Spike. "You still want me?"

"What a silly question. Yes! Let's leave today. As soon as we drop off your sister." *Always be smiling.*

"Guess I'm going with my man," Barbie said.

"Okay, let me finish this," Ava said. She took her hand off the phone. "Sorry, I needed to check on something. Also, get ready to have all my IDs and licenses reissued."

The assistant must have agreed on the other end.

"Good. I'll be in within a couple of hours."

"Wow, I'm impressed," Spike said.

Barbie ran to her sister and hugged her. "I love you so much. I'll keep in touch, and we can visit each other often, right?"

Spike listened.

"As much as we can." Ava flashed a big smile.

Spike often wondered how people would react if they really understood who he was. Actually, he knew what they'd think. *I don't think so. I wouldn't mind visiting Ava after Barbie's gone. Console the grieving sister.* He smiled as he looked at her body and her long, beautiful neck.

"We're gonna go soon, I hope," Ava said. "You'll drop me at my house, right?"

"Of course," Spike said.

Then Barbie hugged Spike. "I love you so much." She kissed him passionately.

Spike kissed her back, though his eyes were open and looking at Ava. He was more of an awkward forced participant. He liked Ava much more. *But that ex-FBI, PI thing is a problem.* As for Barbie, he just didn't care. He wondered if Barbie would even be above ground by Christmas. *Shit! I wonder when the ground freezes in Seattle.*

~

SPIKE DROPPED Ava at her condo and followed her in with Barbie. It was a wreck, with blood and gore all over the second floor and down the steps. Ava looked, then got in her car to go to her office.

Spiked called Magic, then Fluff, who said he'd call Roman. They all met at a Starbucks. Spike parked around the corner, as he didn't want Barbie to see Fluff or Roman. Barbie waited in the car.

When Spike walked in, they were sitting in the back, with no one else around. Fluff and Roman must have found Magic with no introductions. The computer was open, and its back was facing the retail area. No one was smiling.

Fluff stood and stepped into Spike. "What the hell's going on? What are you trying to pull?

"What are you talking about?" Spike asked.

"Nothing's on the drive. Roman took it off Dante's dead

body. There's nothing on it, and I know Roman didn't screw me."

Spike reached into his pocket and held up a thumb drive. "I switched them after I let Dante see the money." He handed it over to Fluff. "Try this."

Fluff's eyes lit up as his face relaxed. He smiled. "You son of a bitch. You had me worried."

"I'm a man of my word ... always," Spike said with a smug smile.

Magic inserted the drive and quickly gave a thumbs-up. He explained what he was going to do and had everyone watch the screen as he did it. He split the bitcoins into four drives. "Okay, I think we're done. You all saw the bitcoins transfer, and then I handed you your thumb drive. You each have two hundred and seventy bitcoins or about $5.9 million as of today. As you saw, that left ninety bitcoins on this thumb drive. That's my fee—ten percent." Magic folded his computer shut, then stood and shook everyone's hand. "Nice doing business with you." His last look was at Spike. "Call me if you need me." Then he left.

Wait a second. Spike walked up to Magic and spoke to him in a low tone.

Roman passed them, patting each on the shoulder while holding a cloth to his mouth. "I gotta go see a dentist for some major work." He shook hands and left.

Spike continued with Magic. "You got the audio files of Dante I sent you?"

"I got it, and it's enough. We can have him say anything you want."

"Good. Hold onto it in case we need it later."

Another handshake and Magic left.

"What happened to Roman's mouth?" Spike asked Fluff as they walked toward the door.

"Let's just say Dante didn't go down easy," Fluff said. "You know how to reach me."

"Keep me in mind."

"Get some training and maybe." Fluff turned to the right.

Spike turned to the left to get Barbie and head to his last stop before leaving Houston.

He went to the bank, where he had a large safety deposit box. He was pleased Barbie seemed to realize she shouldn't ask a lot of questions. Originally, the safety deposit box was the only reason he came back to Houston. He left Barbie across the street at a different Starbucks with a couple of novels she'd bought at a quick stop on the way.

As he stood alone in front of his safety deposit box, Spike placed his almost six million dollars on the thumb drive inside it. *Wow! I'll figure out what I want to do with that later.* Between the money he'd brought back from Mexico and what he'd earned from his one black ops experience, he had about eight hundred thousand dollars in cash. He'd left it in the car. Money wasn't going to be a problem.

Now, who am I going to be? Should I go by my real name, Harry Hunter? By the identity that Magic had created, Michael Smith? Or by Buck?

Fuck it! I'll take all three identities.

He pulled out his laptop and put in a thumb drive. Quickly, he looked at his pictures. They were photos of his kills up until the time Case captured him. He nodded subconsciously. *Lot of memories.* After running through the pictures, he put them back in the first box. *Case thought he got all my pictures.*

I'll keep these as my memory of the innocents. No more killing innocents. No more pictures. No harm in keeping these, though.

He slid the box back into the wall but paused before

locking it. Then he pulled it back out. Spike took the thumb drive with the pictures on it and plugged it into the computer. He set it up to erase and, in a cleansing moment, deleted all the pictures of his previous kills. He sighed.

That was a different life. Help me, God, to stay true to my new calling and satisfy my thirst by killing only bad people.

63

DETOUR

Houston to Seattle

SPIKE ENJOYED the drive from Houston to Seattle. They made many stops, looking at everything available. No responsibility, no looking over his shoulder. It felt like a real vacation. The sex every night was nice. Barbie was very enthusiastic about her lovemaking. He'd smile at her and agree with whatever she said. If it were anything important, he'd speak his mind.

He snapped the rubber band often. She could be annoying, but it was almost forgivable, as it reminded him of a child, though he had very little patience for children. More than once, she did make him think of killing her. *Snap!*

Still, she was company. He'd never taken a trip like this before, going to a new city. *No plan, no place to live, no job.* It felt good, adventurous.

He paid cash for everything.

They spent many hours in the car.

∿

BARBIE WAS LIVING THE DREAM. A handsome man with a real future. A man she loved. She didn't feel his love yet, but she knew he liked her. *I'll do anything for Spike. Anything.*

He could have killed and dumped her in that hole in New Mexico with Buck. *But he didn't.* He could have taken the sixteen million and left her with the cartel to be killed. *He gave up sixteen million dollars to save me. He loves me and just has a hard time showing it.* And he was taking her to Seattle when he could have easily left her in Houston. She smiled just thinking about it.

She loved and respected Ava so much. She wondered if she could get a job as a PI in Seattle or maybe as a policewoman or a nurse. She wasn't sure what she wanted to do professionally, but she felt Spike would support her.

She also wondered how Spike killed Buck so easily. *Could I kill someone? I need to let Spike know I'll do anything for him. I don't want to lose him. I don't want to go to jail. I think Spike is smart enough to keep us out of jail. Maybe we can grow old together.*

∿

SPIKE HAD sex with Barbie in the B-class, cash-only motel outside of Missoula, Montana. *It was great.* It was the last night on the road. They'd make it to Seattle tomorrow.

She sat on the bed, reading a novel with her legs crossed, wearing only panties. Barbie had left *Wheel of Fortune* on the TV, and he was on his laptop.

Spike looked up for a second, admiring her body. Her small, perky breasts were perfect. Her youth was infectious.

He'd gone back to researching the Seattle area when a side ad popped up. He clicked on "Seattle cabins." He found a beautiful area around the clear, glacier-fed, fifty-mile-long Lake Chelan, about three and a half hours east of Seattle, and checked it out. Tons of activities, a cute town, a bookstore, and treehouse cabins with terraces that overlooked sunsets and sunrises. And it was near the 3.8 million-acre Okanogan-Wenatchee National Forest in the Cascade Range. *That's a lot of acres in which to dispose of bodies.*

Why not? He decided to use one of his Michael Smith credit cards, maybe the new him, to reserve an unbelievable modern treehouse cabin overlooking the lake for two weeks. He was shocked when it went through. He thought it'd be booked. "I'll be damned!"

"What's wrong?" Barbie asked.

"Nothing. I just got us a cabin overlooking a big lake outside of Seattle. I figured we'd relax for a while and check out the city on a few short trips. Maybe do some hiking, just some fun stuff."

64

SUNSET

Chelan Falls, WA
Tuesday Evening

Spike checked in and quickly inspected their treehouse. *A treehouse. How cool!* Barbie was in the bathroom. He stood on the deck, which offered a magnificent view of the lake, mountains, and trees everywhere. *Nature! I thought I'd go to Seattle, but God sent me here. To recharge and plan my next step.*

Free again! It was the same feeling he'd had when he came out of the tunnel and sat in the restaurant. *Damn, how long ago was that? A week? And the rubber band.* He looked at the red band on his wrist, realizing he hadn't snapped it in a few days.

A quaint bookstore distracted Spike and Barbie on their way to a grocery store. They went in and each walked out with five or six books. Spike didn't need a Bible, as he'd picked one up during their first night at a motel. He made a mental note to open an account on Amazon under his new name so they could have books delivered overnight. After the bookstore, they stopped to get groceries before returning to their treehouse.

When they got back, the sun was low in the sky. He'd seen several women in the bookstore and grocery store on whom he'd love to practice his hobby but only in passing. He didn't have the itch now. The last week had been so intense. He'd taken the lives of nine people. *In only a week! Time to rest!*

He and Barbie carried the groceries and books into their treehouse cabin. Twenty-five steps to a landing, then a change of direction for another twelve steps to the actual treehouse living area. It looked to be supported by five trees and sat on the side of the mountain, with the back supported by rock. The treehouse had two bedrooms, a full bath, eight hundred square feet, and built-in redwood.

"I'll put it all away," Barbie said. "Take the wine and go relax on the deck."

"Okay, thanks," Spike said. He didn't want to help anyway. He picked up a bottle of wine and a couple of glasses, then awkwardly picked up the books and cradled them in the other arm. "Meet me on the deck when you're done."

"Won't be long." She kissed him on the cheek.

Spike walked onto the deck. He set his books on the table, opened the wine, and poured himself a glass. Standing there, he took a mouthful and held it, shutting his eyes as he swished it from cheek to cheek before swallowing. It was his favorite, a bourbon barrel-aged cab. It had a tiny burn and the smooth sweetness of bourbon, all embedded in a rich cab wine. *Nice!* It was a much stronger wine with the whiskey influence. After two more swallows, he finished his glass. Two glasses would give him a buzz.

Spike poured another glass and took a drink. Then he turned, stood close to the rail, and faced the lake.

From his deck looking down at the mountain, he was overwhelmed by the beautiful sunset, whose vibrant colors reflected in the water. *Awesome!* The lake was further framed by tree-covered mountains. A kaleidoscope of colors. He turned, already feeling a slight effect from the potent wine. He moved carefully, but he wasn't drunk.

Spike sat in a wooden deck chair and sipped his wine. Barbie walked up behind him and topped off his glass with the open bottle as she kissed him on the cheek.

She set down another bottle. "Here's a new one. There's just a little left in your bottle. Take a good drink so I can empty the bottle and take it to the kitchen."

"I'm starting to feel the wine." Spike held up his half-full glass and looked at it as he swirled the deep burgundy liquid. Then he finished it off without coming up for air. "There you go." He held the glass toward Barbie.

She emptied the bottle into his glass. "Enjoy it." She leaned over and kissed him again. "I need to go to the bathroom." She picked up her glass of wine and left.

Spike kept drinking his wine as he sat back with his eyes shut and felt the breeze. *I didn't know life could get this good.*

After a while, he wondered what had happened to Barbie. He set down his glass, stood, turned, and walked into the room off the deck to get a brochure of the area. Barbie ran over to Spike and gave him a passionate kiss, which he returned. They held their bodies tightly against each other, and he felt her warmth. She pulled back and her blue eyes touched him. "Spike, I love you so much."

Spike knew what she wanted to hear. He didn't feel it. He'd never really felt it. "You're special to me too." *I know you're not going anywhere. Don't want to make you any clingier than you already are.* "You're beautiful and so sexy." He kissed her.

"Thank you. I'm so lucky." She gave him a quick peck, then did a silly dance, waving her arms and sashaying her hips. "Catch me, catch me," she said, standing a few feet away.

"Okay, I'm ready." He was smiling with his arms out, his legs slightly bent to absorb her weight when it hit him.

"Here I come." She rocked forward with each count. "One, two, three, here I come." She took a couple of steps and jumped up, wrapping her legs around Spike's waist and hugging him. Once settled, she kissed him again.

Spike stumbled back a little, feeling the wine but holding his ground.

"Let me clean up. Then we can have some fun," she said. "I'm yours forever."

"I know you are," Spike said. *I'm just not sure how long forever will be.* "What have you been doing?"

"Won't take long." She ran off to the bathroom again, waving to him over her shoulder.

He stepped back onto the deck and picked up his wine glass, then walked to the edge of the deck as he sipped. He looked at the long, ugly cut on his arm. The stitches were healing.

That scar will always remind me of a turning point in my life.

The stitched cut brought back many recent memories. But his mind also drifted to the choking old man he'd saved in the restaurant. *Felt good.* He'd also saved Fluff and Roman, and he'd saved the young woman Bubba was holding. *Damn! I've saved four people from dying. God's will.* He snorted a small laugh to himself. *I guess my real count is forty-five and four.*

He sipped his wine and nodded as he looked up from the cut with a smile.

Those thoughts were immediately replaced by the beauty of nature. He revered the scenery and sunset. This was an experience he would never forget. *This moment, right now. Only God could create such a sight. There must be a God. I'll remove only bad people from this earth. God, give me the strength to not be tempted by innocents. And maybe save a few too.* In one gulp, he finished off his glass of red wine. He shut his eyes for a second and breathed deeply.

"Life is good," he said aloud. He smiled and took it all in.

The kill itch will be back! But I'll be ready. He took off the rubber band—for now. *God knows there are a lot of bad people out there. He'll show me the way. But for now, I'll enjoy life and a warm body that loves me. Everyone wants to be loved.*

He took a phone out of his pocket and dialed a number he wasn't sure he'd ever call.

"Hello," said the man with a Hispanic accent.

"Padre, you know who this is?"

"Yes. Yes, I never thought I'd hear from you. Are you alright, my son?"

"Better than alright. Life is good. I even found a woman I think I can trust."

"I am very happy for you," the padre said. "And..."

Spike felt a hard shove on his back. Before he could even drop the wine glass, he went over the wooden railing. Somehow, his phone-free left hand grasped the rail but for only a second. Then he was in a freefall, waiting to hit the ground and break something or die on impact.

65

WHO CAN YOU TRUST?

Chelan Falls, WA
Tuesday Evening

BARBIE KNEW Spike was a little tipsy. She'd put as much wine in him as possible. She knew he had trouble holding her when she jumped on him. *A test.* Then she watched and waited until he got close to the wooden railing. She hoped the fall was enough to kill him, but if not, she'd finish him off. It was just too much money, about eight hundred thousand dollars sitting in their cabin closet.

Then he was at the railing, his back to her, his wine glass in one hand and his phone in the other. *Admiring his last view.* With no shoes, she moved fast but quietly. It was a short distance from the bedroom to the deck's railing. She threw her weight into him, thrusting her shoulder into his back while making sure she didn't go over too. It took only a second, and he was gone. A short yell and a plop.

Barbie didn't look over the railing. She had to hurry. She

slipped her shoes on without stopping and ran down the steps and then down the switchback steps. The tree and house were in her line of sight, and she couldn't see Spike. There was a small trail after the steps, all going downhill. She picked up a rock that she would use to bash in his head and finish him off. Rounding the corner, Barbie could see his body, unmoving. Spike lay on his back about twenty feet down the hill. He must have rolled there. She looked farther out. It was pretty remote, and she saw nobody.

It was slippery with pine needles, wet ground, and the slope of the hill. *It'll be over soon.* Barbie pictured smashing the large rock into Spike's forehead. She'd tell the cops he got drunk and fell over the railing. *Easy peasy! Who's the killer now? My first!*

She slid a little as she stopped next to Spike. Then she straddled him, one foot slightly lower on the slope. She steadied herself and grunted as she lifted the rock and tensed her muscles. She shifted her force to slam the rock into Spike's forehead.

His eyes popped open, and he rolled downhill, taking her leg out and throwing her off balance.

"No!" she screamed.

∼

As Spike rolled, he saw Barbie fall over and drop the rock. It bounced off his back with little effect. The ground was soft from recent rains, and the pine needles had further cushioned his fall. *Thank God.*

Everything hurts, but nothing must be broken. Spike had no time to check his body. It wasn't hard to wrestle Barbie onto her back. She fought hard, but he was stronger and bigger.

"Can't trust anyone these days," Spike said.

"I didn't mean to push you over. I tripped," she said.

"And the rock?"

She didn't answer right away. "I'm sorry. I love you so much. I was just a little drunk."

"Save it. You know, killing you will make me a little sad, but I'll get over it. I thought I had found someone who understood me. I always liked your sister better, but with her FBI background, I just don't think that would ever work."

"I'm sorry. I'm really sorry. Just let me go. I'll never tell anyone. I swear! Please! Give me another chance!"

"I've heard you say that before. That ship has sailed."

Barbie squirmed as Spike wrapped his hands around her neck and squeezed. "No! No! Please!" Then she choked. She writhed.

He stared deeply into her eyes. "God knows you're bad."

She squirmed harder.

He eased up slightly. Barbie gasped for air as she tried to pull his hands off her. Then he squeezed again. "I'll send you back to your boyfriend. Hope you meet him in Hell. Tell him I said hello."

The struggling slowed. She closed her eyes, then went limp.

He released his grip. He wasn't sure if he'd gone too far. Then he felt her chest expand. She was unconscious, not dead. *Good!* He just didn't have the heart to kill her. He wasn't sure why.

Spike sat straddling her, breathing hard. He'd lost the desire to kill her. He knew he'd miss her, and he didn't have many friends. On the ground, within reach, his phone started buzzing. Spike picked it up. "Padre, you still there?"

"What happened? You okay? I heard someone yell. Is anyone hurt?" The priest was frantic.

"Look, Padre, I just got reminded, rather roughly, you can't trust *anyone*. Maybe you're the exception, but I gotta go. Take care of yourself."

"Wait! Wait!" the priest yelled.

"Make it quick."

"'Trust in the Lord with all your heart, and do not rely on your own insight. In all your ways acknowledge Him, and He will make straight your paths.' Proverbs 3:5-6."

"Make straight my paths?" Spike laughed. "Yeah, okay. Thanks, Padre."

"Spike! God loves you. Please, don't kill anyone else. Will you pray with me?"

"Not a good time, and I'm only killing bad people anyway."

"You shouldn't kill *anyone*. Let God judge them—"

Spike cut him off. "I'm counting on that. Say a prayer for me, but I gotta go." Spike hung up. He looked down at Barbie. She had risen into consciousness, but was barely moving as she moaned. Then she opened her eyes and looked at Spike. With grass and mud in her hair, she whispered, "I'm so sorry. Never again. I do love you, but men have always treated me so horribly. The bag of money was there, and I figured someday you'd be like all the rest."

Spike was emotionless. "You shouldn't have tried to kill me. Have I ever treated you badly?"

"No."

"Do you trust me now that I've spared you a second time?" Spike sat on her midsection as she lay on the ground.

"Yes, I'm all yours. I promise I'll always trust you and look out for your best interests because they'll be *my* best interests. Please forgive a broken woman. I won't let you down."

"You understand if there is a next time, there will be no forgiveness?"

"I do." She smiled. Spike knew she realized she would live.

Spike got off Barbie and offered a hand. After he pulled her up, she hugged him like she'd just escaped death. It felt good, and he hugged her back. Then he gave her a passionate kiss.

Covered in mud, with their arms around each other, they started walking up the hill.

"Barbie, a new chapter in my life is just beginning." He stopped and turned her so that she was facing him. Looking into her eyes, he asked, "Do you want kids?"

"Yes, yes!" She started jumping around, hugging and kissing Spike.

"Good. I want a family, and you seem to be the perfect woman for me. Let's go clean up, get something to eat, and maybe start working on it."

"Are we getting married?" she asked.

"Of course. We don't want a bunch of bastards running around."

"I accept. When?"

"Soon. Let's talk about it some more after we clean up and eat."

Arms around each other, they continued up the hill.

Spike felt that a family might help him stay on God's path. He'd still kill bad people. He had to kill something, as it was in his nature. He'd start with some badass training. *All I can get. I'll need it. I liked the black ops, and bad guys don't die easy.*

He'd gotten lost in his thoughts for a second.

I'll get Barbie the same training if she wants it. Could be my partner in crime.

Life is good.
Like Mom said, "Always be smiling." And he was.

The End

Spike's Beginning
A Private Note from The Author, Mike Slavin

THANK YOU FOR READING *SPIKE: 35 Kills and Smiling*. I work very hard to make a novel exciting, believable, emotional, and without a single page that can be skipped.

Spike, was first introduced in *Primed to Kill, Kill Crime 2*. The same charming Spike does battle with Jeff Case, the hero of the Kill Crime Series. Everyone loved Spike, so he continued into the next book, *Wrong Kill, Kill Crime 3*, where he had a side adventure with the cartel in Mexico as Case tried to save his remaining family and stay alive. The ending of that novel is where *Spike: 35 Kills and Counting* seamlessly begins. Case's journey will continue into *Kill Crime 4*, but with some cross over with Spike's journey in his own series.

Jeff Case's universe started with the first Kill Crime. A reluctant vigilante, Case has money and skills, which allow him to seek justice after tragedy strikes his family. He goes on with his team to fight to make the world a safer place as they hunt and eliminate serial killers. And eventually all evil men and women.

As of the writing of this, *Spike 2* and *Kill Crime 4* are both being written.

I hope you enjoyed *Spike: 35 Kills and Smiling*. I always like hearing your comments and questions and I hope you'll write to me at **mikeslavinauthor@gmail.com**. For more information, please visit my **website: www.mikeslavinauthor.com**.

Please leave a review on Amazon and Goodreads if you liked the book. I look forward to seeing what you think about Spike's story!

Dive Deeper into The Adventure: Catch Up Now!

Kill Crime Series
Life-Changing Money (*Kill Crime* prequel short story)
Kill Crime
Primed to Kill, Kill Crime 2
Wrong Kill, Kill Crime 3
Kill Crime 4 - Available 2024

Spike Series
Spike 2 - Available 2024

Southern Death Series
Southern Death-Available 2024

ACKNOWLEDGMENTS

Thank you to everyone who helped me to get *Spike: 35 Kills and Smiling* written and published.

Head Cheerleader Always: My wife, Won Slavin. And my son who drives me to perfection in my writing and editing.

Police Procedure Consultants:

James R. Boy, retired Houston Homicide Detective and a friend, is always there to keep me straight, and share ideas when I box myself into a corner.

CPT Chris Galvez, former police SWAT commander, and still an active on the police force was also always available to answer my questions.

Medical Consultant:

Robert W. Enzenauer, MD, MPH, BG, US Army Retired

Editors: Marni MacRae, and Tonya Blust

Book Cover Design: Momir Borocki

All the Unnamed Professionals:

Thank you to the many beta readers and proofreaders who are too numerous to mention or who chose to remain anonymous. I appreciate the efforts of one and all. There was so much valuable feedback I was constantly surprised.

THANK YOU TO THE READERS

Thank you so much for reading *Spike:35 Kills and Smiling*. I hope you enjoyed the story. If you did, I invite you to take a few moments to leave a review. As an independent author, exposure is everything, and positive reviews help a great deal. I much appreciate your support should you choose to do so.

I love interacting with readers. Feel free to email me at mikeslavinauthor@gmail.com that I might thank you personally. I am grateful for all your support, and I hope you will share the books with your friends/family/book clubs and anyone else whom you think might be interested. Thank you for falling into the Jeff Case series' universe.

Would you like to be notified when more Spike or Jeff Case short stories are posted at the website www.mikeslavinauthor.com and/or when future novels are released? Please visit my website to sign up for the New Release Newsletter at www.mikeslavinauthor.com.

PLEASE LEAVE A REVIEW

Reviews are the life blood of an author.

If you can please take a few minutes to leave a review on Amazon, Goodreads, and anywhere else that you might like to. Even a short review helps, like "Great book!"

If you are not a member of Goodreads, then consider joining this reader community of 50 million+ members for free, then leave a review. https://www.goodreads.com/book/show/55104538-primed-to-kill

On Goodreads, find *Spike:35 Kills and Smiling,* then give the book a rating with the stars under the cover, then a message will pop up, "would you like to do a text rating". Click it and write away.

KILL CRIME SERIES

Life-Changing Money (A Jeff Case Short Story) — Jeff Case has just resigned from the Army and is in NY with his wife. He is on a final interview for a job. When Case steps in to help a defenseless lady, an incredible day unfolds that almost gets him and his wife killed.

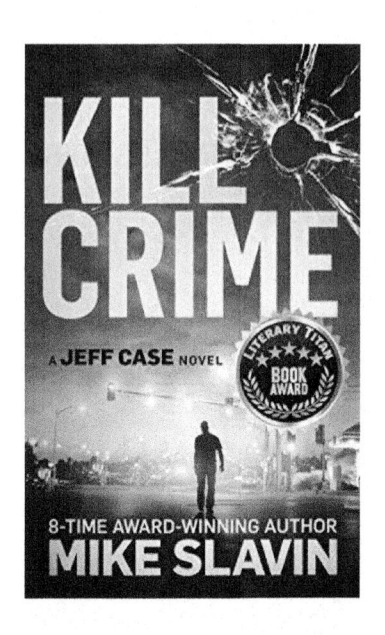

Kill Crime (Jeff Case Book 1)

In the foundation story, former Green Beret Jeff Case finally has it all: money, family, and happiness. But a life-changing event sends Case on a course that could spiral out of control. The story unfolds after the release of a bestselling novel, Kill Crime (book in a book) that urges ordinary citizens to go out and kill a bad guy in order to help society.

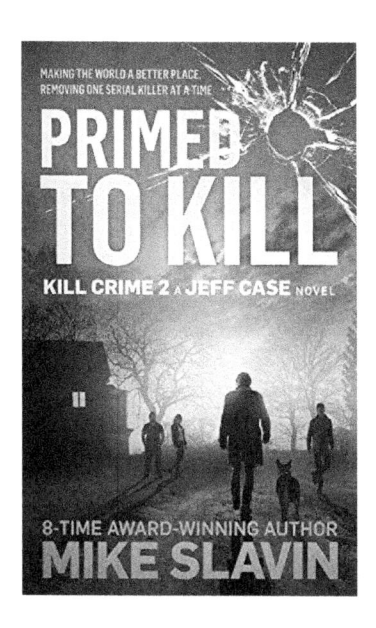

Primed to Kill, Kill Crime II (Jeff Case Book 2)

While helping protect a friend, Case finds himself entangled with a serial killer. Things get more complicated as Case finds more serial killers than most people could handle. A fast-paced struggle to the end, you will never foresee the final twist. Also Introduces Spike, the serial killer everyone, loves and hates. Now with his own series, *Spike, 35 Kills and Smiling*

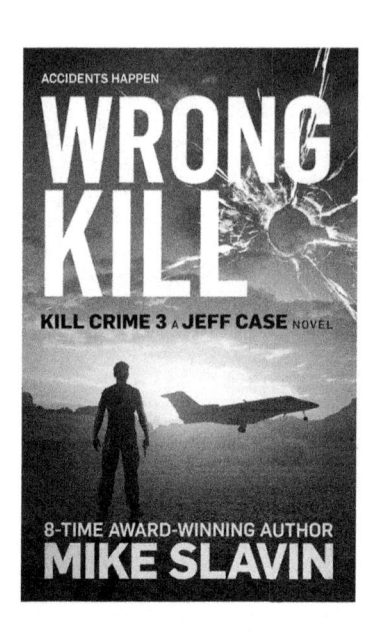

Kill Crime III (Wrong Kill, Kill Crime 3) (Jeff Case Book 3)

Wrong people are killed and that has consequences. The cartel, serial killers, and an old enemy all want to kill Jeff Case. More answers are finally revealed about the true author of Kill Crime, the book within a book, in the series' third novel.

Kill Crime IV and more...

Case does what he can to help everyone he runs into, rid the world of as much evil as possible, and still enjoy poker-playing and some of the other finer things in life.

www.mikeslavinauthor.com

Sign up for announcements and free access to action-filled short stories about Jeff Case and the characters in his world.

ALSO BY MIKE SLAVIN

One Million in the Bank: How To Make $1,000,000 With Your Own Business, Even If You Have No Money Or Experience

I was recruited out of the Army in December 1984 and gave up my lifelong dream of a military career, all for an offer I could not refuse. Then I was fired a year later because of internal partner infighting. Whiplash! Broke and bankrupt, I struggled badly for seven years. Then I wrote a business plan for my everyday ordinary type of business (not a new innovative service or product) over a weekend. In the next three weeks, I raised the seed capital from four people who were neither family nor friends for a total of $203,000 to start my own company. I was a millionaire just three years later, and this book was written to help others do the same. It explains how to start your own business with no money or experience and accumulate a million in three-to-seven years.

Gold Medal Best Business and Entrepreneur Book (Nonfiction Book Awards 2015)

Gold Medal Best Financial Book (Nonfiction Book Awards 2015)

Best Business Book (Next Generation Indie Book Awards 2016)

1st Place Gold Medal Best Informational Book (Feathered QuillBook Awards 2016)

3rd Place Bronze Medal Best Self- Help Book (Feathered Quill BookAwards 2016)

Eric Hoffer Award Finalist (top 10%) (Eric Hoffer Awards 2016)

www.onemillioninthebank.com

ABOUT THE AUTHOR

Mike Slavin lives an interesting life. He survived three helicopter crashes as the pilot, was tear gassed in riots in South Korea, served as an Aide to a U.S. President, has played in the World Series of Poker Main Event three times, and continues to seek out other encounters out of the normal. These rich experiences inform his writing.

Slavin, a West Pointer and a former Army officer, was broke and bankrupt in 1992. Three years later, he was a self-made millionaire. His first book, *One Million in the Bank: How To Make $1,000,000 With Your Own Business, Even If You Have No Money Or Experience*, shares this experience with others and won seven awards. He has since sold his company to take personal care of his wife of almost forty years as she battles with Parkinson's disease. The couple lives in Houston, and *Kill Crime Series* is his first series.

www.mikeslavinauthor.com

Sign up for announcements and free access to action-filled short stories about Jeff Case, Spike, and the characters in their world.

Printed in Great Britain
by Amazon